Kiss of war

CLARA ELROY

Editing: My Brother's Editor
Proofreading: Amy Briggs
Cover Design: Books and Moods

They call this place the City of Stars.

Ironic if you ask me.

City of Soul-Sucking Black Holes seems much more fitting.

A safe haven for the wealthy and corrupt.
A sewer of vice and sin.

Leonardo Bianchi burns the darkest and shines the brightest of all.

My lover turned foe.

Four years ago, my family ruined his, and his tongue got sharper than his jaw. His eyes fostered demons solely reserved for me. They craved to own my soul.

And for the longest time, I took it, I bore his cruelty alone.

But then... then I grew thorns of my own.
And now?

Now it's time for his torment to taste my kiss of war.

Note

Kiss of War is a full-length, interconnected standalone that features strong language, sexual scenes and mature situations which may be considered triggers for some.
Reader Discretion is advised.

Playlist

"Nothing Without You"— The Weeknd

"Prisoner"— Miley Cyrus (ft. Dua Lipa)

"Ruin My Life"—Zara Larsson

"Armageddon"—Lily Denning

"Way down We Go"—KALEO

"Shameless"—Camila Cabello

"White Flag"—Bishop Briggs

"Good to Be Bad"—Talii

"Partition"—Beyonce

For all my hard-working queens.
No dream is too big. Shoot for the stars and straighten other crowns, ladies.

"I threw myself to the wolves, only to learn of the tenderness in their howl, and the loyalty in their blood."

—ISRA AL-THIBEH

Prologue

LEONARDO

A field of death surrounded me as I kneeled next to the marble crypt. The color was stark, a beacon among the tilted and moldy gravestones planted in the cemetery for much longer.

Young blood had been spilled, fresh soil had been dug.

Pebbles poked my knees, the steps leading to the entrance were littered with them. I could feel the pieces of gravel through the thick material of my jeans, a reminder that this was indeed real.

The Massachusetts summer heat was no match for the war brewing inside me as I traced the letters on the plaque. I worked my way up the epitaph—*Beloved Daughter, Sister, Granddaughter & Friend. You are always in the hearts of those you touched. For nothing loved is ever lost and you loved so much*—to the dips and the curves of the year of her death—2017—to her name. My sister's name.

Isabella Bianchi.

1

Blood roared in my ears, and an outburst of warmth burned a path from my heart down to my veins, and on to my hand as it curled over the engraved *I*, my nails digging into my palms.

The end.

This was the end for my twin.

We all died eventually, be it humans, plants, or animals. Death was inevitable and a stepping stone to utter oblivion. It surrounded us every day—sick patients in hospitals, old people in walkers, and junkies in alleyways. We lived it and we breathed it, but we never grasped the full cataclysmic impact it had until we experienced it.

I had a habit of being the most confident person in a room. The one people always tried to please, the one whose smile they tried the hardest to earn. It was a mindset, one my family held close to heart. Lead and others will follow.

Nothing touched us.

Nothing harmed the third richest family in the United States of America, sixth in the world.

Yet... my sister was dead.

The dirt on her grave still hadn't settled. We buried her a mere five hours ago, and I stayed planted in the same spot I'd been in since the start of the funeral. I watched as the lot emptied and relatives and friends returned back to their glitzy cars, some of them chatting lively as if this was a social gathering, a chance to catch up, and my twin wasn't lying dead, six feet underground.

No one cared. No one ever truly cared.

The apathy was a real eye-opener. It forced me to harden my shell, lock in my anger and grief until they overflowed. I felt them everywhere. They drowned my senses, muting my touch with reality. My ears rang, and my eyes stung. I lived in the City of Stars, yet a vortex of darkness hung heavy over my shoulders.

This was Isabella's end, but it felt like my beginning.

One born out of shadows and blood.

I didn't realize Francis Roux traded in his paintbrushes for swords and spears until it was too late. I didn't know he'd developed an interest in the art of war too, until my sister's violated body washed up ashore on Long Beach.

The back of my neck was burned to a crisp, and I tilted my head up, facing the cloudless sky and letting the cruel rays of the overbearing sun ravage my green eyes.

Every breath I took dragged with unearned privilege. Guilt that I hadn't protected Isabella stirred the blood in my veins, and my need for revenge made it race faster. I was blind to my enemies before, but I wouldn't forget their names anytime soon now.

So, with wrath as my witness, I took an oath not to fucking rest until the entire Roux clan faced a worse end than Isabella. The countdown started the moment the thought filled my head, and each sharp inhale coating my lungs counted as a day lost for them.

Chapter 1

Four Years Ago

ELIANA

ELIANA, 16; LEONARDO, 17

The whispers.

That's what I hated the most.

Not that my father was being charged for murder. Not that life as I knew it was coming apart one brick at a time. It was the whispers I cared about.

It started with one person, then spread like wildfire. The whole pier circled around me, sneaking not so inconspicuous glances at the bench where I sat.

I glared at a woman with a stroller, and she wheeled off faster, scared the cornered animal would attack. Scoffed at and looked down upon, that was what I was reduced to.

My skin crawled. I questioned my decision to come out in the first place. Staying home seemed like the wiser decision when my family name was plastered on every social media news outlet out there, but I couldn't. I'd rather suffocate in judgment than the lies the Roux Manor fostered.

Another lady with a stroller wheeled by incredibly slow, and I sighed. What was it with these baby mamas?

Abandoning the bench because I knew they wouldn't stop looking, I reached for the rusted green railing, giving them my back to disguise the fractures on my surface.

And it was a good thing I did. I cringed when I caught my reflection on the waves, the lamp posts hanging over my head aiding my vision.

My face looked borderline unhealthy. Deep black grooves decorated the surface under my bloodshot eyes, making the clear blue color of my irises stand out like a blot on a landscape. Hollowed out cheeks followed before the bloodless form of my lips tied the knot on the badly wrapped present. I resembled a zombie, in its prior to devouring brains form.

Pale.

Alone.

Miserable.

"Are you expecting flowers to spring up in your stead, little vain monster?" a voice spoke behind me. That familiar low timbre sprung me back to the present, my body locking at the sound. Warning signs flashed behind my closed eyelids as I blinked slow.

Leonardo Bianchi.

He had a special aura about him, one that sucked up all the oxygen from a room, replacing it with danger. Breathing became harder as fear coated the walls of my throat. A prickle of awareness ran down my spine even before seeing him sometimes, and this time was no different.

My body protested as I turned around, but I had to

before he sunk his claws in my back when I wasn't looking. Brown hair, the color of chocolate dreams, decorated the top of his head in unruly curls. Eyes like two uncut emerald shards pulled me in, and the slope of his aristocratic nose threatened to slice me if I made a wrong move, right along with the sharp line of his jaw.

In the span of a week, he'd turned a one-eighty. I couldn't blame him, but I also couldn't help mourning what I'd lost. I used to love basking under the light of the candle Leo always kept burning for me. But the boy with a crush had developed into a man looking for someone to ruin.

Me.

His black shirt was open at the collar, framing his lean, muscular body well. Grass stains decorated his knees as if he'd taken one too many tumbles on a soccer field, but I knew it wasn't that. His all black outfit told me all I needed to know.

He'd visited Isabella.

"What are you doing here?"

"Enjoying my front-row seat to a drama called *Roux Family: A Shit Show of Epic Proportions*," Leo taunted. "Gotta say, Narcissus, you make it extremely easy for me to do so."

I smiled, not buckling under the weight of his swift judgments. Keeping up with the charade of the put-together girl was turning painful, though. My mask struggled to stay in place.

"You must be proud. Displaying your obsessions with such arrogance takes a special kind of stupid to pull off. Should I get a restraining order to get you to keep your distance?"

I never wanted him close.

Not when we were ten, and he managed to steal my first kiss, even though I wasn't past the age of believing boys were riddled with cooties. And certainly not at sixteen, when the only way he'd attach his lips on mine would be if he gained the ability to provide me with death's kiss.

"Go ahead and give it a try, sweetheart. Seeing your family swimming in further shit will only make my day brighter." My mock smile shattered, and my heart pounded so hard it hurt. He leaned forward, his six-feet-three inches making me crane my neck. "My word is law around here, Narcissus. I own the fucking world you live in, including the authorities. There is no version of this story where you come out on top."

"And somehow, that still wasn't enough to find your sister. I think running the town with an iron fist is doing you worse than it is good. You're unearthing enemies everywhere, Bianchi." I regretted my words as soon as they left my mouth.

He had every reason to be mad. To hate me. What my father did I—I didn't even want to think about. I avoided it at all costs, but that didn't stop people on social media from tweeting, sharing, and posting about it. It was flaunted at me on every waking moment, and that took a toll when there weren't many sleeping ones.

My father killed a girl. He raped her, killed her, and then left her for dead. I couldn't sleep. I couldn't eat without bile assaulting my throat. Isabella was just one year older than me. I hadn't the slightest idea what Francis was capable of. My dad wasn't *my* dad anymore.

Leo's eyes lit up, and the blood vessels on my cheeks expanded, painting my face scarlet. I wasn't a cruel person,

I'd just been poked restlessly for the past week, and Leo brought out the bitch in me.

He lowered his face to mine, obliterating my personal space. The world around us paused. A mesmerized public prepared to witness the lion tearing into his lamb. A hand curled around my blonde hair, and I froze under his touch, my heartbeat erratic, fear mixing with exhilaration.

"It might have not been enough then, but you'll come to find out I'm very insistent on getting the things I want. And what I want, my little vain monster, is your father's head on a pike if proven guilty." He tilted his head, eyes focused on mine. "I wouldn't mind seeing yours standing next to his either."

That hand tugged on my strands. His face was so close, his intoxicated breath fanned on my cheek. I didn't doubt he could do it. I pulled, but when it came to pushing, no one stood a chance against his barreling form.

"An eye for an eye, Roux."

"Makes the whole world blind?" I spoke past the lump in my throat, quoting Gandhi. "I am not my father, Leo. Don't box me in with his sins."

"The apple doesn't fall far from the tree, and you, Eliana Roux, *you* are the whole damn harvest. I'm past sparing people when the same compassion wasn't shown to my sister."

Leo's green-eyed twin haunted my dreams enough as it was. I didn't need him piling on more guilt. I moved, aiming to detach my body from his, but like a python, he wrapped me tighter in his asphyxiating grip. I sucked in a breath, fisting his shirt.

"Don't you have a better way to spend your time,

Bianchi?" *Asshole*. "Or do you enjoy being a bastard far too much?"

"Hm... being a bastard to you *is* starting to become my favorite pastime. What can I say? Your daddy's cruelty lit a spark in me."

A spark? Yeah, no. The blazing heat his body emitted hinted at a ten foot tall fire, waiting to consume me whole.

"So what? Are you gonna start stalking me now? Did you follow me here?"

"Stalk you?" A condescending smirk bloomed on his lips. "Nah, sweetheart. I'll save you the Ted Bundy experience until after the trial." He twirled a strand of gold hair between his fingers. The jut of his jaw was so close to my lips, his stubble left a trail of electricity and what-ifs dancing on my skin. "But if you must know, I'm meeting Serena. You know? The pretty to your ugly?"

I flinched. The angry little green monster inside of me that lived and breathed for moments like these rose kicking and screaming like a drunk, awakened sailor.

Serena had been my best friend ever since we used to wear diapers to make fashion statements. And Leo was right. She *was* indeed the pretty to my ugly. She had everything. Her mother was there for her, while I only saw mine once in a blue moon. And her dad was a respectable lawyer, while mine was the one needing his services.

Serena was the perfect to my flawed.

"Green looks rather ghastly on you, Narcissus."

I flinched again and pushed at his chest until he finally released me. I gulped in the fresh air that traveled to my lungs, now that his overbearing presence wasn't stifling it.

"You know, with such high self-esteem you possess,

Bianchi, I wonder if that Narcissus nickname should be reversed."

The mop of curls bounced as he shook his head. "The pet name is here to stay, Roux. It suits you perfectly."

I strived to argue, but the butt of the cigarette (I hadn't even noticed he had), came dangerously close to my pinky. He rolled it closed, a few inches away from my hand on the railing, and I tugged my arm back, shocked.

"Some advice for old time's sake, Narcissus. Be a good little girl tonight, get on your knees for me—" A wicked smile illuminated the contours of his face. "And *pray*. Pray for your father's pardon, because if he had a hand in my sister's death, you won't like the outcome."

A pang made a mess out of my insides. They were all over the place, twisting and churning with anxiety.

Much to Leo's disbelief, I did pray. Every day I prayed that this wasn't real. That the next day I'd wake up, and this nightmare would be all but a memory. I didn't want Isabella dead, and I didn't want my father to be a murderer. Why couldn't he understand that?

"Leo!" a high-pitched voice called from behind us. Our gazes both snapped to the source.

My stomach got hollower when a genuine smile pulled on Leo's lips when he caught sight of Serena. She looked like a fairy, a brown bob framed her heart-shaped face, and the knee-high blush dress she wore flowed with the wind as she waved to Leo like a maniac.

I bit my bottom lip, a stinging sensation overtaking my eyes. Serena was supposed to be my best friend, but it seemed like she was settling in on the opposite side of the camp. Her excitement stagnated when she saw me.

Suddenly, her wave felt more like a goodbye rather than a hello, lackluster.

I didn't bother returning the sentiment.

"See you tomorrow, Narcissus." Leo clucked his tongue on the roof of his mouth as he retreated backward. "Can't wait to see how busted those knees look."

"You're late," I spoke as my mom breezed inside the courtroom. She garnered double glances from everyone, reminding me again why she reigned supreme in the trophy wife department. Her chestnut brown hair was highlighted and styled to perfection, eyeliner sharp enough to gouge someone's eyes out, and lips painted blood red.

"What are you talking about? The trial still hasn't started." She took a seat on the wooden bench next to me, her Chanel no.5 perfume wafting to my nose. I resisted the urge to blanch.

Yes, because showing up a few minutes early would be such a bad thing. Riding with me to court, sparing any of your words for me like a fucking mother is supposed to do, would be the end of the world.

I bit back my words like always. Mother and I didn't have a conventional relationship. Her signature frozen glare had shut me out a long time ago. I no longer asked for questions when I knew I wouldn't find any answers. Trying to reach out to her was like drawing water from an empty well.

"All rise. This court is now in session," the bailiff said.

A blanket of dread fell over my shoulders when the judge entered. I was hyper-aware of Leonardo's presence on the opposite side of the court. It forced my muscles to tense into immobility.

Opening statements began, and my father's resigned stance had my heart pounding. Why would someone that was innocent look so ashen? Fear and uncertainty were palpable around him, dripping onto the tawny floors of the courthouse. He glanced back at me, his crystal blues were glass-like, and his blond hair askew as he rubbed it to oblivion.

Anxiety twisted my stomach in knots, but the lawyer—Carter Laurent, Serena's father—cherry-picked for us was impeccable. He held his ground with compound sentences that left even me feeling confused by the end of the questioning.

"Your Honor," the opposing attorney motioned to a flat screen TV. "According to the witness's statements, Isabella Bianchi was last seen alive walking out of a restaurant on Elm Street with her friends. She got in her car and simply vanished until she was discovered three days later on Long Beach, a mere ten-minute drive from the place she was last seen. Now, I think I speak for everyone when I say that alien abductions are not recurring anomalies."

The ice of the murder trial melted slightly as the lawyer garnered a few chuckles from the jury. I coiled further, drawing invisible Tic-Tac-Toes on the skirt of my gray dress, waiting for the other shoe to drop.

"Let's all witness as Mr. Roux is spotted near the location, Isabella Bianchi, but also three more girls, Zena Steele, Kira Vang, and Emily Haviliard, were reported missing the very same day and still haven't been found."

"Objection! Assumes facts not in evidence." Mr. Gideon popped out of his seat.

"Sustained," the judge ruled. "Mr. Hunt, please stick to the information that is already in the record."

XXX, *cross.*

OOO, *cross.*

I doodled harder on my thigh when my father's silver Mercedes flashed on screen, like a beacon of guilt. Security footage from a store nearby caught his license plate and profile as he drove. There was no mistaking the aquiline shape of his nose. A white timestamp at the bottom of the screen linked him to the wrong place, at the wrong time. He wasn't seen doing anything incriminating, but the coincidences were too many to sweep under the rug like that.

My ass was numb by the time Dad was called to the stand, and Mom kept throwing me *"behave"* glares because I couldn't seem to keep still anymore. My feet bounced, fingers twisting and overlapping.

"Mr. Roux, would you agree that you looked up to Lorcan Callahan? You found inspiration from him, isn't that correct?"

I swallowed hard, knowing where the persecution was heading with this. They wanted to take a hit at Dad's character, and this was the perfect place to strike. Dad knew it too. Shadows gathered in his eyes, but there was no point in denying it. He'd only dropped Callahan's name about a thousand times during interviews.

Keep your head up.

Don't let me down.

I can't lose you too.

I traced the words on the roof of my mouth. I was Daddy's girl, always had been, and it was hard being anything else when Mom was never there.

"That's correct. I think he was brilliant."

Indeed he did. Art should always be telling a story. It wasn't about how beautiful a painting was, it was about the message behind it. That was the mantra my dad lived by. His art centered around depicting the most immoral parts of our society, psychotic, just like Callahan's.

"Lorcan Callahan passed away in the early twenties, out of self-mutilation, right? His cause of death was widely reported. It's not every day someone drinks paint or tries to carve his body to become "one with his art." So how brilliant can a man be when he harms himself as part of his creative process?"

"Art isn't sane or logical, Mr. Hunt. It takes you where it wants to take you. Sometimes you just have to hold on and hope the ship doesn't capsize."

I squeezed my eyes shut, recognizing my father's colossal mistake. Our lawyer tried to object again, but the judge shut him down.

"And where did your art take you, Mr. Roux? Your paintings feature mostly human subjects in various stages of duress, particularly females. How do we know you didn't try to become one with your art as well?"

"I didn't!" Dad raised his voice. "Art is subjectiv—" he started, but the prosecutor cut him off.

"Thank you, your honor. I have no further questions."

Irritation dilated my father's gaze. He sat back in his seat, muttering words I couldn't make out.

I risked a glance at Leo when the prime piece of evidence was brought forth. My stomach churned as Ms. Bianchi broke down crying in his arms when the lawyer uncovered that pieces of Francis's hair were found on Isabella's clothes the day she disappeared.

"Don't look at them," Mother snapped, her cold marble

gaze fixing me in place. "You're only giving them more power that way."

"They lost their daughter," I croaked out. "Because of Dad."

"We don't know that, yet," she hissed. "Now keep still and stay quiet. Don't attract any unnecessary attention."

I couldn't.

I couldn't keep doing the same thing I'd been doing for the past two weeks. Ignoring the evidence that kept piling on. Supporting Dad when he was the villain in this story.

A growl of irritation rumbled from Mom's throat, but I didn't care. I had to get out of that courtroom. Keeping my head down, I exited the trial, my black pumps clicking on the laminated floor. Bile rushed up my throat, and I managed to reach the bathroom in time, spilling my guts all over a porcelain sink.

I gagged. My tears burned as they slid down my face, leaving a charred trail forged by Leo's loathing. There was no turning back after this. He'd ruin me, for that I was sure. Heaven has no rage like love to hatred turned. Nor hell hath no fury like a Bianchi scorned.

Chapter 2

Three Years Ago

LEONARDO

The scent of weed made my nose itch and my head swim. Smoke slithered out of my mouth, floating past the sliding doors and getting lost in the inky black night.

"And? How did the bastard die?" Ares Alsford asked, yawning as a brunette straddled his thighs, sucking on his neck like she was auditioning for Twilight.

"Hell if I know." I took another hit of my blunt. "The fucker is dead and that's all that matters."

Three stabs to the gut, one after the other, after getting in a row with an inmate.

Of course, I knew how Francis Roux died. It was all I could think about. Part of me rejoiced while the other hungered for more of his suffering. Death was too fucking kind for him, but unfortunately, prison hierarchies weren't within my jurisdiction. August the thirteenth—he died exactly a year after he was convicted. If it were up to me, that day would become a national holiday, ridding the world of one more sicko, but I'd settle for a balls-out party.

Slouched on my sectional, I had an eagle's eye view of the entire first floor and the back porch. I observed the havoc that the horny teens reaped, crushing my blunt on an ashtray.

I'd lost track of how many people showed up. My house looked like what I imagined a pan full of STDs would. Couples making out on loveseats, groping each other on the dance floor, and sneaking hand jobs in the hot tub. The private rooms on the second floor were protected by actual walls as opposed to the floor-to-ceiling windows on the ground level, but what you couldn't see, you could hear.

Groans and slaps of flesh infiltrated the air as music pounded from the loudspeakers. I took a peek at the front door out of force of habit. It was open, people were milling around, red Solo cups in hand, but the one I was looking for wasn't there.

"Why do you keep staring at the door every five seconds for?"

I turned back to Ares, catching his honey-colored eyes laughing at me. The slight crack my neck produced mocked me and made the smirk on his face stretch bigger.

"I'd say there's a pretty obvious answer to that question," Kai hiccupped.

"Well, did you have to point it out?" Reaching forward to grab his beer, Ares effectively scooted the girl that had been plastered on his lap the whole afternoon off. His brown hair looked like it'd braced a thousand monkeys trying to pick lice off him. That was how much she'd been running her hands through it. "I wanted him to tell me why."

He whipped his head in my direction. "Come on, man, you know you shouldn't bottle up your emotions. Tell us what's wrong," Ares continued, sounding like some online therapist that never bothered to finish high school and prescribed crystals as a healing method.

"Good thing you're pursuing business in college, asshole, because psychology ain't cutting it." I leaned further back on the sofa, stretching my stiff neck.

"Cheers to that!" Kai knocked back his beer as one would a shot, only to end up wearing the contents a few seconds later.

I snuck one more glance at the door when Ares pulled Kai into a headlock, messing up his brown hair.

Nothing. Nada. Zilch.

And here I thought Narcissus had a little more bite in her.

I didn't even know why. Eliana never bothered to fight back. I stole her best friend, fucking paraded her in my arms like a trophy, and she let me. I turned her other friends against her, and she settled in well as a lone wolf. Rumors spread, one nastier than the other, and she kept her head down, minding her own business.

She was miserable. I knew that much. She'd gone from looking like a kid to aging a thousand years in the span of one.

Yet that wasn't enough for me.

I wanted her to feel what I felt—angry, mad, fire flooding her veins. Eliana was getting the easy way out; she was cutting my joy of watching her deteriorate short. I didn't want to bring down a zombie. I wanted to bring down a bull;

I wanted her to experience the insanity that sparked up my nerve endings to oblivion.

My head snapped back when I heard a thump. Ares and Kai were spread on the ground, tipped over because they were so fucking high. "You have got to be the stupidest people I know." I watched them try to wrestle their way up the couch.

"At least I'm not obsessed with the girl I claim to hate." Ares didn't miss a beat, settling back on the couch with a huff. "Don't you think it was a little much? Inviting her today?"

Ares, ever the protector of the underdogs. Gucci shoes, leather jacket that cost more than a middle-class family's income, he made for a shitty James Dean impersonator. And an even shittier animal rights advocate.

"Do you think Francis Roux stopped to think it was a little much to assault and kill Isabella?" I asked, and his gaze sliced to the floor. "No. Because if he had, my sister would be here today, and we wouldn't be having this conversation."

"And you're looking to turn into a sociopath too?" he muttered, sending a rush of annoyance down my spine.

"Why not? You'll be the first on my to-kill list," I warned. *Fucking get off my dick.* I took a sip of my beer, cringing when the lukewarm liquid hit my throat. "Where the fuck is Serena? Feels like five hours since she left to grab us drinks."

"She's not your fucking errand girl."

"And yet she'd suck my dick in a second if I told her too."

His face purpled, and I realized what the third degree was about. He didn't care about Eliana, never so much as made a peep about her before. This sudden case of mouth diarrhea came because he was too much of a pussy to ask Serena out, so he got on my nerves instead.

"You're a son of a bitch, Bianchi."

"As long as we're talking about my father, I agree, Alsford." I shrugged, getting on my feet, and the room spun slightly. "Check his pulse. The last thing I need is someone dying on my property." I motioned to Kai, who hadn't made a sound for the past fifteen minutes, slumped against some white throw pillows.

Hauling my ass to the kitchen to get my own drink, I ignored everyone that tried to talk to me on the way. I had plenty of acquaintances, but not many friends. Genuine people were a rarity when you were the heir of a billion-dollar oil company. Fake masks were part of the package, though, and I'd gotten pretty good at unwrapping them. Little did they know my father planned to fuck my ass raw and make me earn my position.

Actually, I wasn't even sure I was the sole successor of BB Oil anymore. Daddy dearest had been a busy man the past year, fucking anything that moved while mom drowned her sorrows in giggle water. He'd taken her out today. He figured he'd celebrate life's hard-on with his wife.

"I still can't believe you slept with Leo." The words floated on over to my ears as I tugged the fridge's French door open. The kitchen was empty, even though the dark granite countertops were overflowing with spilled drinks. I shrugged it off, grabbing a Corona from the top shelf.

"Yeah, me neither." A higher pitch this time. "I heard Bianchi only dates college girls, you lucky bitch. How was it?"

That statement wasn't entirely true. I didn't discriminate based on age (within the legal confinements), but I did stick to screwing women and not girls. I had enough drama in my life, and teenage girls were drenched in it. I slammed the silver door shut, leaning against it and honing in on the shadows in the hallway.

"He gets an A-plus from me," the girl in question answered, sighing dreamily. "Seriously girls, no other man does it like Leo. He went in so hard and fast, I swear my bones started to rattle at some point. I had to tell him to be a good little boy and take it slower after my second orgasm, or I'd end up needing a wheelchair."

A flurry of squeals hit me right in the head, and I winced. God, what an overactive imagination. I didn't even need to fuck girls anymore apparently, their dreams with me alone got them hospitalized. Rolling my eyes, I pressed forward. This chick obviously had potential in writing—the same kinds of books Isabella used to read, with the bare-chested dudes on the covers.

"Is that so?" I asked into the hallway. Four terrified screams pierced my eardrums, one more than the original three I had in mind.

Serena was curled into herself, resting her back on the wall. Three girls crowded her, but I knew it wasn't her relaying the fantasy. Not only because I hadn't ever touched her, or the other three. It was because she looked wounded, hands curled over her chest, stance weak.

"I don't usually make a habit out of sending my dates to the ER. Can you please enlighten me on which one of you got me to act like *a good little boy*?" My words came out slightly slurred as I ran my gaze across them.

Mediocre. Mediocre. Pretty okay. And Serena.

"Did I say little?" *Pretty okay,* spoke up after managing to close her mouth.

Blue eyes and silver hair, I examined her, running my tongue under my top teeth. The nose ring threw me off, and

I didn't know why. The liar looked like the dirtied up version of Eliana. So freaking similar my dick started stiffening. But I was fucking high. Any girl with her coloring didn't seem too far off for my crappy vision.

"I'm sorry. We both know there's nothing little about you." She giggled, ruining the fantasy.

The two other girls followed suit, and Serena's full brows pulled in a frown.

I stared at her, my expression blank. *Pretty okay* started taking on the hue of a tomato the more silence stifled the narrow hallway. Nope. I one-hundred percent didn't know this Daenerys Targaryen wannabe.

"Right. What was your name again?" I asked. "Might need to send you a check for those medical bills, apparently."

"Umm..." Hairline fractures spread over her confidence as she threw a quick glance at her friends *and Serena*. "Adriana Franco, remember?"

Mediocre number one and *two* snickered, and it could have been the alcohol and weed running through my system, but I felt kind of bad for her. People made up shit stories to look cool all the time, and all she did was give me an ego stroke.

"Riight..." I drawled. "Why don't you stick around tonight then, *Ariana*? I feel like I gotta add some pluses to my rating."

I was a bastard by nature.

Ariana had an uncanny resemblance to Eliana, and I spent the better part of my afternoon waiting for her to burst down the front door and blast my balls to Mars. Her pussy seemed to own me, but I'd rather cut my veins and bleed to death before getting my dick anywhere near her. So, the second-best choice would have to do.

Disbelief coated *Pretty Okay's* eyes, and she nodded dumbly. Winking, I grabbed Serena with me before heading on out.

"Oh, so now you remember I exist?" she hissed, rolling her wrist in my hand.

"Well, I thought you'd gone extinct when you never bothered to show up." I threw my arm over her shoulders, plastering her side to mine. Her gaze grew heavy—overloaded with emotion.

"Yeah... for some reason, your pieces of ass love sharing details about your sex life with me."

"And? You love listening?" She didn't have to stick around, and there was a reason why they loved doing it. Serena had a nasty habit of swearing up and down that we were a thing. The only reason why I didn't combat it was because, in a weird way, I needed her. I valued her as a friend, but most importantly, I valued the reactions we garnered together. "If you're into voyeurism now, you can come watch me fuck Ariana tonight."

"Her name is fucking *Adriana*, asshole," she spat, bitterness lacing her voice.

I stopped in my tracks, my sneakers squeaking on the hardwood floor. Serena did too, looking at me with crossed eyebrows.

I didn't usually waste my time advising other people, 'cause at the end of the day, they would do whatever they wanted. But I'd make this one exception for Serena. She'd given me so much, even unknowingly.

"Some advice, Serena? Desperation isn't anyone's type." My eyes sliced to Ares, who had a different girl on his lap this time. He wasn't a nice guy. Those were a rare breed in Astropolis. But for her, I knew he'd try to be less of a cunt.

Just like I'd been willing to change for someone else a long time ago. "Sharks are poisonous to humans, babe. Look for other fish in the sea."

"What if I want the biggest, most dangerous one?"

"Then I suggest you start looking for a whale," I dead-panned, and she swatted at my chest.

"Yo, Bianchi!" Ares cut our conversation off. "Look! I found us a stray."

I turned around, sizing up whoever he was pointing to, only to come up short.

Red toes peeked at me under strappy heeled sandals, then legs. Legs for miles with a sheen of golden glitter that spoke of getting touched by the sun and kissed by the tide. A wave of crushed pink broke off all that bare expanse of skin, the dress (that looked more like a fucking negligee) wrapped around a toned body, stretching thin across the girl's generous chest.

The liquidity that coursed through my veins ebbed away. I turned rigid, an unmoving slab of stone, following the trail of wavy golden strands up to the wet dream's face.

Pause.

Breathe.

Re-fucking-wind.

My lips thinned with the effort to keep the fire that bloomed between my bones tucked inside. She came. Eliana Roux showed up in all of her broken glory. Atoms of defiance stifled the air. Her fight rubbed off on me from the upward tilt of her chin and the fact that *she* had parked her ass between Ares's thighs, most definitely warming up his boner.

"What the fuck do you think you're doing?" I boomed, dousing the tension in the room with a healthy dose of gasoline. People pressed harder against the walls, all eyes awaiting the continuation of our nasty broken record.

"Got your invite, Bianchi, and I thought I'd bless you with my presence. What's wrong? Is your corset on too tight?" She tilted her head, trying to look cute. "You look like you're about to have an aneurism."

"He does seem a little tense, doesn't he?" Ares piped in, folding his arms over her womb. I traced the movement, committing the bones I needed to break to memory.

"You either must be really dense or seriously mad to show your face here." Serena gave her two cents, and I felt her presence next to me as she moved forward, staring at the same train wreck as I was.

Eliana's top lip curled with disgust when she looked at her former best friend. "If those are my only two options, I'll take the latter, seeing as you've permanently booked the first one."

I hooked my arm over Serena's shoulders, drawing her closer and tracing the exposed skin of her decolletage. Narcissus's arctic blue glare turned to me, and a smirk danced on my lips. Two can play at this game, but only one will get out of it with a broken jaw.

"It's okay, Serena. She can stay as long as she doesn't weird out the guests." *One finger, two...* I edged past Serena's lacy black shirt. She turned to putty in my arms, pressing harder against me. "This is a party in her father's honor after all."

I was a user, but the little mouse had given me something to play with. I wanted to sink my claws in so deep, her blood left a permanent mark on my skin, like war paint.

"Cool," Kai said. I took my eyes off of them for a second to see that they had formed a circle of guys and girls, some on the ground and others on the couch. "We were playing spin the bottle. You wanna join, or do you prefer sitting there and glaring at each other?"

"Just out of curiosity," Eliana spoke up again. "Are all your parties reminiscent of your elementary school days, Bianchi? Still hung up on your 'king of seven minutes in heaven' glory days?"

"Nah, Narcissus. These days I only need about two minutes to bring heaven to earth." Her jaw tightened, and her throat worked with a swallow.

"A taker, not a giver. I see." The wheels in her head worked overtime to twist my words. "Figures. The only person Leonardo Bianchi is ever truly capable of loving is himself."

"You can run with that idea if you want." I let out a dark chuckle. "It lessens the sting, doesn't it?"

"What sting?" She planted her elbows on her knees, leaning forward, and Ares all but came in his pants when she wiggled her ass, getting comfortable.

My hand fell from Serena's shoulders as I advanced their way. The people in the middle broke off, facilitating my upcoming destruction. I felt my nostrils flare and my need to humiliate her rise.

"The one that has you clenching your legs every time you see me, Narcissus," I spoke out loudly. "The one that has you running home, shoving your fingers knuckle deep in your soaking wet cunt, because you know I'd never touch you even if you were the last woman left on Earth."

She rose like a set of flames licking the walls of my kingdom. It didn't matter though, everything that I adored had turned to dust already. I had nothing left to lose. Satisfaction raced under my skin when her soul turned inkier by the day, morphing and turning into a mini-me.

I heard the sting her slap produced before I felt it. Her hand struck out like a tornado, acrylic fingernails leaving a trail of blood on my cheek. Her orange scent wrapped around me in waves, seeping into my skin like alcohol ravaging an open wound.

Eliana was all consuming and oh so fucking dead.

I heard her gasp as she retracted her hand, but I shot out before she could flee. Wrapping my fist around her wrist, I tugged her close, pinning her to me, the struck look on her face doing nothing to sedate my bloodlust.

"*Out. Now*," I snarled once, and the scuffle of feet that followed was immediate. There was noise around us, so much noise, but it all paled when I focused on her.

"Leo, man." My gaze snapped to Ares, who stood stiffly off the side, looking like he'd love a barbwire fist flung at his face. "It was a joke. Don't do anything you'll regret."

"A joke, huh? I bet the stones outside are laughing. Leave, before I make you leave," I warned in a low voice. The fucker glanced once at Eliana but left like I instructed.

When had they gotten so close?

I looked back to the wilted daffodil in my arms. Our chests were flush, but she was bent as far back as she could go without falling on her ass.

"You come looking for a fight and I'll give you a fucking war." My other hand wrapped around her delicate throat, squeezing lightly. The apple of her throat bobbed against my palm. "Don't ever hit me again."

"Or what? You'll hit back?" she hissed, her blues turning electric.

"And don't confuse me for your father either."

"I would never. You don't need your fists to destroy me. My back is already mangled and bloody, but you just won't stop twisting the knife."

I leaned closer, a cruel smile staking claim on my lips. "I won't rest until I've pierced your ugly black heart, Eli. You take what's mine, and I obliterate everything that is yours."

"What is mine, you fucking bastard?" she asked, her bottom lip trembling before she bit down on it. "You've already taken everything. What more do you want?"

"You're still standing. That means something's left in that shallow life of yours to steal."

"I hate you," Eliana said, hand wrapping around my arm and snapping my hold off her. I let go without resistance, my point already made. Either awake or asleep, Narcissus would always find me starring in her nightmares.

"Thank you."

That means I'm doing my job right.

I looped my pointer around a ringlet of sunshine, tugging the golden strand of hair. Hard. "These pretty feathers of yours, babe? Not only will I ruffle them. I'll strip them off with hot wax."

Glaring at me like I was the scum of the earth, Eliana left without a word.

She did wave her middle finger at me in goodbye though.

I'd danced on her father's grave and invited her to join the party. The battle was over. This was where the real war began.

Chapter 3

Present

ELIANA

LEONARDO, 21; ELIANA, 20

If there was ever a time to run as far away as possible from the ivy-covered, French château I called home, it was now. There was a Porsche Carrera 911 parked in my driveway. Fallen leaves stirred around the flashy red number. It fit right in with the manicured lawns and wrought-iron gates of our zip code. Although it probably fell a little flat next to the Ferraris and McLarens, Mr. Miller, next door, loved revving up at odd hours of the night.

I paused, taking my earphones out and sweeping my pony away from my sticky neck. The bite of fall was evident in the air as September rolled in. Still, something inside me pleaded to stay outside of the manor, even if I died of frost-bite, dressed in my workout gear and drenched in sweat after my morning jog.

I didn't get many visitors, let alone ones that showed up unannounced, but I had a feeling this was no guest. It was a once in a blue moon occurrence, one that would have the pleasure of smelling my repellent post-workout odor. I could already see her scrunching her nose in displeasure at the sight of my lackluster appearance.

Sighing, I left the oak trees of our garden behind and tucked my earphones in the pocket of my leggings. In my opinion, whoever thought of combining leggings and pockets deserved a lifetime of supply of orgasms. I thrived in comfy clothes, even though blade-like stilettos and blinding uncomfortable dresses were the go to in my social circle. The dancer in me spoke louder and prouder than my stuffy upbringing.

Climbing the short front steps, I brushed past the hand-crafted gold leaf iron and glass entrance. My house dripped with opulence, fully equipped with marble floors proudly displaying mosaic medallions, multiple stairways, and a bathroom for each day of the week. The Corinthian columns and statues that made you shit your pants in night light made me feel like I lived in a museum and had to tiptoe around not to break any of the couple thousand dollars' worth of decoration.

I moved through the cold halls, stopping dead when I reached the living room. Even with her car parked outside, I had to rub my eyes *twice* to make sure I wasn't hallucinating.

Dear old mommy was sprawled across a gold ottoman sofa, her legs propped up on some silk tasseled pillows, Jimmy Choos staining the light fabric because she couldn't be arsed to remove them. Why go through the trouble when dry cleaning money was mere change?

"I understand David; you did the best you could." Claire Roux spoke into the phone attached to her ear.

I took an automatic step forward, my ears twitching at the name that escaped her lips. The detective I'd hired to look into my father's death.

The familiar pang that followed when I thought about that night didn't disappoint. It came back with a vengeance, making a mess of my stomach and forcing the acai bowl I'd had for breakfast up my throat.

Three years, and you still haven't moved on... A voice in the back of my head cackled.

It was hard to do so when you were raised as Daddy's girl for sixteen years straight. Only to find out the person you loved the most killed for sport. A part of me died when Dad got sentenced to life in prison with no possibility of parole. It might not have been the death penalty, but I still went through the stages of grief just the same, bypassing a few pesky fillers when it suited me.

First came anger. I was angry at him, myself, my mom, God, the trees outside. Anything that lived, breathed, and made sounds, I wanted to hurl it at the burning orange orb in the sky with my nonexistent Herculean powers.

I refused to look at Dad when he got ushered away in handcuffs. I could feel his pleading gaze rubbing all over my body, but the puke threatening to spew out for a *second* time held me back. The angry beast, otherwise known as Leonardo Bianchi, on the opposite side of the aisle, made for a more convincing case, as his stare seared me in place, lasering the space around me.

Then depression sunk its dark talons in deep. I cried over the calls from Clarkson Jail, I left to go to voicemail repeatedly, and lost weight as fast as my friends fluttered away from the PR nightmare that buzzed around the Roux name. I didn't know whose fall was faster, harder, and more bone crushing. Mine or Lucifer's? Our life stories matched as well. Disgraced, fallen, and loathed.

Acceptance came last, reluctantly at first. Blame by association, embarrassment, and my very own grief for Isabella were some of the things that kept me away. Guilt gnawed on my insides when I answered my first phone call from Dad. I didn't speak, just breathed into the receiver like an idiot, listening to his voice for the first time in seven months. By the time I managed to digest my darker than kohl legacy and schedule a visit, it was too late.

"There was a fight in Clarkson Detention Center today, Eliana. Knives were pulled, lives were lost. Your father was one of those lives." Mother did me the honor of hand-delivering the piece of information, a tan peppering her silky skin. She looked so immaculate, so put together, so unbothered, while I was dying inside.

The gaping wounds I attempted to stitch together were dealt with a killer blow there was no turning back from. Whatever his faults, I was devastated. I cried while others rejoiced. And Leo knew. Leo saw all as if he was fucking omnipresent. Feeling for my father wasn't something I was allowed to do. It represented betrayal in its deepest form, in Leo's mind.

"Yes, yes. I know, it's not your fault. Honestly, this was a dead end to begin with. I don't even know why Eliana sent you on such a witch hunt," Mother continued, oblivious to my presence. "Alright. Well, thank you for your patience, David."

Since when were they on a first name basis?

"What did *David* say?" I startled her with my sudden appearance.

Her feet dropped from the ottoman as she clutched a single line of pearls outlining her slender throat. I cringed when I saw the dirty footprints on the fabric.

On the outside, one would think that the queen had given birth to a hood rat. Mother was all prim and proper like always, dressed in an olive-colored sundress that complimented her crystal blues, not one hair out of place. I fidgeted with my messy bun, plucking stray strands behind my ears.

"Why, hello to you too, Eliana," she replied, winded.

"Hi, Mother." I flashed her my teeth. "Long time no see, huh?"

Her attitude dropped at my jab, and she decided to forgo any other formalities.

"David said exactly what he's been saying since the first time you decided to push forward with this nonsense investigation. That there is *no* evidence supporting anyone had it out for Francis. Inner-gang rivalries and leveling the score is pretty common in prison. Unfortunately, what happened wasn't extraordinarily new."

"As far as I know, Dad wasn't in any gangs." I folded my hands over my chest.

"I don't think our knowledge extends that far, Eliana. I know you want to cling on to whatever you can. Trust me, this isn't easy for me either." Her face looked like she was clenching her ass cheeks together, in order not to rip one out. Mother got off the couch, her heels clicking against the marble floor. "I'm worried about you though. Getting wrapped up in made up problems is not healthy. You're digging yourself down a rabbit hole."

For better or worse, I was sixteen when Dad was put

away. I wasn't completely clueless. I knew how to fend for myself. Our housekeeper at the time, Melinda, part-timing as my nanny, let me sponge up enough life skills to make it out alive. I had a hard time believing mommy here was worried about me, when at the first opportunity she got, she took off on a world tour.

She tried to pat my cheek, but I grabbed hold of her hand in time. "Oh, that's rich, Claire. I'm sure you'll be worrying yourself all the way to Milan later tonight." I dropped her limb as if it was diseased. *"Unfortunately,* not everyone is as great at moving on as you are. If I remember correctly, you refused to spend a dime on figuring this out, so I fail to see how this was hard for you."

"Because we don't have money to waste on stupid causes. We're living off an inheritance, Eliana. It's going to run out eventually."

She was so full of shit.

I wasn't allowed access to *my* inheritance without her say so, until about a month ago when I turned twenty. The number was astronomical, good enough for the children of my grandchildren to survive and thrive on.

"But we do have enough money for your bi-weekly trips to the LV store?" I curved a brow. "My *fucking* father died, Claire, and their story isn't cutting it. I want to know how."

"Mind your language," she hissed, smoothing her hands over her dress. "You did not go to the best schools only to come out speaking like a whore."

And you just love fixating on the innate when I make a solid point.

"Too little, too fucking late to be scolding me on my choice of words, Mommy." I backed away, painting on a petulant smile. "Now, if you'll excuse me, I have places to be.

Please refrain from walking on the tabletops with your heels on too."

I made for the spiral stairs, hoping I wouldn't have to see her face again for another year. I didn't believe in shooting the messenger, but she seemed to come around solely when bad news was in order. I could live with the mommy issues I had. I wasn't that desperate for her attention.

I'd find out what happened.

With or without help.

I wore a strapless chiffon dress, with lace flowers sheathed around my back like a wrap scarf. My hair was up in a messy French twist, some loose strands lightly caressing the nape of my neck. I wanted to scratch it raw, and I didn't know whether it was because my hair tickled or because all the glares behind my back weighed a ton.

Pillan's was an auction house that rivaled the likes of Sotheby's and Christie's. It was established much later, but the name was just as notorious. They were known for selling controversial pieces, be it artifacts that were supposedly *"borrowed"* by the British centuries ago, or more recently pieces created by disgraced artists. There was no such thing as bad publicity in their dictionary.

And it worked.

Beyond the glitzy chandeliers and rush of the art world's blood sport, people also showed up for the headlines, hiding behind the, *"separate the art from the artist"* excuse. Bad people could create good art. It was proven plenty of times before. A fat bank account didn't care as long as the eye was pleased. Besides, artists didn't get compensated or royalties from their works being sold at auction houses.

I would know. Francis's most ambitious piece was up for grabs tonight. The commission required for the evening sale had cost an arm and a leg. This was a work I didn't want to miss though. A gift addressed to me by my father.

Sipping on a champagne flute, I tuned in on the mindless chatter of socialites and artificial white smiles of businessmen filling the room. I didn't fit in their canvas, despite my Carolina Herrera dress and Aquazzura bow pumps. I was ignored until they ran out of topics to talk about—their source of entertainment for the night. I couldn't care less. I was here for one reason only. To get back what rightfully belonged to me.

I choked on my last sip of champagne when I felt a sharp push from behind. The first thing that flew through my mind was, *did they jump people for underage drinking now?* The second, *I'm about to eat a mouthful of wood.*

Alas, my face never met the floor. A hand wrapped around my midriff, steadying me and causing the glass in my hand to bump against my teeth again. God, if this was who I thought it was, I'd be suing his ass in the event of a chipped tooth. Struggling in his hold, I set myself free and turned around, a scowl fixed in place.

"Oh, I'm so sorry." A virile voice, somehow not registered in my brain, slammed home. "Are you okay?"

I blinked, my pre-disposed stance melting away. Leo's face full of sharp edges and expressive eyes that looked like a flattened grass field after a storm, just got knocked down a peg or four. The guy before me filled all the vacated top spots in my personal, *hottest males on planet Earth* list.

Not to worry. Leo still held the top three in my alien one, right along with his spirit animal, Loki.

Dressed in black, skinny jeans, and a form-fitting white shirt, he didn't immediately catch your attention among millionaires with flashier clothes than Donatella Versace. His sun-kissed skin, tightly coiled black hair that fanned over his gorgeous face like clouds, sure made you look twice, though.

"I'm really sorry. I kind of lost my footing there and tripped." He apologized, waving his hand at a waiter over his back.

"No, no, accidents happen. It's okay." I set my empty glass on a passing tray, smoothing my hands over my dress. "*I'm* okay, just a bit startled."

The guy stared at me openly now, running his eyes all over me. I resisted the urge to fidget with the tulle of my gown. He looked familiar, but no matter how much I ravaged my brain for information, I came up blank. I didn't know every resident in Astropolis, that would be absurd, but a face like his would definitely linger.

"You sure? You looked ready to tear me a new as—" He cut himself off, risking a glance at his surroundings. "You looked pretty angry," he finished off with a well-practiced smile.

"Yeah, I like to scowl without reason sometimes. I find it to be a very beneficial exercise for my facial muscles."

What the hell did I just say?

Well, at least it was better than saying *my scowl dropped because you look like a gold-plated rendition of Adonis.*

A smirk split his lips, and he leaned against the wall. "Really? All I've heard is that you can develop wrinkles early on. You should stop. We wouldn't want such a pretty face aging before it's due time."

I arched a brow, resisting the tug of my mouth. "I think I'll be safe."

I didn't acknowledge his comment about my looks. I still appreciated it, though. I wasn't starved for validation or anything like that. I knew I was above average in the beauty department, no matter how much my outfits, features, and hairstyles were picked apart.

Blue-eyed blondes weren't as much of a rare breed in Astropolis, but I didn't fit well within those misconstrued beauty standards. With a sharp jawline, slightly uneven brows (they were sisters, not twins), and an off-kilter nose, symmetrical wasn't an accurate synonym for me. Still, everything blended well together.

Off-beat when unchaperoned, yet at harmony with each other.

I didn't mean to be conceited; it was simply the truth.

"That you will." His smirk extended to a smile. "I'm Cole, by the way."

I gripped his extended hand to shake. The calluses scratching against my skin made me wonder how a pretty rich boy like him got hands like those in the first place. It was refreshing. People who attended these auctions weren't your average run of the mill hard workers. Their hands were smoother than a baby's butt.

"Nice to meet you, Cole."

"I didn't catch your name."

Stick around long enough, and you will.

"That's because I didn't throw it." It was my turn to smirk as I dished corny comebacks like it was nobody's business.

I affirmed my suspicions that he wasn't a local when he asked for my name. I wasn't the queen of Astropolis, but I *was* the villain. Everyone knew my name. Cole could pick up Page Six tomorrow, and he'd learn all about it. Bianchi was rumored to make an appearance today too. They'd be all over it. The king of the food chain hated me, so in turn, the sheep in his court had to go along with it. The herd mentality was ingrained in their pea-sized brains.

He dipped his chin, amusement evident in his hazel gaze. "Very clever."

"Aren't I?" My smile was bitter as I backed off. A bidding war awaited, and I was looking forward to spilling Bianchi's blue blood. "See you around, Cole."

"Wait—"

I didn't wait.

I wasn't a prude. I just didn't like fraternizing with people from my social circle. The only time their leash was extended was when they got an order to bite, and Lord knew I didn't need one more scar to add to my collection.

I regretted my decision to opt-out of telephone bidding about thirty minutes into the auction. Claustrophobia gripped my throat tightly. There was a sea of seats with barely any space separating them. I was stuck between two balding middle-aged men that didn't know how to use their fucking paddles.

No, you can't spank the air, Jimmy. Or the people around you, as a matter of fact.

"All right, let's move on to lot number thirty. God's Answer, by Francis Roux on the screen." I breathed a sigh of relief when the auctioneer announced the next piece. "Starting at two-hundred thousand."

I swung my paddle up so hard my hand cramped, and I had to drop it again, massaging my arm. It seemed I got his attention, though, and the auctioneer pointed at me. "To the gentleman in the back. Do I hear seven-hundred thousand?"

Gentleman?

I whipped my head back, and of course, *he* made an appearance. Leonardo loved collecting goods that weren't his, flaunting his cash around in a way only new money would. He sat right behind me, paddle perched between his long fingers, a casual grin on his face.

"You're not winning this time." I didn't bother showing my shock. The feeling was growing pesky after four years of battling all kinds of volatile demons.

Leo rested his ankle on his knee, swinging the paddle in his hand when the auctioneer continued spouting numbers, his voice falling into a cadence. "Finally grew a backbone, princess?"

"I figured the stick up your ass was permanent, hence the round the clock bitch treatment." I smiled sweetly. He was dressed like a fucking daydream, his suit clinging to his muscles like Velcro.

Business major.

Upstanding citizen.

BB Oil heir.

Leo's future was bright, overshadowing the nightmare hiding underneath. That part of him he reserved just for me, always giving his worst and never letting go. The least I could do was fight back, up my survival chances.

"How can she be so shameless?"

"Utterly Disrespectful. But what can you expect with a father like hers?"

I swallowed past the lump in my throat, ignoring the chatter around me.

"Would you like to have one too, Narcissus? I know plenty of places that would accept a blonde Lana Rhoades knock-off in no time." He leaned forward, and I saw he was holding paddle number 666. How fucking fitting. "Might help you loosen up."

I had a list of insults lined up on the tip of my tongue. That was what we did. We could go off offending and humiliating each other for all eternity if we didn't also have to eat, sleep, and shit.

But I didn't.

I turned around because I wouldn't let him derail yet another aspect of my life.

"At four-hundred and eighty thousand." The auctioneer used his hands like a traffic cop, keeping up with the bids in rapid fashion. "Do I hear five hundred?"

Again, I raised my paddle.

Again, he outbid me.

The circle went on and on until I was squirming in my seat at the uncomfortably high sum.

"Why the hell do you even want this piece?" I hissed over my back. "You're about as artistic as pineapple on pizza is sane, Mr. *Statistics is fun*."

He used to tutor me way back when I was struggling with math. Men were multifaceted creatures, but Leo was a multifaceted asshole.

"I've always wanted a free standing toilet paper holder." He shrugged, and I wanted to crack his blasé demeanor with an icepick. "And pineapple on pizza tastes fucking awesome. Bite me, Narcissus."

"Aren't you supposed to be Italian?"

"Aren't you supposed to be winning?"

My body acted on autopilot, abandoning the wooden chair, and my mouth dropped the words faster than my brain could register what I was spewing. "Two million."

A glint entered the auctioneer's eyes at the prospect of a higher commission. My dad's glass statue had fallen in worth, but it was about to make its buck if Leo continued to fight me over it.

It was mine.

It was fucking me.

God's Answer: Eliana.

The sculpture was vivid and visually illusive. I was lying on a blue pillar, my hand reaching out to the sky, hair strewn all around me. Details so precise that up close, you could probably see individual strands of hair, carved to perfection. Dad made it in my honor. God's answer, that was what he always told me I was to him, that's why he named me Eliana.

"Two million. With the lady at two million, do I hear two point five?" The repeated question filled the room, and no one offered more. If they did, they'd be losing, not profiting.

"Five million." Leo's cool voice slashed through the air.

"Seven," I shot back.

"Fifteen."

The auctioneer was struck speechless. He didn't even have to intermediate. We were doing all the work for him.

Was it worth it?

Losing almost twenty percent of my bank balance to win a petty war? Leo's cocky grin flashed like a reel before my eyes. The upward tilt of his lips and the arrogance laced in his gaze. It physically hurt; the need to raze his kingdom.

I quickly sucked in a breath, basing my stupidity in spontaneity. "Twenty million."

"Thirty-five."

Get in a ring with a billionaire, and you will lose.

I rolled my lips in my mouth when the auctioneer's gaze bounced back to me. *Forty million. Say it. Don't let him take another part. He already has a whole trophy shelf with pieces of your soul.*

"Do I hear, thirty-five million, five hundred thousand?"

No, but he could sure hear the sound of my heart cracking against my ribs and crashing into a million pieces on the bottom of my stomach.

I could ponder however high I wanted, hell, give away my entire inheritance, and set a new record. Leo would still outbid me. He had the means. He had the power. And most importantly, the drive to pursue this tirelessly.

I didn't bother shaking my head, just plopped down on my seat with a thump.

"Aand going once... going twice... and sold! To the gentleman in the blue suit."

The pound of the gavel echoed, lingering in my ringing ears. Next lot, next piece, the auction moved on. Only we remained in a constant loop of one-upping each other. I closed my eyes when his pine scent tickled my nose, and his breath skated over my bare back. He was so close, but I was used to the devil barring down my neck.

"Even after all these years, and you still try to fight it?" Goose bumps formed on my neck and down my spine.

I gulped down the bitter smile that threatened to splay

over my lips. "Isn't that why you chained me here in the first place? To amuse you?"

"You think I find this funny, Narcissus?"

"I know you enjoy it," I snapped. "Destruction must taste sweet if you're willing to spend thirty fucking five million dollars for it."

I didn't hear his reply. Every head swung to the exit when a loud crash sounded from beyond the room, like a ton of solid glass, breaking into a million tiny grains on the ground. Scattering sounds filled every ounce of the space for a breath. It was as if I was right there, at the epicenter of the earthquake.

"What was that?"

There was an uproar of activity as people rushed out the room, flashy dresses and stuffy suits scrambling like chickens in a henhouse. Cool as a mint, Leo leaned forward, the smirk painted on his lips imprinting on the skin of my arm like a stamp. I stayed put, his touch networking its way down my body, until I was as frozen as an ice sculpture.

"Destruction laying the ground rules for reconstruction." He followed a trail up my shoulder first with his lips, then the tip of his nose, stopping when he reached my ear. "Paint me as the villain in your story Eli, and I'll gladly play the part. At least I can still sleep soundly at night knowing my legacy isn't stained with blood, knowing my support lays with the fallen and not those who buried them."

Gasps spilled inside the now deserted room. My mouth was open, struggling to regulate my breaths, but it wasn't me. It was from the outside. From whatever shit he'd orchestrated this time. Leo didn't do bullying at a high school level. He went the extra mile, wrapping his ugliness with a corporate level bow.

He was no villain.

He was a monster.

I forced my muscles to work, twisting more of my body on the chair that felt slick beneath my thighs. Curls for days and long lashes assaulted me, paired with pouty lips that invited you to take a dive into the underworld. His face was a hair's breadth away from mine, yet our mindsets were oceans apart.

"I *never* supported him. Not once after he was found guilty."

"So, what are you doing here?" A finger curled under my chin.

"I wanted that statue back. I—" I thought better of what I wanted to say. It didn't matter, really. This was another ploy, another scheme. "I don't have to explain myself to you. You'll hold on to any word as admission of guilt."

"You can have it back." His hand dropped from my face, and my jaw almost scattered to the floor as he got on his feet. A smile twisted his features until he resembled a well-fed devil. "In pieces."

I bit down on my left cheek, littering my wooden chair with fine crescent marks. "You didn't."

"Why don't you have a look for yourself?" Leo turned around, making his way to the door. He might as well have dropped pebbles on his path because I couldn't stop my legs from following behind him.

The walls blurred as I tried to match his gait, but even my height was no match for his stride. Lungs burning, I stopped abruptly when I caught sight of a gathered crowd in the hall, glimmers of blue peeking through their forms.

I knew what I'd find there, yet I still shouldered past the people. They gave way easily, and a shattered sky spread beneath my heels. Glass crunched, crumbling further, vulnerable under the weight of my carelessness.

Keep it together.

Keep it the fuck together.

Even though this wasn't my first rodeo, hurt slammed into me repeatedly, like North Atlantic waves ravaging rugged cliffs. I shook like a leaf, vaguely aware of the buzz around me.

If anything, the bastard knew where to hit. My dad's sculpture was crushed beyond resemblance. *I* was crushed. Leo broke whatever version of me he could get his hands on.

Chapter 4

Three Years Ago

ELIANA

The skin around my elbows was rubbed raw and bleeding.

My knees stung, decorated with beads of blood that seeped through my skinny jeans. A russet hue stained the blue fabric, commemorating my broken promise.

I was betraying my own damn self.

I vowed never to step foot inside his house again, yet here I was. Repeating and not repairing, jumping over fences, evading guards by hiding behind polished bushes, just so I could scream at Leo. I was risking jail time to plead for my freedom. How ironic.

My clammy palms stained the crinkled papers in my grip. A bead of sweat rolled down my back as I pushed the gray door of his room open. In my defense, I'd knocked beforehand, and no one answered.

The room was as chaotic as Leo. White duvet half on the king-sized bed, half spilled on the floor. Clothes *everywhere*. On top of his dark gray dresser, over his hamper and around it, as if he'd cannonballed them there and missed the mark.

Not surprising.

He wasn't famed for his aim. His left hook, however, was a different topic. Leo took boxing classes for as long as I could remember him.

Light on my feet, I moved further inside, taking in the training bag and some red boxing gloves abandoned on the floor by his desk. It was radio silent, except for the sound of the shower. So when the door swung shut with a soft click behind me, I jumped.

"Fucking hell," I muttered, fisting my green crop top and tugging it down subconsciously.

I couldn't afford to be timid. That was what got me here in the first place.

I was naïve in my thinking. Leo didn't pull any stops, had lost his moral compass, and messed with my fucking college applications.

My future.

He'd robbed me of my ticket out of this town.

Astropolis—Greek for City of Stars. Ironic if you asked me. City of Soul-Sucking Black Holes seemed much more fitting.

Squaring my shoulders, I started for the en-suite bathroom, following the trail of steam that slithered out in smoky swirls. Anger and hurt fueled my steps, and just a little bit of hope, too. Maybe he could undo whatever he'd done. Maybe I still had a chance to escape.

Holy steam.

Even with the bathroom door open, steam had built up,

and condensation stuck to the dark tiles like glue. My gaze raced from the black quartz floor to the single pane walk-in shower, and the breath I was about to inhale stuck in my throat.

Holy buns.

Perfect. Muscular. Wet. Bronzed. Buns.

His ass was so perfectly round and firm, my mouth watered. I tried to chalk it up to the cinnamon bark scent that conquered the air in the room. In reality, my mind assaulted me with pictures of sinking my teeth into those flexing back muscles. I felt like a pervert, but I couldn't stop looking.

Saliva pooled in the back of my throat, and I choked, drooling over my enemy. Drooling over the guy that picked apart every aspect of my life and throwing spears like he was training for the Olympics. He got the thrill of his life whenever the victim fell prey to his ways.

"Who the fuck—" His voice was muffled over the sound of water crashing against the floor.

But I heard him.

And he saw me.

The need to duck and hide washed over me like a tsunami. His gaze paralyzed me... *okay*, maybe it was the water running down his pecs. Or the fat droplets that peaked over the dips and peaks of his abs. Or the trail they followed down the V-Line of his lower abdomen or...

No.

I snapped my gaze back up, shutting out any unnecessary distractions. He eyed me like he'd seen a ghost, unsure if I was really there.

"Narcissus?" His voice was sharp as he shut off the shower. The papers in my hand wrinkled further with the effort it took not to give him the satisfaction of my ogling. Then he threw open the glass door, releasing an onslaught of steam that hit me right in the face.

This was a bad idea.

Naked as the day he was born, he looked formidable. He was supposed to be looking small, caught off-guard. Yet he had no qualms about his nudity or the fact that I'd ambushed him at his own home—the space where I wasn't allowed to be.

The place between my thighs clenched when a slow smirk tugged at his full lips, lighting up his moss colored eyes. I willed my cheeks not to heat up. He was on the spot, not me.

"Bianchi," I quipped, crossing my arms over my chest. "I have to talk to you."

His gaze fell to the rolled up papers in my fist as he extracted a white, fluffy towel from a rack next to the sinks. "What makes you think I will listen to you and not call security to have you thrown out?"

"Oh, you're going to want to hear what I have to say." I spit through my teeth, keeping my gaze on the ceiling.

Through the corner of my eye, I saw him shaking out his wet hair and using the towel to wipe the precipitation off his chest, but he hadn't moved to cover himself up yet. He stood there gloriously naked, and I was turning embarrassingly red.

"Will I?" Leo inquired, abandoning the towel on the sink. "Plead your case then, Narcissus. You have five minutes before I throw you out."

"Oh did I just get the upgraded escort?" I scoffed.

"I was afraid you were after my virtue at first, but you've been here for three minutes already and can't take your eyes off the ceiling." The scent of deodorant tickled my nose as he went through the motions like I wasn't even there. "Do you think if you stare hard enough, your guardian angel might come down and rescue you? Because you're facing serious jail time right now."

"You mean the virtue that's lying in shambles in a poor girl's backseat?" I retorted, turning to him. "And if you think I'm the one facing serious jail time, you're in for a surprise. You might be rich—*richer*—but you're no god."

"Is this some reverse psychology trick you're trying out? If so, it's not working out well, Narcissus, and I suggest you get straight to the point. My patience is running thin."

I bit my lip, munching on the dead skin. Him being naked wasn't good for my brain. All the blood it needed to function was rushing south.

"Put some clothes on. I'll wait for you outside." I turned on my heel, banging the bathroom door shut.

I heard him grumble some expletives under the thin crack of the door and tiptoed around his bed. I sat on his gaming chair, and an itch to pick up his comforter and fold it slammed into me. The inner neat freak in me was coming out when I should have wanted to bleach the walls white and give him the mental asylum he so desperately needed.

It was a coping mechanism. I always did my laundry when I was mad or upset. Something about folding clothes and hugging a fresh load warm from the dryer soothed me.

The raging bull emerged from the bathroom, a towel wrapped around his narrow hips. My blood pumped faster when he locked his eyes with mine. He walked over slow like a lion stalking its prey.

"That's you dressed up?"

"This is all you're going to get. And if you don't start

speaking soon, it will be me throwing you in the back of a police cruiser."

Tired of all the back and forth, of him stealing every ounce of oxygen from the air, I threw the papers I was holding onto the bed. They plopped on it with a sad, heavy thump. There were a lot of papers, a lot of *rejections*, a whole stack of them.

"What is this?" He asked, bending to pick them up. I didn't reply, just watched him thumb through them with coolness.

When he'd finally looked his fill, and I'd picked the skin around my nails enough for it to pinken, he looked up, a crease marring the space between his eyebrows.

"So you went through all this trouble just to show me how intellectually incapable you are? I already knew you were dumb, babe, there's no need to flaunt it like this."

I abandoned the chair, annoyance flaring in my chest. "I have a 4.0 GPA, and higher SAT scores than you could get in your dreams, Bianchi. Don't talk to me about 'intellectual incapability'."

"Stanford? Yale? Princeton? Penn?" He listed off the names, letting the papers drop on our feet one after the other. The whole floor was covered with my defeat and his win. "These schools don't look for the next rocket scientist. They look for leaders. They value experiences over achievements. You could be Stephen Hawking on paper, and it wouldn't matter if you're bland on every other aspect of your life."

"Then why did Dane University accept me? They're just as renowned and highly competitive to get into. Conveniently tucked right in the outskirts of Astropolis, a mere twenty-minute drive away. That's where you're going too, isn't it?"

Leo took a step toward me, and I was so mad that his face looked like the perfect punching bag. Fear of doing more damage to myself than him held me back.

"If I'm not mistaken, your family threw several millions in donations a few years back. Hate to say it, Narcissus, but nepotism isn't gonna end anytime soon."

"This isn't nepotism; it's you! You messed with my college applications. I know you did!" I hissed, pointing my finger at his chest. I wished I could have drilled a hole through his torso just to see if his heart would bleed red or black.

My bets were on the latter.

"That's a pretty theory you got there and an overactive imagination. Is your narcissism trickling into psychopathy now?" He eyed me like I needed special care. Deflecting and turning the blame on me like a proper snake.

"You knew I wanted to leave this town, and you couldn't let me be, could you? How is it that my applications were rejected from every other university? You had something to do with it. I'm a hundred percent certain."

Leo grabbed a hold of my hand, dropping it back by my side. The mocking glint in his eyes made an appearance again. A staple of his.

"Yeah? And where's your proof, Eliana? I can also fling empty accusations around, but will anyone actually believe me? No. Because there. Is. No. Proof."

Leo turned around, reaching for his dresser, *dismissing* me. My heart slammed harder against my ribcage, and I felt this insatiable need to hurt him. Hurt him as much as he hurt me.

This thing between us, it was a festering wound that if we kept rubbing, it would get infected. That's why I wanted to leave. I wanted to escape him and our toxicity. I wasn't twenty yet, so I didn't have access to my inheritance. College was my way out, and he'd robbed me of it.

It was getting harder to breathe. The need to strike out, to break away from the suffocating walls he'd build around me, spilled over like an overflowing river. My balled fists met his back before I could think about what I was doing. There was a flash, and suddenly bloodlust was the only thing in my mind.

"You will undo whatever you did and let me be!" I screamed over my lungs, pounding my hands on his unmoving back. "Let me fucking be! I'm not asking for happiness, just less pain. Less you!"

Leo rotated in place, but I didn't stop. I hit his chest again and again, and he let me. He didn't try to contain me or fight back. Maybe deep down, he knew he deserved this and worse.

He was a heartless beast that once cared too much.

And I was guilty of being born in the wrong family.

Our knees cracked on the floor at the same time as we both folded over the weight of our past and grim future. The scabs on my knees most likely opened again, staining Leo's pristine white carpet.

I was exhausted, my face was wet, and my body hurt from the physical extortion. I didn't know how much time had passed. All I knew was that we lay on the ground in a rare moment of tranquility. He let me rest on his chest, keeping his hand tucked behind my head so I wouldn't slip.

"I hate you so much," I whispered, pulling at the sparse hair over his sternum in weak protest.

"I know." My head bounced with his steady breaths. "You bring it up every time you see me."

"Why do you never say it back?" I looked up, catching the way his jaw locked as he stared at the ceiling.

"I don't hate you, Narcissus. No matter how hard I try, I can't. You're the fire to my smoke. You keep me going. You keep the flames blazing. And for that, I can never hate you."

I didn't pay much attention to the way my chest tightened. I literally barreled through his walls today. That was why he was opening up. We'd go back to hurting each other when our five minutes were up.

Feelings were inconsequential. Revenge took the front stage, the main character in our tragedy.

"Then why are you acting like you want to put me out?" I croaked.

Leo glanced down at me, his abdominal muscles tightening under my palms. "Because when we go down, we'll go down together. You numb the pain, but you don't take it away. It's still there, dull and throbbing."

You never let me try, I wished to say.

I didn't though, I kept my mouth wired shut.

There was no turning back from what we'd become.

Our dream couldn't take place in a city where shadows thrived.

The boy with the crush and the girl doing little to nothing to stop his advances were buried under the weight of bad blood.

Chapter 5

Present

ELIANA

I stabbed my cupcake with a fork until it resembled nothing but granulated cake and crumbs. Beans N' Cream was a favorite among the students, a mere ten-minute walk from campus. The built-in bookshelves, warm brown sofas, delicious coffee, and homemade treats created the perfect ambiance for university students glued to their Macs.

A lo-fi hip-hop playlist acted as background noise, right along with Leo and his friends, three tables over. Their obnoxious laughter floated over, and I was this close to storming there and jamming my fork into their eye sockets. Starting with Ares, the loudest one.

My paper lay abandoned, and I felt a headache coming on, but I refused to go. Perhaps I was enjoying the *fifty ways to murder Leo and his friends* reel my mind played on repeat way too much.

"If only looks could kill." A voice I vaguely recalled broke me out of my stupor. "Those guys would be ten feet under."

"Unfortunately, they don't," I replied, turning my head and meeting Cole's gray gaze.

Cole from the auction.

I took in his plain white shirt and ripped jeans. This was the second time I was seeing this stranger in a week, and he'd approached me first on both occasions.

"Mind if I sit?" He pointed at one of the vacant seats at my table, a coffee cup and greasy brown paper bag in hand. I didn't have to look to see what was in it. Beans N' Cream's infamous pizza, loaded with fat and cheese. Every establishment had a weak link, and this was theirs.

"Um... yes. I'm sorry, but I don't know you."

Did I resemble a hedgehog whose spikes flared whenever I was approached? *Affirmative.*

Did life teach me to be cautious with people's motives? *Also, affirmative.*

"Well, that's why I'm here. We can get to know each other. You go to Dane, right? I just transferred from California."

I stared at him for a beat. The guy *was* scary hot, but also kind of creepy. My inner bitch poked her head, ready to shoo him away. I blamed her for the next words that escaped my mouth.

"I'm sure someone else here will appreciate your hobo-chic getup. Why don't you go bother them?" I locked my ankle around the leg of the chair he'd targeted, tugging it closer.

He smiled, undeterred. "You see, I'm feeling kind of on the fence about it. Your six-figure wardrobe hasn't helped you gain plenty of friends, now has it?"

He referred to my red, floral print designer dress, and my eye twitched at his observation. Indeed, everyone was paired up in study groups or coupled up, and I was all alone.

"Beat it, Cole." I threw him a tight-lipped smile.

"Don't mind if I don't." He placed his things on the table, scooting my laptop out of the way, and parked his ass on a seat. I hissed, reaching down to rub my ankle. He'd knocked my foot out of the way when he scraped the chair back. "It's a free country after all."

Another round of laughter traveled from the table containing the bane of my existence, just in time. "A lot of people would beg to differ. You have the resources to attend Dane. Don't tell me Mommy and Daddy are a bunch of sweet high school teachers."

"I don't even know your name, sweetheart, and you're already asking what my parents do for a living?"

"I doubt you haven't heard all about it by now," I replied flatly. If he had indeed transferred to Dane, he would have caught some talk by now. It was the second week of classes.

"I want to hear it from you, too. Is that so bad?" He raised a brow, taking a sip from his coffee. I wondered if he was still referring to my name or all the gossip surrounding it.

It is often said we had a devil on one shoulder and an angel on the opposite. I was personally acquainted with my devil, feeling his labored breath on my neck every now and again.

Turning my head left, I met Leo's disapproving eyes. How he seemed to hate on both of us at the same time without looking cross-eyed was beyond me. Mona Lisa who? We had Bianchi throwing daggers in all directions.

I shook my head, retracting my gaze. Cole was making enemies already, and he'd been here all but five minutes. A bizarre sense of responsibility had me warning him off.

"If you don't want your first year here to be one straight from hell, then you should probably stay away from me, Cole."

Don't get it wrong, I was far from bending to Leo's wishes anymore, but I didn't want to bring someone else into our bullshit. He tended to drive away every guy he saw me with. Thankfully, I still had freedom of movement, other-wise I would've been a twenty-year-old virgin.

"Call me a glutton for punishment, but I have a stronger affinity for hell than I do heaven."

My tense shoulders sagged. "So that's what it is then? You're a masochist?"

"Why are you offering to be my mistress?" Cole teased back, finally biting into that awful looking pizza.

My face scrunched up when he started chewing it. "I'll pass, seeing as you've already found your source of pain for the day."

"Your loss." He shrugged. "You'll be the one missing out on all this goodness." Using the pizza slice, he gestured to his body, stretching his muscles while doing so.

"I believe I'll be able to manage Don Juan."

"Suit yourself, sweetheart." He didn't deflate at my rejection.

"Will you stop calling me sweetheart? I think we've established I'm anything but that by now."

"What should I call you then?" he asked, with a stubborn

tilt of his chin. "Since you still haven't offered me your name."

He was already acquainted with it; he just wanted to see me bend first. And fuck, I would. Leo hadn't stopped staring since I first caught his eyes. I could feel his gaze rolling all over me, and I bet Cole could too. The fact that his ass was still firmly planted on a chair opposite me was admirable and deserved a bone.

"Eliana Roux," I offered with a sigh.

Cole widened his eyes comically. "There you go. That wasn't so hard, now was it?"

"Don't make me make you forget it."

"No, that's not possible. You'll have better luck trying to erase an elephant's memory."

And here he was giving me goldfish vibes. A smart person would've heeded my warning. I bit on my bottom lip, containing a smile. I'd become so engrossed in our conversation, I didn't notice the looming shadow over my head until it was too late.

I gasped, shocked, when a cold, dark liquid was doused over my head. It splattered all around, catching the backpack by my feet and making a mess out of me. My hair dripped, and the liquid slid down my spine, leaving behind a disgusting sticky residue.

"Ohmigod!" A nauseating voice I recognized as Caroline King called. The bottle-blonde replacement of me in Serena's life. "I slipped while on my way to throw my leftovers in the trash."

"What the hell is wrong with you?" Cole touted for my behalf, picking my drenched laptop off the table.

What was wrong with them was never outgrowing their

kindergarten sandbox hierarchy phase. Developmental delay.

"We're so sorry, we didn't realize they were aiming for a different kind of garbage bin." I didn't have to turn around to know Serena had a sickly sweet smile on her face.

Muffled giggles echoed around me, but shame didn't follow. This wasn't my first rodeo. I wiped a drop of coffee that had rolled on my forehead with a napkin before snapping my head back, meeting Serena in all her Celine wrap dress glory.

"Really?" I asked her, resisting the urge to wipe the smug look off her face. "I'm sorry your aim was so off then."

"Here." I curled my hand around my cup of coffee, popping the plastic lid off. Still scorching. Perfect. "They're going to the right trash can now, that's for sure."

I threw the coffee, drenching them in return. A course of adrenaline zinged through my veins at their pained moans. A rush of satisfaction. This time there were no laughs, only horrified gasps. Caroline shrieked, doubling over and covering her face with her hands.

Drama queen, I aimed for their chests.

"You fucking bitch!" Serena blew her hair over her shoulder, looking down at her dress. The dark fabric was stuck to her body, not doing her any favors in helping her cool down. "You burned me!"

"Your mother should've taught you not to play with fire." I bared my teeth.

She surprised me by letting out a dark chuckle. Usually, Serena flipped out at any mention of her dead mom. "She might have not, but Claire probably won't skip over the lessons."

I jerked my head up at Mother's name, my eyebrows

crossed in confusion. If that was supposed to be a clever comeback, it had missed the mark by a few football fields. What the hell was she talking about?

"God, you don't even know, do you?" she scoffed, using a few rolled-up napkins Caroline handed her to wipe her neck.

"*Serena.*" I heard a chair scrape against the floor. Rolling my gaze to Leo's direction, I found him on his feet, staring at Serena in warning.

It seemed everyone was in on the joke but me.

Unease washed over me despite trying to stand my ground, unflinching. What could she possibly tell me that was worse than the shit I'd heard before? I grew from the drama. Serena lived in it.

"Why don't you enlighten me then?" I twisted back around, the sparkle in her eyes making me want to duck and hide in my imagination. I knew that look. It had graced her face way too many times before when she took a jab at my walls.

"Carter and Claire got engaged last Friday."

The pounds of my heart got shallower, my chest caving in and giving out.

I didn't hear her right.

I mustn't have heard her right.

I shook my head. "No."

I felt a ghost touch on my shoulder, but I shook it off, focusing on the knives disguised as words Serena continued spewing.

"Yes." Serena nodded, overzealous. "Welcome to the family, *sis.*"

I clenched my teeth, hoping the bite of pain would eradicate the pricking in my eyes. I didn't want to believe her.

Serena was fluent in two languages, English and gossip. But why would she lie so publicly? Why would she fabricate such a story?

Hysteria and logic mixed like two crushing wavelengths, battling each other for dominance. My spine met the sharp edge of the table as I leaned back for support, looking for crumbs of dishonesty in Serena's face.

I found none.

Her cruel smile was in place, stance confident even drenched in coffee. But there was also disgust she couldn't fake in the way her upper lip curled. She found the idea of our single parents marrying just as nauseating as I did, if not more.

My mom was engaged.

To Serena's father.

And she never bothered to tell me herself.

My veins filled with liquid ice as I dug my nails in my palms. Serena had a pretty face, but with a heart like that, I wouldn't approach her with a ten-foot pole if I were a guy. In fact, the only reason why I'd get close would be to slap her with Cole's pizza slice. She'd soak up so much oil she wouldn't have to use moisturizer for a year.

I shook my head, clearing out my thoughts. I'd deal with Mother and my new *family* on my own terms, not in front of an audience.

Turning back around, I tried to disguise the shake of my hands by shoving things into my bag as fast as I could. Likely dead laptop? Check. Keys? Check. Phone? Check.

"Where are you running to, sister?" Serena asked.

I didn't let my face show how much that word grated on my nerves. We used to be sisters, not anymore. All she was to me now was a stranger that liked tearing me down, so her obsession would let her suck his dick.

I ignored her foul existence, looping the bag through my shoulders.

"Want me to drive you home?" Cole's voice was almost overpowered by all the talk around me.

I threw him a smile I hoped didn't look like a grimace. "Thank you for the offer, but I can drive myself."

My heart hammering in my chest, I rose up, stealing one last look at Leo. He was staring at me, the mirror image of a blank canvas. In a room brimming with malice and drama, I stole a piece of his frigidness, coating the protective film over my bones.

Stepping forward, I shed the dead weight off my back. I wouldn't give my last breath to save any of those people, so why should I let their opinions affect me?

The bell of the café's door sounded as I let the crisp afternoon air embrace my body.

I had a rogue mother to deal with.

Thursday.
Friday.
Saturday.
Sunday.

I'd given her plenty of time to tell me. Tell me of her engagement to *that* family. She couldn't be bothered to walk through the door for a second time this month, though. Couldn't make a call or even send a fucking letter to let her daughter know of her engagement.

My standards were low already, but I didn't expect such

disregard when everyone knew. *Every-fucking-one,* after Serena's little Regina George meltdown at Beans N' Cream.

So I cut Claire's allowance off. Froze her Amex and withdrawal rights. I figured nothing got her running faster than money. She'd shown up on my twentieth birthday after she'd missed my last three. On the very same birthday, I got full access to my locked bank account.

Prenuptial agreements were all the rage in my dad's side of the family. Considering their wealth spanned back generations, they probably got spun one too many times and learned their lesson. Mother didn't inherit a cent, although she got to spend plenty from my trust.

Her well ran dry on Tuesday. Hence, it was time for her to make an appearance. I was driving back from campus after a long drawn out math class, and I was feeling irritable already. I was good at math, but I didn't particularly enjoy it, or the thousand whiteboard pictures full of laws and equations I'd have to copy down on paper later.

Pulling up the driveway, I saw her through the windshield. Mother was leaning against a pillar, almost blending in with her white halter dress, tapping her foot repeatedly against the floor. A motion that got more restless when she noticed my car.

She straightened up when I exited the BMW, banging the door of the X6 unnecessarily hard.

"Now, what did the floor ever do to you that you're tapping it so viciously?" I smiled when her eyes flared up as I breezed past her. There was something about getting under her skin that just got to me.

She followed me inside, almost nipping at my heels. "Would you rather I tap my heels against your face?" Came her seeding response.

"Ouch!" I threw her a look over my shoulder, making my way to the kitchen. I needed coffee and Tylenol stat. "You were never one for negative reinforcement, Mommy. What's changed?"

"What's changed is that my card got *declined* at brunch today. Not once or twice, but three times, so I definitely know it wasn't a fluke," she hissed at me, looking like a snake that would like nothing more than to wrap around my neck. "Stacee had to step in and pay for me, and that bitch lives to prove me wrong. Her sly remarks were in abundance after... what happened." She took a brief pause before finishing her sentence, as if the mere thought of her card getting declined was preposterous.

"Oh, the horror!" I exclaimed, passing through the kitchen's arched threshold, on a one-track course toward the De'Longhi coffee machine.

I wasn't allowed to say anything else. Mother continued showering me with her complaints, so I made sure the capsule I chose contained coffee darker than the kitchen's onyx countertops.

"So then I went to withdraw some cash, because I thought maybe there was a problem with my card, but lo and behold—I can't! Again!" She paced across from me, beyond the isle. "Oh, but if you think that's where my adventure from hell ended, you're in for a surprise..." she continued, and I debated how many painkillers I should take.

I popped two in my mouth, washing them down with a glass of water. Mother was lost in her bubble, gesturing wildly as notes of roasted beans filled the air when the machine started spewing out my drug of choice.

"I had to ask for a ride here because my car was all out of

gas, and I couldn't afford to fill up the tank. I was almost stranded on the side of the road!"

If only you went through so much effort to see me.

I kept that thought locked in my head, ignoring the prickles underneath my eyelids. "You should consider changing to a Tesla then. They're much more environmentally friendly, and you can charge them at home," I said. Me, the gas-guzzling SUV owner. "Oh, but that's right." I snapped my fingers, cocking my head. "You can't afford one, can you?"

She stopped pacing abruptly, her head whipping in my direction, as I settled on a stool resting my cup on the kitchen island.

"Well, don't feel too bad. You could always trade in your current vehicle."

"What the hell are you saying, Eliana? What happened to *my* money?" she bellowed, wrapping her shaking hand around her neck, twirling the pearls there.

"What money, Claire?" I took a sip, watching her clutch her pearls tighter. "You haven't worked a day in your life, so do enlighten me. What do you mean by '*your money*'?" I peppered my question with air quotes.

"I haven't worked a day in my life?" she scoffed, eyes rounding. "I gave birth to you, you ungrateful brat. I raised you!"

"Your prices are a bit too high for a surrogate, don't you think? And as for the raising me part, please refrain from the bullshit, Mother. I don't have Alzheimer's just yet."

She started pacing again, her pace slower this time. "Well, what do you plan on doing? You want to leave me penniless?"

If the news about her engagement were true, she'd

hardly need for anything. Carter Laurent owned the biggest law firm in Astropolis, and one thing rich folks always had on standby were lawyers. It was safe to say, business was booming.

Mother had been here for more than ten minutes, though, and still hadn't said a word about her alleged engagement. One last ember of hope curled in my stomach, and I wished what Serena said was a lie. Not because I expected Mother to stay a widow forever. Of course not, I wasn't stupid. She was still young, bound to find someone, but did it have to be Carter?

Serena was already as pleasant as nails on a chalkboard. I could only imagine how much worse she'd get after officiating our step-sibling status.

"Of course not," I said, and her sigh got stuck in her throat when I continued. "You can keep your jewelry. You'd probably be able to live for a good two years if you pawned it. Or you know... you could look for a job. Become a waitress, barista, whatever your heart desires." I toyed with her a bit more, waiting for the volcano to spill out.

Her expression turned murderous, and you'd think I'd suggested she went to a local alleyway and picked up men for money.

"You disgust me, Eliana. How could you be so cruel?" She pointed her finger at me, acrylic nail looking sharp enough to gouge my eyes out. "I guess you are your father's daughter after all."

My exhale burned as it came out of my nostrils. I crossed my legs, rolling my ankles. The sudden urge to remove my sneakers and hull them at her face until she needed a second nose job was overwhelming.

I'd seen her attack others before when she felt threatened. I'd never been on the receiving end. She was a master manipulator, but I wanted to show her that shit wouldn't work with me. I didn't get a chance to do so though as she continued her tirade of stomping all over my heart with her Louboutins.

"I'm sorry to burst your bubble then, but I got engaged to Carter Laurent. I won't be needing your money." She got closer, eyes unnaturally bright. Almost brighter than the huge rock on her ring finger.

Mother shoved her left hand in the air, letting me get a good look at the oval cut diamond. Although I knew, air still punched out of my lungs at the confirmation. The rock was of the highest clarity, and it must have cost a pretty penny.

A wave of nausea hit, and I cupped my hand over my mouth. This was a stab in the back, from the person that was supposed to *have* my back.

Claire wasn't oblivious. People talked in Astropolis. Adults loved getting involved in their kids' lives. She knew I wasn't having the best time ever since the trial and that Serena was a big reason why.

"That's right," Mother responded to the disbelief portrayed on my face. "I was even going to invite you to our engagement party, but now I'm having second thoughts. My kid, my own kid, wants to cut me off. That's absurd!"

"Would you, now? When was that going to be? Before or after the whole town found out?" I wet my dry lips, rage and hurt seeping through my pores. *They'd told Serena before me.* "Actually, don't answer that. I don't need how low I rank in your totem pole."

"Eliana, you're acting like a jealous child!"

"And you're going to marry the father of my nemesis, which by the way she was so delighted to let me know so in front of everyone. I had to find out that you were engaged from *her*."

"Nemesis? Are you talking about Serena? She's been nothing but kind to me ever since Carter introduced us."

Yeah, but she'd been horrible to me.

Spreading up and down that I'd sucked off the football captain under the bleachers or that I slept with the math teacher for an A. Serena made up whatever bullshit she could to tarnish my reputation.

I never spoke up, though. It didn't serve me in any way, not when I was out-numbered. And it wouldn't do me any good to do so now. Mother was as selfish as they came, so long as her back was safe, she didn't give a shit whether the wolves had me for lunch, dinner, or breakfast.

"Why did you never introduce me to Carter, then? Why do I have to hear everything last?" I asked, crossing my legs.

"I-I..." She started, eyes blinking rapidly. "I was going to introduce you, Eliana, I've just been busy."

"Having brunch with Stacee. *Got it.*" I plastered an arsenic smile on, feeling my eyes water and hating myself for it. "Well, Mother, this has been fun." I hopped off the stool, draining my coffee cup on the sink. I couldn't stomach more than a sip. "Congratulations on your engagement. I have to go study."

She caught my upper arm in a tight grip when I tried to walk past her, her fingernails digging into my skin. "And the money? Are you going to give me access to the inheritance?"

"Whatever for?" I freed my arm from her hold, biting back a hiss when her nails scraped against me. "You just said you didn't need it. Let Carter take care of you. After all, this won't be the first time you played the role of the dutiful trophy wife."

Her eyes widened, and she took a step back as if I'd burned her. I'd feel bad, but it wasn't my fault she hadn't gotten a good look in the mirror in a while.

"You'll regret this, Eliana," Mother tutted as she slipped her purse back on. "Keep pushing everyone away, and you'll end up alone and miserable."

She stormed out of the kitchen, leaving me to deal with the knots in my chest. I closed my eyes when I heard the front door slam shut, letting misery carry me into the arms of self-pity.

Chapter 6

LEONARDO

"Did you know that auras are real?" Ares asked as we shuffled out of Dane's double-doors.

Heavy clouds kissed the high roof of the main building, and the enclosed courtyards were devoid of the usual crowd. The air was peppered with the scent of petrichor, but it'd been hot as balls when we rolled in for the first period. I was underdressed, in khaki shorts and a blue Ralph Lauren tee, but I didn't mind the slight sting of cold, fall bleeding into summer.

"Auras, as in multi-colored wavelengths around a body, that hold the essence of one's personality?" I asked, fishing the keys of the R8 from my backpack.

"Exactly." He tilted his body in my direction as we ducked under a sandstone hallway, just as heavy droplets of rain touched the soil past the archways.

"Did *you* know my second last name is DiCaprio?" I mocked.

"Any relation to the movie star?" Ares played along, sliding a cigarette out of his red Marlboro pack. He swung it in my direction, but I declined. My family was already riddled with addiction. I didn't need to add one more to the mix.

I was no saint. I had the occasional drink and blunt, but in moderation. Still living at home a few months shy of graduating college to take care of my alcohol dependent Mom had its effect.

"Only in good looks, I'm afraid. His tastes run a little too young for my liking," I said dryly.

"Come on, man. I'm serious. Oren, the physics nut from second period, told me about it. Apparently, our bodies emit light that is undetectable to the naked eye." He puffed out a plume of smoke. "I bet I know what color your aura is."

"What would that be, Alsford?"

"Tar black, with specks of green reserved for Eli and her new beau."

My jaw locked automatically, and I was glad I declined that cigarette. Otherwise, I would've ended up biting it.

"What *beau*?" I spat out, the rainfall turning heavier by the second.

"The one you almost had for lunch when he sat his ass on Eliana's table at B&C last Tuesday."

I inhaled more of his rancid smoke as my nostrils flared and my right eye twitched.

Cole Wright.

I didn't like him.

I didn't even know where the fuck he'd sprouted from. Everyone knew everyone in Astropolis. We were a metropolis with the mentality of a small town. He was like a ghost. Except for his name, Caroline didn't know anything

about him, and that girl was Dane's unofficial gossip ency-
clopedia.

Ares's next exhale came out in puffs as he laughed at the
memory. "I was sure you were going to end the night at the
police station."

"I don't think your prediction was entirely wrong. You
just lucked out on *which* night I'd end up in a police station,"
I retorted.

"All I'm saying is there's nothing wrong with admitting
you have a tiny infatuation with the girl. Your brain needs to
catch up with your body, though. Acting like an asshole to
your crush is a kindergarten move, not to mention a dick one
as well."

I shot him a dirty look, holding back the mean right hook
his face called out for. "Are you sure you're not the one with
the crush? You keep bugging me about her consistently."

"Sure." The asshat coughed out a laugh. "Run with that
if it helps you sleep at night. Although, I happen to think
using Eli's thighs as ear warmers would be better."

"I've got plenty of ear warmers already. I don't need one
more."

"You can never have too many."

"But you can have plenty of STDs. When was the last
time you got tested, Alsford?"

"Last week after Astor's party. I'm clean as a whistle."
He chuckled, crushing his cigarette under the weight of his
combat boot when we reached the end of the hallway. "You
don't happen to have an umbrella, do you?"

I didn't have an umbrella on me, even though I should
know better, living in Astropolis. A *very* thick curtain of rain
and several Italian and German cars stood between me and
my R8.

"You aren't made of sugar. Make a run for it, pretty boy."

"You aren't made of sugar either, yet I don't see you making a move."

I slipped my phone from my side pocket, checking the time. It was four in the afternoon. Walker Gym, home to the theater and performing arts department, was shut down at this hour and opened back up in two hours, or so. Eliana liked to practice there during this time. I'd catch her sneaking in whenever I parked my car on the north end of the campus, and maybe I'd snuck a peek *one* time.

My rank on the creep-o-meter took a sharp rise that day, but at least I wasn't bordering Edward Cullen's territory. I was about to move a few places up today too. Ares did a great job of warming my blood, and I felt like paying Narcissus a visit.

"I actually forgot I had a meeting with Mr. Stanton to go over some course material. Fucking Managerial Accounting is kicking my ass this semester." I clapped his shoulder. "You go on; I'll meet you at Kai's."

"I took out the bike today. I can't drive while it's pouring. You were gonna drive me," he growled.

"Should've checked the weather app," I said, retreating. "See you later. Hope you don't catch pneumonia."

"Yeah? Well if I don't, it won't be because of you," he yelled behind my back as I made my way down the hall again.

Ares was wrong.

It wasn't Eliana I was attracted to. It was the unattainable, forbidden tasted sweet momentarily, and then the rotten aftertaste hit. We were like slow poison, spreading through each other's system, and whoever got to the heart first won. I'd yet to find out what the prize was, and not for lack of trying either.

I took a right, bypassing the Romanesque style tower that housed some of the finest eighteenth-century literature. If I hadn't known that the university was older than my great-grandpa three times combined, I would've seriously thought the architect was a Hogwarts enthusiast.

I broke my speed when I reached the gym's back door. I could already hear a sweet melody spilling past the crevices of the building, and once I slipped inside, it wasn't hard to follow the trail the vibrations left on the vinyl floors.

I tugged open the third door on the left and was assaulted by Sia's high note as "Bird Set Free" burst out of the speakers. It drowned out everything else, even the doors creak, and so Narcissus remained oblivious. But I saw, and my cock swelled in my pants, appreciating the view of her in a blush leotard and tights, her hair up in an elegant twist.

The elastic tie was holding on by a thread as she performed pirouettes like she was gliding on ice, seamlessly. Light from the overhead window display bled into her routine, her form fading slightly at the edges.

Eliana was always dreaming with her feet and painting with her whole body. Even when she was simply standing I could often get a glimpse of the dancer in her, from the ramrod straight arch of her back to her left foot being on pointe whenever she waited in lines.

Okay... so maybe I was bordering Edward Cullen's insanity after all.

My brain had gotten the memo to stop ogling her, but my dick still needed some convincing. The poor sod decided to make his move when the song changed, and "El Tango De Roxanne" bounced off the mirror walls.

Eliana cut her one-woman show short, reaching for the controller to change the song, but stopped dead when I grasped her waist, molding her back to my front. A breathless gasp escaped her, and my brain decided to play the sound on loop.

"That's a lovely outfit you're sporting, Narcissus," I announced my presence, and her locked muscles loosened. I didn't know how to feel about her getting accustomed to my rampage. "Got it off Goodwill?" I leaned down, my lips feathering over her shoulder blade.

"Bianchi," she groaned like I was the bane of her existence. "I guess I shouldn't be surprised you're here. You're like a bad rash I can't seem to get rid of."

"I hear congratulations are in order." I chuckled into her skin. "How is the happy couple?"

A growl like sound escaped her mouth as she twisted around in my hands. Loose pieces of blonde hair grazed my chin, and her claws found their way up my bare arms.

"Did you have something to do with it?" She hooked her fingers around the nape of my neck, twisting her bare legs with mine.

I kept my arms in place as we circled each other, the heat of her body rubbing off on me as we pretended to dance. In reality, we were creating new ways to hurt each other.

"Sorry, I delegated my cupid duties to Eros a long time ago. Now I'm mostly doing groundwork for Zeus."

"And here I was certain you were serving Hades," she replied with a vicious smile, twirling in place. I caught her fist in mine when she turned around.

"We aren't that close, but he does lend me his hounds whenever someone needs a bite in the ass to fall in line."

"Would you be talking about me, pray tell?" She kept her chin up, defiant till the end.

"I don't know, you tell me. Have you done anything that deserves a little nip, Narcissus?" I tugged her forward until her right leg bent and her left stretched long behind her.

Her body swooshed along with my movement instinctively. The perfect follower when music ravaged both of our eardrums and her skin touched mine. Lighting it up with friction.

Her arms locked around my ears, and I teased her thigh with my fingers before grabbing it and wrapping her bent leg around my waist. Eliana's breath hitched in my ear, and frissons traveled straight to *both* my heads when I felt her full chest rubbing all over mine.

"I never do," Eli whispered, the outline of her lips gliding over my rough scruff. "Your sadistic mind sure loves creating scenarios just to punish me though."

She'd never know how much she was punishing *me*.

By just living.

By being a walking, talking distraction and destruction.

By plaguing my thoughts like an incurable type of cancer.

I should've let her go when I had the chance. Thrown her out of Astropolis and let the big dogs have her for lunch. I wished I'd never kept her here, but if wishes were fishes, we'd all be casting nets.

"I'm not punishing you, Roux, simply reminding you of your place."

I hiked her up, resting her full weight in my arms, and made a spin. She threw her head back, and her hair burst out of the confinements of the tie. My pulse throbbed harder when her long, golden locks cascaded in waves down her back, like a touch of sunshine bursting through a gloomy sky.

Fuck, if I kept this up, my balls would run off screaming.

"Really?" she asked, short of breath when I brought her down. "If that's all, I can just set a daily alarm on my phone, and we can skip talking to each other ever again."

"Now, where would the fun in that be?" I raised an eyebrow, guiding her feet back with mine. She gave away, the light in her frosted eyes omnipresent.

"I wouldn't exactly call keeping my sanity intact a tragedy in the making."

I made an abrupt stop, and she clung to me tighter than before as she worked her legs in tune with the melody. Despite the strain of her body, her face looked relaxed, like she could do this routine in her sleep.

"Who knew the rigid Leonardo Bianchi could dance?" A tentative smile pulled at her lips, her love for the art over-coming her hatred for me for a slight moment.

"My father taught me a gentleman should always know how to dance."

An inaudible laugh escaped her throat, consumed by the music. "And I suppose that gentleman, is you? God, please enlighten me on how your father's teachings went so wrong."

"Sure, I will." I fought to keep the smirk on my face when her intoxicating scent swished with our movement. "Right after you tell me how your father's teachings went."

"As incredibly as yours, I suppose." She glared at me, and I dipped her whole body down again, this time out of spite. I nudged her foot out of the way, and she dropped like a bag of hot potatoes. If I wasn't holding her hands, her tailbone would've had a lovely time cracking against the floor.

She still was where I wanted her, though.

On her knees and disoriented.

I grabbed her hair lightly, leading her up, but she didn't come without a fight. Narcissus had her own tricks up her sleeve. Smiling like a maniac, her face hovered close to my nether region, and my dick almost saluted her when her tongue peeked out, tasting her full bottom lip.

I tugged harder, and this time she followed, a hiss falling out of her parted mouth. "So, you sought me out just to antagonize me?"

"Among other things."

I.e. dancing with her until the song came to an end with Ewan McGregor belting out words like his ass was on fire.

So, I took a detour, big deal.

The last of the melody melted away, just as I tried to melt her walls off. She'd become harder to read over the years. No matter how much my hold tightened physically and mentally, she didn't let up.

It was okay, though.

I craved a good challenge as much as she loved dishing them out.

"Are you going to finally tell me what you came here to say, or do you plan on keeping me company all night?" She pushed against my chest until I let her go.

Eliana walked the distance to the speakers, shutting off the music and my ears almost thanked her for it. I stopped by my abandoned backpack next to the mirrors, kneeling next to it.

"Seeing as the only emotion I'm willing to extract out of you is one opposite of pleasure, I'm going to have to pass on your sleepover invitation. You would enjoy that way too much."

"My, my." Her voice seemed closer than before, the

mocking lilt laying underneath sheathing over me. "You really must be that good, or the groupies that have been keeping you company lately are nothing, but a bunch of pathological liars."

I twisted at the waist, catching her trying to look over my shoulder to get a glimpse at what I was fishing out of the bag. I had a feeling she'd wish she'd never asked once she opened the blue box.

"Wouldn't you like to know?" I noted dryly, keeping the box propped between my arm and side as I got to my feet again.

"What is that?" Her eyes gleamed as she locked them on the packet.

I stared at her face for a minute, memorizing the pout of her lips and upturned nose. One of the rare times she was so relaxed in my presence, but then again, I didn't make it a habit out of dancing with her.

I almost felt bad about giving it to her until the contents rattled as I extended my arms, and the thought vanished. "A consolation gift."

She cocked her head sideways, squinting at the box in suspicion.

"Is a snake going to jump out at me?"

"Do I look five to you?"

"Are we talking physically or mentally? You gotta be more specific." She tucked a stray hair behind her ear, wry amusement coloring her tone.

"Take it," I hissed, glancing at the analog clock above the door. Mom's babysitter had been gone for an hour now and I was sure she'd cracked into her second bottle of gin.

"Alright, alright." Her fingers curled around it and once I was sure she had it safely in her grip, I let go. "Woah, what did you put in here? Rocks?" Eliana asked as she struggled with the weight.

Not unless rocks cost you a small fortune, sweetheart.

"You'll find out soon enough," I said, dragging my bag from the floor. "Say congratulations to the happy couple from me, will you?" I smiled as I backed off.

Eliana had learned to roll with the punches over time instead of tucking her tail between her legs. And while I found her offense gleaming, her *defense* was a bit lacking.

The blind spots were just begging to be poked at.

ELIANA

Fool me once, shame on you.

Fool me twice, shame on me.

What if a person had fucked you over close to a hundred thousand times, and you kept letting it happen? Who did the shame fall upon then?

The joke was on me.

Letting my guard down, letting him *touch* me, dance with me, *grope* me. His hand definitely slipped in places it shouldn't have, but why should he care? He had no qualms about taking. I was the only one that ended up breaking time and time again under the weight of his cruelty.

My hands shook so hard the box dropped on the floor, and a wave of deja vu hit me with full force. I was at Pillan's again, my father's statue crushed beyond recognition, the whispers of crunching glass filling my ears as people stumbled over the remnants of *me* on the ground.

What did I expect?

You expected him to be a decent human being for once.

But Leo was no mere mortal. He was a divine asshole. Decent wasn't in his dictionary. Or humanity for that matter.

I didn't want any consolation prize.

The real win would come when I broke him back like he ripped me to shreds. When I opened up his chest, and his black heart stopped pumping out hatred and pain, so much fucking pain.

Quickly, I got on my knees, hissing at the slight bite of cut glass on my skin, but I had no time to linger on it. I had to gather the spilled shards swiftly if I wanted to make it before he left campus.

Almost mechanically, I collected all of the fine blue grains, trying not to pay any mind to how bloody or mangled my palms got. It was a price I was willing to pay to win the war.

Once satisfied, I secured the top over the packet again and shot to my feet, racing to the door Leo had disappeared from a mere two minutes ago. If he'd taken the long way, he was probably eight minutes away from the parking lot, and with the shortcut? About three.

It didn't take me a long time to decide on a road. I leaped into the rain, taking the pelting on my shoulders, and *ran*. I ran like my life depended on it, like my dignity cost more than a few nickels and meant more than an anecdote Leo could share with his degenerate friends later.

I was worth it, damn it.

I was worthy of love and happiness, no matter the nightmares Bianchi wanted to rope me into. He could star in them alone if that was what he desired. *I* just wanted to be free. To live without him breathing down my neck and dissecting my actions and words as if he were my own personal god.

It was getting dark, and the rain was so heavy, I could only see a few meters in front of me. Soon the green patch of grass beneath my feet gave way to the asphalt of the parking lot. Overhead lights illuminated the space, and I finally caught sight of him, a few steps upfront, sandwiched between a Volvo and a more modest Prius on the left.

"Bianchi," I called out, but he didn't hear me. "Leo!" I repeated, making sure my voice was as clear and sharp as the fat droplets of water that were soaking me to the bone.

His head snapped in my direction when I called his name. My lungs were close to collapsing from the physical extortion, but I didn't stop until his angry eyes touched my furious ones.

"Back for round two?" He asked, licking the water off his lips. "So soon?"

"You know me," my teeth chattered, but I held my ground. "Not one to miss out on all the fun."

"You liked the present?" Leo eyed the ticking bomb in my hands, his polo shirt sticking to his chest.

There was five feet between us, and my aim remained steady as I lifted the box, holding it as if I was about to serve it. Because I would. "So much so, I came to give it back. Seems only fair you get to bear the fruits of your labor."

I didn't give him a second to digest my actions. I wasn't even sure what I was doing myself. All I knew was that I was hurt, and I wanted to hurt him back.

Leo's eyes widened, and at the last minute, I cocked my hand lower until the broken glass hit his chest and neck. I wanted to make an impression, not blind him. The particles consumed the air between us, swallowing him whole. A delighted shudder made its way down my body. The pieces became one with the rain, spearing the dark space around us with prisms of light.

Throwing things felt glorious lately.

Every action had an equal and opposite reaction. Newton's third law. Not even Bianchi was exempt from the rules of science, and he'd do best to remember it.

Leo's guttural growl rose above the whistles of the wind, and I took a cautious step back. My hair went flying across my face as I did so, and some of the airborne glass shifted, nicking my cheek. I hissed, stopping short.

"And where do you think you're going?" His gruff voice was closer than before. I felt his touch branding around my forearm as he slammed my back against the parked Volvo, locking me there with his body.

Oxygen refused to travel down my windpipe when I got a close up look at his face. Heavy lashes shielded outraged green eyes, and water beads made their way down his smooth skin before getting caught up in his scruff. A spur of laughter escaped me at the sight of blood on his Adam's apple. My mouth watered, and I wondered what vindication tastes like.

He narrowed his eyes, the lines of his face getting harsher. "Laugh it up, Narcissus. Laugh it up before I give as good as I receive."

Shivers raced down my back when he slid impossibly closer, his hands sliding down my arms and fisting my wrists.

"What are you doing?" I jerked my head back, banging it against the Volvo.

"Helping you lick your wounds, little monster. You're going to need the energy for what's yet to come." His nose blazed an electric path up my cheek, which his tongue followed, igniting my damp skin on fire.

"What the f—" I gasped. My back arched, getting involuntarily closer to the hard planes of his chest. It felt like the thin pieces of clothing weren't even there. We were soaked—me, in more ways than one.

He was fucking licking my face.

And I was letting him.

Jesus Christ, I liked it too. I ached for his tongue to slide an inch to the right and slip into my parted mouth. I wanted to taste the coppery tang of my blood on his tongue.

He detached his hot mouth from my cheek entirely too fast. I almost whimpered at the sense of loss when his heat subsided. *Almost.* I didn't want to give him the satisfaction of knowing he had an effect on me.

Leo's chuckle bounced against my skin. "Bummer, that was a dose of happiness cut short."

What the hell was I doing? Why was liquid heat coursing through my center? We were in the middle of a parking lot, exposed as could be. Anyone could pass by and see us. See how he unraveled me.

I straightened, gaining back some of my resolve and rolling my wrists against his hold until he freed them. "You *are* a licensed specialist in cutting my joy short, Bianchi."

"You sought me out, Narcissus. Not the other way around. Could it be that deep down you enjoy the inflicted misery?" He smirked. Eyes dead on my body, asking why I still stood in front of him. I caught my lower lip between my teeth, rolling it.

I achieved what I'd sought out to do.

I should leave.

Just then, the Volvo's alarm went off, and I squealed, detaching my back from the cold metal.

Air fought to find its way down my lungs as the rain

didn't seem to let up. I was only wearing a leotard, tights, and pointe shoes. I was shivering so hard now that Leo stood a respectful distance from me, that my body almost folded.

"Worry about your own wounds, Leonardo. If that tongue gets close to me again, I'll rip it from the root." I struggled to let out.

Bloody and bruised, he turned his back on me first, laughter spilling from his lips. Leo slid into his car effortlessly, with every intention of showing me that I was beneath him.

Chapter 7

ELIANA

Engaged.

The gold letters printed in a loopy font stared back at me mockingly as I applied a layer of lipstick.

Please join us for an engagement party celebrating Claire Roux and Carter Laurent. Saturday. October 12th, 2021. At seven in the evening. The Laurent Laurent residence - 756 Dawn Hill Lane. Astropolis.

I'd kept the invitation close ever since it was delivered to me. I didn't know whether to be pleased or annoyed that she actually went ahead and invited me. Claire didn't do it out of the goodness of her heart. I knew that much. People would talk if her sole daughter skipped her engagement party.

My intentions for attending weren't entirely innocent either. I wanted to see *Claire LeGoldDigger* in action, despite the acidic taste that hit the back of my throat every time I thought about her and Carter together.

Sighing, I dropped the lipstick back in my clutch when my phone buzzed with a text, alerting me of my date's arrival. Cole and I shared a math class, and somehow, he'd roped me into letting him tag along. He was all too eager, and I didn't want to be alone when I knew Serena would show up with Leo.

The Great Gatsby inspired mini dress hung off my body like a dream. Its neckline, deep but not plunging, still tasteful. The crystals embroidered on top of the virginal white fabric caught the light of my room and left me feeling dizzy in love with this masterpiece. It reached my mid-thigh, and the equally bedazzled Jimmy Choos adorning my feet stole the show from then on.

Ruffling up my hair one last time, I was out the door, my Prada clutch in one hand and invitation in the other. A sleek black Mercedes waited in my driveway, fully equipped with tinted windows, disregarding state laws blatantly.

"Don't you look positively bridal," Cole greeted.

A musky trail underlined the leathery scent of the all-black interior as I got in the car, pressing my head against the headrest and fastening my seat belt.

"It's an engagement party, no?" I said cheekily.

"Yes," he drawled, stepping on the accelerator. "An engagement party where you're supposed to be the guest."

"Really? So are guests banned from wearing all white?" I fiddled with a little knob on the dash that changed the ambient colors of the interior. My question was rhetorical since we both knew wearing white was frowned upon. I wasn't in the business of extracting smiles from people I didn't care about anymore, though.

"Not if they look as gorgeous in it as you do," Cole humored me, taking a turn down Wheeler Street.

I settled on a blue shade, bathing the car with light, and turned to get a good look at him. He was one to talk. Cole filled out his navy suit handsomely and with his curly hair combed to perfection; it was difficult to take your eyes off him.

"You don't look so bad yourself. Finally decided to drop the hobo act?"

He scoffed at my rather lousy compliment, hands caressing the length of his body. "Of course, I don't. I look fucking amazing."

"Jesus Christ. Put your hands back on the wheel, Narcissus." The last word ricocheted off the windows, bouncing inside my head. I had to stop my brain from the automatic route it took down *Leoville*.

"There's nothing wrong with a bit of self-love," Cole replied, his hands thankfully clasping the wheel yet again.

"Only a little condition called big-headedness."

"So? Everyone loves a cocky bastard, even if they won't admit it. Aren't they the ones every good girl ends up choosing at the end?"

Hell if that wasn't true. The ability to put up with all kinds of bullshit had been ingrained into us women since we were young.

"Unfortunately for you, not this girl," I said, yet something about my answer rang disingenuous. I shifted, glancing at the flashing lights out the window.

"And here I thought, getting splashed with hot coffee would warranty some basic level of appreciation. Or you know, eternal gratefulness."

I felt the need to clarify my stance, even though his tone was mocking. "I do like you, Cole. I do. You're funny and *kind.* But dating and relationships are off the table for me right now."

My life was complicated enough as it was. I didn't need to add more fuel to the fire. When a beat of awkwardness filled the car, and his hands tightened around the wheel, I feared I was too blunt. Or worse, way in over my head. My mouth opened, poised to make matters worse, but he beat me to the punch with an uncomfortable chuckle.

"Ugh... you're not really my type; sorry to burst your bubble. You see, I'm more interested in sausages than buns."

It took me a few seconds to decipher his metaphor, and when I did, my eyes went as wide as they could go. Cole was one of the most rugged guys I'd ever seen. Girls were attracted to him like moths to flames at Dane, but I guessed him never giving them the time of his day should've clued me in.

Cole was gay.

And I'd just gone and embarrassed myself with my big mouth. That would teach me to judge a book by its cover again.

"That has got to be one of the *wurst* metaphors I have ever heard." I blurted, and his eyes squinted, catching the typo in my speech. Bratwurst was a weakness of mine.

"I see what you did there." An amused smile bloomed on Cole's lips.

His jokes helped me relax, and by the time we pulled up at the Laurent's driveway, I wasn't feeling like I was walking to my death sentence. Cole parked next to a line-up of palm trees that admittedly looked like the gateway to hell. Bright beams of light shone on them from the ground, casting daunting shadows between the branches.

This estate was a significant update from their previous

home. Tangible wealth was evident in the air as people were being ushered inside by a small army of butlers.

"Ready?" I asked as I met Cole in front of the car.

"As ready as I'll ever be. You?"

"Well, it's not every day your mom gets a new life partner, but Carter's a great guy." My voice caught, and I masked it up with a cough.

Intertwining our hands together, I let him drag me toward the Italian style villa. The multi-story home screamed of extravagance. Buttery white paint embellished the high arches of the halls, and elegant multi-colored flower beds rested amidst renaissance sculptures. With sprawling gardens and the ocean as a backdrop, it felt like lake Como had traveled to Astropolis.

"Eliana!" My gaze snapped to a suited up Carter, standing by the double doors. "So glad you could make it, dear."

At approximately six feet, with sun-kissed, golden hair and a chiseled jawline, I had to give it to Claire. He looked fucking great. Nausea bubbled up my throat as I realized how much my mother gained by giving me up. A bigger, better house, a husband that didn't look a day over thirty, and a prodigal daughter. A top-tier, brand new family with an untainted past.

I was nothing.

The pack runt they were forced to tug along to keep up appearances.

"It's good to see you again, Carter." I tried not to recoil when he went in for a hug, patting my back.

"Please, call me dad. We're going to be a family after all, right?" he asked, and my face dropped before I could control my reaction. "Kidding, I'm kidding." Carter laughed, and I joined in with an awkward smile of my own.

He went on to greet Cole, and I had no choice but to turn to my mother's direction, whose presence I'd become an expert at ignoring. She looked good, albeit a tad bit generic, dressed in a red silk gown with a slit running down her thigh. What she lacked in fashion choices, though, she made up for with the genes she was blessed with, and regular Botox treatments.

Her lips pulled up on a smile, whose credibility I questioned. "Eliana, it's good to see you, sweetheart."

"I wouldn't miss my own mother's engagement party for the world."

Claire leaned in for a peck, her small frame struggling to reach mine, but I didn't aid the process. She blew me an air kiss instead, whispering in my vicinity. "Interesting stylistic choices, my dearest daughter."

"I know right, don't you love it?" I played with the crystals, as her eyes took me in, showing me just how much she adored it.

"Must have cost you a pretty penny."

"Indeed it did, but if I can't go all out for such an important milestone in your life then what is it worth having so much money for?" I batted my eyelashes.

The vein in her forehead looked ready to burst. After Cole and I congratulated them on their engagement, we made our way into the grand foyer, yours truly smiling like a maniac.

"Psycho at five o'clock," Cole warned, right before the second wave in need of tackling hit.

"Look who decided to bless us with her presence." Serena's words dripped with sarcasm, her hawk eyes trained on me.

Leo was by her side, always by her side. Their outfits even matched. The black and white colors of his suit complemented her A-line dress perfectly. Knowing Serena this was carefully curated. I didn't look at him. My chest felt heavy, and stepping into Leonardo's minefield would only lead to a burst.

"Serena, missed me already?"

"You know I just can't live without you, my special little stepsister." Serena's hand tightened around her champagne glass.

"And you are?" Leo cut the strained atmosphere with even more tension, directed at Cole.

"Cole Wright." He extended a hand, but Serena was the one to shake it when Leo ignored the limb's existence.

"Serena Laurent. My, my, Eliana, at least your taste in men has improved." Her brown eyes twinkled as she took a dig at me.

Don't say it. Don't say it. Don't say it.

"Well, one of us had to break the cycle."

I said it.

Cole choked on a sip of champagne he'd snagged from a passing waiter. And if Serena had been chewing any gum, it would have stuck on the porcelain floor with how her mouth dropped. It was Leo's burning green orbs that alighted the smirk on my face, though. I raised a provocative brow, eager for his response.

Before he could most likely tell me to drop dead, the clinking of glasses from the backyard alerted us that it was time to find our seats. Serena's airy laughter grated on my nerves as Leo wrapped a hand over her shoulders, whispering something in her ear and stepping out.

"Ever heard of being the bigger person?" Cole asked as we followed.

"I have, but I enjoy being the bigger bitch more." I smiled, and he shook his head at me.

Fairy lights hung off every inch of the backyard, which was the size of a small football field. The alluring smell of white gardenia bouquets decorating the dozen or so circular tables mixed with the scent of freshly cut grass.

Cole and I were stuck on the kid's table. We were grouped together with all the other guests' children, some of them still teenagers, right along with Serena and Leo. They even brought us virgin cocktails. How cute. Half of these people had a local drug dealer at their beck and call, yet here we all sat, drinking mocktails. At least I was able to get off, by imagining Leo's drink was laced with cyanide. Other than that, we ignored each other's existence.

"Hello everyone, thank you for joining us tonight." Carter took the stage, with Claire hanging off his hand. Muffled talks quieted down, and we all tuned in to listen.

"As you all know, we are gathered here tonight to celebrate mine and Claire's engagement. It's been a long time coming, and I am beyond ecstatic I get to spend the rest of my life with the person I love and my best friend."

Awws, filled the air when Carter swooped down for a peck. Bile raced up my throat, and one glance at Serena confirmed that she wasn't faring much better. I wanted the ground to open and swallow me whole, so I didn't have to look at my mom, frenching someone other than my dad. I was close to retching when they finally pulled apart.

"So, I would like for everyone to grab a glass of their

favorite beverage and join us for a toast." He raised his wine glass, and everyone followed suit, everyone, but me. "To love, soul mates, and second chances!"

When Carter's lovely speech—that lacked some seasoning in my opinion—was up, we were served Escargots à la Bourguignon, as hors d'oeuvres. I refused to touch the snails, no matter how much Cole tried to coax me into trying one.

The tables buzzed with talks, and I slipped into a natural conversion with Cole. Turned out, he was born and raised in Massachusetts but moved to California four years ago. Whenever I tried to breach the topic of his family, he'd deviate from my original question in a matter of seconds. Instead, his *sexcapades* were more interesting to talk about. He was telling me all about his experience on a Ferris wheel when we were interrupted.

"Soo, are you guys *like* step-sisters now?" a Barbie looka-like from the opposite end of the table asked, drawing all eyes on Serena and me.

"That would be us," I chimed in when no one else took the bait.

"But don't you *like* hate each other? There are mentions of you two all over Crestview High. Some of the bathroom stalls still have your names scribbled on them."

I was aware. There was one difference though. One name was surrounded by tiny hearts and the other deroga-tory terms. I cleared my throat, refraining from biting in again. There was only one direction this was going to, and that was south with both Leo and Serena here. There was power in numbers.

"If you'll excuse me, I have to use the restroom." I

dropped my napkin on the table, squeezing Cole's shoulder before leaving.

I'd never been to Serena's new place. They moved in after we cut ties, so a member of the staff was kind enough to show me which direction to take. I came across a spiral staircase when the hallway that led to the guest bathroom filled my vision.

I stopped short, feeling an itch to climb the first step. *It's been a long time coming,* Carter said during his speech. How long exactly? And why did Mother never bother to tell me anything about him during this long time? No whispers, nothing. I was simply plunged into the thick of it, and forced to accept that she was engaged to a man I'd never heard her mention before.

An unshakable suspicion led me to step forward, and a burning need to be rid of my doubts landed me at the top of the staircase. I didn't know what I was doing. All I knew was that if someone caught me, I'd be in serious trouble.

My heart thrummed in my chest as I turned left and marched down a long hall, keeping my pace brisk. Several futile attempts later, I stumbled upon Carter's room. I knew it was his because I could already see how Mother's influence affected the decor.

From the snow white curtains that she loved to include in every room, claiming it made the space brighter, to the mosquito net around the king size bed. She was really anal about mosquitos, even opting out of a trip to Thailand once when I was fourteen.

I let my eyes roam over their bedside tables as I stepped further in, stopping my scan when I spotted a half-open laptop on a mahogany desk. I didn't even know what to look for, but I guessed emails or texts were a good idea.

Halfway to the desk, the gleaming edges of a bronze picture frame caught my attention. The room was too dark to make anything out. A large set of doors gating a balconette blocked any light from breaching, so I tugged one open, allowing for light to spill inside.

Bin-fucking-go.

I moved closer to the bookcase, examining the picture. It was them kissing again, under a lit-up Eiffel Tower. Needles pricked my eyes as I grazed my thumb over my mother's hair.

Ginger.

Her natural hair color.

She only started dying it brown five years ago, wanting to hide the persistent white hairs that betrayed her misleading claims of being in her early thirties.

It all started before my dad's trial.

Before he chose Carter's firm to represent him.

Their confirmed infidelity filled my chest with searing pain. It hung heavy inside me, dangling like a piece of information that left me hungry to know more.

I didn't get any time to dwell on it before I was forced back to the present, though.

"Lost your way to the bathroom there, Narcissus?"

Even if I had a stroke and forgot who that voice belonged to, the fucking pet name gave away all the answers. My blood ran cold as I spun around. Breeze picked up from the open balcony, chilling my flushed neck.

"You seem to have taken the same wrong turn I did, Bianchi."

His gleaming eyes were closer than I expected, and I backed up, running away from the carnal feelings his taut body awakened in me. He followed suit, and it wasn't long before the cold railing of the balcony dug into my back. My hands connected with his chest in an attempt to stop his advance.

I was super close to kissing the ground below.

"Mhm." His whiskey induced breath skated along my cheek. "Seems like I did, and what a glorious destination it led me to. Breaking and entering seems to be your pièce de résistance."

My hands tightened on his suit as his molded over the contours of my waist. A silver flask gleamed from his pocket, sticking out like a gray cloud in a clear sky. Someone obviously couldn't be bothered with the no-alcohol rule, and it seemed sobriety wasn't in the cards tonight.

"For a girl you seem to hate, you sure do love bumping into me. A glorious destination, was it?"

"You do have your charms." Leo's hands slid from my waist and onto my ass they went, squeezing hard. An embarrassing yelp escaped my mouth when I felt cool air grazing past my quickly dampening panties.

Okay, tipsy Leo made for a touchy-feely Leo.

"I'm glad my body amuses you," I squeaked out, blanketing my statement with a healthy dose of irony.

For the first time since he'd initiated any close proximity between us, I didn't move away. Watching him hold Serena so close, hug her, kiss her cheek, stand up for her, it had my stomach twisting in all kinds of knots.

I reached up to bite his long neck in retaliation to another squeeze. My lipstick smeared over his hot skin, leaving a little scarlet letter—a visible present for *her* to obsess over later.

"Put your teeth away, woman," he hissed when my love bite tricked into a hate bite.

"I will when you stop squeezing my ass like it wronged

you." I flicked my tongue over his pulse, feeling the warm beat of his jugular under the sensitive skin of my lips.

"But it did. It's too round for its own good." Leo almost *whined*, and I snapped back to look at him, my mouth falling open. His pupils dilated further when he glanced at my lips, and I felt something stiff press against my thigh.

Did I say he was tipsy? Scratch that.

He was *hammered*.

"Were you snooping?" Some of the haze from his eyes cleared up. "What were you hoping to find?"

My overactive pulse threatened to crack my facade, so I went back to nuzzling his neck, breathing in his pine scent with a shudder.

"Maybe I was waiting for you to find *me*. Something in your expression told me you didn't like my date. What's the matter, Bianchi, can't handle a little competition?"

"As always, you think too highly of yourself, *Narcissus*." He said, latching his hand in my hair and straining my neck, so I had to look up at him. Warmth filled my womb at his possessive grip.

"Is that so? Then I guess I should head back. Let him take me home and invite him inside. Do you want to know what will happen next?" I taunted as our breaths mixed. "He will tear off my dress, bend me over the counter and fuck me until the ache between my legs disappears. But I'm a greedy bitch, honey, so I might just let him take me on the floor, the bed, maybe even let him eat me out on the dining table too."

His grip turned bruising, and I struggled to maintain my train of thought when his chest flexed, blowing out angry exhales. "You're not only a greedy bitch. You're a suicidal one too."

He snarled as his mouth closed in on mine for the first

time in years. A shiver raced down my spine when our lips touched. I gasped out my shock at the feel of him, something I thought I'd never get to experience again. Leo took advantage of that, and there was nothing tentative about the clash of teeth and tongues that followed. His full lips felt different from what I once remembered, rougher. As if the cracks on the surface sought to carve me out.

My heart accelerated to dangerous speeds, and I sucked in a quick inhale when he pulled me up, sitting me on the railing. My legs fell open, and he didn't hesitate to step between them as I clutched his shoulders, tugging closer, unsure which fall scared me the most. Tingles rushed over my breasts as his firm body took and gave plenty in return.

Our pelvises brushed when he hooked my bare leg around his waist, and I whimpered in his mouth when his hardest part tried to seek refuge in my softness. The pure male groan he released in return vibrated through my being, making my head swim.

I dug my heel into his spine, sharing some of the pulsating pain that rippled down my body, and he smacked my ass in retaliation. My fingernails scratched his scalp, squeezing a throaty laugh out of him. *Snap out of it*, a voice in the back of my head screeched, but the sound of our anguished moans filled every nook in my brain.

Everything was fuzzy, and I had difficulty distinguishing right from wrong. We were submerged in a pool of pent-up emotions and hormones. Dragged farther down the rabbit hole with each velvety stroke of his tongue on mine. A low whine of sorts distracted me, but I didn't pay it much mind. I was too busy biting Leo's lip until the coppery taste of blood exploded on my taste buds, trickling down my chin and his scratchy stubble.

A blanket of light fell over my closed eyes, and I stilled. Leo's arms stiffened around me, and our inexplicable need flushed away as a moment of clarity ensued. We disconnected. Cheeks red, lips raw, we stared at each other, shocked.

"Fuck." I flinched, and if it wasn't for Leo's hands around my waist, I would've plummeted to my death.

Our eyes widened when voices carried from the inside. Disoriented, I was of no help, but thankfully Leo was quick to act. He circled his arms around me again and moved to a more shadowed part of the balcony. Blanketing my body with his against the wall in an attempt to blend in.

"Did you have to wear white today?" He whispered against my mouth, pressing me back.

"I'm sorry I'm not a psychic, and couldn't foresee you attacking me in Carter's room." I hissed back, licking my swollen lips.

"Oh please, you didn't hold back either, sweetheart," he spat, more reclusive than before.

My heating cheeks were responsive enough, so I didn't grace him with a verbal answer. Holding on to Leo's suit jacket, I strained to listen in on the conversation when I recognized the speakers, Carter and Claire. Technically, I wasn't eavesdropping. The voices drifted to my ears, the evening breeze carrying the echoes to us.

Well, duh, they were screaming.

"...how are we going to afford it, Claire? You said you'd get her to reconsider giving you a portion of the will." Carter's voice boomed with anger I'd never heard him possess before.

Claire's response was inaudible, most likely trying to

console him. Things had taken a turn from the happy-go-lucky couple image they previously tried to pacify us with.

"No, I won't calm down. I did *everything*. Everything to get to this point. I protected you, got rid of your problems, while making sure our asses were clean. Now I want the reward I was promised. Get your ball-busting daughter under control, or I will take care of her. I swear I will, Claire."

Daughter?

Unless Claire had any other extramarital children I wasn't aware of, he was talking about me. The heat that previously coated my body, evaporated into a mist of dread. Leo's eyes burned a hole through the side of my face. I could almost see the questions forming in his head, but we both kept still. More hushed words by Claire followed, as she calmed her fiancé down, and then the slam of a door signified that our stealth had paid off.

"What was that about?" Leo asked, taking a step back.

The threads of a carefully curated lie started unraveling, and I bit my lip to keep it from trembling. What was it all about? I wanted to know too. The adulterous picture in Paris came to my mind again, stamping itself inside my eyelids until it was all I could see. Why would Carter care about my inheritance? He didn't need money. His castle of a home spoke plenty about his wealth.

What have you gone and done now, Mother?

"Your guess is as good as mine," I whispered, shrugging.

"Did you cut Claire off?" He advanced forward again, striving to push me in a corner until I spilled my guts out.

He'd find he didn't have to push much. I was super close to spilling my breakfast, lunch, and dinner all over his Oxford's already. The desperation in Carter's tone struck a chord within me, and the promise of violence had my knees weak. Fear attacked my system, mostly because I never heard Claire defend me. Did she not care?

"Eliana?" I felt Leo's soft touch on my forehead, and he came into focus again as he smoothed the crease between my eyebrows with his finger. "Do you know what they were talking about? You can tell me."

His voice had dropped a few notches, suave and seductive. My mouth opened as if bound by a spell, but I capped my words back in, not surrendering to his allure. The feeling of being boxed in had me sidestepping him, and his hand fell from my face as I stood in front of the billowing curtain, the fabric softly teasing my ankles.

"Did I miss the memo where the two of us are best fucking friends, and I have to share all of my life's secrets with you while we braid each other's hair? Fuck you, Leo. I don't have to tell you anything."

I quickly made my way inside the vacated room, moving toward the door, but Leo spoke again, stopping me short.

"I will look into this, Eliana, and you know what? If my suspicions pan out, I might just fuck you. Judging by your reaction out on the balcony, you might just like it too."

Blood rushed to my cheeks when he stood next to me, a smile stinging his mouth.

"What are you talking about? What suspicions?"

"Ah," he shook his head condescendingly. "I'm sorry, sweetheart, but if my hair ain't braided, my mouth will remain shut."

I started to argue, but he dismissed me by peeking into the pocket of his suit jacket. A fluff of white rushed for my face, and I flinched back before I realized he'd thrown a handkerchief at me, his initials L.B. engraved at the bottom left.

"Here. In case your cunt needs a little pick me up."

I paled, gasping at his audacity. He simply winked, the douchebag jumping out of him as he sauntered to the door.

I gripped the handkerchief tight, hearing the silk rip underneath the pressure of my nails.

Fucking bastard.

My head buzzed, not knowing what to think about first as I exited the room a bit later myself. I flushed the handkerchief down the toilet after using the bathroom, and even though he didn't see it, it made me feel better.

Chapter 8

LEONARDO

"Let me guess. What errands did you have to run this time?" a pissy Ares greeted me, nursing a glass of bourbon by the soft-lit bar.

We were supposed to meet outside of Bella's, a club my father owned. Once a month, he unleashed his lackey—me—to oversee the manager's progress. Whenever I fucked with him, he liked to order me around under the guise of: *money doesn't grow on trees, son. You have to contribute more than you take from this family.*

Money didn't grow on trees, but it sure as hell bloomed once you'd planted the seed. The old sod didn't work that hard. He paid people to do the hard work for him. Instead Alessio Bianchi, spent his time sampling pussy from all four corners of the world behind my mother's back.

"I see you took the liberty of coming inside already. Although I don't need any escorts to make a grand entrance, it would have been nice having you there." I slapped his back when he went in for a sip, resulting in him spitting the amber liquid back in the glass.

Grinning, I ordered a glass of bourbon myself and sat on a metal stool by the bar, looking at the jam-packed crowd as Ares recovered from his coughing fit.

"So not only do you show up thirty minutes late, but you also try to murder me and expect me to wait outside in the cold. You're really winning best friend of the year award there, buddy."

I wouldn't have been late today or yesterday if Eliana picked up her phone. I spent the better part of my weekend chasing after her like a scorned lover. Not only would I get her to tell me what she knew, but I'd also make her sing it out like a canary.

Carter's words didn't sit right with me. The fact that he'd threatened his stepdaughter had my eyes rolling to the back of my head and my blood pumping faster. If he actually went along with it, he wouldn't escape my fist meeting his face.

I didn't even know why I cared. She wasn't my problem, and I'd done my fair share of damage on her as well. Call me possessive, I guess, but I didn't want anyone stepping foot in my territory. Eliana was mine to toy with and mine to end when the time came.

"We don't live in Alaska, drama queen. Your nipples ain't gonna freeze and fall off if you stay outside for longer than two minutes."

"It would just kill you to apologize, wouldn't it?" Ares tugged the collar of his blue shirt away from his neck, quirking a brow.

"I'd drop dead before my mind even conjured up the thought." I smirked into my glass as I took a sip.

"Exposing your weaknesses that easily? You'd be a blast to interrogate."

I shrugged, placing my drink back on the counter. "I could be misleading you, throwing you a bone. Empathy tends to weaken people's walls."

Slurred laughter floated over from one of the lilac couches in the VIP section. The kind of obnoxious tone only rich fucks possessed. The kind that surrounded me my whole life. I turned toward the familiar sound, catching the manager treating his job like a field day. Waiters hovered around him and his friends, as if on speed dial, catering to their every need.

Oscar Harrison didn't come from money. According to his resume, he'd busted his ass when he was young, gotten into a good university with a full-fledged scholarship, and made the right connections, thus climbing up the social ladder. However, people got too wrapped up in their own arrogance. Making it didn't mean you stopped working for it.

Everything needed a base level of dedication—family, jobs, *pussy*. You couldn't expect BJs on the daily when you weren't giving anything worthwhile in return.

What *Oscar* needed was a harsh reality slap. Our clientele had slipped significantly in the past few months, and that couldn't fly. The revenue from Bella's served as mere change in the grand scheme of things, but that wasn't why the club was important. We named the building, hell the whole pier the club was located on, after my sister.

Bella's Pier.

I clapped Ares's shoulder, cutting off whatever he was saying, and nodded in Oscar's direction, so he got my message. Manager or not, this wasn't a playground for him and his buddies to fuck around in.

"All right. Let's fuck shit up." He downed his drink before we slipped off the stools.

The security guard did a double take when he saw us but quickly rushed over and parted the ropes. Empty and half-full bottles of Grey Goose and Dom Perignon lined up the tables. The closer to Oscar, the more the bottles on the tables. The hierarchy was clear as day. Old money, new money, crooks. Everyone blended in yet stood out altogether. They had the same goals, yet their confidence and pockets set them apart.

"Get this! And then I tell her; if you want to keep your job, you better bust your ass for it, sweetheart." Harrison and his friends cackled like a bunch of hyenas. "She dropped on her knees faster than lightning."

Ares tensed behind me at his words. Oscar's thin face looked hollowed out, with his yellow teeth on display for everyone to see and all I wanted to do was bash them out of place. He hadn't seen us yet, but his shit for brains buddies were starting to feel the strain in the atmosphere when they noticed our looming shadows.

"Want to say that again, Harrison?" I hissed.

His head snapped in our direction, and I saw the dark cloud hovering over my shoulders mirrored in his expression.

"Mr. B-Bianchi?" Oscar stuttered, fixing up his slouched form on the couch. "We-we weren't aware you'd be visiting us today, sir."

"We came to see how hard you were busting those cheeks, Oscar," I replied serenely, eyeing his friends as they started fleeing one by one. I made a mental note to have them tracked down later.

Ares *tsked*, shaking his head. "I hope you've been

spreading them wide open because so far, I'm not impressed."

I huffed out a humorless laugh. It didn't matter if his asshole was fucked raw and bleeding. He was out. Sexual assault was not to be treated lightly, and I'd make sure to tie him up with so much litigation that his grandchildren would need lawyers.

"Mr. Bianchi, that was nothing. I was simply kidding. Mere locker room talk among some close friends." Oscar's cheeks turned crimson. His throat worked around those lies.

Resisting the urge to curl my hand around his bobbing esophagus, I slid in next to him on the couch, and Ares followed suit behind me. Oscar shrank at the foul smell of violence in the air, his previous vulgarity draining away.

"Save your locker room talk for elsewhere. This is a place of business, and the law mandates equal opportunities and *treatment* for men and women. Now tell me, Oscar, is that any way to talk about your female employees?"

"No, sir. No, it isn't, and for that, I apologize," he croaked, pressing farther into the arm of the couch. "I was just celebrating the launch of our new dance team here at Bella's, and thought I'd invite some people over to see what a good job our staff had done preparing for tonight."

"Dance team?" I cut my tirade short.

I hadn't heard anything about a dance team in any briefings.

Leave it to my father to want me to be the voice of authority while keeping me out of the loop.

"Yes." Oscar nodded vehemently, checking his Rolex. "The performance is about to start any minute now."

As if on cue, beams of light flashed from the stage, a few

feet away from the VIP section. Smoke slithered out of the fog machines, curling over the onyx floor.

"At least this time I won't be bored to death while you bully your employees," Ares whispered next to me.

I still heard him and threw a glare his way, but my focus was on Oscar. He tried to weasel his way out of the booth when he thought we weren't paying attention.

"Oh, no you don't." I tugged him back by his tie. I wasn't done with him. An investigation would be put forth, or he would be promptly fired.

It all depended on how shit the performance was.

My gaze fleeted to the stage when a remixed version of "Partition" by Beyonce dominated every sound in the club. Conversations hushed as everyone tuned in for the show. It must have been promoted pretty heavily. One look around, and there was barely any space left.

There was a flash then darkness engulfed everything. Squeals turned into roars and wolf-whistles when the lights flickered back on again, and with them came five dancers. They were all wrapped up in identical white dress suits, their backs aligned against silver poles.

I settled back on the plush couch when they started snapping their fingers, building up to the performance. My balls jerked along with the vibrato of the music as they shed their suits, revealing sparkly beige leotards hiding underneath.

The music was so loud, I was fully emerged in the melody and dipped my toe in partial deafness. I grimaced as my eardrums pulsed, but like any red-blooded male, I couldn't help the upward tug of my dick. Partially clad dancers did tend to have an effect, and coupled with the sensual twist of their hips, every guy in the room stiffened.

What a great time to be stuck in such close proximity with two other men.

The crowd lit up even more—if that was possible—when the beat dropped, and the dancers spun around, lithe bodies moving in full synchronization. Their moves were more tuned for seduction rather than showmanship—soft, not controlled, and sharp. They flowed with the music, handling the poles with confidence.

"Dude!" Ares's voice barely echoed from beside me.

"What?" I sliced my gaze to my dick after managing to unglue my eyes from the stage. Nope. My boner wasn't visible. What the hell did he want?

"Look at the dancer in the middle. Isn't... isn't that Eliana?" he asked, and my eyes immediately flew to the direction he was pointing at.

Fuck me sideways.

Fuck me sideways with a rusted rod.

It was her.

It was Eliana.

The content smile painted on her face, her graceful movements and flaring hips—it was all her.

I didn't fucking know how Ares noticed her before me. The heat that swirled below my belt was because of her. She worked me up like no one else. Being in her presence felt thrilling and agonizing at the same time.

My chest fluctuated with harsh, sharp breaths, and I didn't know whether to hop on the stage, crush her body to mine and kiss the shit out of her luscious mouth. Or drag her by the hair, and lock her into a nearby office so no one else got to see her this naked.

Or I could drag her into a nearby office and fuck the shit out of her for going out this naked.

God, what was wrong with me?

I was suddenly thinking like I time traveled from the stone age. And for a girl I should despise no less.

Eliana was born to be a performer. Like a Narcissus in the bloom, she attracted everyone's attention. I tore my gaze off the stage for a second, glancing around. Men squirmed in their seats as their girlfriends glared at them. Even Ares looked enamored, so I elbowed him.

"What the fuck is wrong with you?" he wheezed, bending forward.

"Muscle spasms." I stretched my arm out, a few inches away from his face, and he rolled his eyes. "I can't seem to keep my limbs in check sometimes."

The very vivid display of curves and *sex* did numbers with the customers and magic for my body. A jolt of electricity shot through my system when the girls took a bow. Oscar's face was enough to shoot down my mood though. He was hovering so close to me, he might as well have been sitting on my lap, waiting like a dog for a rewarding pat.

I would deal with him later.

"I'll need a member of the staff to show me to your office and have the dancer that was in the middle meet me there," I ordered, refraining from using her name.

"Ms. Roux?"

I nodded, not lingering to hear any more questions.

Getting off the couch, I addressed Ares. "I'm not sure how long I'll be. You can leave if you want."

He tipped his head back, eyes hooded with warning. He could smell the upcoming destruction too. "Be good."

"Aren't I always?" I lied, yelling over my shoulder, and his laugh followed me all the way up to the office on the second floor.

A timid knock sounded after twenty minutes. I tightened my hands on the mahogany desk, parking my ass on the edge of it, my back facing the door. She'd been hiding under my nose this whole time. I peeked into her file. Eliana was employed for two months now. Even though this was their first performance, she helped choreograph and plan half a year's worth of shows.

She was helping keep Isabella's memory alive. How fucking fitting.

I ground my teeth, speaking through my clenched jaw. "Come in."

The door opened with a soft click, and her faint voice broke the silence. "Mr. Harrison? I was told you requested to see me?"

So proper.

So good.

I wondered how fast her manners would fly out the window when she realized that I was *not,* in fact, Mr. Harrison. The rancid smell of cigar smoke hung heavy in the air after I took the liberty of breaking into Oscar's stash. He wouldn't be needing them anymore, anyway. I didn't want him anywhere near her vicinity.

"When I lose about ten inches in height and all of my hair, then you can go ahead and call me Mr. Harrison. Right now? You'll call me Mr. Bianchi," I drawled, turning my head sideways to take her in.

Her eyes widened in disbelief, and for a brief moment, she clutched the door handle behind her, ready to flee. Her need to outwit me, though, didn't allow her to run off. Squaring her shoulders, she dropped her hand and moved farther inside. Eliana recognized she was the prey in this den, but she dove right in, eyes wide open.

"What the fuck are you doing here?"

Yes.

Manners never stood a chance.

I swallowed down a dark chuckle, turning around and planting my knuckles on the desk. "That is not a way to talk to your boss, Ms. Roux."

Technically the boss's son, but I didn't bore her with the details.

"Boss? You're not my boss. What have you been smoking, Bianchi?" She scrunched up her nose, staring at the ashtray that held the still-burning cigar.

"You got a job at a club named *Bella's,* but okay, that didn't ring a bell. You see me standing in the manager's office, but then you still continue to fight me. *And* you performed half-naked on *my* stage." I counted her strikes, and it seemed like she'd run out of lives.

Realization kicked in, and she fisted the sides of her gold sequin dress. A tiny little thing that didn't leave much to the imagination, it wasn't any better than the fucking leotard. Eliana wasn't all skin and bones, so she filled it up nicely, the material stuck to her body like second skin.

"So what?" The stubborn tilt of her chin got sharper, her lips painted a signature red tilting at the sides. "You're going to terminate my employment already?"

She said it as if I couldn't do it.

Abandoning the desk, I approached her, circling around her form. Like a sicko, my inhales became faster when her head swiveled to follow my movement, hair spreading a delicious orange scent.

"I believe it won't come to that. *If* you give me what I want," I said, stopping in front of her.

She peered up at me through narrowed eyes. "Should I file a sexual harassment lawsuit then, *Mr. Bianchi?*"

"Don't be daft, Narcissus. The only time I'd consider touching you would be if I was blackout drunk." I threw her a pointed look. "Or if you were begging for it. Which, even in that case, you'd have to be extremely and tremendously desperate for it."

"What do you want?" She sighed out a resigned breath, crossing her arms over her chest.

"I want you to tell me what Claire and Carter were talking about." I parked my ass on the table again. "What '*everything*' did he do, and what does he want with your inheritance?"

I'd spent the past few days racking my brain over it, but I always came out blank. Carter Laurent was in the millions club. Why he needed access to Eliana's money was beyond me. And he was marrying her mother, who little miss *my jaw is wired shut*, threw in the street apparently.

"Why? Did you start doubting your little girlfriend's father? Is the spotlight finally off of me?" She glanced at the ceiling, mocking me.

"Don't play with me, Eliana." I struck out before she could act. Grabbing her wrists, I tugged her flush to my chest, and her minty gasp landed on the skin of my neck.

Limbo was worse than hell.

"Are you going to make her life hell too?" She fisted my shirt in annoyance. "Because if so, direct me to the sign-up sheet. Right after I highlight my name under the '*I'm letting Leonardo Bianchi be annihilated by curiosity*' one, of course."

"The only one that will be annihilated here is you. You need my help. Judging by Carter's words, he's not above stepping over you to get what he wants."

Her answering laugh was dark and smoky. "And what? You, Leonardo Bianchi, are going to be my protector? Am I being punk'd right now? Please pinch me so I know I'm not dreaming this up."

I did her one better and bit her exposed shoulder, tasting the bitterness of her perfume.

She was back to squirming, and I removed my teeth slowly. "You must be delusional if you think I'm going to help you after you made my life a living hell for the past *four* years. It's only fair you get to burn a little, too."

My jaw clenched, and I regretted not clamping down harder.

Maybe that would give her the reality check she so desperately needed.

"You think you're the only one that suffered, Eliana? The only one whose lungs don't fill up all the way? The only one that was wronged?" I bit out, wanting to wrap my hands around her delicate throat. "Try again. I lost my sister. My *twin*. Isabella was *sixteen*. She got to experience nothing, unlike you and me. You want to play this game? Let's play, Narcissus."

There were days where all I could do was breathe after Isabella passed.

I didn't eat, couldn't sleep.

Just stared at the ceiling, thinking how I let my sister slip away from my fingers like that. How a fucking useless artist brought upon the demise of one of the most powerful families in the world.

It didn't make any fucking sense, yet... the evidence was there.

Eliana stopped struggling, and her frosty eyes melted,

giving way to remorse. "I'm sorry," she whispered, her heavy lashes shielding her eyes as she looked up at me. "I guess there's no fault in telling you, but…"

"But, what?" I pressed.

"I want something in return." A slow smile spread on her face, and all of a sudden, she didn't look like my nemesis. She looked like temptation.

Her hands smoothed out, and she went from creasing my dress shirt to releasing the first button and then the second, and the third. I tilted my head sideways, plucking her hand from my chest. My balls protested, and my dick roared to let her keep going.

"How about you get to keep your job? Is that good enough?"

"Nope," She shrugged. "Not good enough. I don't need the money after all."

Eliana freed her hand from mine, diving back to unbuttoning my shirt. Warm air grazed my abs, her short pants falling directly on my torso. She didn't want me. I knew that much. It was my humiliation she was after. The world paid in cash, but we paid in misery.

"Spit it out," I barked, ignoring the manicured nail that made its way down the dips of my stomach.

"An apology. I want an apology for treating me like Satan's spawn."

Three words.

Eight letters.

I am sorry.

I could do it. It was a small exchange for getting what I wanted. All I had to do was open my mouth and spew out those three damned words. But just as I started to speak,

Eliana took a step back. The grin on her face double the size now. Serene and unnerving.

"On your knees."

I stopped short, but my heart picked up the pace. She couldn't be serious. Oh, but she was. Her face was painted with a blasé expression, foot, tapping rhythmically against the floor, telling me she wouldn't volunteer any information willingly if I didn't give her what she asked for.

"Eliana..." I warned.

"What? Don't you want me to share what I know?" She shrugged one shoulder. "Then apologize. *On your knees.* Chop, chop, handsome. I can't wait all night."

I bit my tongue so hard, blood flowed, thick and warm.

My knees protested, but I reluctantly dropped to the floor, hyper-aware of how my large build stacked against her significantly smaller form. At least I was eye level with her crotch, right where the wave of gold ended and the field of tanned skin began, so that was a silver lining.

"I'm—" The words refused to come out, stuck somewhere in the back of my throat. I glared at the floor, giving it another try, and this time they spilled quickly, almost too quickly. "I'm sorry."

Eliana's fingers tangled in my hair, and she tugged my head up, meeting my green gaze with her piercing blue one. "What are you sorry for?"

I laced my hands around her calves, and she hissed, jumping closer. My chin grazed her stomach, and I saw her throat bob as she waited expectantly.

"For treating you like Satan's spawn as you so poetically put it."

"Elaborate," she drawled.

I dragged my fingers up slowly, and her eyelids fluttered.

I might have been the one on my knees, but I wouldn't be the only one affected. She couldn't get my obedience without a strip of defiance. It was there, alive and pulsing, much like the state of her clit right now.

"I'm sorry for isolating you, breaking your dad's statue, and ruining your chances of going to an out-of-state college." Two truths and a lie. "Do I really have to list everything? We'll be here for a while."

My fingers teased the bottom of her dress, an inch away from the curve of her ass, and Eliana squeaked, almost tripping as she jumped back from my arms.

"Gosh, you suck the fun out of everything." She threw her hair over her shoulder, letting her red face breathe.

I wasted no time getting off my knees as she smoothed her dress over her toned legs. "I did what you asked, now speak."

Bypassing me, she reached for the burning cigar on the ashtray. It was almost done, but that didn't stop her from sucking on it as if she needed an outlet. Her cheeks hollowed out, and she popped her hip on one side, staring at me like she was debating if she was going crazy or not.

"I saw a photo in their room. They were kissing and hugging, in Paris, under the Eiffel Tower of all places," she started timidly, shuddering at the memory. "And it makes sense, they're engaged, right? Couples have memories together, whether etched in history or frozen in pictures."

"What's your point?" I asked, and my blood warmed when she took another inhale, stalling.

"My point is." She blew out a puff. "My mother started dying her hair brown when I was fourteen, but in that picture, it was ginger, her natural color. Which in turn leads me to believe that they started dating long before anyone knew anything about it, when my dad was still in the picture."

I pursed my lips, staring at her as she abandoned the now finished cigar on the tray. Them dating when Francis was still in the picture was skeptical. Him losing his shit two years later, led to a slippery slope full of questions I didn't have answers to.

"So they wanted him out of the picture? Is that what you're alluding to?" I barked out a laugh, but the thought didn't seem that crazy considering what I heard. "If that was the case, why didn't your mom just file for a divorce?"

"Do you know any logical person from our social group that doesn't push for a prenuptial agreement before they marry? Because if you do, I'm all ears."

She was right. No one in their right mind would sign a legally binding document without taking some precautions first. No matter how much they loved their significant other.

"This doesn't make sense. What would Carter need the money for?" I shook my head, dropping on an armchair that lined up the front of Harrison's desk.

He was desperate for it, that was for sure. All the talk about how their asses were clean, getting rid of their problems, and how he'd go after Eliana had me questioning if the sky was really blue or not. What stepfather would talk about his new daughter like that? I didn't know what to fucking believe.

The only thing I was sure about, was that I couldn't let it go. It was a shadow of doubt I couldn't get rid of. Ever since the engagement, I'd been plagued with dreams of clearing Francis's name. All because I was tired of fighting *her*. Of scratching the wounds between us raw, until we were starved for each other's blood, of denying what I fucking wanted. Hating Eliana required effort. It didn't come naturally.

She mirrored my movements, sitting on the chair opposite of me and heaving a sigh. "I don't know that yet. My head's been a mess thinking about this shit. In fact, I can't believe I managed to get my point across when I'm not even sure what my point *is*. It feels exactly like how it did when Dad was first accused. I don't want it to be true."

My heart raced as her accusation started taking shape in my mind. It materialized in the form of a black cloud, raining acid on my lungs. If what she was saying was true... If Francis really had nothing to do with it, then we were both fucked. Me—in more ways than one. I'd fucked her over because of this.

"I'll help you figure it out," I said, and her head made a sharp turn in my direction. "What you're saying could very well lead to Isabella's case reopening, and if they're the ones to blame..." I chuckled low, the sound drenching the stale air of the room with bloodlust. "Let's just say, there won't be a good end for them."

She stared at me as if I'd just told her Eminem and Tupac had a love child, disbelief exuding her body in waves. I extended my left hand between us, itching to feel her skin on mine.

"Deal, Narcissus?"

"You believe me?"

"I'm not saying I don't. I think there's more to this story, and if there is even a small shadow of doubt behind my sister's death, you best believe I'm looking into it. So..." I thrust my hand in her direction again. "Deal?"

Tentatively, she reached for a handshake, her unsure

expression doing funny things to my chest. She didn't trust me, and I didn't blame her.

"I can't believe I'm saying this, but it's a deal, Bianchi."

We sealed the agreement with a shake and cemented it with unspoken words. I wanted to crush the flare of hope that bloomed in my chest with both of my hands until it deflated like a balloon.

Chapter 9

ELIANA

"Hello, Narcissus." Leo stood propped against my car's trunk, looking pristine as ever in his Burberry outfit, his arms and legs crossed.

I felt underdressed as he examined me, clad in a plaid, black dress and army boots, jean jacket haphazardly thrown over my shoulders. There were huge dark circles under my eyes that even the five layers of concealer I'd put on this morning couldn't disguise, and my complexion was ashy. Sleeping was a luxury these days. Keeping up with my over-turned life *and* exam season was turning out to be difficult.

"Hi," I mumbled, looking around at the few people that lingered, taking peeks at us. Most students were holed up in the library, but it was past eight pm now, and people were starting to flee home.

"Change of plans," he drummed his long fingers on the shiny blue surface of the BMW. "We're heading to your place. My mom's not feeling well, and my father just flew in, so I can't really waltz home with you by my side. No offense." He peppered his words with a cold smile.

No offense taken.

I understood why I wasn't welcome in his home. I wasn't jumping at the prospect of going there in the first place. I didn't want to revisit all the memories it held or witness the havoc my family had wrecked.

"Can we do this some other day?" I asked.

I was drained, running on only four hours of sleep, and on top of that, I hadn't had anything to eat since lunch. Unless the two energy drinks I'd downed to keep me running counted.

Operation *catch the bad guys* would have to wait a bit longer.

"No," Leo replied curtly. "It's been a week since you agreed to this, but all you've done since then is avoid me. And this time, I actually did nothing to land in the proverbial doghouse."

He stepped closer, and I strained my neck to look at him. I hated the dip I felt in my stomach when Leo's cologne wrapped around me, all pine and male. My lungs burned for him when he was around, reaching to absorb more of his scent.

Huffing, I hitched up my bag. It weighed a fucking ton after all the literature I had to borrow. "Yeah? Well, don't worry. You've done a lot of other bullshit to land you in the doghouse for an infinite amount of time."

"I apologized."

"I'm afraid it's gonna take more than a half-assed apology from your part to right what you did wrong, Bianchi."

"Look, you can stay mad at me all you fucking want, I don't care. Your ass is getting in that car tonight even if I have to carry you and strap you to the seat until you can't move an inch, and we're finishing off the talk we started on Saturday." His eyes burned me in place, making any wick of sleep fizzle away. "Do I make myself clear, Narcissus?"

My body heated with the need to fight back, tooth and nail like we always did. My mind prevailed, though. We were extremely exposed, and he was shameless. No matter how much I hated to admit it, Leo would most likely win this quarrel. Leading other people to public meltdowns was his thing. Like he did last Saturday when a nervous Oscar Harrison interrupted us, and a shirtless Leo almost chewed his ear off.

"Fine," I spat. "But we're grabbing something to eat. I'm starving. You can tail me if you want. I wouldn't mind avoiding you as much as possible during this ordeal."

He shook his head, reaching to take my bag off my shoulders. "I don't think so, Eli. I don't trust you enough not to gun it to hell in order to escape me."

"I mean, hell doesn't seem so bad when Satan has taken permanent residence on Earth."

"Cute." He cocked his head, looking at me as if I was a brain dead little puppy.

A sigh of relief escaped my mouth when he took over the weight, handling my bag as if it held nothing more than feathers. I unlocked the car, and he threw it on the backseat before settling in on the passenger's side. I caught a brown blob in my peripheral vision just as I was about to sit.

Serena.

She was looking at us, frozen, as Caroline kept up a one-sided conversation. Satisfaction hit me in waves, and I winked at her, shutting my door extra slow.

"So, what are you doing, driving around in a mini-

SUV?" He adjusted his seat, buckling up. "Do you have any kids I don't know about? If so, the white leather? Not your brightest idea."

I started the car, gunning it out of the parking lot. "When your sports car leaves you squashed on the side of the road, I'll be the one streaming it on the internet and laughing."

"And if you're ever involved in a car chase, I'll be the one whose dust you'll eat as I leave you behind." Leo snorted, reaching for the radio at the same time as me.

"The chances of me ever being involved in a car chase are zero to none, but I get why you would. After all, you can only spew so much shit before you have people gunning for your neck. How is Annie by the way? Any news from Australia? Or was it Austria? I can't remember where her parents shipped her off to."

I smiled when he dropped his hand, rubbing it over the length of his face, and continued my last playlist.

Annie, his high school sweetheart, was the closest to a relationship he'd ever gotten. She'd stuck around for two whole months before her parents sent her to a university overseas for reasons unbeknown to me. If I had to guess though, it probably had a lot to do with her very public melt-down when she discovered Leo's interpretation of the word *fidelity*.

"I haven't thought about Annie in years, but she clearly left an impression on you, I see."

I bit the side of my cheek, trying to keep my smile from slipping and my face from twitching. Watching him parade so many girls in his arms was hell. My heart never failed to clench painfully whenever I saw his mouth sliding over theirs.

"The girl could perform Liszt's La Campanella without missing a note. Of course, she left an impression on me. It's one of the hardest piano pieces of all time."

His answering laugh was a touch sexy and a lot mocking, and I upped the volume on my steering wheel, letting The Weeknd drown out our conversation. Stepping on the accelerator, road signs and elm trees blurred as I thanked the Lord for the lack of traffic. Being trapped in such close confinements with Leo was testing my sanity.

"Where are we?" Leo looked up from his phone as I parked on a gravel patch of land.

A charming little bar stood perched on a hill, vines donning small purple flowers stretched all over the structure. The tavern was a far cry from the turbulent atmosphere you'd find a few blocks away.

"El Vitale, a restaurant near Breezy Peak. You can see the entire city stretched beneath your feet and the food is delicious, even though the neighborhood is a bit rough."

Turning the car off, we stepped out together. Mini olive trees were nestled under a canopy of heat-lamps inside the restaurant. It was pretty cramped at this hour, but the receptionist managed to find us a table by the west-facing deck. Astropolis looked like a castle floating in a cloud as we settled on our bistro chairs and ordered some food and boozy slushies.

Leo stared at the skyline while I looked at him, destroying the napkin in my hands. The strong line of his nose intimidated anyone he came into contact with, while his intelligent green eyes, arched brows, and air of superiority sent them running. Hardly anyone stood a chance against this debauched aristocrat.

He was definitely an asset.

An asset that if I was smart, I would refrain from pissing off. The Bianchi's were powerful allies to have. If anyone knew what powerful friends in high places meant, it was them.

Then again, there was a part of me that couldn't let go. A part that wanted to cause him as much hurt as he did me. I wanted to leave some scratches of my own on his soul.

"How do you know about this place exactly?" His gaze turned back to mine after getting his fill of looking around.

I blinked, snapping out of my thoughts. "Figured I'd never run into you or any of your bloodhounds here. The stench of poverty is too much for their stuck-up noses to bear."

My response got a smirk out of him. "Crafty, huh?"

"Yes, and as time goes by, I turn even craftier." I paused, smoothing my hands over the white linen tablecloth. "So if you're planning on double-crossing me, if you're planning on messing with me in any way, just know I won't hold back."

The waitress materialized next to us, handing us our drinks. My hand curled around the cool base of the mint green cocktail, and I took a sip drenching my parched throat.

"Let's get one thing out of the way, Narcissus. No one wants to see this through more than I do. You scratch my back, I'll make sure no one takes a bite out of yours." His teeth gleamed, and I wondered if there was a double meaning behind his words. "I called for a truce, and I intended to keep my end of the deal."

I stopped sucking on the pasta straw, stringing my hands together underneath the table. Putting my faith in his hands felt wrong, my mind kept screaming that I knew better. But I had to take the plunge.

"Alright. Let's get to business, shall we? What did you have in mind?"

"I hired a private investigator," he said out of the blue.

I choked while taking a bite out of the complimentary bread, my eyes nearly bulging out of their sockets.

"Well, this is starting out great. And you didn't think to ask me? You have to have all sorts of connections to frame someone and not to mention fucking traffic human beings. How do we know this P.I. of yours is trustworthy?"

"He *is* trustworthy." Leo plucked the piece of bread out of my fingers, and my eye twitched, watching it disappear down his throat. "I trust him, he's a good family friend."

"Really? Since when does your family keep private investigators as close friends, now?"

They were considerably below their tax bracket.

"I never said that was his sole specialty." He released a blinding smile, straight white teeth on full display, a walking ad campaign for Colgate.

I shook my head, retracting my gaze. He didn't offer any more details, and I didn't ask for any.

"So, has he told you anything yet?"

"Jesus Christ, Narcissus, I hired a P.I., not God. He is proficient, but even he needs more than twenty-four hours to gather any worthwhile information."

Our conversation halted when our food came. A plate of steaming hot pasta was placed in front of me, and my mouth salivated at the smell of the shrimp and scallops wafting in the air. Pasta Pescatore was one of my favorite dishes.

Leo got an herb-crusted filet mignon that looked straight out of a food column, and I waited until the waitress left before diving in. Popping a scallop in my mouth, a little moan escaped me. After not eating for almost half the day, this tasted heaven sent. I found Leo looking at me funny when I opened my eyes.

"What? Do I have something on my face?" I asked, reaching for my non-torn napkin.

"No." He cleared his throat, going back to cutting his steak into perfect little pieces. "Nothing."

"You know, the fact that you call me Narcissus is seriously hilarious. Seeing as out of the two of us, you are clearly the one that is more vain," I said conversationally, taking the liberty to keep going when he ignored me. "In fact, I bet you were expecting the waitress would slip you her number."

"That's ridiculous. Do you really believe I'd be thinking about another woman while on a date with you?" he mocked, not giving in to my attempt at starting a fight.

"Your reputation *does* precede you and... wait—" I stopped mid-sentence and he followed suit, a forkful hovering just outside his parted mouth. "This is not a date, what the hell gave you that idea?"

Leo rolled his eyes, leisurely going back to chewing his food before deigning me with a response. "I don't know. It might be the fact that we're spending time together, sharing a meal and we *still* haven't gouged each other's eyes out." he checked off an imaginary list in the air with his index finger. "Yeah, that pretty much sums up my idea of a date."

"I'm surprised you even have one since you're so fond of skipping them. And besides, I have no romantic interest in you whatsoever, Leo. This isn't a date."

"Hm... you see your mouth is saying something, but then again, that same mouth was saying something different a few weeks ago. At your mother's engagement in case you've forgotten."

My cheeks heated, and I was surprised he still remembered.

Taking a sip of water, I swished the liquid inside my mouth, ignoring the knot in my throat. "I was simply humoring you, testing the goods half of the female population at Dane raves about. Pretty sub-par skills, if you ask me. Seems there is more hype than actual talent."

"That's interesting. Do you always moan that loud when you are not satisfied? If so, do you cry when you are?" His question turned my face beet red, and I broke the stare first when a devilish smirk spread on his lips. "Yes, I bet I could make you cry out of contentment."

I felt Leo's eyes slip from my face, to my throat, and then lower. All of a sudden, the room's temperature dropped, a counteract of his cold gaze on my body, whose instinct was to harden upon his inspection. He chuckled once he realized my knack for skipping bras as a part of my daily routine.

The sound brought the remnants of a long sealed memory to the forefront.

"Why are you sitting out here all alone?" *the boy with the electric green eyes asked. They were big, bursting with energy and emotion, something that lacked from my stance.*

I ignored him, focusing on creating whirlpools in the frigid water with my toes. My cheeks were decorated with dried-up tears, so I hid my face behind a curtain of blonde hair, sitting slouched next to the pool.

He didn't bow to my rejection like I'd thought he would. The air stirred around me, and his feet sent ripples across the water as he settled down next to me.

"Is this about, Claire? I'm sorry she didn't show up today. I knew the recital meant a lot to you. But if it counts for

anything, I thought you looked amazing. You did incredible, Eli. I couldn't look at anyone else besides you."

I felt my hair brush over my shoulders as he tugged my mane behind my ear, his finger tracing the side of my jaw. My gaze snapped to his, and I was taken aback by his proximity. Our flat chests were an inch away, and I could see some frosting lining up his upper lip. Guilt swirled in my belly. It was Leo's and Isabella's eleventh birthday today, and while everyone was having a good time inside, I was too busy throwing myself a pity party on the front porch.

"No," I shook my head, trying to contain the sting in my eyes. "It's nothing, I was just feeling a little tired and needed some fresh ai—" My voice cracked, betraying me, and the tears I was trying to hold back spilled forth again.

It was *about mom.*

I didn't know why she was ignoring me. She promised, promised, to show up today, yet her seat was empty when I got on stage with the rest of my classmates.

My heart hurt. It physically hurt, but when Leo wrapped his hands around me, hugging me, it beat faster for an entirely different reason.

"You don't have to lie to me. Even if she wasn't there, I saw you, and I couldn't take my eyes off you. You shone brighter than any other dancer on that stage."

Warmth found its way in my chest, and I hugged him tighter, craving his validation. While all the other boys gave me a mean headache, Leo had this pull about him that made me want to spend the whole day with him. And that wasn't good. Serena, my best friend, liked him, and I had no business stepping between them.

Leo ran his fingers through my hair, and before I knew it, we were looking at each other, sharing the same air. My breath hitched, and my eyes closed as his mouth dove to mine, seeping from my lips.

Nervous waves made their way down my body, but after a solid five seconds of feeling the pressure of his pout on mine, I relaxed, weaving my hands around his neck.

I'd never been kissed before, never felt the need to, but with Leo, it seemed as if he was expanding my world to a myriad of sensations.

I gasped when he sucked my bottom lip in his mouth, drinking in my surprise. He pried my lips open with his tongue, and an unfamiliar sound burst out of me, same as the ones the girls in mom's movies made when they finally got to kiss their hero.

Leo groaned, wrapping the length of my hair around his wrist until we were impossibly close. I felt so good. Like I belonged. Like I had an ally that wanted me near instead of throwing me away.

He pulled back for a quick breath, his translucent skin bathed in pink highlights from the lowering sun. "I've waited for this for so long," Leo whispered feverishly against my mouth. "I like you, Eli. I really like you—"

His words blurred when I heard hushed giggles from the living room. The girls—they were coming outside to catch the sunset. Serena was coming outside. And I'd just kissed her crush.

I, Eliana Roux, just had my first kiss.

With my best friend's crush.

Dread took pleasure's place in my heart, like a cruel understudy that threw the main lead under a bus.

I didn't think. I acted.

My ears were ringing with panic as my hands slid from his nape to his chest, pushing until he snapped back. His body *flailed, shock mixed with hurt flashed in his eyes as he broke the calm surface of the pool, sending a huge splash of water my way.*

"What the hell?" Leo sputtered, his hands slapping the chlorinated water.

I winced, my gaze jumping over my shoulder when the whispers got closer. "I'm sorry," I said through trembling lips. "I'm so sorry. I like you too, Leo, I do. But I can't do this."

I slipped away before he caught a glimpse of the embarrassment on my face, but over my shoulder, I thought I heard his chuckle. If there was one thing I knew about Leo, was that he never backed away from a challenge.

I cleared my flushed throat, snapping back to the present. "You can keep wondering that, seeing as that's all it will ever be. An unanswered enigma."

"Never say never, Narcissus."

"*In this case, I will.* And since when are you so interested in knowing how I sound or what I do when I come? Been having a dry spell lately?"

"What can I say? Unlike you, I liked the goods I sampled and am man enough to admit it."

"Right, well..." I glared at my half-empty plate, eyeing the shrimps like they were the ones to blame for me losing this battle. "If we're done here, I'll take my leave." I decided to cop out before I lost the war too.

Scooting my chair out, I stood up and threw some cash on the table that would more than cover the bill. Further perpetuating that this was *not* a date.

"So twenty-first century of you." He laughed hoarsely, stretching his long arms wide. "Aren't you going to offer me a ride home too? You know, walk me to the door and all that."

I dropped my wallet in my pocket, ignoring his taunts.

"You're the son of an oil tycoon. You can afford an Uber, Bianchi."

Against my better judgment, I swooped down, cupping the side of his face as if he would disappear if I pressed too hard. I heard his sharp intake of air as I kissed his cheek. A myriad of sensations wrapped around me, suffocating my lies. I *did* like the goods I sampled too. And if I wanted to beat him to the punch, I'd play him before he played me.

"Thank you," I whispered against his skin. I didn't have to elaborate on why, we both knew.

Leo looked caught off-guard when I pulled away, and I smoothed my thumb over the line of his stubble. His pink lips were parted, the black in his eyes dominating the green.

"Do inform me when the P.I. gets back to you with news."

Reluctantly, I dropped my hand once I received a robotic nod in response, strutting back to my car.

This could get addicting if I wasn't careful.

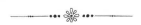

LEONARDO

"Alessio, please don't leave."

My mother's sobs were the first thing that greeted me when I entered my house, a harsh reality slap. While Eliana's short dresses and inability to stand bras were... distracting, bringing back memories I'd pushed to the bottom of my mind, I had to get my shit together.

Breaking into the living room, I caught Mom clutching on to my father's suit jacket for dear life. She had a glint in her eyes. A glint that was always there after polishing off her third bottle of Pinot Noir for the day.

"What's going on?" I asked, immune to shock.

Dad tried to shake her off, but she was determined.

"Leo!" my mother exclaimed upon hearing my voice. "Your dad, h-he's trying to leave again."

I looked at him confused, taking in the suitcase next to the waiting next to the beige sectional. He shook his dark head at me, catching on to my thoughts.

"I am just going on a business trip, that's all, Barbara. I'll be back before *Monday!*"

"Like you said you'd be back before Saturday last time, right? I'm starting to believe that's code for *you won't see my face for a month,*" I snapped.

I couldn't miss the difference in their appearance.

Mom looked like she'd just gotten out of the eye of the hurricane after battling all kinds of debris thrown her way. Her white shirt was hanging off one shoulder, and her brown hair was piled on top of her head in a messy ponytail. Dad on the other hand, save for a wick of sweat lining up his forehead, looked like the definition of cool. His suit was freshly cleaned, straight from the dryers, and a healthy tan donned his skin, an F.P. Journe watch sitting pretty on his wrist.

She was deteriorating, and the fucker couldn't give less of a shit.

My fists itched, and I felt like breaking all kinds of glass in the house. Everyone grieved Isabella's death in different ways, but by far his was the worst.

Indifference.

Bottling up his feelings until he was numb.

Maybe that was why Mom felt so much.

She had to do twice the work.

"Must you do this now?" he had the gall to ask.

I clamped my mouth shut because I actually gave a shit about my mother. If it wasn't for her, I would've fled this house the very second my ass got accepted to college. Someone had to stick around and take care of her though, and that person obviously wasn't her husband.

Mom's wails got harder when I grabbed her shoulders, hauling her to my chest. My heart swelled like an overblown balloon, ready to burst when her voice cracked and her tears stained my shirt.

"Thank you, son." Alessio smiled tightly, patting down his suit.

I didn't do it for you, you fucking cunt.

"You just got back. Where are you going?"

"New York. I have to go over some contracts with Brandon, and he can't travel right now. His wife is on her third trimester."

His go-to lawyer, the devil's advocate.

"Don't you think it's time to send her to a rehab facility? This has gone too far." I said this with her still present, knowing she was too wasted to understand what I was talking about. "I'm graduating in a few months, and even though our garage is the size of a small house, I don't plan on sticking around for most of my adult life too."

His eyes, identical to mine, fell to Mom that was curled up in my chest. For a split second, I thought I saw sympathy flashing through them, some longing too, but I might as well have imagined it. Seeing things, I wanted to be true.

He quickly went back to fixing the creases mom had left behind. "We'll talk about it after I return, Leonardo. I have to go now, otherwise, I'll miss my flight."

Translation: that particular conversation would be put

off indefinitely because I was already aware of his decision on the matter. A hard, firm no. A dead daughter, a rebel son, and now an alcoholic wife? He hated supplying the press with ammunition when the choice to just ignore the problems in his life was within reach.

I watched him drive off, wondering if it was best he stayed away permanently.

Chapter 10

Eliana

The digital clock on the bedside table was the first thing that greeted me when I woke up. The flashing neon red numbers irritated my already groggy eyes.

God, it was three a.m.

Who the hell was calling me at three fucking am?

I had no intention of holding a conversation over the phone this late, but when I caught the caller ID through my squinted eyes, I knew I'd get no more precious beauty sleep.

"Hello." My voice came out hoarse, and I reached for the glass of water on my nightstand. "What's the matter, Peter?" I asked the security guard in charge of the night shifts.

"Ms. Roux, I'm sorry to bother you this late, but we have a bit of a problem." He paused, and I heard some rustling on the other end of the receiver. "There's a girl here claiming she won't leave until, and I quote, *you come down and face her.*"

What in the...

"Who is it?"

"She says her name is Serena Laurent, and she seems intoxicated." *Of fucking course, it is.* "What would you like us to do? Should we call the police?"

They should.

I should've ignored her sorry, attention-loving existence and had her ass arrested for waking me up before the butt crack of dawn.

Alas, I didn't.

Curiosity might have killed the cat, but what people tended to forget was that it had eight more lives to go.

"No, I'll be there in a minute."

I hastily tugged on some jeans, keeping my silk sleep shirt on, and made my way outside. Leaves crunched under my fuzzy unicorn slippers, and I regretted not changing into something more sensible. I had no time to spare, though. Serena's screeches could be heard to the moon and back, and if not me, then probably one of the neighbors would call the police.

The iron gates looked scary, solely illuminated by the light of the stars. With Serena rattling the bars and trying to climb up top, the creepy factor went through the roof.

"What is the matter with you?" She stopped when my bewildered voice sliced through the breeze. She had done a lot of shit, but this by far took the cake. "Are you crazy?"

Serena was a mess, and certainly higher than a kite, a fucking plane even. Her disheveled hair and clothes clued me in on the situation, and her actions sealed the deal. She came all the way out here wearing a sexy nurse costume, probably straight out of a Halloween party.

The glossy sheen in her eyes got sharper when I

approached, and she rattled the gates harder, like a caged zoo animal. "Why don't you let me in, bitch? You haven't even seen crazy."

There was a crunch from behind before a voice startled me further.

"Do you want me to call the police, miss?"

My heart lurched, and my hand coiled over my chest as I jumped, not expecting the intrusive echo. It was bad enough that I had one wild animal to deal with on the front, now I also had to watch my back.

"Jesus, could you give me a little warning first, Peter?" I eyed the buff security guard. "And no, that won't be necessary."

I wanted to hear what she had to say. What the hell was so important that led her to such dramatics? I'd get to the end of the rope, even if it meant exploiting her enraged state.

"You can let her in," I ordered.

"But... miss..." He looked between me and Serena, unsure which one was the true sicko. My pointed look made him resign, and soon the gate unlocked.

Serena didn't even wait for the doors to fully open before storming inside, even bumping her left shoulder against the metal during the process. I took a step back when she charged at me with the momentum of a thousand armies, wanting to sink her talons in my skin. Peter swooped in and caught her around the waist, so she never made contact.

"Let me go, you big-headed oaf." She struggled against his hold, her hair smacking his face.

"Why the hell are you here, Serena? It's the middle of the fucking night." I glanced behind her back, catching her car parked sloppily by the edge of some bushes. "And did you drive under the influence?"

"What if I did? Are you gonna lecture me, *oh perfect princess*, Eliana?" She cackled, her head lolling back. "While you're in the process, why don't you teach yourself to keep your hands off things you shouldn't touch?"

A light bulb clicked in my head, and genuine bewilderment traveled through my body. "You put other people's lives in danger over some guy? Over Leo? Is that what this is all about?"

"Oh, please. Don't act holier than thou. You're about as rotten as they come. You and your slut of a mother are made out of the same cloth!"

My breath turned labored as the impact of her visit hit me. Most children would consider taking after their parents as a praise, but she specifically knew I wouldn't.

Serena was my shadow up until four years ago. She saw when Claire prioritized going out with her friends over taking care of her sick ten-year-old. Saw my disappearing birthday presents when Mother got jealous of all the attention I received. She was there for every single undermining comment, lie, and micro-aggression.

I didn't know how she still managed to shock me. Serena had done way worse, but somehow this comparison cut deeper than anything else she could've thrown at me.

"Cat got your tongue?" Serena continued when I failed to reply. "Of course you have nothing to say. You always wanted what was mine. You Roux women sure love popping where you don't belong. I won't let you kill me like she killed my mom. I won't!"

"What?" I asked, my posture turning rigid.

Serena, on the other hand, was turning more animated by the second, and Peter was struggling to hold on as she twisted and turned in his arms. A tremble ran down my spine, enveloping my body until my hands shook.

"Claire killed her! Mom couldn't handle her stealing her husband under her nose. I saw them with my own fucking eyes four years ago. The only thing that whore is good for is opening her legs and mouth. Just like you to follow in her footsteps."

I should've known their affair would've had a ripple effect. You didn't throw a stone in a pond and expected the waters to remain calm. Serena's mom was damn near perfect. She never drank, never smoked, so when she overdosed, no one expected it.

"She didn't—Amelia overdosed. Claire didn't introduce your mom to drugs, Serena." My voice came out hoarse. I knew I was lying, but my heart fought to retain some of the dirt off my mother's soul. "She didn't introduce her to alcohol either. She did not hold the pills to her mouth. *She* is not to blame."

Serena suddenly slumped in Peter's arms, looking at me as if she didn't recognize me. I wasn't sure why I defended the indefensible. It was like my stomach dropped, and my mouth opened, spewing out shit faster than I could process.

A downside of Serena's finally relaxed posture? Peter's hold loosened.

I saw the shift in her eyes. That split second of bipolarity where she went from dazed to raging. Recognizing danger was moot when you didn't have the means to defend yourself, though.

Serena charged; lithely slipping out of Peter's arms, she was before me within seconds. I stumbled when she shoved me in the chest, her eyes burning with anger and body reeking with the stench of alcohol.

It all happened so fast, I didn't realize what was going on until my back crashed against the ground, bits of gravel digging into my skin as Serena straddled me.

I saw stars, nebulas, fuck the whole damn galaxy as she delivered blows with rapid succession, not giving me a moment to breathe, a moment to regroup.

I tried to latch on to her hands and failed miserably. The pounding pain on my face, my back, my head, *everywhere*—it rendered me useless. I was nothing more than a human punching bag, a vessel for Serena's frustrations.

She did kill her.

She overdosed because of you and your slut of a mother.

She was everything I had.

She was fucking everything I had.

Now you want to take him too?

I was chained under her body, blistering under the heat of her punishment. Strike after strike, the only thing I saw was red. Blood stained her hands, dripping off my split lips and seeping into the ground below.

My oasis came in the form of distant sirens piercing through the fog in my brain. They managed to pull the unyielding viper off me, but I didn't feel any less crushed. My face was maimed, and my soul was bleeding. What hurt the most, though, was the nauseating contentment that gripped me when I saw her being escorted in the back of a police cruiser.

Things were never supposed to turn up like this, but we were nothing if not the byproducts of our parents' fucked up actions. Pawns in a game started long before our time.

Instead of breaking the cycle, we continued to feed into it.

Just like any other human on Earth, I lived for those lazy days. The ones where I could curl up in bed with a good book and avoid all kinds of responsibilities. Sick or not, I made it a point to take at least three days off from school.

This once, though, I would've preferred for my day to have been another mind-numbing routine. My face; an assortment of black and blue bruises prevented that.

God, it fucking hurt.

And remembering who gave them to me... now, that cut even deeper.

I squinted my eyes, trying to glide the brush smoothly over the canvas I was working on, but regretted it just as soon, hissing at the resulting pain.

"Fuck," I muttered when my hand went off-kilter, smearing the acrylic paint.

"It doesn't look that bad to me." My hand decided to take yet another detour, spooked by the sudden invasion of privacy. "Scratch that, now it does look dreadful. Unless, of course, you are going for a more abstract style."

I didn't even know why his voice scared me when I knew he was coming. I chalked it up to the trauma of his past habits *and* the past twenty-four hours.

"So, is this where the old man painted his masterpieces?"

I didn't have to turn to see that Leo was taking in the art studio in my house. It was on a whole separate wing, Dad didn't like to be disturbed when he was working. With a high glass roof and lots of natural light flooding the vast space, even if one didn't have a creative bone in their body, they would still find it in them to feel inspired.

"Yes. The same masterpiece you took upon yourself to

destroy was created here too." I bounced back, bitter, while trying to patch up the smeared paint with a wet brush, dabbing off the excess color.

"If it brings you any solace, there were approximately another *one-thousand-three-hundred-and-one*, other artworks spared."

Yeah, because he couldn't get his hands on them. It wasn't like he spared them out of the goodness of his heart. Did he even have any goodness left in his heart? My chest squeezed in annoyance, and my brushstrokes became more aggressive.

"You said the P.I. called?" I kept my back to him.

My hair was piled up high on my head in a messy bun, and I had on a plain white shirt and boyfriend jeans with paint remnants on them. I could safely say I wasn't appropriately dressed for human interaction. And the state of my face deemed me inappropriate for *any* type of interaction.

"Damn Roux, bad night? Are you hiding dark circles the size of Mars there, is that why you can't face me?"

His mocking words had the exact effect he intended them to. A flustering heat unruffled inside me, and I rested my brush on the easel before turning around.

"I don't know, you tell me? How bad *are* my dark circles, Bianchi?"

His widening eyes didn't provide me with any satisfaction. He stood there frozen, looking like a statue of a Greek god brought to life, while I looked like a freaking dalmatian.

"What the fuck happened to your face?" He galloped in my direction, and I had to place my palm on his chest to put a cap to his advance.

It flexed beneath me with shallow, angry breaths, as if he was ready to tear apart any person I snitched on. I tried to nip the fuzziness that grew in my heart in the bud. His interest was endearing, but he wouldn't be this riled up when he found out who did it.

"I woke up and decided to face plant the floor for the thrill of it," I deadpanned, but his upper lip curled, showing me he wasn't in the mood for games.

"Who did it?" Leo hissed.

Unadulterated viciousness swirled beneath his greens, hitting me with waves of despondency as I failed to contain my heart's rapid acceleration. A curl from his cocoa brown hair grazed his forehead, and this bizarre need to sniff it hit me.

"Why? Would you avenge my honor?" I goaded.

"If some deadbeat had the balls to put his hands on you, then I imagine he wouldn't mind putting up with someone his own size. And even if he did, I don't fucking give a shit," his eyes scanned my face as if he could find clues behind all the scratch marks. "Who did it, Eliana? Tell me, and they're fucking dead."

I couldn't help but cringe. Serena was half my size, and the damage she managed to inflict wasn't only skin deep. It spanned deep into my mind, her words ingraining on my conscience.

"Great," I replied, pushing my shame down. "When can I expect to see Serena in a hospital bed then?"

As predicted, he stumbled back, and my hand met with empty air. I wrapped it around my midriff, not knowing whether I wanted to laugh or cry.

"What?" Leo asked, stunned.

"It was Serena. She showed up at three in the fucking morning and started spewing some crazy shit." My eyes closed of their own accord as I failed to hold my composure.

I hated being weak after so many years of being my own protector. It was unnatural to me how my body slumped in resignation. In front of a person that wouldn't hesitate to shatter me on the first sign of fragility, no less.

Fingertips pressed against my swollen face. The rough pads soft against the bruised skin. My eyes flew open when his hand enveloped the side of my profile in a cradle, with gentleness I wasn't aware he possessed. I stood still, scared I was dreaming his touch up, that if I blinked he would disappear.

"I'm sorry," he said as if he was the one to blame.

"What for?" I murmured, resisting the urge to nuzzle my face against his warmth. "For once in your life, you didn't do anything."

"We were at a Halloween party last night, but I didn't feel like pretending I hadn't heard what Carter said. I ghosted her pretty heavily, and I guess she took it out on you."

"She is not used to your leash being extended that long, huh?" My hard-earned sarcasm shone through.

He didn't laugh at my stupid joke. His sharp gaze slipped through the cracks of my demeanor, figuring out that derision was my defense mechanism, and didn't acknowledge it. Instead, he smoothed his thumb down my temple before sneaking his other hand behind me, forcing my body in a bear hug.

My head throbbed at the sudden pull, but my shell-shocked mind kept me from voicing any complaints. This was the first time he'd touched me in years. *Sober and voluntarily.* And it felt like home, like jumping in your bed after a month-long vacation.

I sunk into his embrace effortlessly, reacclimating myself,

and we fit so well together it frightened me. The pressure his strong arms applied was perfect for my aching bones, a sweet pain that gave you the giggles.

"I'll take care of her," Leo promised, smoothing a hand over my messy bun. "Can't have you dead before we figure out what's going on."

Before we figure out what's going on.

The mush inside my brain that battled my need for self-sufficiency got flushed away by a cold dose of reality. *He doesn't care about you, you silly girl. Only what you can do for him.* I resisted the urge to push him away violently. I didn't want him to know I cared.

"*Don't worry.*" I slurred the words, detaching from his hold. "Serena has already been dealt with."

His hands stayed laced behind my neck, massaging the knots that had formed and forced my vision to stay rapt on his confused greens.

"She'll be rotting in a jail cell for the next forty-eight hours. At least until her daddy comes to the rescue."

"You called the police on her?" His eyebrows met, and he took a step back, scrubbing a hand down the length of his face.

Thickness coated my throat as I blinked extra slow, trying to contain the sting in my eyes. Was he worried his little fuck buddy was okay?

"Technically, *I* didn't. My security did. I was too preoccupied facing the mentally unhinged ape banging her fists on my face." I rearranged my cramped feet on the stool I was sitting on and winced.

"This will put an even bigger target on your back than before, you realize that right? Carter will now have a bigger reason to come after you."

"He already had one to begin with." I shrugged. "What's one more? Besides, if he doesn't, Serena will. My mother living with them is not going over well with her."

Couldn't blame her. Claire Roux wasn't the most pleasant woman to live with.

"What did Serena say?" Leo cocked his head sideways, leaning his weight on the table behind him that held all of the art supplies.

I gave him the watered-down version of what happened, forgoing some of the gory details I wished to forget.

"Did she never mention anything to you? About the affair? She found out around the same time of my dad's trial, caught Claire and Carter together apparently." I shuddered at the thought. While I would've liked to have known as well, I didn't think I could handle the visuals.

"I don't think she did." He wrinkled his nose in thought. "I'm not really the most attentive person, and deep conversations weren't really a thing between Serena and me."

"Right, I assume your relationship was more *physical*." I bit down on my tongue.

A smirk graced his lips, and he traced my movements as I picked up my brush again. He surprised me by snatching up a brush of his own from the table and dipping into the green paint.

"You know, Narcissus, I'm starting to believe you like darkness more than you let on." He got behind me, and the hair on the back of my neck rose to full attention.

Reaching forward, his arm touched mine as he started blending the colors. The grass turned darker, making the fireflies gleam brighter. Leo's breath fanned my neck, splaying over my collarbone, a mix of mint and cinnamon.

"How did you reach that conclusion?" I asked as he

worked his way around me, bringing in more and more depth.

I felt his abs brush against my back, forcing my spine to straighten.

"Light and fun doesn't really do it for you. You spark in the shade, love challenging the shadows for dominance, but be careful, Eli. Too much play, and you'll be swallowed whole."

Chapter 11

Eliana

Hot water surrounded my marred flesh.

I could tell it wasn't good for the bruises one day after the incident. My whole body pulsed to the rhythm of my heart, but I was craving a relaxing afternoon. A glittery bath bomb with some Baileys for company was just what I needed.

Light from the windows in front of the clawfoot tub gleamed off the marble walls and brass fixtures. Tipping my head back, I inhaled the sweet chamomile scent and let my head wander.

He shouldn't monopolize my thoughts like this.

Especially not for all the wrong reasons.

Leonardo grew inside of me like fucking fungus. The more time I spent with him, the more desperate I was for his attention. Instead of being the manipulator, I was being manipulated, one smile at a time. The tension between us was palpable, and I was starting to remember why everyone fucking worshiped the ground he walked on.

The lethal combination of sarcasm, crass, and abs had a mind-numbing effect. He was slowly, but surely, inking his way back to my heart, despite my vehement denial.

I'd crash and burn when the time came, but behind the brick walls of my house, I felt shielded. And horny. My pussy had become slicker than an oil field after the past two hours we spent painting.

His nose would wrinkle when he smiled, and I'd catch myself imagining him using it to nudge my opening. Using his pearly whites to scrape along my clit, to nibble and bite it.

I groaned, my blood raced under my skin, and the apex of my thighs throbbed until I hungered for something solid inside of me. I bit my lip as my hand trailed a path from my belly to my needy bundle of nerves, circling and rubbing.

Ian Somerhalder, think about Ian Somerhalder, you dumb bitch.

I couldn't, though.

God, I tried, but Leo's green eyes always came on top.

My breathing turned labored when I imagined his electric gaze on my wet soapy breasts while he fucked my cunt with his tongue. He reached over, his thick fingers squeezing the pliable flesh and rolling my pebbled nipples with his thumbs.

I gasped. My whimpers echoed across the painfully empty bathroom, and I rubbed harder, faster. I masturbated to the idea of him, hating myself for wanting to know how the real deal felt like. For wanting more, when I should be running for hills.

My legs sent ripples across the water as they shook on either side of the tub. Liquid swished against my sensitive breasts, and my neck stretched. I refused to let the scream that crested at my lips out.

Ian Somerhalder. Ian Somerhalder. Ian Somerhalder.

Chris Hemsworth?

Nope, not a chance.

Nothing but the taste of forbidden pressed through my skull.

I clenched my core, trying to prolong the sweet torture, but I was too aroused. The heat, low in my belly, intensified until I couldn't hold myself back anymore. Spasms racked my body, my orgasm galloping forth and shattering through my inhibitions. Moans slipped out and the shakes were overwhelming, like nothing I'd ever experienced by myself before. I came so hard liquid gushed out of me.

I squirted.

Fuck, he made me squirt, and he wasn't even here.

It petrified me how much power he had over me.

Sweat and water pooled together along my collarbone as I tried to catch my breath. I didn't even know I could squirt. It had never happened before. But of course, it was Leonardo Bianchi that got it out of me, the overachieving bastard.

Drowsy by that post-orgasmic glow, I relaxed my tense muscles, submerging my shoulders under the water. I had to get him out of my system, absolve him from my bloodstream. I'd never been this needy before. I got by fine with casual sex. Didn't get attached. Didn't linger. Maybe that's what I needed from him to get my mind to calm the fuck down.

Sighing, I reached for my glass of Baileys. The thick liquid burned sweetly down my throat and reminded me of —*I choked*—my own fluids... that I was currently bathing in.

I shot up from the bath, my mouth releasing sounds that would win a baby pig singing competition. My flailing body dripped water on all four corners of the bathroom as I tried to balance myself. But with nothing short for empty air to hold on to, my ass sunk back down to the tub. The impact reverberated through my injured spine.

"Fuck." The curse ripped from my mouth. In what previously was a shout of ecstasy, now one of pure pain escaped the confinements of my larynx.

There you have it, Eliana. Not even masturbating can be painless when it comes to Leonardo Bianchi.

I was looking for someone to blame for my own clumsiness, I knew that, but the words rang true. Leo was trouble, and if I wasn't careful, I would burn myself in the process.

I'd texted Cole to see if he wanted to meet up. I needed some fresh air. I was surprised when he agreed to take a walk by the pier. I didn't have someone to vent to for so long, I'd forgotten how it was to simply have that option.

Freshly showered and with a new set of bruises decorating my ass, I sat on my plush vanity chair. The light bulbs surrounding the mirror painted my face in a harsh light, and my lower lip trembled as I reached for some heavy-duty makeup. Although, I wasn't sure if even that would be able to hide the damage.

I didn't have time to feel too bad for myself, though. My phone rang and I reached for it with some hesitation, knowing who it would be beforehand.

"Hello, Mother," I answered the phone with a resigned sigh.

"Eliana," she exclaimed, with the kind of tone parents

possessed when kids were caught eating candy before dinner.

"How come you're gracing me with a call, Claire?"

"What the hell were you thinking?" she hissed over the receiver. "Getting your sister arrested? What are people going to say?"

If she knew Serena got arrested, then she must have known the actions that led to her being thrown in a cell in the first place. As expected, there was no concern over my well-being. Her own daughter's well-being.

What strangers thought of her was more important.

I ignored the pinpricks behind my eyes and set the record straight. "First of all, Serena is not my sister. In fact, I am not even sure I can call her a stepsister, seeing as you retired your title as my mother a long time ago. Second, I don't give a shit about what other people say. They talk about us regardless. And third of all, I was too preoccupied protecting myself to worry about Serena's ass getting thrown in jail."

"Serena is half your size! I seriously doubt she was able to cause that much damage!"

"That's because you don't care enough to find out. On top of hitting me, she drove under the influence. She was definitely drunk and high when she got here."

I heard some whispers on her end, not loud enough to make anything out, but I knew it was Carter. And it wasn't long before the rustling ended, and his voice filled the other end of the line.

"Eliana, how are you?"

"I've seen better days," I replied sarcastically.

Placing my phone on the creme white vanity, I put it on

speaker. I had to meet Cole in an hour, and they didn't seem to be letting up anytime soon.

"So have I," he answered a question I never asked. "I know we don't know each other very well, but based on your mother's words, I never expected something like this from you, Eliana."

Funny, she'd never mentioned him.

"What would you have me do, Carter? Just lay there so your daughter could extract her anger?"

Which is what I did, but that's beside the point.

"No, of course not, but we could have handled this privately. You could've had your guards hold her down, locked her in a room... anything, besides calling the police!"

"Excuse me. Next time I'll make sure to think about my attacker's reputation in the middle of getting assaulted." I slowed down the application of my foundation when my strokes got a bit violent.

I heard an angry exhale of air through the phone and imagined Carter pinching the bridge of his nose. Something about this whole exchange got me madder, more stubborn. If he really wanted to hurt me, then he should know that I wouldn't go down easily.

"I am really sorry about what happened, Eliana. You have every right to be upset. But you have to understand Serena has been going through a rough patch recently with some medical problems, and that might have set her off the wrong way."

"What kind of medical problems?" I couldn't control the way my heart clenched, wanting to know what was wrong with her.

"It's not my place to say." He let me down with a sigh. "She asked us not to tell anyone."

I didn't know if I believed that. She was out partying and had enough energy to jump me like an agitated rottweiler. Then again, not all diseases had an impact from the get-go. I'd let it slide for now though. Lies had a way of coming out.

"Okay." I swallowed my protests down. "Do you need anything else? I really have to go." I knew what he wanted, but I'd enjoy the humiliation of having him spell it out for me.

"I wanted to know if you were planning on pressing charges. Keep in mind Serena will have an ironclad defense if this is ever taken to court."

I missed my father every day, even when I shouldn't have. But today I missed him the most. However skewed Carter's vision on this topic was, I envied the way he defended his daughter. The way my mother never did, and the way my father couldn't do because he was six feet underground. Moisture pooled in my eyes, threatening to ruin my blue eye-pencil.

"Are you threatening me, Carter? Because if this case is indeed taken to court then let me tell you something. I have video footage, I have witnesses, and I even have proof your daughter was under the influence." My case was sealed tight this time. There was no way he would be able to turn this on me. "Not to mention enough money in my bank account to hire a lawyer from the Goldberg firm."

His biggest competitors in Astropolis.

"Eliana, please..." he insisted. "I'm sure we can come to an agreement. Serena can apologize, and we can call it a day. Do you really want to alienate yourself from the only family you have left?"

The word family wasn't a title you could simply slap on any household. Family meant loyalty, devotion, and love.

Bloodshed on the battleground was thicker than any water in the womb. We weren't a unit, nor would we ever be. And as much as I loved him begging, I didn't plan to press any charges. I preferred bringing Serena down a notch or five on my own, not because she was stupid enough to lay her hands on me.

"I will not be pressing any charges." A sigh floated from his end at my words. "Unlike you, I don't go around threatening family."

"I apologize, sometimes I can get irrational and protective over Serena. But thank you so much. It's wonderful that you're able to be open-minded about this. Does that mean you're available to meet so we can get her released immediately?"

"No." I applied a layer of mascara, and I felt like if it was him doing it, he would have poked his eye out at my answer. "I'm a little busy at the moment."

"We can't just leave her there."

"Sure we can. She'll be released within forty-eight hours after no charges are pressed." I never claimed to be a saint. She wouldn't get out of this completely unscathed.

"Yes, I'm aware of the law." Came his strained response.

"Great then. Have a wonderful day, Carter!"

"Eli—" He started, but I cut off the line.

His little lunatic spawn already got more mercy from me than she deserved.

I spotted him from the back. His tightly coiled hair and broad shoulders were a dead giveaway. Sitting on a bench by the pier, he enjoyed the night's view of the waves crashing on the shore. The lulling sound forced me to inch forward, bypassing a family and their cranky child.

"Wow..." Cole greeted me once I materialized in front of him. "Looking good, killer."

"You should have seen the other girl," I joked back, taking a seat next to him and stealing some of his popcorn.

"What? You went all Mike Tyson on her?" He pretended to throw some punches in the empty air in front of him, and I rolled my eyes.

Ever since I called and told him about the incident, he had been texting me fighting memes the entire day, and my ribs hurt from laughing at them. So I muted him, but I was so glad he cared enough to make me laugh. Cole Wright was an unexpected light that I was so grateful had put up with my darkness.

"Not exactly, but I do believe I left her with some long-lasting mental issues." I imagined getting arrested did have its virtues.

I rested my head on his shoulder and got lost in the sounds of the night mixed with the activity of the hyperactive people mulling around us. I stole his bag of popcorn too, which resulted in him giving me the stink eye.

"So, what do you plan on doing now?"

"I don't know." I shrugged. "Enjoy this few more hours I get without worrying about what Serena will do or say next?" I popped a kernel in my mouth and threw one his way, which he caught like a pro.

"You mentioned you had a video of the assault?" he asked while chewing.

"Yes, my security cameras kept a record of everything."

"Have you looked at it yet?"

I detached my head from his body and leaned forward.

The saltiness of the ocean tingled my nose as I took a deep breath. "No, I haven't. It's not something I want to revisit."

This outing was because I wanted to get my mind off her and Leo and my father and Claire, and everyone else that complicated my life. I wanted to just be for once, and Cole was ruining it for me.

His hand connected with my back, rubbing in between my shoulder blades until some of the tenseness ebbed away. "Maybe you should."

"Why is that?" I looked back at him, perplexed.

"I was thinking you should release the video." He paused, gauging my reaction before rushing to explain. "Anonymously through social media, for the world to see."

"What could possibly drive me to do something like that?" I gulped down nervously, the anxiety of that sort of outcome already gripping me. That would be like leading myself down the crucifixion aisle while wearing a blindfold and drenched in gasoline.

The sound of a barking dog made me lose focus, and I turned, watching a six-foot-four guy being dragged by his Mastiff as it ran toward a Pomeranian excitedly.

Cole dragged my gaze back to his, his index curling underneath my chin. "Think about it. Isn't Serena perceived as Dane's princess and the perfect daughter of Carter Laurent?"

"More along the lines of Dane's queen bitch," I muttered under my breath.

"On the other hand, you have been painted as this monster simply for being blood-related to one."

I blanched but didn't dispute his claims.

It was true. Serena was the white swan while I was painted tar. Nothing touched the princess, but everyone seemed to want a piece of me. Own and disrupt my soul like it was a piece of cake to them. A game.

"What if we managed to reverse the roles already premeditated to fit you?" Barely there lines decorated his forehead when his brows raised in question. "Turn her into the aggressor and you into the victim, your rightful titles," he said as if he shared my grudge.

"Why do you care so much?" I asked, genuinely curious.

His eyes flashed with an emotion I couldn't quite put my finger to before he shrugged with a smile. "My family used to foster strays when I was younger. Guess that habit stuck with me. I'm a sucker for the underdogs."

He did not just compare me to a stray.

I flicked his nose, and he laughed, leaning away from me.

"Regardless of your noble intentions, no actual harm would come to Serena. The Laurents are not simple individuals, they are a brand, and PR companies are very much a thing. They could turn a video of her kicking a cat, to gently nudging it out of ill's way."

I knew this because the same thing happened with my father when his image was still salvageable. They even had me doubting everything, and I was in the front lines. Manipulation was a part of our daily lives, from fake commercials to false personas.

"She is not the only one who can afford a good reputation." The light in his eyes never dimmed.

I didn't give a shit about reputation. Why spend years building something up when it could be ruined in a matter of seconds? However, I also saw Cole's point of view, and if I wanted to not end up in a ditch somewhere, I had to be more strategic. Sympathy points were an invaluable asset and could influence an entire jury.

Warmth built in my chest as I looked at the stubborn tilt of Cole's jaw. He didn't know how much he'd helped me in that very moment. "Thank you for the idea, Cole. I'll think about it, I promise." I squeezed his hand.

"Anything for my—" A violent cough gripped him before he could finish his sentence.

"Are you okay?" I asked, patting his back.

"I-I'm fine, I'm fine," he said in between deep gulps of air. "I've been feeling a bit under the weather lately, that's all."

"Must be all that thinking you've been doing," I teased and regretted it soon thereafter because I ended up with mussed, popcorn filled hair.

Chapter 12

Leonardo

Serena was... well, an acquired taste, but I was starting to grow tired of her brand of crazy.

I knew the moment she was released because my phone started blowing up with texts. I hadn't tried calling her since I doubted she was allowed unlimited phone access while in custody, and I was itching to pick up. The text and drive law was there for a reason, though, and I wasn't partial to looking like a squashed ladybug on the side of the road.

Serena didn't really want me; she liked the idea of me and what I could do for her. She liked being gawked at and admired. Having a pretty face was an asset, but influence? That was where the real power lay.

Breathing out a sigh, I lifted my gas-happy foot off the pedal when a red light appeared. Another notification pinged on my phone, and I reached for it in the passenger's seat.

Serena: Seeing as you're too preoccupied to answer my calls, I'll be waiting for you at your place. x

"Of course, you will," I muttered, throwing my phone on the seat again.

The light turned green, and I stepped on it, earning honks and flip-offs from several other drivers. I didn't care though. The need to wrap my hands around Serena's neck washed over me when her name fell from Eli's lips.

Air punched out of my lungs when I saw Eliana all bruised up—her face, collarbone, and neck. She was covered with scratches and welts, and it would take at least a full month to heal.

Guilt, thick and palpable, gripped me.

The one emotion that eluded me for so long came back with a vengeance. It not only haunted me but ate my black heart alive. Spending time with Eliana, getting to know her again... it was testing my loyalty to Isabella.

My teeth hurt as I ground them together, flying down the road that led home and doing a haphazard parking job. Serena's mood swings around my mother were the last thing I needed right now. Tucking my phone in my back pocket, I jumped out of the car and was inside the house in a matter of seconds, following the airy laughter from the hallway to the kitchen.

My mom and Serena were standing behind the kitchen aisle, nursing matching glasses of chilled white wine. I immediately knew it wasn't Mom's first for the day. How? Well, it was past seven in the evening, and she'd never give alcohol to a minor if sober. Even if that minor was twenty.

A stickler for the rules, that was the kind of person she was.

"How come we don't see you around as much, Serena?" Mom asked, taking a sip.

"Serena has been too busy taking up boxing classes lately, Ma." I marched past the foyer, dropping a kiss to my mother's pale cheek.

Mom jumped and Serena avoided my gaze. Other than gulping down the remaining wine in her glass with a newfound urgency, she didn't let the chips in her demeanor show. Her back was stiff as she sat on a black kitchen stool wearing a pink checkered skirt and a white blouse whose sleeves she kept tugging past her wrists every few seconds. To disguise her recent detour down to the APD most likely.

"Oh boxing, how lovely." Mom patted my forearm in greeting. "Did You know Leo has been taking boxing ever since he was young too?"

"I know, Barbara. After all, if it weren't for Leo, I wouldn't have gotten that good at it by myself. He helped me out a lot." Serena smiled, injecting a barb into her sweet words.

She had moved on to shifting the blame to me already. No sense of responsibility. I bet she actually believed her delusions. I'd put her shifty behavior on the back burner for too long now. Convincing myself that her laugh, her voice, her face didn't annoy me because I needed her.

I needed her to hurt Eliana.

"No, I think Serena can cause quite a bit of damage all by herself. Don't be too modest now," I countered without even blinking.

Serena winced at my response, reaching for a refill. My mother, unbeknown to the tension suffocating the room pushed her glass forward eagerly, so Serena could top it off again.

I snatched it away before she could, addressing her. "Mom, if you don't mind, Serena and I have to talk about a class project."

Oh, she didn't mind, alright.

Shifting in my grip, she let me have the glass, snatching the whole bottle off the table. She looked like a ghost and moved like one too in her white tunic. "Alright, I'll leave you two kids alone then."

A pounding headache enveloped my head as I turned back to Serena.

She didn't wait a second to pounce. "Eliana complained about me, huh? Is that why you've been ignoring my calls?"

"Besides the fact that I was in between classes all day, sure that's a reason too."

"God, what a whiny bitch. I didn't even hit her that hard." Using her thumb, she wiped the precipitation off her glass.

"I think her face would beg to differ. She looks like a fucking abstract painting of blues and blacks."

"Well, she probably *let* me go off on her, so she could have something to use against me." Shrugging, Serena whipped her chestnut hair over her shoulder, running with denial as her theme for the night.

My shoulders bunched up, and fuck, now *I* needed a drink.

I chugged whatever was left in my mother's glass before I did anything I regretted, like dragging her to the door by her extensions.

"Are you self-aware at all, Serena? You can't simply go off attacking people like that and expect no repercussions."

Especially in Astropolis, where more than half of the population had insured body parts.

"Yeah? And why not? I simply did what was on everyone's mind." She finally focused on me, her eyes swimming with annoyance that I wasn't falling in line. *Sorry sweetheart, those powers only work on Ares.* "Why are you even arguing with me about it? I assumed you'd love it. She got what she deserved."

"In what world would I ever be fine with you going off and assaulting people?" This wasn't Krypton or fucking Tatooine. "What? Did you have some fucked up fantasy that I would join you for a second time, too?"

"Up until a few weeks ago, you would have been fine with it. What happened? Did the little whore spread her legs for you, and all of a sudden your fine with her existence again?" She roared back before clapping her hands mockingly. "Bravo Leonardo, *bra-fucking-vo*. Isabella would have been proud."

The mention of my sister's name in her petty war had my blood pumping. She didn't deserve to know it, let alone speak it out loud with such confidence.

"Keep Isabella's name out of your mouth." I pressed forward, and she stumbled out of her stool at the storm brewing behind my eyes. She'd gained immunity to my lightning because I'd been too fucking soft with her, but she'd soon learn again. "And I suggest you move on because you're starting to sound like a fucking psycho. I know I have."

I threw that last bit in there as an afterthought. It was total bullshit. When I fixated on something, nothing stopped me from getting it. I fought for it, bruised mouth, bloody knuckles and all.

It was just that my obsession as of late was starting to trickle from hate to lust.

"You are such a fucking liar. You just want to fuck her. You always have," she hissed, her voice metallic. "Is that what it is? Haven't had your dose of whores lately?"

Serena was a safe distance away, but not far enough to escape my grasp. My hand shot out, and I gripped her forearm, tugging her struggling body to mine. Apprehension and lust shone in her eyes, as I pressed her against me.

"Do you feel that, Serena?" I asked, grinding my pelvis against her taut stomach.

Her half-mast eyes squinted at me, eyelashes clumping together. "Feel what?"

"Exactly." My answering smile was cruel. "If I was sexually deprived by my whores, you would have gotten my dick hard already."

Silence fell between us, heavy and loud.

In a delayed reaction, her mouth dropped open as if it took her some time to digest my words, roll them over in her mind, and make sure she understood them correctly. She stumbled back as if slapped when I merely touched her.

"You're a bastard." Her hands pushed at my chest, and I let go, confident I got my point across.

"And you're getting on my last nerve. Why did you beat Eliana up? I heard it had something to do with me."

"Partially." She winced, embarrassed. "Her fucking mother went and got herself knocked up. As if it wasn't bad enough that I had to suffer through both mother and daughter's existence, now I have to share DNA with them too."

Jesus. I took a step back, not expecting that particular answer. *Holy fuck.* Knocked up as in with a baby? *No, with a watermelon. Of course, with a fucking baby, dumbass.*

"Isn't she like forty?" I found myself asking.

"That's what I thought too. Shouldn't her eggs be shriveled up by now? But apparently, she still has a chance of conceiving. A slight one, but it's still probable."

There was an inseparable tie that linked Eliana, Serena, and me together. One of grief. I pitied her, I *understood* what she was going through, but I couldn't find it in me to pull her out of the turbulent waters.

She knew about the affair, blamed her mother's death on Claire, yet kept her mouth shut around me. I wondered if she also knew something bigger was going on behind the scenes, and that was why she kept everything in until it overflowed.

I moved closer, my gaze level with hers. "In any case, there is no excuse for what you did. The least you can do now is be grateful Eliana didn't press any charges."

"Why don't you transfer my heartfelt thanks," she taunted, eyes dead. "After all, you sure do love meeting with her."

"I don't think you have any idea what I love doing, Serena."

"I'll get off your hair then, since it sure as hell is not me."

I blew out a breath, my eyebrows meeting in an amused frown.

You're right, it's not.

I'd been tempted to sleep with her. Serena was all too readily available and relatively attractive. But I couldn't see her as anything more than a friend. I met Serena before I did Eliana, yet she still wasn't the one that lingered in my mind. Not to mention, Ares, with his not so subtle crush, would freak.

And what was I if not a fan-fucking-tastic friend?

Slowly, I moved out of her path, leaving the coast clear for a swift exit.

She didn't move for the longest time, just stared at me as if she could make me break down and beg her to stay. A frown marred her forehead when I didn't let up. Although if she didn't wrap this up soon, I'd leave her here to stare at the wall by herself.

Finally, with a huff and a roll of her eyes, Serena grabbed her bag off the aisle, moving to the door. She didn't glance back, but I knew the view of her russet brown eyes, turned molten, would greet me if she had.

After making sure she had left the property and wasn't sulking in a corner somewhere, I grabbed my phone to call Eliana, but decided against it. We'd be together tomorrow, I'd tell her then.

Face to face.

Literally, just as I placed my phone in my pocket, it rang with a call.

"Hello?" I answered with a sigh.

"Hey, sunshine," Ares greeted.

"What's up?"

"We're heading over to Astor's. Wanna come?"

Saint Astor.

Captain of the football team and asshole extraordinaire.

Despite what his name would lead you to believe that motherfucker was anything *but* a saint if his monthly orgy parties were anything to go by. I had participated in a few, but at least I wasn't the one that hosted them.

I hesitated.

Breathy moans and needy groans filled my head. The ghost touch of Eliana's lips broke through the chains of long locked memories.

Her back was pressed against my mattress, math book long forgotten on the floor. I held her in place, my weight strewn over her smaller frame.

Her dad was going to be here any minute to pick her up, but I didn't want to let go yet. Not when she finally gave in. Not when I finally made a move after two weeks of tutoring her.

I spent two hellish weeks of watching her parade around my room in barely there skirts. Two hellish weeks of her cutting my advances short for reasons unbeknown to me. I knew Eliana liked me. Her moans spoke plenty of that, her legs gripping my waist tight even more so.

But something held her back.

That something melted away, though, the minute I really made my move. I attacked her when she sat in my bed, her book perched between her hands. I dove straight for her mouth, fighting back tears of relief when she didn't back away.

She was soft underneath me. Her skin was like silk, smooth and unblemished as I ran my hands over her stomach, making my way up.

"One week, Leo." She breathed against my mouth, her hands clasping my cheeks tighter until there was almost no space between us. "I'm giving us one week, and then we're through."

"One week," I mumbled back, knowing full well I was lying. You aren't getting rid of me that easily, Narcissus. "One week, and then we're through."

I closed my mouth over hers again, kissing her, touching her, getting consumed by the mouthy blonde that owned my world until everything slowed down and there was just us.

We never made it to a week, though.

Only three days of heavy petting and make-out sessions behind locked doors before her father doomed what hadn't even started.

"Yo, are you still there?" Ares's voice pierced through the memory.

I should have gone. Under any other circumstances, I wouldn't have thought twice about joining, but the thought of meeting Eliana tomorrow held me back.

"I'm not feeling like partying tonight. You guys have fun though." I moved up the stairs to my room.

I failed to catch the reply, my shirt muffling my hearing as I removed it to get in the shower.

"What was that?"

"I said, are you sure? I heard Eliana will be there."

I stopped dead in my tracks.

"Eliana Roux?" I asked for confirmation, even though there were no other girls named Eliana that I knew of.

But what business would Eliana have attending Astor's party? People only went there to either fuck or get fucked. And no one else would be fucking her if I had anything to say about it, and I had *plenty* to say.

"Yes, *Eliana Roux*." He stressed the words.

"Why would Eliana be there?" I bit down on my tongue until it stung.

"Do I look like I'm her keeper? I just heard Astor's girl was bringing her along."

Astor again.

Maybe he was in the business of sharing what was his, but I very much liked my territory landlocked. A sharp sensation hit the back of my throat as the realization that I'd fucking kill any poor bastard that dared to touch her, settled in.

Eliana was mine.

She'd been mine when I loved her.

She'd been mine when I loathed her.

She'd be mine as long as I wanted to fuck her too.

Whatever fun she'd had until now, it was about to be cut short. We spent years running circles around each other. She ran in my veins, and my name was etched in her soul. It was about to be etched on her ass too, if she kept testing me. The only time she would be allowed to have some motherfucker's hands all over her would be after I was six feet under.

Hell, even then, I'd come back and haunt her branded ass.

"I'll be there." My response was gruff, and I hung up before I got to listen to Ares's self-satisfied laugh.

My split-second decision was followed by the quickest shower of my life. I didn't take much time getting ready either, settling for some gray checkered pants and a generic button-up shirt that I didn't have the patience to fasten all the way.

I made sure to check on my mother before powering my R8 and descending down the driveway. She was passed out in bed, but I still called in our housekeeper in for an all-nighter.

So, Eliana Roux was off seeking adventures, huh?

I planned on giving her one that would last her a lifetime.

Chapter 13

ELIANA

I was in a glass museum.

The kind of place where you feared your touch alone would stain the shiny countertops and stainless-steel appliances. Cold. Impersonal. Prudish. The house was so alike, yet at the same time couldn't be more different than its owner.

Saint Astor was everyone's favorite golden boy, but something underneath that amber gaze rubbed me the wrong way. There was a touch of frost extending past the warmth everyone was so enamored by. A kiss of ice fogged up the Sahara stone tiles he glided over while socializing with guests.

"You've never been to one of Astor's parties, but you both attend Dane University?" Madison Higgings asked, diverting my attention from Saint.

The redhead was a coworker from the club, and after

completing our rehearsals for the day, she invited me to tag along to a party.

I shook my head no.

The star quarterback was miles out of my league. His shiny gold hair and even shinier legacy knew privilege that rivaled mine. Saint was the heir of the Falco fashion house. One of the first haute couture brands originating from Paris, catering to the elite and aristocrats for more than a century.

"Oh boy, you're in for a treat then." Her high cheekbones peeked with a smile, as she clinked her negroni with mine and didn't elaborate further.

"How do you know Saint exactly?"

"We met at a Falco runway show. I was one of the models walking the summer collection. We clicked, and now we just like to hang out every once in a while." She crossed her gazelle-like legs.

I couldn't judge her for going out with a guy three years her senior. Astor blurred the lines of age when it came to attracting the opposite—and same—sex sometimes. The bleachers were jam-packed with women of all generations whenever he played, and no, it wasn't because they suddenly discovered their undying love for football.

Before I could reply, Saint's large build brushed past me as he bounded over to Madison. Not bothering with words, he plopped a very *wet* kiss on her mouth as a greeting.

"Uhm." I cleared my throat, slightly uncomfortable.

Their lips clung together, fighting to detach from each other's hold. Even apart, though, Maddy's doe gazed still looked lethargic while nonchalance dripped off Saint as he appraised the low neckline of her black dress.

Throwing a heavy hand over Maddy's bony shoulders,

he turned to me, eyes shining with inexplicable mirth while taking me in. "Roux? What are you doing here?"

Yeah, I definitely understood why Maddy went after him.

He was just so... large.

His muscles flexed, stretching the Falco logo—a red hawk—on his white shirt, over his pec. Saint's six-foot-five build made his appeal in football clear. And the slight crook of his nose was a welcome break from the perfect symmetry of his jaw and lips.

He raised his blond eyebrows, waiting for my delayed response.

"What does one do at a party?" I questioned back defensively, trying to break out of my red shell.

"Hey, I'm not complaining. Feel free to stay however long you like." He released a slurry smile, catching on to my wariness. "God knows Bianchi isn't all that generous when it comes to you."

"Bianchi isn't anything when it comes to me." I managed to bite out, barely making sense, yet he still understood.

"Sure, he's not." He chuckled.

People often underestimated Saint. Sure, he was a hot jock, but he was no meathead. The perceptiveness in his gaze could lock down the route of the labyrinth in your head in seconds. The mere thought of making an enemy out of him sprung shivers down my arms.

Winking at me, he pecked Maddison's pouty lips before retreating with a group of friends. A sigh I didn't realize I was holding hostage escaped my mouth when he was out of proximity.

"Bianchi?" Maddy inquired.

"I don't want to talk about it." I shook my head,

proceeding to change the subject. "So, you also work as a model, in addition to being a dancer?"

"Yes, I'm trying to gather a sufficient amount of funds to attend med school after I graduate from my current bachelor's degree."

She had the lithe body of a dancer, the face of an Irish pixie, and the brain of a genius? I expected jealousy to grip me, but all I felt was pride for her. Madison was a prime example of what women were capable of and didn't constrict herself to fit any stereotypes.

"That's amazing! Do you know what you'd like to specialize in?"

"At the moment, I'm thinking, dermatology. I want to own my own skincare line one day, but we'll see."

Must've been nice having your life all figured out. I didn't know what I'd have for lunch tomorrow or if I wanted to drop out. Biotechnology wasn't for me. I only stuck with it because my dad always raved about the importance of a college education. What I truly loved was dancing, but I'd lost a few important years of training after... everything.

Not to mention, I could very well end up not having a future altogether.

Cold sweat broke out along my body, and I tried to loosen up by downing the rest of my drink. When I settled the glass back on the Lemurian blue countertop, Maddy's mind was miles away as she looked at the couches in the living room.

I followed her wistful gaze to Saint. He had his tongue shoved down a girl's throat while pawing a different girl's ass as she ravaged his neck with bites and licks. My head swiveled back to Madison as soon as a manicured hand reached for his zipper.

"We're not serious," Maddy explained, bitterness lacing her voice.

It was clear that she was bothered. We all had our vices, and an asshole with commitment issues was hers. Saint lived to prove the meaning of his name wrong, a ferryman of Hades, collecting broken hearts wherever he went.

Thinking of assholes, another one magically materialized next to me, so I didn't get a chance to warn Madison to run before it was too late. Maybe it was the universe's way of telling me not to offer unsolicited advice if I didn't plan on following it myself.

"Long time no see, Eliana." Ares threw a hand over my shoulders, smiling down at me.

"We see each other every day, Ares."

"Sorry, I meant to say, long time no talk."

"Yeah, you've been rather busy." *Chasing after Serena's skirt.*

My dig went unnoticed as he had already lost interest in me, turning to a sulky Madison. "Won't you introduce me to your friend?"

I'd rather not, seeing as she already had one douchebag to deal with, I didn't want to overfill her plate by throwing Ares there too.

"Won't you introduce me to yours?" I rested my back on the countertop, smiling pretty at the brawny guy next to him.

He looked like he ran people over for a living and didn't wait for an introduction. Instead, he grabbed my hand abruptly, bringing it to his lips, warm brown eyes fixated on mine as he kissed the back of it.

"Devin, pleasure to meet you."

Okay, I was either tripping or everyone was very touchy-feely at this party. Ares had bypassed my rudeness of not introducing Madison and started chatting her up, oblivious to my discomfort.

"Pleasure to meet you too, Devin." I tried tugging my hand back, but he wouldn't let go, getting close enough that his heavy cologne flowed through my nostrils.

"What's your name, sweetheart?" He asked, his hand migrating to my upper thigh area. I squirmed, but my body language didn't deter his advance. That was, until a voice boomed behind him, making my heart loop in my chest.

"Her name is none of your fucking business, and if you want to keep your limbs, I suggest you take your hands off of her."

My breath hitched at the threat, and one peak beyond Devin's shoulder had Leo filling my line of sight. His expression was thunderous, like a pile of TNT about to detonate at any given moment. My heart skipped a beat at the uncalled possessiveness I found lurking there.

I didn't know when this predator had become my knight in shining armor, but I was immediately at ease in his presence.

"Who the hell are you?" Devin asked, turning his body to confront Leo. His hand tightened on my thigh upon closer inspection. I winced at the twinge of pain, clawing my nails down his skin so he'd let go.

In tune with my expressions, Leo's eyes missed nothing. Not needing any more motivation to feed the hysteric energy around him, all hell broke loose as he lunged for Devin, yanking him away from me.

As if tied to them by an invisible string, I stumbled off my stool. I didn't make it far, though, paralyzed by the violent turn of events. The touching was a little over the top, but Leo was breaking through the glass roof with his... with his... jealousy?

Yes. *Jealousy*, I realized as Devin face planted the floor beside a forming crowd.

"The guy who had the decency to warn you." Leo crouched down to his eye level. "Too bad you weren't smart enough to heed it."

"Oh my god." I cupped my mouth as Leo delivered the first blow. A grotesque gush of blood slipped from Devin's nose, staining Leo's knuckles red.

I rushed forward but stopped short. I couldn't break them up. All I'd accomplish was getting elbowed in the face. Leo's name ripped from my mouth as a last-ditch effort. Devin's face was turning into a bloody pulp.

Even consumed in his bloodlust, he heard me. His head turned in my direction, and Devin took full advantage of his distraction, throwing a bruising punch of his own.

I thought I'd enjoy a sight like this, Leonardo Bianchi finally hit back, but my heart broke at the brief look of pain on his face.

Not one to be discouraged, Leo dove right back in, determined to make Devin's backhanded punch the last he'd ever be able to deliver. I got closer as the stakes got higher, hoping my hundred and twenty-pound body would be enough to pull them off each other. No one else seemed to be doing anything, too caught up in reveling in the outlandish dominance display before them.

"Oh, no, you don't." A foreign hand grasped my upper forearm, tugging me back. "You've done quite enough, sweetheart." Saint looked on, vexed.

"I didn't do anything." I crossed my arms petulantly, but my words fell on deaf ears.

Assigned to stay put, I watched as they tried to pull Leo off of Devin. The lump in my throat grew thicker when he didn't seem to let up. Leo was so engrossed in the mechanical movement of his arm, going at it with unparalleled viciousness.

It took almost four brawny football players to manage to break up the brawl. Two holding Leo by his arms and the other two dragging a bloody Devin away. My stomach churned at the sight, and a wave of nausea hit me.

We were coming full circle.

Dragging other people in our toxicity.

Leo's chest fluctuated with the remnants of his adrenaline. I could hear his sharp, short breaths, even above everyone's whispers. Finally, somewhat in control, he pushed the guys that were holding him off, his wrathful gaze connecting with my horrified one.

He prowled closer with gusto, as if it was only us two in the room. Like a gazelle caught in the hunter's unrelenting gaze, my legs moved backward in an attempt to flee.

I wasn't quick enough, though, and the next thing I knew, I was looking at Madison and Ares upside down when my stomach connected with his shoulder.

"Oh my god, where is he taking her?" Madison asked, concerned.

"Eh, it's okay. That's just their version of foreplay," an unbothered Ares replied.

"Leo, put me down." I hit his lower back.

In response, he let me slide down his back while taking the stairs two by two, making the fall sharper, and I squeaked, latching on to him again. He released a dark chuckle and tightened his hands on my bare thighs again.

"Where are you going?" I demanded.

He didn't answer, and I slammed my balled fists on his back again. The only attention I got was an answering slap on my ass that rendered me speechless, long enough for him to reach his destination and slip inside.

I was set upright, and the sudden change in inclination left me dizzy. Taking advantage of my weakness, he pushed me back. My hands flailed, and my hair swayed over my face as my ass met the mattress below me.

"What are you doing?" I screeched. "Are you completely out of your mind?"

He didn't waste his breath. Leo got on top of me, locking my squirming body down by straddling my waist. I sucked in a sharp breath when I felt him. Felt all of him. He fisted my hair in a tight grip, stretching my neck and our lips almost met. Separated by nothing save for a few inches of warm air.

"What am I doing?" He released a harsh chuckle. "What the fuck are you doing at one of Astor's parties?"

"I don't need your permission to go out. Don't confuse me for an obedient little girl, Bianchi."

"Oh, baby," he rasped, his breath tingling the surface of my cheek. "You wouldn't even know what an obedient little girl is."

Annoyed by the effect he had over me, I thrashed under him, attempting to throw him off. Leo released my hair but didn't let me go. He never let me go. His hold turned to my wrists, boxing them over my head, joining our bodies tighter together.

I couldn't breathe, couldn't speak, couldn't fucking think without him consuming me. His tight muscles ignited a spark inside me I'd long forgotten existed.

"What the fuck are you doing here?" he repeated,

grazing my ear with his nose, following up the path with a flick of his tongue.

"A friend invited me." I gave in, shuddering away from his tangible heat. "Not that it's any of your business. I don't get what you're so worked up over, it's just a party, and last time I checked, you had no say over where I go or what I do."

His thick throat worked with a mocking chuckle, and I bristled.

"Let's get two things straight, Narcissus. One." Leo smiled down at me, but I didn't dare confuse his smile for kindness. It was more of a show of teeth. "Stop kidding yourself. What you do is my business. Where you go, what you wear, who you fuck. Simply put you're mine."

I stilled. Lust dug at my insides, despite his infuriating thoughts over my ownership. This was so wrong. We were a recipe for disaster, and yet my stomach quivered at his possessiveness. I couldn't help but want to bathe in the waters that led my obsession with Leonardo Bianchi deeper.

"Two, this is not just a party," he mocked. "This is a fucking orgy, and that loser downstairs would've been the least of your worries if you'd stayed for ten more minutes."

My mouth dropped open. I guessed that was the *treat* Madison was talking about. Nevertheless, that wasn't the information stuck in a constant loop in my mind. The word *mine* penetrated the cracks of my heart, threatening to ruin me.

"Don't be delusional. I am not yours as much as you're not mine. You've confused the pain we love inflicting upon each other for something more because that's all you know," I lectured condescendingly. "And if I want to attend an orgy, I fucking will. You are no one to stop me."

"No one, huh? Then why do I live in your mind rent-free, sweetheart? You'll do yourself a favor if you just admit it already." He ground his hips on mine, and my skirt rode up, right along with my need for him.

"Leo, we c-can't." I grappled with my last bit of sanity.

His darkened eyes lowered to my shirt, and I knew he was so far gone he didn't care about right or wrong. My nipples peaked at his interest, and he got closer, wrapping his hot mouth around a peak over my mesh shirt. A cry built inside of me, spilling when he sucked harder on my flesh.

His laugh vibrated against my delicate skin, and a gush of wetness soaked my panties, dripping down my lips. All too soon, he detached his mouth from my breast, and my jaw unbound, releasing a whimper. I wanted to tug him back down again. Feed him with more of my skin.

"What's the matter, baby?"

A slew of curse words sat at the tip of my tongue, but I didn't want him to win any more than he already had. So I bit them back.

"If you're not mine, then who else gets you this worked up, Narcissus?" He snarled. Sliding his hands down my arms, he wrapped a big palm around my throat, eyes flashing when they felt the erratic beat of my pulse.

Only you.

Only you have the power to ruin me. That's why I hate you.

His other hand tugged at my legs, and they all but fell open, wrapping around his waist. His hard cock rested snuggly between my thighs as he palmed my ass, squeezing until my eyes rolled in the back of my head.

"Answer me," he commanded. "Who else makes your pussy drip? Whose touch do you crave? Who do you belong to?"

His lips traced mine, teasing, driving me crazy. I felt crazy. Deranged with need. "You," I mouthed against his mouth, soundless.

"Out loud, Eliana. Say it out loud."

"You," I breathed, desperation seeping into my voice. "You. Always you."

His relief mixed with my terror, that constant terror that never stopped me from giving in. It wasn't enough. Nothing ever was enough to withstand Leo.

He rewarded me with a tug of my lower lip, and when my tongue swiped out to taste his, he slipped away once again. A frustrated groan filled me. He kept throwing me scraps that didn't pacify me.

"That's right. All fucking mine," he growled.

My yelp was muffled by his lips as he dove straight into my mouth. I breathed a sigh into his exploring mouth, relieved when his minty breath finally touched my taste buds.

Liquid fire coursed through my nerve endings as his lips started their descent down my body. And I felt rather than heard my shirt rip, cool air prickling my exposed breasts.

"You did not just rip my sh—" My words gave way to a bewildered moan when his mouth *really* touched me, devoured me. Leo's tongue and teeth began a bewitching dance of nips and licks, smoldering my body with their silent assault.

He could probably feel my pounding heart underneath him, could tell how easy it would be for him to break it to pieces. My vulnerabilities were stripped bare for his taking.

Desperation clung to my core. I needed something to fill the void, and he had the perfect tool. Tugging at his hair, I didn't wait. I took what I wanted, grinding against his hard-on like an ambitious stripper crippled by student loans.

"Fuck, Eliana. You drive me fucking crazy," he croaked against my exposed flesh, his hands flexing on my ass, keeping the steady rhythm of our erotic grind going. "I'm betraying my own blood for you. You walk into a room, and I can't fucking think straight. You talk back, and fire fills my lungs. I don't know whether to bend you over right then and there or kiss you until your lips are bruised."

You destroy me, the thought swam in my head. What's stronger? Spoiling something or blowing it completely out of orbit? The tortuous split between duty and lust crackled between us.

So, so wrong, yet so fucking right.

"That sassy, luscious mouth, all mine. Will you part those beautiful lips for me tonight? Let me hit the back of your little throat?" He sucked my plump tit in his mouth like a starved man.

My head met the plush comforter beneath us with fervor, brain swimming with stars and thighs tightening around him.

I could fucking come from his dirty mouth alone.

His lips feathered down the valley of my breasts, and I groaned when the weight of his erection disappeared from my pussy, right along with my panties and skirt. His expert fingers slid the clothes down my legs slowly, giving his tongue time to swirl teasingly down the expanse of my belly.

Pinning my knees open on either side, he took his fill, looking at my bare pussy, the red color ripe by arousal. "God-damn, you're dripping." His tone was pained. "Soaked through and through."

I'd fantasized about this moment for years. Little old me

even looked forward to a future. A relationship with none other than Leonardo Bianchi. *Insert eye roll.*

"Take your shirt off," I ordered, trying to balance out our uneven ground.

"Making demands now, are we?" he asked mockingly, but his shirt disappeared over his shoulder. He was as impatient as me to explore the crippling chemistry between us.

I'd seen his taut bronze chest a thousand times before. An exhibitionist by nature, Leo loved showing off his body in public. And I didn't really blame him. With a stature like that, it would have been a shame if he was born modest. Reaching forward, I couldn't help gliding my fingers down his torso, enjoying the peaks and dips of his abs.

Cupping my face, he brought his mouth to mine, feeding me his rough groans and stealing my breath away like the fucking selfish bastard that he was. *His, his, his.* Everything had to always be his.

I broke the kiss, holding him off by the cross on his neck. "A catholic prodigy."

"You can say I have a knack for bringing people to their knees."

"You mean you have a god complex." I quirked a brow, twisting the chain until it dug into his skin.

His thumb found my clit, and my hand jerked, breaking the clasp of the necklace. The cold piece of metal slipped down the chain, and we both followed its descent, watching a disaster unfold in slow motion.

The square edges of the steel pressed into my sex, and the chilling contrast between the temperatures was welcome, calming my engorged need.

That was until Leo twisted the situation down a path I'd never taken before. A devilish grin spread over his face as he curled his fingers around the pendant, pressing it harder against me. Rubbing me with it.

My cheeks took on the color of sin, but I couldn't help my reaction toward his blasphemous perversion. I didn't like it. I fucking loved it. Thrived on the forbidden and inconceivable.

Hell.

I'm going to burn in the fiery pits of hell for all eternity.

A moan ripped from my mouth, drowning the myriad of emotions swarming my head. Shame, embarrassment, guilt, but most importantly I was so fucking turned on. My chest stuttered with broken gasps, and I clutched his bulging biceps as he stroked my clit with the cross.

"But is it really a complex though?" Leo asked, his grin touching my lips. Without any forewarning, he sunk a thick finger inside of me, and my back arched at the intrusion, my sanity unraveling thread by thread.

"Oh my fuucking god." The weight of my head became too much to bear, so I let it fall back as he went to town with his fingers. Inserting a second digit, he pushed inside of me like he was looking for a hidden treasure.

Leo decorated the surface of my neck with punishing kisses, sucking my skin into his mouth and muttering filthy muffled words. I rolled my hips to the rhythm of his fingers, clawing my nails down his biceps.

I hope God has a sense of humor 'cause there is no sane way to explain this.

"You're sick," I accused, my tone high-pitched.

He licked a nipple before clumping down on it with his teeth. The high of the pain was so profound my ass scooted off the mattress, meeting his thrusts with excitement.

"We're both sick, Narcissus, you should have known that

by now." He penetrated me ruthlessly, and my abdominal muscles flexed with lust and desire. "You're cutting the circulation off my fingers with that tight pussy of yours, Narcissus. I can't wait until you're stretched on my dick, filled to the brim with nothing but me, little monster."

I whimpered, tugging his head back to me. I fused our mouths together, wanting to forget that this was him. That this was Leo, finger fucking me to oblivion.

My greatest enemy, my deepest regret, my unrelenting obsession.

I was swimming in ecstasy. The sinister nature of our passion made my body cramp with yearning, the steady fire burning beneath my skin becoming unbearable. Fevers scorched my being until my core was ready to combust.

"Leo." My moan was lost in his mouth. He swallowed my cries, hungry for more of me. "God, Leo, please," I begged for relief.

"Please what?" he teased, making me eat my past taunts.

My eyebrows took a nosedive, and I couldn't come up with a comeback of my own. I was so close. My climax was almost through the threshold, and only he could provide the final push to ultimate release.

"Please make me come." I nudged my nose with his and saw the moment his eyes softened, his slow blink making time stand still.

Leo's fingers curled upwards, and my heart faltered. The feel of the chain grinding against my folds and the bite of metal digging into my fleshy nub unraveled my most prolific desires.

I tried to hold my cries back, but I was too far gone. The orgasm ripped into me with the power of a whiplash. A murky tsunami took over my brain, and all I could do was ride the waves and pray I made it out alive. I shook all over, my hands twisting in his hair and wrapping around his shoulders. Bringing him closer and closer and closer. I didn't want more, yet I couldn't get enough of him. I absorbed his scent and his touch in my skin, brimming with need.

Not only out of orbit, I realized. He blew me out of this galaxy. My body was floating in inky darkness as the aftershocks slowly ebbed away, and my lungs filled with air again. Stretching and knocking my ass back for trying to survive solely off of him.

Jesus Christ.

I slumped against the foreign mattress, my body covered with a thin layer of sweat. "I'm guessing there was no sentimental value behind that cross?" I said on a sharp exhale, hands still making a mess out of his brown mane.

"It was a gift from dear ol' dad... I'm just honoring his lovely treatment, *in spades*." He muttered the last part, and I had difficulty grasping his words, seeing as his fingers were still leisurely moving inside me. Exploring still.

"What?" I asked, but the frost had already settled over the green leaves in his eyes. It was not up for discussion.

He withdrew his fingers and the necklace, and the squelching sound my pussy made when he did so further reddened my already cherry cheeks.

But Leo wasn't done.

He dangled the necklace between us as one would bloody sheets in a Sicilian marriage. It glistened under the partially lit room, polished with my essence. Throwing me off-kilter once again, he parted his lips, sucking the cross right in his sinful mouth, groaning at the taste, my taste. "Heaven liquified."

I squeezed my eyes shut when he reached forward to kiss

me. The ache between my thighs came back with a vengeance when my musky flavor exploded in my mouth, one stroke of his tongue at a time.

Way beyond the moral ineptness of it all, my hand traveled to the bulge of his pants, breasts sliding against the hard planes of his chest. I was hyper-aware of his every movement, fine-tuned to his desires as if made specifically for this very moment.

The sense of destiny heightened in the air, begging to be consummated.

My fingers fumbled as I worked his zipper down. There would be no turning back after this. All chances of cordial friendship would go up in flames. It seemed both of us were too eager for the impending doom, though.

Insistent knocks from the door somewhat cleared the haze in my brain, and we pulled apart, my hand still fisting his dick over his slacks.

"Guys." More knocks. "My room is off-limits for guests." An urgent voice said.

My eyes widened when I caught sight of Saint's headshot on the wall, and Leo followed my line of vision, looking pained at the interruption.

Leonardo Bianchi just fingered me in Saint Astor's bed.
Great.

As if this couldn't get any more fucked up.

A giggle escaped me, a kind of laugh that belonged to a crazy person more than a happy one.

"I'm sorry," I said in between chuckles, when his eyes darkened and his body hardened. "It's really more sad than funny."

"Yeah, for him. Because I'm gonna kill him."

Chapter 14

ELIANA

A honk went off outside my front door.

Both his actions and personality were loud. Apparently, averse to technological communication, that was all the warning I got that he was here.

I hated myself for what happened yesterday with Leonardo. And for how my hand rushed to my hair, fixing up the flyaways in my peripheral vision.

God, I was done for.

I even wanted to mess with his emotions, bless my heart. But the only one that would end up getting strung along here would be me. My body was still trying to recover after yesterday. I was teetering the edge between *what the fuck did I do,* and *I want to do it again. I want him to pound me against the wall until I can't feel my toes.*

Not even the dirty look Saint graced us with when we exited his room could stop my libido from running. I should be mortified that probably half of the people at the party knew something was going on. If the fight didn't clue them in, then me leaving in Leo's shirt most certainly did.

The killer's daughter and the victim's brother.

We would make for such cute headlines.

It was scary how he got me to spell out things I've been denying to even myself for years. He was such a skilled manipulator. Cold-blooded and silver-tongued, Leo trapped you in his snare, uncaring of how much you bled as long as it was for him.

I was betraying myself by caving into his touch, craving his tongue and sinister mind. My moral compass pointed in all different directions when he was around. Leo turned off my ability to feel anything but him, and that wasn't safe. He had the power to be catastrophic.

Barren trees laced my driveway, the kiss of winter was eminent in the air, yet my jean jumpsuit still clung to my body weirdly. A thin sheet of sweat blanketed my skin, and nervous flutters wrecked my belly as I stepped out.

I was no psychic, but the prospect of today turning out good was slim to none. It was a cliff in front and current in the back type of situation. No matter what the P.I. told us, no fall would be less painful.

I tried to muffle the shake of my hands as I reached for the handle.

"Should I be flattered by your imitation, Narcissus?" he greeted.

My brows pulled together, and I buckled my seatbelt before turning to look at him. He was wearing a jean jacket and a black pair of Diesel pants. Our looks were hardly similar but probably still an eyesore for any onlookers.

"I couldn't help it. I wanted us to have our own little double denim moment," I teased.

Spearing me with a thousand-watt smile, he put the shift in drive, reveling in the engine's loud purr by speeding down the driveway. The awkwardness after I left with Maddy and not him yesterday didn't seem to linger on to today. I wasn't ready for the aftermath, but it needed to be addressed for both of our mental sanity.

"So..." I started. "About last night."

"What about it?" he asked because a world where Leo wasn't difficult was pretty much non-existent.

"Do you think it's wise for us to..." I toyed with a few stray strings from my jumpsuit, confused about our label.

"To fuck?" he deadpanned.

"To get involved," I inwardly winced. "We're still looking into your sister's murder, and my father could very well still be the main suspect."

His grip turned white around the steering wheel, but I didn't regret asking it. Feelings were an innate part of the process, much to his disbelief. Involving any sexual activities would give him that extra edge to plunge my world into destruction more easily.

"Don't think too much about it. We're just having some fun, Eliana." He took a sharp left I felt down to my stomach.

Right, *fun*.

Fun that apparently makes me only his. *Fun* that had need swishing at my insides every time I saw him. *Fun* that had him beating random ass dudes because they touched me.

Maybe I was looking at this wrong. He didn't want me. He just wanted to *own* me. But I wasn't about to sit back while he was free to do anything and anyone he pleased.

"I'm assuming we're free to date other people then. This is just some harmless fun after all." I detested the words as soon as they left my mouth.

Another sharp turn, and I held on to the oh shit bar, glaring at him for wanting to put me in an early grave.

"It will be a cold day in hell if that ever happens. I don't share. If I did, the fun would be more deadly than harmless for all parties involved."

His green eyes sought mine, and even though he stepped on the accelerator, the thought of a crash wasn't the reason I wanted him to stop looking at me. I needed a barrier between us, a veil, separating his magnetizing hold from influencing my thoughts and decisions.

"Eyes on the road, Bianchi." I cleared my throat. He smirked at the catch in my voice but did turn back to cruising the road safely. Well... as much as going a hundred miles per hour could be considered safe. "So I'm supposed to stay celibate while you get it on with everything that moves? Because if that's your thought process, you're delusional."

"I am capable of monogamy, you know."

I couldn't help but scoff at that, my eyes rolling to the back of my head.

There was a rumor about why his parents named him Leonardo, and it involved his and DiCaprio's innate ability at driving girls mad. I could see it. My Leo, hanging out in Saint Tropez, on a yacht full of supermodels. It wouldn't surprise me. Him at an altar, however, pledging his life to another person forever... now that was laughable.

"What's so funny, Narcissus?"

"The only thing you've ever been monogamous toward is your hand, and that was when you were thirteen. I don't know where you find the confidence that you'll keep it in your pants from."

"But I won't." I whipped my head toward him, not expecting that bold of an answer. "I'll keep it in yours." He graced me with a smile, soft and seductive—and just a bit wicked.

I couldn't help but feel the stubborn tug of my lips when he reached over, grasping my thigh with his corded hand. His fingers grazed my sensitive inside, and heat spread along his lethal touch.

"Whatever." My gaze fled to the sky, enamored with making shapes out of clouds, so I wouldn't linger on his taunting exploration up my leg. "We'll see if you'll still be all in after today."

Part of my reluctance to accept that my dad had nothing to do with this was because I didn't want to hold on to false hope. I didn't believe in the law of attraction. Out of experience, I knew that a positive mindset only led to life kicking you down harder than before.

His fingers squeezed my skin tightly before releasing their hold on me, and going back to strangling the hell out of the steering wheel instead. I was reluctant to give him too much power because he wasn't a benevolent god. He'd take any leeway I provided him with and abuse it when things went south.

"What difference does it even make if it's my mother that's involved in your sister's case rather than my father? How does that make me any less of a monster in your eyes?" I continued, unable to stop myself.

They were both my parents as much as I wished otherwise sometimes.

He shook his head, frustrated that he couldn't turn to look at me. "It's different because you're more loyal to Serena than you are to your mother. I never saw you as a monster by association. I just hated that part of you still loved your father despite knowing what he did. Or at least what we thought he did."

My throat constricted, and I didn't reply.

It was true, and the hateful smile that greeted me every day in the mirror knew it. I loved my dad despite knowing the extent of his madness and supposed disturbed morality.

Save from the click of my clear heels on the laminated floor, tense silence followed our wake down the hallway to the P.I.'s office. Every step weighed on me, but I kept moving, planting one foot in front of the other.

The only thing keeping me from screaming, *"I don't wanna do it!"* and locking myself back in my gilded cage, was walking right behind me, blocking any possible exit routes with his large body.

Coming to a stop in front of a wooden door, I tried my best at a knock, but the shakiness of my limbs caused me to drop my hand back down again, resting it limply against my hip.

Impatient with my reluctance, Leo reached over me, his thick arm rapping against the surface with more force than necessary.

"I think he heard you already," I hissed, stopping his fist from leaving an indent on the door.

Indeed he had. The door flew open, and the man that greeted us was your typical forty to fifty-year-old. A mostly bald scalp, with a few sparse hairs here and there, and a beer belly that hinted at a strenuous alcoholic lifestyle.

"Leonardo, welcome," the man addressed Leo with familiarity, going in for a handshake. "Nice to see you again."

"Well, I can't say I'm all that excited to see you, Ethan," Leo replied, and my eyes bugged at his rudeness. "This is Eliana Roux." He gestured at me, while I was still eyeballing him for his impolite reply. The P.I. took his words in stride, though, and while ill-mannered, he had a point. Neither of us was happy with the circumstances that led us here.

"Pleasure to meet you, Ms. Roux." He shook my hand too.

After inviting us inside, I elbowed Leo's stomach while Ethan's back was turned. The strained groan escaping his lips, while barely audible, brought a smile to my face. The answering pinch on my ass, though, all about wiped away any crumbs of humor.

He threw a little smirk my way that had me gearing up for retaliation, but Ethan gestured for us to take our respective seats before I could do so.

"Leonardo, you asked me to look into the Roux case." His chocolate eyes briefly fleeted to me, making my lips thin. "And any possible involvement by Carter Laurent and Claire Roux."

Leo nodded at the statement, his hands pressed calmly by the sides of the armchair. I, on the other hand, couldn't seem to keep my limbs still. My legs bounced in sharp, jerky movements, straight-shooting from the floor up.

"My initial background check hinted at a pretty vanilla life. No criminal record on either of them save for the occasional parking ticket, social media accounts squeaky clean. Everything was locked tight." He thumbed through some files on his desk. "On the surface that is."

Ethan and Leo exchanged a quick look that would usually leave me asking for more, but this time I decided to keep my mouth shut. First of all, Ethan White sounded like the second coming of John Doe. Second, this office—with no nameplate on the front, no secretary, and on a pretty nonde-script building in a middle-class neighborhood—didn't really scream professional private investigator. More so, profes-sional dirt collector for the wealthy.

"So I did some digging, reached a few mutual acquain-tances, and it turns out Carter Laurent is in the process of filing for Chapter 11 bankruptcy." He paused, and I didn't know about Leo, but I wasn't aware of what specific types of bankruptcies entailed.

"What does Chapter 11 bankruptcy mean?" I asked.

"It means that Carter Laurent is trying to keep up appearances while buying some time to regroup and reorga-nize his business affairs, assets, and debts. His firm will remain open during this process, but if he doesn't find money fast, then things will start heading south for him really quickly."

I tried to gulp around the lump in my throat, but to no avail. The comments about Carter's economical instability made sense, all things considered. What I was curious to know was how he managed to throw parties more lavish than the Vanderbilt ball, and upgrade to sprawling mansions that rivaled the Rockefeller estates, if he was truly on the verge of bankruptcy.

"Then that solidifies their motive. They had a reason to get rid of Francis." Leo scratched the edge of his bitter smile. "What a friend, fucking your bitch behind your back and locking you up in jail afterward."

"Yes, that would indeed be the case." Ethan casually nodded in agreement. "His money problems stemmed four years ago and he has barely been able to keep afloat ever since."

"If he's struggling to 'make ends meet', then how is he maintaining such a luxurious lifestyle? He is basically living the dream of every American."

"Did you know that debts and mortgages peek through the curtains of almost every American dream, Ms. Roux?" he lectured, and my cheeks burned hot as a furnace.

I didn't want to believe it.

Didn't want to believe that everything was for nothing. My father lost his life and I spent precious time hating him aimlessly.

"Not to mention, he and Claire Roux, your mother, were recently engaged. Now, if my information doesn't elude me, and according to some bank statements I managed to get ahold of, she has been quite the helping hand," Ethan continued, plunging the knife deeper in my gut. "She did have unbounded access to your inheritance before you turned twenty, did she not?"

My hands shook, and I pressed my fingers harder on the leather armchair. My temperature ran high when I had the undivided attention of both males in the room. I nodded, not trusting my mouth to spew out the right words.

"There you go. Carter found his new money source." He grimaced, staring at me. "For a short while, that is."

The caution in his eyes lingered in my aura. He didn't speak any more words, but I felt the warning signs flashing behind his browns. He had stumbled across other cases like this, men like Carter and the obstacles on their way.

I smoothed a finger between my brows, trying to ease the unrelenting ache between them. The dingy office space aided my worsening mood. It mostly consisted of earthy tones reminding me of being dragged through a muddy field, with only a tiny window on the far-off distance breaking the monotony.

"How does this tie together with the trafficked girls?" I heard Leo ask. "What role does my sister play in all of this?"

This time Ethan grimaced for a whole different reason. One that told me he didn't have all the answers.

"I haven't been able to figure that part out yet," he admitted, and Leo's face dropped. "But," Ethan rectified. "I did find an address that Francis Roux paid frequent visits to. It's a two-story home on Long Beach with a view of the ocean."

Long Beach. The place where Isabella's body was found washed up ashore, the blue waves painting the coast crimson. I wanted to reach out, pull Leo's tightening fists in mine, but fear of my bones crushing under that white-knuckle grip held me back.

"I wasn't able to enter. My relationship with the law is complicated, but I choose not to obliterate every imaginary line. The home didn't look suspicious, but was considerably below the tax bracket of someone like Francis Roux."

Eyebrows crossed, Leo turned to me. "Do you own any property near Long Beach?"

My dad was an only child and had a family legacy spanning back to Victorian times. He had made it big as an artist, but a lot of our wealth was inherited. Gold didn't stray far from the hands of the rich.

We had a lot of properties spanning across seven territories, some purchased, others inherited. I had visited quite a few during summers in the French Riviera and winters skiing down the powdery slopes of Aspen, but I'd never heard of a summer pad so close to home.

"No," I shook my head. "Not that I know of."

"But there is a possibility you might and not know of it?" He pressed.

"No, Leo, there isn't. I don't know what my father was doing there, but he had no assets listed in Long Beach, at least not any that he passed down to me," I mumbled, shooting down his theory and regretting my vehement manner when the light in his eyes dimmed.

"I want that address, Ethan," Leo barked at him, running a hand through his hair, lacing the curls with frustration.

I understood his annoyance. He came here looking for answers and got more questions instead. Guilt gnawed at my heart for stumbling upon a four-leaf clover and getting what I wished for, yet at the same time didn't hope for.

"Yes, of course."

Ethan scribbled the address on a piece of paper. Leo snatched the information out of his hand as soon as it reached his field, skimming over it with impatience. He squeezed any information he could out of the yellow post-it note, as if it was the key to paradise.

And maybe it would be.

Maybe it would provide him with the closure he needed to let Isabella rest in peace.

"Why Isabella? That's what I don't get. Why target one of the richest families in the world? It must have been a hell of a job, covering up their tracks," I addressed Ethan.

"If they really wanted to frame Francis, Isabella would've been the safest bet. Three more girls went missing before her, but no one really pays attention until the rich girl disappears. They had to put your father up against someone more influential, someone that had the power to ruin him."

I leaned back in my seat, focusing on deep breaths as his words started making sense.

"Is that all?" I asked, ready to bolt out of the door of this jinxed office.

"That's all," he confirmed. "I will call if any new information surfaces."

We didn't waste much time on goodbyes, and my feet burned a path to the entrance of the building, not even checking if Leo was following me. My lungs craved sweet air, however, blackened and polluted by the gas-guzzling machines all around us. But not even the chill of the winter night could flush away the pain of the twenty lashings my soul received tonight.

Chapter 15

LEONARDO

"I think you missed our turn." I heard Eliana squeak in concern.

I had, and I was past the point of return.

I'd hired Ethan to get to the heart of the issue, and instead, he'd eaten away at the edges. I wouldn't tolerate any more fucking bones. I wanted the whole damn steak.

My sister's murderer was still free.

Sitting idly by while they had the time of their lives shitting all over Isabella's memory was no longer an option.

Broken jaw, ruptured spleen, shattered dreams.

A wave of red-hot madness slammed into me, and my foot pressed harder on the accelerator. They had dumped her mauled body on Long Beach as if she was nothing, a no one, without any protection, because her family didn't care. *I* didn't care.

I wasn't there for her.

"Leo, where are we going?" Eliana voiced her concern again.

The tightening of my jaw was all the answer she got. Isabella had been a splinter in my soul ever since she left. I always felt her there. But lately, that splinter had turned into a stake lodged in my throat, and every breath burned as it traveled to my lungs.

I wouldn't let her down again.

I couldn't.

Eliana's irrational streak spiked, and I found the car swerving close to the edge of the cliffside road as she punched my arm. She didn't hit hard, but I took it there, turning her squeaks of annoyance into shrieks of concern.

"What is wrong with you?" she panted, her eyes wild, the *oh-shit* bar and glove compartment becoming extensions of her hands as she clutched them in fright.

"You're the one punching the driver."

"Because you were ignoring me!"

"I don't talk and drive, sweetheart. Unless, of course, you decide to get handsy."

"The law is *don't text and drive,* asshole, but I guess I'm too distracting." She didn't know the half of it. "Now tell me where we're going."

"We're checking out the address Ethan gave us." She would have eventually caught up. There was no point in holding my cards so close to my chest.

"Leo!" The unbreakable wax seal of her rationality gleamed once again. "We can't just storm there. We have no plan. That's a recipe for disaster!"

"I want to know who killed Isabella. I don't care about any plans," I bit out.

My gaze connected with Eliana's ocean eyes, that looked

at me as if I'd officially lost my mind. Maybe I had. My veins felt void, shriveled up by an all-consuming revenge.

"You can wait in the car; you don't have to get involved," I offered her a way out, hoping she would let me down. Her personality had bled too far off the designated box I'd shoved her in. She made me feel again. Made me want more than I was willing to give.

"That's not the point, Leo. You know I would follow you, *regardless of how stupid it would be*," she huffed in disbelief. "But we can't afford to do anything rash. Please, pull over so we can talk about it."

Against my better judgment, I listened to her advice and pulled over on an extension of the road that wasn't asphalted. Gravel kicked underneath my tires as I floored the break, otherwise we would have nosedived into the crashing waves below.

"I'm sorry about today," Eliana said, not waiting for the engine to cool one bit.

I didn't have to ask what she was sorry for. Sliding the window open, I breathed in the clean air that smelled of algae and salt, staring into the blue abyss. It felt like I was on a never-ending roller coaster ride. At first, the surge of adrenaline was everything. The sparks of fire between the sliding steel fueled you to be on the go, but soon the nausea of the dips and twists caught up with you.

"I am so fucking tired of everything," I blurted and closed my eyes, trying to combat this sudden case of mouth diarrhea.

A cool palm wrapped around the heated skin of my bicep, and my eyes snapped open when her weight shifted. Eli bypassed the center console and slid on to my lap, locking me in place by resting her legs on either side of me.

Whoa, escalation.

"This wasn't the talk I had in mind, but I ain't complaining." I sucked in a breath, sliding my seat back. "For future reference, I prefer you in dresses." My hands squeezed her thighs before trailing to her jean-clad ass, being helpful and settling her better on my legs.

"I'm sure you do." Her fingers threaded through my hair, thumbs massaging my temples in circular motions that made me want to purr, and return the favor by kneading her ass. "Now talk to me, Bianchi. What's eating away at you?"

I had never been good at opening up. My soul was stained and no one wanted to see the ugly inside. Except for her.

My Narcissus.

Never scared to dive headfirst into my darkness and swim in the murky waters like a pro.

"I failed her, Eli." I blamed the full moon and her damned touch for getting me to sing like a canary. "And, as you saw today, I'm continuing to disappoint her."

"You failed her?" Her blonde brows crossed. "What are you talking about? You're doing everything you can to see this though."

"Yeah, *now* I am." I grasped her wrists before they lulled me to sleep. "But where was I when she got out of the house that day? Why didn't I ask her where she was going or who she was going with? Why didn't I call her even fucking once like a concerned brother should?"

Frustration built in my chest at the memory of the day Isabella was kidnapped. I dismissed her presence altogether because of some trivial fight I didn't even remember anymore.

"So, you're blaming yourself for not being an overprotective jackass?" she said with fiery resolve, pursing her inviting lips.

"I didn't get to say goodbye, Eliana. All because of my negligence and pride," I sighed out. I could have prevented it. I *would* have prevented it if I hadn't been an egotistical bastard with such tunnel vision.

"Oh, Leo." Eliana wrapped her arms around my shoulders, her sweet orange scent invading my nostrils, and I breathed in her affection as she settled her head on the crook of my neck in a hug.

My heart was full at her generosity, dancing in tandem with hers, both crushing against each other at our connected chests. I smoothed a hand over her head, enclosing her in my arms, holding her tight.

I forgot everything but her when she was around, either plunged in red-hot anger or seeding need. She was selfless, helping me even after four years of reigning hell on her life, but I didn't know how far her altruistic nature could extend. Didn't think she'd allow us to be more than an outlet to lose ourselves in.

Maybe in a better world, we could've made us work.

"You didn't know what was going to happen. Don't villainize yourself for things you had no control over," she mumbled against my skin, placing a scorching kiss on my jumping jugular.

"I should have been a more involved brother."

"And given the time you would have been." Eliana pulled back, looking at me with earnest eyes, light hair, a halo around her head. "You were just a kid Leo. Both of you were, and the opportunity to grow into your relationship was stolen from you."

I wanted to believe her, but my wounds had years to

develop, and not even her balm was enough for them. Infection had taken hold, my toxic thoughts, infusing the illness deeper.

"We are going to find out what happened." She pronounced her words slowly as if she was talking to a stubborn child. "We're not going into this blind anymore, and we aren't wasting energy hating the wrong people. We have to think things through if we want to see the perpetrators behind bars."

Releasing a sigh that was lodged in my throat, I leaned back on my seat, holding on to her round hips. "I know, but my excitement gets the best of me every time a vision of the Laurent version of Bonnie and Clyde in orange jumpsuits flashes in my head."

Her lips split in a sad smile that I wanted to breathe life into. I wanted to plunge my tongue in her mouth, and my stretching dick in her pussy until neither of us could remember the depravity in our worlds.

I licked my lips, staring lower, at the generous decolletage of her jumpsuit, and my cock didn't need much convincing to come to life. After all the twisting and turning she had been doing on top of me for the past ten minutes, I was rock hard and ready to be sucked dry of my sorrows.

Before I could close my mouth in on her perfect rosebud lips, she leaned over the other way, reaching for her purse.

"Here." She handed me a white roll, which upon closer inspection turned out to be joint. "I was saving it for later, but I feel like you might need it more."

A genuine laugh, a deep, hearty one spilled forth, and I couldn't remember the last time I'd laughed authentically. Well, *would you look at that*? Even little miss perfect bent the rules sometimes, so there was still hope for the rest of us.

"What?" she demanded haughtily. "You're not the only one that's allowed to smoke."

"Oh, I know," I grabbed the joint from her fingers, chucking it in the backseat. Her confused eyes traveled to trace its landing, but I pulled her gaze back to me, holding her chin. "And I'll rip Kai's hands off if he ever deals to you again."

"How..." Her mouth fell open, and she thought better of it, snapping it shut again.

"You can keep your blunt, Narcissus. I've got more strenuous activities to get things off my mind." And it involved keeping that pretty mouth wide open. I was stiff as a flagpole, and my jeans were aiding the pain.

"Like what?" the seductress asked, even though she felt me pressing against her, her eyes turning half-mast.

"Let's see." I tugged the zipper of her jumpsuit down. It zipped on the front, lucky me. "I suck your tits off real nice, and you get to put that rebel mouth to use for me tonight."

Her thighs quivered around me, and I knew my bad girl was down. I palmed the velvety skin of her breasts, rolling my thumb around her beaded pink pearls, and she moaned at the brief touch. God, I loved her tits. They were porn star worthy and mouth-watering, barely contained by my hands and spilling all over the place. And fuck if I wasn't ready to come just by touching some boob, as if I was fucking fourteen again and feeling Susan McAllister's breasts in a closet.

"Have you ever sucked a man off, sweetheart?" I growled through my teeth, my paws massaging her tits as she dry humped my cock.

"N-no," she said, and I was pleased by the answer, until she ran her mouth again and ruined it. "They usually do all the sucking for me."

I slapped her tit, hard enough to sting, but not so much so it lingered. Eliana's squeal soon turned into laughter as she pressed harder against my straining jeans.

"Laugh now while you can Narcissus, because soon your eyes will be watering." The threat I spat cut off her smile, but only because she leaned forward, crushing her lips with mine, expelling her excitement in my mouth.

I opened the driver's side door and wrapped her legs around my waist, shooting for the backseat. Her nipples hardened against my shirt when the chill night air wrapped around us. Deciding to forgo the original plan, I pressed her bare back against the side of the door as our tongues mated.

"Leo," Eliana hissed once the cold metal kissed her spine. "Not out here," she protested in between nips. "It's freezing."

Yes, out here.

I wanted to see her. See the moonlight shining off her pale skin and rosy nipples. See her blonde hair reaching her ass in ecstasy. See the ocean reflected in her eyes, both in color and depth, as she unraveled on my tongue.

I wanted to see her wild.

Just for me.

"I'll warm you up."

Letting go of her swollen lips, I moved down her body, taking her jumpsuit with me. Her chest fluctuated with inconsistent breaths, sharp and raspy after I couldn't seem to stop kissing her body—her tits, the narrow valley between them, her ribcage, and her round belly button. I ravaged every bit of skin until I got to the gold.

The tight material snagged deliciously around her flared hips, and it took me two harsh tugs until it fell forgotten on the gravel, bringing me level with her bare pussy.

"No panties?" My voice lowered, and I loved her adversary toward the redundant piece of material.

"Or I could be wearing some, and they're just invisible." A coy smile spread on her lips.

The view up was as glorious as it was filthy. The fullness of her chest begged to be touched, bit, and sucked. I'd get to them eventually, in fact, I had plans of spending entire days pinching, twisting, and kissing her tits until she came from that alone. There wasn't such a thing as an overachiever in my book, but for now her pussy was on priority boarding.

"Let's find out then." My gaze never strayed from hers as I pressed a kiss on the light strip of hair decorating her pubic bone.

Fuck, her scent alone drove me crazy.

Tightening my hand around her right leg, I draped her long limb over my shoulder. My cock gave another painful twitch at the sight of her dripping pussy spread open. Shit, she was wetter than the ocean. I bet I could just slide right in, but for the moment, I settled for taking her cunt in my mouth, needing to taste that pretty pink slit.

"God!" came her breathy response, barely audible over the sounds of the crashing waves.

A mountain full of issues couldn't keep me away, so when her taste hit my tongue, I was a goner. High of sucking Eliana Roux's perfect pussy. She was delectable. Dripping honey down my throat and chasing away the salt in the air.

I focused on her clit, pumping it into my mouth and firing up all her nerve endings. Fucking intoxicating, that's what she was. Her taste sent my dick flying and my need roaring.

Refined strokes were my go-to when it came to bringing a woman to orgasm on my face. But with Eliana, I couldn't keep that cap on my control. The need to let loose until I'd tasted all of her was as high as tourists in Amsterdam.

Her body grew heavy the more my tongue ran rampant on and in her pussy, and she rode my face like the perfect cowgirl, holding on to my head. I didn't miss a beat, watched every rapid rise and fall of her chest, heard every breathless gasp and anguished moan. The sound of my name from her lips had precum leaking down my shaft, staining my boxers, a mess that she'd have to clean up.

She broke down my steel walls like they were nothing but a glass partition. Easy to shatter, impossible to fix. Creating labyrinths and loopholes within each other's minds came easy to both of us, remembering the way back was where things got tricky.

I grazed her clit with my teeth, knowing my girl liked a touch of sting with her pleasure, and moved my tongue inside her opening, stuffing her tight hole.

"You'll be the death of me," she said with her whole chest, throwing her head back on instinct as her abdominal muscles convulsed.

You already killed me, sweetheart.

Any chance of peace was shot down the moment I saw you for the first time.

Watching her come from my position was like seeing an avalanche crest. Her back arched off the car, and I had to keep my hands steely braced around her hips, so she didn't fall forward.

"Ohmigod, ohmigod, ohmigod," she chanted to the sky.

God complex my ass. No one had made her come harder than I did, and that was a fact. I was wearing her arousal all over my face like war paint, and her screams stretched over the Atlantic, waking the fish.

"Get in the car," I ordered after pecking the soft, wet flesh of her pliable body one more time, getting off my knees. I was ready for her screams to be muffled by my severely neglected cock.

Her glazed eyes looked about ready to do anything I told them too, and I couldn't resist a kiss as I reached behind her for the handle. I pinned her against the door, letting her taste how ruined she was for me.

"Get. In. The. Car," I repeated against her mouth.

"Bossy," she muttered the word like an insult.

"You fucking love it, sweetheart."

She didn't argue with that, just retaliated by slapping me with her hair as she turned around. I huffed out a laugh that trickled to a groan when she bent over to crawl inside, her bare ass sticking up in the air. I couldn't help myself. My hand automatically slapped the expansive skin, the sting echoing around us.

Sucking in a sharp breath, she hit me with those narrowed blues, but want was more prevalent in her gaze than annoyance. I raised a brow, shedding my shirt and pants, and her attention fell directly to my dick as it sprang free with excitement.

"That's a whole ass mammoth," Eliana exclaimed, her eyes rounding.

My stomach rumbled with laughter at her ego boost. I might have not gotten to split her legs open first, but I sure as hell was excited that I'd be the only one those beautiful red lips parted for. The thought of other assholes enjoying what was mine touched on uncharted territory inside me, and the one thing that kept me from hounding her for their names was that I only had myself to blame.

I should've pulled my head out of my ass and claimed

her sooner. I shouldn't have spent so much time hating the wrong person. That was a mistake that cost me precious time and a different future. One that required a miracle to happen now.

"Don't worry, Narcissus, I like it when they choke."

I got in, shutting the door behind me with more force than necessary.

"They?" Her breasts jiggled in tune with her outraged voice. "I am not one of your disposable fuck buddies, Leo."

So that didn't earn me any brownie points, but it at least got her to bleed some jealousy too. Nothing one-sided was ever fun.

"I'm sorry." I settled on top of her. My cock rested on her thigh and she jumped at the slight touch, nails raking my shoulders. Taking a nipple in my mouth, I smiled at her around it, and if lust had a face, it was staring right back at me. "You're my most important fuck buddy."

She tried to swat my head, but I grabbed her delicate wrist before it made contact, treating the other one the same way too. "Now, it's your turn to do the sucking for a change."

She bit her plush bottom lip, her throat bobbing as she nodded, willing to give it a try. Unbeknown to her, Eliana had been the obsession of my wet dreams ever since I was old enough to have any. It was funny that she was worried. Unless she bit my dick off, there was no way of this going... north? 'Cause it was certainly gonna head south.

"Show me?" she asked, fisting her hand around me and squeezing until my eyes rolled on the back of my head, and my body straightened up, putting her first in line for my fire. Pert nose shining with a sheen of sweat that I had put there, coated lashes blinking slowly at me. She awaited further instructions.

The view from up top was euphoric. Pure surrender, yet a coil of strength gleamed underneath. I wouldn't have it any other way. I enjoyed her teeth and nails as much as I did her submission.

"No hands," I instructed, voice gruff. "You're taking it all, sweetheart. Lord knows you've tortured me long enough."

Her mouth fell open, and I resisted diving my hips in her awaiting heaven. "I tortured you? Are we really turning the tables now?"

"Come on now, Eliana, the damned dances, the skin-tight clothes, the short *skirts?*" the last word came out like a hiss, and my hand caressed the top of her head, tracing her hairline with my thumb. "Always running away and leaving me hanging? You knew what the fuck you were doing."

She shrugged, arching her brows. "I won't apologize for it. You deserved it."

"Not with words you won't." My hold on her hair turned rough, gripping the tresses on the crown of her head tight until her neck was exposed and her mouth was a few short breaths away from my erection. "Take me in, Eliana."

My order rolled over smoothly. Hands gripping ass, she gave an experimental lick, sampling the small drops of precum as if they were her prized possessions. A clenching jaw accompanied her teasing as I watched her tongue glisten against my swollen tip.

"You're not licking an ice cream cone, sweetheart, but sucking a lollipop." Although I appreciated the occasional sweet, slow torment, I was overworked enough as it was. I didn't want to come unless it was deep inside her hot mouth. Her brows furrowed, but for once, she listened. Her wet heat enveloped my head as I guided her.

"Fuck," I groaned when her doe eyes stared up at me, mouth stretched and cheeks hollowed, drawing me deeper. "That's it, baby, suck it."

My breaths turned uneven as she followed my lead, gaining momentum and bobbing her head up and down. Watching my cock disappear past her full lips had me coiling my body tight to prevent coming prematurely. For never sucking dick before, she sure knew what she was doing. It would be so easy to let myself go with the tempo she adopted.

Sucking, licking, rolling her tongue.

Eliana was a fast learner, and I had no control over the words that escaped my mouth. Some sweet, others down-right filthy. Her enthusiasm got to me the most. She was hungry for more, which was why she let me take over.

I caressed her mouth, stretched around me, and the little hums she produced teased my sensitive head as I hit the back of her throat. *"Fuck, fuck, fuck,* my fantasies never did you any justice, little monster," I growled, guiding her head to take more until her nose hit my base.

Her muscles were relaxed, facilitating my intrusion. She had a so-called mammoth down her throat, and her gag reflex was barely acting up. Heat spread from my balls and up my thighs when black streaks of mascara pooled under her eyes.

Hottest shit I'd ever seen.

Even thoroughly destroyed, Eliana had a sex appeal like no other. She twisted me up in so many knots, I required special attention to function. The slurping sounds her mouth produced were like music to my ears. Beethoven didn't stand a chance next to master composer Eliana Roux.

She moaned around me as she slid me out of her mouth,

saliva and precum pooling from her lips and dripping down her chin.

"You fantasized about me sucking your dick?" Eli licked the underside of my veiny shaft before flicking her tongue over my slit.

"My creativity knew no bounds when it came to all the ways I could shut you up." I groaned when she sucked my crown into her mouth again, almost punishingly.

The air in the car grew humid as the sloshing of my flesh invading her wet mouth dominated everything. A thin layer of condensation coated the windows as Eliana upped her suction. I moved my hips faster, wanting to hear her gag on my dick, and when she finally did, I couldn't hold back anymore.

"Shit, I'm coming, baby," I warned.

My balls tingled, fuck, my everything tingled. Even my soul was shaking as she elevated the pressure, not letting me slip out and swallowing every thick rope of liquid that slid down her throat. She took it like a champ, not wasting a single drop, and I was all about ready to go to hell and back for her right then and there, if it meant she'd let me do that again.

Her mouth released me with a pop, and it took me a minute to regain my senses. She'd literally hoovered the life out of me. I sagged on the back seat next to her, tugging her naked body on top of my sweaty chest.

"I think the words you're looking for are; you're amazing, incredible, fucking phenomenal Eliana," she teased, trying to catch her own breath.

"You are amazing, incredible, fucking phenomenal, and out of this world." Her head snapped up and she stared at my mouth in disbelief. I was completely serious. She was all that and more—and not just because she gave amazing head —she fit every piece in my puzzle.

"You actually mean it, or should I take that as you calling me an alien?" She swallowed, her weak tone disputing the joking nature of her words.

I chuckled, shaking her with me, and then proceeded to bite her nose into submission. Proceeded to peck her stained cheeks and leave a deep kiss on her mouth. I didn't want for the sun to rise. I wanted to spend my whole time savoring her under the stars because, for once, my worries, thoughts, and ugly feelings were put on hold.

But illusions didn't last forever, and reality was a tough pill to swallow.

Chapter 16

ELIANA

W as ignorance truly bliss?

The blush tennis skirt, white cotton crop top, and matching vans adorning my body didn't seem to agree with Thomas Grey's opinion.

Once again, I reverted to my old habits, molding myself to the image others painted of me—the perfect daughter, brat, spoiled princess, stuck-up bitch, attention seeker. I could go on forever, but it was safe to say that if ignorance was the shit, I wouldn't be going crazy bathed in it.

Claire invited me to lunch, and while my stomach lurched at the thought of having to see her face again, I had to come. Holding a blindfold over the world's eyes was a must, even if it meant smiling at the person that didn't hesitate to plunge a knife in my back.

Astropolis Country Club.

The worn sign, pasted under some shrubs, warned me on my way to the dining veranda. It seemed to scream "enter at your own cost." Sighing, I pressed forward, past the vegetation. Life was a double-edged sword. It didn't matter which path I took. Something would eventually come up and bite me in the ass. Why shouldn't I go for the killer blow first?

Nothing much had changed ever since I frequented the country club when I was a kid. The pleasant scent of the Jacaranda trees wrapped around me, making me nostalgic for those simpler times. They were spread strategically across the veranda, providing shade and making for a beautiful view with long-lasting indigo blooms.

I adjusted my sunglasses when a field of green stretched across the horizon. The sun's rays glared at the large expanse of land reserved for golfing and some man-made lakes that broke up the monotonous viridescent hue of the lawn.

I didn't have to look hard to spot my mother. She and her socialite friends seldom changed their designated table, right at the edge of the rail, the best seat in the house.

She didn't wave or smile when she saw me. No, Claire never greeted anyone first. Everyone else always had to. And maybe it was the indifference painted on her face because people always did. They bend over backward to please her. *When smiles aren't handed out easily, we walk the extra mile to win them.*

My eyes strayed to Carter's as I got closer. His gaze wasn't as impassive as Claire's. A steady fire of hatred burned beneath the mask he flicked in place the moment our eyes met.

"Good afternoon, Eliana." He shot up from his seat, and a hush fell over the table at his greeting. "You're looking good."

"Thank you, I'm doing great." I lied through my teeth, but I wasn't about to bleed in front of a table full of sharks. A lot of Carter's lawyer associates were present, and my smile stretched extra thin when I caught sight of Mark. The one that had represented my dad.

"You're late." Claire spoke first after I'd addressed everyone but her.

"Well, some may say that I lacked proper attention growing up, so any classes of etiquette were glossed over." I sunk into her cold hug as one would a coffin to the ground.

Her arms turned stiff around me and an awkward laugh lilted from her mouth. "Oh, Eliana, always one for morbid humor."

"Yup, that's me, dark humor extraordinaire," I mumbled, proceeding to take the only free seat available, beside Stacee, Caroline's mom, on the rectangular dining table.

I couldn't even get a cocktail to wash down the smoked salmon toasted baguette I ordered. Claire's eyes shot laser beams at me when I flipped through the alcoholic drinks section of the menu. It was times like these that I hated living on American soil.

"So, Eliana, how is college going?" Stacee asked, brown eyes swimming with mirth. "I imagine choosing a local campus must have been difficult after everything that happened with... you know... your father."

Out of all of my mother's friends, she was the one I hated the most. The kind of person that peaked in high school, and never grew out of it, seeking drama like it was a lifeline.

"I'm assuming adjusting would have been much easier if the fact that my dad went to prison and then got murdered wasn't thrown in my face every few seconds. But other than that, I'm settling in just peachy, Stacee."

I felt a shudder move through the table, beginning from Carter sitting at the head, all the way to me. They didn't expect me to share my thoughts so explicitly. To remind them that they were hanging out with a murderer's family, willing to forgive and forget so long as it benefited them.

Stacee's lips twisted into a smile she tried to paint as sympathetic, but the joy of me playing into her hand could not be masked. "Is that so? Are people giving you a hard time about that?" She egged on.

"Why don't you ask your daughter? She can answer that question better than I ever will." I smiled into my glass, taking a sip of the cool lemon water placed in front of me as Stacee gasped dramatically.

"Are you accusing Caroline of anything?"

"Well, I certainly ain't saying we're best fucking friends."

"Okay!" my mother cut in, her fingers white around the stem of her Bellini glass. "Carter and I have some exciting news to share, that's why we invited you all here today."

"Yeah, we planned to bring it up after lunch, but you know what they say, God laughs when you tell him your plans." Carter stared at me as if I were the root of all his problems.

My mother cleared her throat, clasping Carter's hand in hers and squeezing lightly. Removing my sunglasses, I stared at the Cheshire-sized smiles on their faces, and a sliver of anxiety curled in my belly.

"We're..."

They were what? Were they moving to Africa? Did they decide to go on a spiritual journey and live with monks in Thailand? Maybe retire early in a villa along the Spanish coast?

Whatever it was, I was on board with them disappearing, so I could forget all about their existence.

"... having a baby!"

The ringing in my eardrums must've been playing tricks on me. They were having a *maybe*? What was a *maybe*?

I looked around lost as congratulations rang all around me like empty words between a husband and his mistress.

Not a maybe, but a baby.

A fucking baby. Fuck.

She would be bringing a baby into her fucked up world. What could possibly lead her into making such a stupid decision? Lord knew she failed at parenting the first time around. Did she want a second chance to succeed? Words of encouragement had me grinding my teeth together. Everyone hyped them up while I felt sorry for the unborn child.

"Eliana?" The film in my ear dissolved when someone called my name. My eyes befell Claire again and her mumbling mouth, but I couldn't make out a word of what she was saying.

"Pardon me?"

"I said, aren't you going to say something?"

Suddenly, the weight of everyone's gazes fell on my shoulders, and questions like "Are you mad?" and "Why do you want another mentally impaired child as part of your legacy?" seemed like the wrong thing to say.

So I went with the second-best choice. "You're adopting a baby?" Maybe that's what she meant, seeing as she was pushing fifty, having a baby biologically would be hard. There could still be hope for this child if I could cancel the adoption in time.

"No. We're having a baby. I'm pregnant."

My hand itched to grab Stacee's Bloody Mary, but I wasn't sure whether I wanted to down it or douse us all with it until we made for an accurate depiction of Scream Queens.

"Aren't you past the baby-making age, Claire? How could you possibly be pregnant?" I could literally hear the sound of every jaw drop around the table. My bluntness wasn't self-serving in any way, but I wasn't about to sit down and congratulate them for bringing another child into this world to ruin. At least I had only one psychopath for a parent. This kid was going to have two.

"Don't talk to your mother like that," Carter, the knight in bloody armor, replied.

Before I could tell him to bite me, though, Claire butted in. "It was an unexpected, nevertheless happy surprise for us too, Eliana. There is no need for a temper tantrum." Her gaze fluttered around the table.

"You're right, Mother." I plastered on a pretty smile. "How could I be upset that I'm learning about this over a brunch table filled with strangers."

I'd never been this mouthy with her in front of company. People's perception of us was the only aura of normality left in our relationship, and I guess I didn't want to lose that last thread of hope. But no more. That cold exterior of hers would melt and judging by the sweat shining off of her forehead as streaks of light peeked through the tree branches, it was already on its way to becoming a puddle on her shaking feet.

An awkward cough and a few scuffles later, the guests announced they were off to play some golf. Not everyone left willingly, though. Stacee had to almost be dragged away from the table, enraptured by our conversation with a sly smirk.

Claire's distraught gaze turned into one of a mad rottweiler foaming out of its mouth as she turned back to me.

"Look at what you did. Are you happy now, Eliana? Got all the attention you wanted?"

"Quite the contrary, Mother. I worry about this unborn child seeing as the both of you couldn't keep Serena in check and let's not even start with how great of a job you did raising me."

"Spare me the waterworks." Carter smoothed a hand over his honey blond swoop, completely skating over everything I said. "This was our happy moment, and you twisted until it became all about you."

"Well, Serena had her time to shine, seems only fair I do too," I snarked, and judging by the popping vein on his forehead, I hit the nail straight where the sun didn't shine. So this was what drove Serena off the road. Medical problems, my ass.

"You..." he started again, and I itched back on instinct at the vehemence with which he started his sentence. Only he didn't get a chance to complete what I was sure would have been a very colorful response.

"What's up everyone?" Leo's commanding vibrato sent my pulse into overdrive.

They both snapped their attention to him.

I didn't turn. I could feel his presence behind me, chills broke down my back, but I was too enraptured by the strained smiles on both their faces. Carter would love nothing more than to send him on his merry way and rip me a new one, but you just didn't do that to a Bianchi.

"Leonardo, hi!" a flustered Claire replied, probably grateful that this conversation was cut short. "We were just about to have some lunch. You're more than welcome to join, right, Carter?"

"Right," he assured with a sour face.

"My friends just left, so don't mind if I do." Leo deliberately scraped the chair beside me against the floor. "Hello, Eliana." His face came into view and my mouth watered at his smile in combination with his light pink polo shirt.

Whoever said pink wasn't a manly color clearly hadn't seen Leonardo Bianchi rocking it. Delicious thick blue veins disappeared under the cotton material, which was paired nicely with some white cargo pants, a pair of square sunglasses, and just rolled out of bed unruly hair. He looked like he came straight out of a GQ magazine shoot.

"Hi." My voice came out squeaky, and I cleared my throat, reaching for an abandoned glass of mimosa resting on the tableware next to me. I was sucking his dick like my life depended on it less than a week ago, so why was I suddenly shy?

"Are you celebrating anything important? This is quite a spread." Leo gestured to the table full of untouched food, from croissants to berries, even caviar, basically a waste of money. Claire's friends were all size zeroes and survived on fruit smoothies.

"Claire is pregnant, so we thought why not celebrate over brunch." Carter narrowed his eyes at me, and a smirk dominated my lips. "Serena told me she mentioned it to you already, and we wanted to personally share the news before the whole town found out. You know how Serena gets when she's excited."

Didn't we all? And... *wait, what?*

My head did a one-eighty, and Leo met my furrowed brows with a purse of his lips as he proceeded to shatter the fragile trust that had bloomed between us. "Yeah, she did. Congratulations on your pregnancy. I hope everything progresses well."

Why?

Why did I expect any shred of loyalty from him?

It was my own damn fault. I let his words wrap around me until all I could hear was him. His smile blinding my eyes until he became everything I saw. And his aura suffocates my spirit until everything started and ended with him. *Open your fucking eyes. He doesn't care about anything but himself.*

My lymph glands struggled to swallow, swollen from a thick fleece blanket of emotions. A heaviness crushed my eyelids, and I squeezed my eyes shut, trying to relieve the ache, but it wouldn't go. I needed to leave. Save whatever dignity I had left.

Searing heat radiated from my thigh. Even my bone sizzled below, protesting against Leo's touch as he kept me in place, unbeknown to Carter and my mom. He was a portrait of cool, calm, and collected while I was struggling to breathe.

"Thank you, Leonardo." Mom looked pointedly at me as she spoke. "I appreciate your kind words."

I scoffed at that. Leo, ever the kind person. Now, if she'd said two-faced conniving bastard, with a mean, cruel streak, I would have agreed.

Realizing the progression of my thoughts, he pinched my thigh with a smile on his face, and I raked my nails over his hand, drawing satisfying beads of blood. He gave away nothing, as unfeeling as a statue.

Leave, leave, leave.

I needed to escape before I did anything I regretted.

"I have to go." *Make a voodoo doll of a certain green-eyed devil.* "Enjoy the rest of your meal," I announced, knowing he had little control over the matter and had to let me go. He worked his jaw as his gaze pierced the side of my face before his hand fell away. I didn't want to look at him or them.

The people that always served as my downfall.

Grabbing my bag, I ignored Carter and Claire's whispered insults, instead hyper-aware of his silence. It lingered until the valet had my keys in his hand and was bringing my car around.

Why the hell was it so hot today? I scratched the back of my head, weaving my nails through the hair at the nape of my neck. Sweat had coiled it tight, and the unrelenting sun had baked it in place.

I didn't feel so good.

"Eliana." His voice boomed behind me, and my legs unlocked.

I didn't need a damn valet. I'd get my own car.

"Eliana, wait up!"

As if adding wait up would make me stop. In fact, I started eating the distance between me and the pimply teenage valet faster. He still hadn't reached my car, possessing the efficiency of a sloth.

And I never did either.

My arm almost popped off its socket as when the self-serving asshole got what he wanted. Turning me in place, he had the audacity to look mad at me. Eyes glittering like rough emeralds and jaw looking extra bone crushing.

"Did you not hear me?" Leo hissed.

"Of course I heard. I think the whole fucking country club and the gnomes upfront heard you," I hissed back.

"Then why did you keep walking?"

"If you really have to ask that, then I should've been

running instead." I tugged at my arm, but he didn't let up. "Let go, people are watching."

I looked around to all the eyes we'd attracted. A glare from Leo was all it took to send them scurrying. As most of them were employees, I'm assuming they weren't keen on losing one of their biggest customers.

"Look, I was going to tell you about Claire." His mouth was set tight.

"When did you find out?" I asked, giving him the benefit of the doubt. Blaming him was a knee-jerk reaction of mine. He breathed and I accused him of stealing my air, but it was difficult not to do so when that was all I knew.

"The day of Astor's party."

Two weeks ago.

God, I hated him.

Hated him to pieces.

I moved to leave again, but his hand was branded on my arm. "Hear me out. I just didn't know how to tell you, Eliana."

"Yeah, you knew my mother was pregnant before me, but were too busy sucking my face and couldn't take five minutes to tell me that much."

"Your pussy too, Narcissus, I don't do half-assed jobs."

"Ugh, you're disgusting," I spat, but my core clenched at the memory. And he knew it, knew the power he held over me, body, mind, and soul. And perhaps that was the most dangerous thing of all. "Why do I always have to know things last?"

I sucked in a breath when he tugged me closer, one hand fisting my waistband, the other fixing my hair behind my ear.

"Look, you've got to be more careful with what you say. I didn't come here today because I give a fuck about Claire's pregnancy, but because the rest of their friends were already mouthing you off. You already have a target the size of a bull on your back sweetheart, don't paint it red too."

I knew I was poking a sleeping bear, but the thrill of it waking up and giving me the chase of my life didn't scare me as much as it should. I was bored of all the inertness, chasing a tail with no end and getting shit on during the process.

Leo was right though, I wouldn't get anywhere by acting like a spoiled brat. My nostrils burned with an exhale, and as much as it killed me to do so, I voiced my agreement. "Okay, I'll behave better next time. Can you let go of me now?"

Instead, he pulled me closer, both hands pulling at the base of my spine until I was forced to stare up at his smirking face. "That depends. Do you need some behavioral lessons to help lessen the learning curve? Because I've got a knee that craves your weight and a palm that wouldn't mind reddening your ass."

My ass was still as white as a sheet of paper, but my cheeks turned the color of a beet. I didn't find his words embarrassing. My body just warmed up to the idea of his palms cracking against my skin.

Leo groaned in approval when he saw my reaction, pupils dilating as he made to trace the flushed skin with his lips.

"Miss, your car is here." The valet's shaky voice snapped our lustful bubble, and we both pulled apart, remembering where we were. Rolling my lips in my mouth, I turned my back on the hormone inducing beast that was Leo.

"Thank you," I squeezed out, snatching my keys from his hand.

Leo's feet burned hot on my heels, following close behind. "You're not coming home with me," I stated.

"I know, I'm doing the gentlemanly thing and opening the door for you," he said and reached for the handle.

"Opening a single door won't make this go away."

"No?" A brow raised. "Well, I at least got a close-up view of your ass too."

I glared at him as I sat down, wishing I could scorch the fine hair on his chest, so they didn't look so damn distracting. He was still wearing that damned cross. Catching my gaze, he palmed it, thumb rolling over the gold with precision.

"Call me, in case you do end up needing my help." He winked, and I pulled out of the parking lot before I caved.

Leo's answering laugh followed me all the way to bed that night, when I slipped my panties aside, and spent some quality time with a buzzing pink lady-killer because I certainly did *not* need his help.

Chapter 17

ELIANA

Even though I powered my phone off, a consistent buzz rattled my brain. Sleep eluded me. No matter how hard I shut my eyes, they failed to glue together in slumber. A blanket of uncertainty crushed me under its weight, smothering me with heat.

The need to check my phone was palpable. My hands fidgeted with the Egyptian cotton sheets, a dew of sweat clinging to my skin. Carter, Claire, and Serena circled around me like vultures eyeing their next meal. The gifted family that never graced my wishlist.

While I once thought that unconditional love and loyalty were the golden standard for every household, I now knew that blood, secrets, and lies were the only things that run through mine.

"Fuck it." Shoving the covers off me, I departed from the bed, making my way downstairs. Dad's cure to a restless night had always been a glass of warm milk with a teaspoon of honey, and since I didn't have any sleeping pills lying around, I'd make do with what I had.

Every light in the house was on full blast. I wasn't a wasteful person, but I hated walking around in the dark. It didn't help that tonight, I expected Serena to sneak up on me at any given moment and beat me to a bloody pulp.

I took Cole's advice and released that video. A bubble of jealousy burst when I finally hit the post button. I'd come to the conclusion that being just equaled a loss of opportunities. If Serena could be cruel and thrive on top of it all, why couldn't I? Why was I drowning in a pool of good intentions?

That was why I avoided my phone like the plague, and the milk tasted sour sliding down my throat. Momentary bursts of braveness were my forte, but I still had a long way to go when it came to dealing with the aftermath.

A brave coward.

It didn't make sense, yet at the same time, no title had ever felt more fitting to me. The world could have gone up in flames, or I was worrying about a drop in the ocean, and the video was already taken down before any real damage was done.

The devil worked hard, but Carter Laurent worked harder.

Either way, I wouldn't allow myself to look until dawn. It was already two in the morning, but I'd put it off until I couldn't anymore.

Honey pooled on the bottom of my glass as I chugged the milk. It didn't help a wink. Was this why bad people couldn't sleep at night? Were their demons tugging at their conscious every second, begging for attention like yapping puppies?

I didn't even know why I felt guilty. It wasn't like she didn't deserve it. Serena had an unparalleled obsession with me. Reached past mountains in her brain to shift the heftiest load of blame to me. Yet, the role of judge and jury sat heavy on my shoulders.

I'd stooped to her level. Hurting her because the real villains sat behind walls of steel, hiding under cloaks bathed in blood.

I rinsed my glass, staring at the window above the sink. Darkness swirled at the edges of the pool and the entirety of the lawn. The maple trees Dad and I planted for my thirteenth birthday aided the spooky atmosphere, casting daunting shadows that stretched tall along the walls of the pool house.

"What the hell?" The usual pang that followed every time I thought of my dad was cut short. One of the shadows shifted, and I didn't know if it was the wind or something else.

My breath fogged up the window as I raised on my tiptoes, leaning forward to get a closer look. The silhouette moved faster than the slight breeze outside could ever make it go.

Shit, shit, shit.

The sound of the glass slipping from my fingers barely registered in my brain. This was it. I'd finally pushed until there was nothing left to pull. Had they sent someone to kill me?

Oh fuck, oh god!

I'd left my phone upstairs, and there was no way security could ever hear me from the gate. My breath got caught in my throat when the shadow moved again, this time closer, propelling toward the window.

I stumbled back, my hands gripping the aisle behind me, and a banshee shriek bubbled up my throat when... a fucking *squirrel* leaped on the sill, staring at me as if I was a lunatic.

"Oh my god," I exhaled roughly, my chest heaving. "I'm going insane," I spoke to the squirrel, and it tilted its head at me as if it agreed.

Yeah, positively delirious.

I gathered the broken shards of glass quickly, and by the time my eyes flicked back to the window, the squirrel was waving its bushy tail at me in goodbye. After double-checking every lock in the house, just to be sure, I hightailed it back to my bedroom. Sleep might hate me, but creating a fort out of my covers and hiding there until orange dusted the sky didn't sound half bad.

It was still dark out when I heard a loud crash coming from downstairs. It sounded like a muffled army of elephants had plowed past the living room walls and belly-flopped into the pool.

This time, I a hundred percent knew I hadn't imagined that.

Cold sweat broke out in hives over my skin as I clutched the covers to my chest. I was blonde, but I didn't want to also be the stereotypical character in horror movies that run headfirst to the villain. A little voice in my head whispered, *Leo would like to say hi*, but I silenced it immediately, my toes touching the frigid floor.

It was just a little crush. The mansion was old, damages were part of the package.

I snatched a pair of scissors on my way out because, yup. What was more intimidating than a girl in a pink robe holding a pair of crafting scissors? But I didn't want to call security. I was sure this was nothing more than a misplaced item, or worst-case scenario, my mind playing tricks on me again.

Holding a breath, I headed downstairs slowly.

"Hello?" My stomach tightened as I reached the base of the stairwell, the scissors clutched tight in my clammy hands. "Is anyone there?"

Rounding the corner of the living room, nothing seemed amiss. The white sofas looked pristine as ever. No one ever sat on them anyway. The framed pictures were all in place, serving as a constant reminder of the lie I'd been living my whole life. And no ridiculously priced vases were shattered on the floor. The house was a perfect vessel of its previous inhabitants. The ones that ruled my life even after they'd abandoned it.

I took cautious steps forward until a shining object on the corner of my vision caught my attention. Lungs frozen, I twisted in place, already feeling the ghost touch of a barrel's heat.

My breath shuddered in my lungs when all that lay in wait, though, was some broken glass on the marble floor, from a framed picture a few feet away, having met its tragic end.

"See?" A whoosh of relief escaped my mouth. "It's nothing." I let the scissors go, taking the frame in my hands, careful of all the broken glass around me.

It was a picture of me, and my dad, from a fishing trip east in the Florida Keys. My face was all scrunched up and red, the opposite of his toothy smile. Francis and his friends had a good laugh at my expense that weekend.

I'd sobbed until my lungs dropped when I had to put my

little ten-year-old hand inside the bait jar. I had to face my fears according to Dad, but it felt like I was falling farther down in them when the slimy fuckers went to town, sliding in between my fingers.

I caressed the picture, wanting to jump in and see my father happy and healthy one more time. Get a chance to say a proper goodbye, unlike the dreadful shit show that took place in the courthouse that day. The mood was spoiled rotten the last few days of his supposed freedom. Sadness sliced through every pore in his body.

No one believed him. Not even me, his daughter.

A tear slipped down my cheek, when at the same time I heard a curse from behind me. A very loud tangible curse, uttered in Spanish with an underlying vibrato that could only belong to a man.

My heart leaped in my throat at the intrusive voice. I had no time to react, a large shadow engulfed my body, and a hand soon followed, pulling at my hair until pinpricks of pain aligned with his touch.

"W-who are you? What d-do you want?" I croaked, but all the answer I got was my face being shoved against the floor, and my hands seized. Fallen glass split my skin, and I hissed as blood trickled down the side of my face.

Primal fear pounded through my veins and stifled the air around me. It felt like that last intake of air right before you plunged down from an ungodly height had been extended, and now I was stuck in a constant loop. One that my stupidity contributed to.

God, *I was the dumb blonde in the horror movies.*

And now I'd die alone, like I'd always been. A bitter curse that hung over my shoulders like a dark cloud.

"I-I have m-money," I whimpered through the pain as my

assailant's knee connected with my back, robbing my breath and ability to struggle. "It's all cash. Please, you can just take it and go. I-I won't call the police."

Salty tears and metal bloomed in my mouth. I couldn't move, paralyzed from his strength and my terror.

I don't want to die. I don't want to die.

God, please, I don't want to die.

"Shut the fuck up." A gruff male voice sounded, muffled. I tried to peak at him from the corner of my eye, but all I saw was a dark blob. A sob ripped from my heaving chest when I felt the sharp point of a knife piercing through my robe. "Not a word."

He tightened his hold in my hair, lifting my head a tad from the floor, I almost retched at the pain from the cuts. Controlling my movements, he brought me eye level with the shattered frame I was cradling in my grip not too long ago.

"Do you see that picture?"

I nodded, instantly regretting it when my scalp caught fire.

"A piece of advice, little girl? Shut your mouth and don't go digging too deep." He forced my face closer to the photo. Amidst my terror, a picture of Melpomene and Thalia flashed in my brain. The comedy painted in my father's smiling face reflected back as tragedy in mine. "Unless, of course, you want to end up like Daddy here."

My bloodstream froze. Icy fear trickled through my veins.

Daddy had been telling the truth. Each and every day, the stack in his favor got taller, but this time the villains had admitted it themselves.

Francis Roux had bled in a jail cell all by himself, with the whole world against him.

Maybe I deserved such a death too.

But I couldn't go through with the thought. I trembled all over when he pressed against me harder. I tried to peel my head off his hand, struggled against his hold, but he wouldn't let go.

They said life flashed before your eyes right before you died, but I saw nothing. I had no life, only pain as the back of my head bore the brunt of a blow. Pain and panic were the only things that remained constant.

"So, you live here alone?" The police officer with the balding head asked me the same question for the thousandth time.

I couldn't even roll my eyes at his repetitiveness because if I did, an unrelenting pang on the back of my head would soon follow. I learned that through trial and error when I first made the call to 911, the flash of my phone, irritating me beyond belief.

Every little movement of my eyeballs made the pain worse. It was like my nerve endings were being tugged like a harp, and I was sure I'd suffered a concussion. But no, the brute was sent to inspire fear, and just enough bodily harm to leave a mark. Besides my face, the rest of my body felt fine, save for some bruising. I was thankful I wasn't touched in ways that would leave scars more permanent than some flesh wounds.

My shaking hadn't seized from the minute I'd called the police. What if he came back to finish the job? What if one of the paramedics that touched me was him? I didn't see his face. He could've been anyone. Maybe the police officer, sitting right in front of me too.

I threaded my fingers together, resting them on the heavy oak dining table as I looked at the middle-aged man. He sported what I'd call a donut belly, excessive fat deposits on his pink cheeks, and a pretty high-pitched voice for a man.

Okay, so it wasn't him. But the line between law and anarchy had become so diluted, it was difficult to catch the thread.

"Miss, we won't be able to help you if you don't cooperate. Please answer the question. Who resides in this house?"

Oh, I was cooperating all right.

Who has keys to the house? What did you see or hear? Who has been inside your home recently? Do you have any idea as to who the perpetrator might be?

I'd answered every question they'd asked of me over the past two hours, save for the last one. I had plenty of ideas, but sharing might've gotten me thrown in jail sooner than the charges against said perpetrator would be dropped.

I was starting to get tired because all they'd been doing for the past hour was repeating questions I'd already answered. It was like *I* was being interrogated. Like they wanted to get me to trip up and discover cracks in my story.

"Officer Allen, I answered that question four times already, and my answer still remains the same. I, Eliana Roux, am the only person that resides in this house."

"Well, alright," he grumbled, looking around. I got it, we were currently in the dining room that seated an entire family and then some. It was bizarre that a college student lived in this cold house all alone.

A knock sounded on the door before a young police officer came inside, his soft features unmarred by the stresses of this particular job. "Sir, we retrieved the CCTV footage," he said to officer Allen, who dismissed him with a nod.

"That will be all then, Ms. Roux." He got off his seat, clutching his notepad, and I felt relieved. "Please don't refrain from calling us if you remember any information that might be relevant. We will look into this and get back to you as soon as possible."

"Thank you, officer," I replied and showed him out, my movements stiff.

I'd gotten the shit beat out of me twice in a month and a half. I just couldn't catch a break. First, I was beaten bloody by Carter's spawn and now cut up by his lackey. At least I assumed him to be.

Although I shouldn't have been feeling relieved when the brigade of police cars exited through the iron gates, a breath of peace escaped my mouth. The grounds had been swept from corner to corner. No stone was left unturned as they scrambled to find any piece of evidence.

The sun had also started to slice through the darkness of this long hellish night. The first rays of sunlight caressed my skin, and I couldn't help but feel grimy, covered in sweat and dried-up tears and blood. The roses sitting pretty in a flower bench in front of the Ionian columns mocked me as they came awake under the warmth, dewy and crisp from the chilly night's air.

Jealous, I hovered nearby, plucking a white rose and questioning if I'd ever be that carefree and fresh again, full of life to give. The answer was a thorn in my finger, as even the rose recognized that I wasn't cut out to be a flower.

"Probably not," I murmured.

One bad thing about branding yourself as unbreakable was that people forgot you were human too. And they seemed to recognize that as the only thing they didn't do was handle me with care.

Something wet landed on my finger, and it took me a second to realize it was my own tears.

I couldn't remember the last time I'd cried. It'd been sucked dry of tears a long time ago. After all, I would have been doing nothing but lay in a pool of my tears if I'd let everything affect me. In all the craziness and action, I'd forgotten how cathartic the simple act of sobbing your heart out under the stream of the shower was.

That was exactly what I did. And while the clean water washed away the grime from my body, my tears took with them some of the scars from my soul.

Not all. Simply too much had happened to me to get out of this unscathed. Everything left a mark, and at the end of the day, I was only but a collection of memories, good and bad. I just had to be careful not to let the good overpower the bad, otherwise those scars would bleed and bleed until nothing was left no more.

Thoroughly rubbed off, dressed, and dry, I found myself wanting to see the one person that for the longest time had been my bad. He numbed the pain better than any other drug.

I'd found solace in someone that was supposed to be nothing more than another thorn wedged in my body, yet somehow he sprouted vines and locked himself in. I could always lose myself in his words. His fire was consuming and overwhelming in a way that made me forget all of my worries and simply let me be.

But I couldn't.

I wouldn't be the one to break first after all he'd done.

So, I settled for some ibuprofen and chamomile tea instead.

Chapter 18

LEONARDO

I woke up on the wrong side of the bed that morning.

Daddy dearest, still hadn't returned from his several month long "business trip", so I had to spend the entirety of my waking moments watching out for my mother's sly ways. And just when I thought I'd confiscated all of her stash, a good ol' bottle of Johnnie sprung up in her hands out of thin air.

Little Miss Priss wasn't picking up my calls, and what was worse was that I didn't fault her. I was going to tell her, but then one thing led to another, and my head was all wrapped up in her pussy. My balls were starting to shrivel up from all the inaction lately, and it didn't help that my brain was conjuring up all sorts of ways to punish her.

Bite, slap, nip, and then chase it all down with kisses and licks.

Only a few hours had passed since I left her, but it felt like fucking eternity. There was this unease in my chest at the way we left things, like battery acid coursing through my veins.

That's how I found myself behind the wheel, driving past the Roux mansion's gates. I came to a screeching halt before her front door, taking the stairs two by two before ringing the bell.

"Peter, I told you I'm fine." Eli's voice traveled past the door's crack as she shoved it open, slightly annoyed. It was better than coffee and sent a zing through my system that activated all of my body parts. "You don't have to check in on me every hour."

"Confusing me again, Narcissus? I don't know if I should start taking it personal—" I stopped dead when my gaze fell on her face, taking in what she was trying to hide behind her hair. "The fuck?"

Fury wrapped around my chest, turning my breathing labored. I grabbed the door before Eliana could slam it shut and moved inside as she backed away, hunching her shoulders in defeat. I didn't let her get far. I chased after her, letting the entrance slam shut behind us.

"Don't touch me." She slapped my hand away when I tried to hold her. "How the hell did you get in, Leo? I swear this is the last thing I need right now."

"I'm in your approved guests list," I seethed, getting closer again, hating how she tried to cower away from me. "Now stop running, and let me see you."

Eliana sighed as if deliberating how easy throwing me out would be. She figured out the chances of that happening would be zero to none when she squared her shoulders and let me look my fill.

A wave of deja vu hit me, only this time her wounds were ten times worse.

"Jesus, Eli." Red bathed my vision as I clasped her shoulder. She let me, and I tugged her closer, examining her skin thoroughly.

Bruises the color of lavender blooms decorated the left side of her pale face, and scabs that would leave faint scars wrapped around them in twisted harmony. Her lips were chapped, and she tugged the bottom one inside her mouth, teasing the violent cut with her tongue, looking at me with vulnerable eyes.

My gaze drifted over her, catching every little contusion that would eventually fade away. While the superficial cuts filled me with primitive fury, it was the stabs on her soul that were my undoing. Dread swirled in my gut at the ripple effect that this would have.

"I'm going to fucking kill her." My nostrils flared when Serena's face flashed front and center in my mind. I didn't care that she was a girl, as she certainly didn't care that Eliana was a human being. Every time she winced in discomfort, I wanted to blow shit up, starting with the Laurent's house. "It was Serena again, wasn't it?"

"It-it wasn't Serena." Eliana fiddled with the edge of her light blue dress, playing with some loose strings. Her hair fell forward, hiding her injured cheek as she grew uncomfortable the more I stared at her, waiting for answers.

"Don't ever hide from me, Eliana." I tugged the blonde curtain behind her ear. "You'll always be the most beautiful person I've ever seen, even if you do look like you fought with the meat grinder and lost."

My joke touched base, and my heart soared when she giggled. The sound was magnetizing, and her smile lit up her whole face. She looked like a better version of Tinker Bell. Radiance shone through the gloom.

"Now, tell me what happened." Intensity bled into my tone again, but I was barely holding back for her sake.

Eliana finally opened her mouth, and when she started talking, it was like a dam broke. Like she was opening up for the first time in forever.

"Someone broke into my house, Leo. I-I don't know who. I couldn't see his face because he had me pinned against the floor the whole time." She shuddered at the memory, and my jaw clenched, fireworks exploding behind my lids, but I let her finish. "He threatened me. Told me that if I went digging in too deep, I'd end up just like my father. Dead."

I embraced her shaking form without thinking, holding her tight and easing some of her shock. I knew we were playing a dangerous game, with players far more experienced than us, but I thought we were being careful. Well, that naivete came back to bite us, and Eliana bore the scars.

"Did he... did he do anything else to you?" I swallowed hard. "Hurt you in ways that I can't see?"

My relief was immediate when her head shook against my shoulder, but short-lived. She was in pain because I hadn't been there. Eliana always hid behind walls of steel, always one step ahead, so I didn't think... I never thought this would happen.

"You should've called me. You should've come to me the second you had the chance, Eliana."

"Come to you? To the guy that withheld information from me, that acted as my bully for four years, that chained me to my past?" She scoffed, looking up at me as if I'd lost my mind. "No, thank you. Whatever this is between us, it can't get any further than it already has. Physical wounds will heal eventually, but I don't think I can survive you cutting me off for a second time."

"I apologized for that, Eliana, and I'll keep apologizing if that's what it takes for you to forgive me. I'm sorry. I'm sorry for seeking to erase my pain by hurting you as well, but as for chaining you to the past, I never did. I never messed with your college applications."

Not in the way she thought I did anyway.

"I can't deal with your lies right now, Leo." She slipped past my embrace, and I grabbed onto her arm, pleading my case.

"Call me a bastard, an asshole, a fucking douchebag if you must, and you won't see me resisting those claims. I know who I am, and that's no liar. I did not mess with your college applications."

"No." Eliana shook her head, a glossy sheen taking over her eyes. "You admitted it. That day at the club? You admitted it!"

"I told you what you wanted to hear, what you wanted to believe. I don't know why those schools didn't accept you, but I had nothing to do with it."

I did pull some strings to get her in Dane. No matter what her father had done, she didn't deserve to be destroyed over it. Especially when her place was well earned. Hurt? Yes. I wanted to hurt her, and I did. I wasn't a complete fucking psycho, though. No one wanted the bad rep that came with Eliana, but they wanted those Bianchi donations more.

I'd take that knowledge to my grave. Eliana was a prideful person. She'd hate me more for making it easy for her.

She shook even harder, and I let go, scared she was going to injure herself more in her current state. "I swear Eliana, I didn't have anything to do with it."

"Then why did you let me believe you did? For three fucking years, you let me believe that you'd taken away my choices!" She yelled at me, wincing when the wound in her lip reopened.

"Because I wanted you to hate me!" The truth slipped out of my mouth, stinging like sandpaper on my tongue. "I wanted you to not be able to look at me. I wanted you to think I was nothing but a fucking monster. You were a stake lodged in my heart. Every time I thought about you, I felt like I was tainting Isabella's memory, letting her down in the worst possible way."

Her chest mirrored mine as we both breathed hard. We were so used to inhaling lies that questioning the nature of our words came naturally. A headache enveloped my skull, lessening only when Eliana's gaze softened, and she took a tentative step forward.

"And now I'm not anymore?"

"Preying on your negative emotions was my way of keeping you at bay. I can't fucking stop myself from wanting to make you mine whenever you smile, and I can't fucking stop myself from wanting to hunt down anyone that put their hands on you." My palms fisted at my sides until I felt my nails digging into my skin. "You're like a drug I can't quit Roux, working together is only making your effect stronger."

"Well, you accomplished one thing. I did think you were nothing but a bastard..." She bridged the gap between us, trepidation dripping from her movements. "... yet, at the same time, I also couldn't forget the little boy that gave me a shoulder to lean on. The little boy that pursued me endlessly, and for as much as I still fucking hate you, I can't get you out of my mind either."

Like Buffy hated Spike, little liar.

Her arms came around my shoulders, and I held on to her waist, dipping my head until our foreheads met and breaths mixed. She looked at me as if she was really seeing me again for the first time after years. I honed in on her features, taking in her unsure wide eyes and parted mouth before dipping down, sealing our reconnection.

Our mouths met halfway, fusing with a kiss that held the weight of our lies. The pace was languid as we prodded past the shields we always kept lifted between us. It still filled my lungs with air, making the hazy clouds in my brain soar.

Eliana was the first woman outside of my family I felt so linked to. The paradox of what we'd become didn't escape me. Our situations were tailored so that we'd never see eye to eye, yet hatred had a habit of leaving trails of desire on its path.

If there was anything I was good at, it was getting so lost in her touch, I couldn't find the route home anymore, and as much as I wanted to keep kissing her, I pulled back before it could get any further. She'd been beaten bloody mere hours ago, and I couldn't sit back, twiddling my thumbs.

"Get ready to hate me even more," I murmured against her lips once we detached.

"What now?" she whined softly.

"We're moving in together." I threw the words at her like it was a done deal.

Her eyes went wide like saucers. "Um, care to repeat that?"

"We're moving in together."

She blinked two times, and I felt the need to kiss her eyelids until the pain seeped away.

"Don't be ridiculous. Won't your parents think it's weird

you're moving out all of a sudden? You can't just leave, and I most certainly can't stay with you."

"You're not staying with me. My family owns a cabin close by. And trust me, my parents are nothing to worry about." I couldn't stop the bitterness that laced my tone, and she caught it.

"Why?"

"Well, for one, my father treats our house like a hotel, and two, my mother is more interested in what shade of brown her newest whiskey bottle is. Tawny or cinnamon."

Eliana saw past my sarcastic smile, and clutched her hand over my heart, feeling the rapid beat underneath her fingertips. Rage, hostility, and stress all roiled together.

"Since we're apologizing, I'm sorry too. So sorry I never peeked under your tough exterior to see that you were also hurting."

I sucked in a sharp breath, holding back a wince.

"You have nothing to be sorry for. I was acting like a jackass, and you owe me nothing. I made your life miserable, and I liked it too, Eliana. If anyone should be feeling remorse here, that's me."

She leaned on her tiptoes, kissing my neck and the wound on her lip scraped my skin. I wanted to brand it to memory, file it under the things I should take better care of.

"We're both sorry. How about that?"

I pecked her smiling lips. "I'll take it."

I pulled away before either of us deepened the kiss, touching her ocean blue gaze with my moss green one. "Do you want to keep going? I definitely understand if you don't. Your safety comes first." I knew the words were true as soon as I uttered them. I wouldn't jeopardize her. In fact, I kind of wanted her to pull away. "I will do my damned best to protect you, but I won't make empty promises, I don't know our opponent well enough to do that."

"No." She shook her head. "I'm scared shitless, I won't lie. But we're in this together. I'm not giving up now, not after everything."

God, I wanted to kiss her.

And if we made it out of this alive, keep her.

My Narcissus wasn't a kitten. She was a whole ass tiger.

"Alright, let's get you to bed, sweetheart. Your eyes look like they're going to start bleeding out soon if you don't get some sleep."

Eliana mock punched my arm and squealed when I bent her knees under my arm, carrying her to my car. She wouldn't be staying here anymore.

Sleep was the last thing I thought Eliana Roux would be doing when she stepped foot in my room, but fate had a habit of slapping you across the face.

She looked tiny on my king-sized bed, engulfed by the navy blue sheets. The bruises were stark against her pale skin. Eli was entirely too breakable when she slept. She'd dozed off a few minutes after I tucked her under my arms, body pasted against mine.

It took me more than twenty minutes after she fell asleep to find the power to unglue my body from hers and stop staring like a creep. I hated to even blink. My mind loved conjuring up all sorts of ways to dismantle the poor fuck that had put his hands all over her. The possibilities were endless, and I made sure to give Ethan a call and make him get on it, to turn them into probabilities.

I had to deal with my mom. The situation had gotten too out of hand, and if her husband didn't care enough to get involved, then I would.

I found her in the kitchen way past eight a.m. She was eating breakfast, a glass of whatever poison she'd chosen today on standby.

"Good morning, Mom."

She jumped slightly at the invasion, not seeing me walk through the kitchen's entrance. Any doubts I had about sending her to rehab without my father's say so all about disappeared when I took into account how thin and brittle she'd gotten. It looked like her robe was wearing her instead of the other way around. Her brown hair lacked their usual shine, while her gray eyes were hollowed out and bloodshot.

"Good morning," she grumbled back, one of the rare times I found her sober.

"How are you?" I asked, tugging the glass away from her. She resisted my hold, her blush robe slipping past her bony shoulders, but she released the glass from her grip once she realized I wasn't about to let up.

"Just peachy," she sneered, extra touchy when she didn't get her way.

Great, I couldn't wait to see how she took the next piece of news.

I sat on a cherry stool beside her, snatching a piece of bacon off her plate. "I have some news for you," I said slowly, taking a bite.

Her head snapped up from her jelly-covered toast. "What news?"

Like a band-aid.

"I'm enrolling you to Lakehouse Recovery Center."

"Lakehouse Recovery Center?"

"It's a drug and alcohol addiction treatment center."

"I know what it is!" she hissed. Her grip on the fork got tighter and I got tenser. "What I want to know is, why would someone on their right mind enroll me there?"

I expected denial, so she really wasn't pulling out all the stops here. Although, this time, I wouldn't humor her and brush the fact that she had a problem under the rug for the sake of being perfect. No one was. We were all flawed creatures, and I didn't care what the fuck people were going to say or how my father would feel. All I wanted was for her to get past this intact because I loved her. Seeing her downturn spiral fucked with me and my morals.

Watching her slip away while I, her son, did nothing was purely evil. And if I didn't want to be another Alessio Bianchi, I had to show consequences the *fuck yourselves* door.

"Do you really want to go down that road, Mom?"

Like a spooked deer caught in the hunter's fire, she sprung up from the chair she was sitting on. "I'm not going, and you can't make me."

I stuffed my mouth with bacon again to avoid saying anything I'd regret later. Her collarbones stood out like jugged mountains, and it didn't take much more for the tap of lies to start spewing from my mouth.

"How can you be so sure I can't make you, Barbara? You've been around Dad for almost half your life. You must be well aware by now how vast his sphere of influence is."

That was true. He could move mountains if he wanted to, yet that same resolve was lacking when it came to his family.

"He is in on this... this intervention?" she scoffed, gesturing in the air.

"Yes, he is." My lies stacked three stories tall.

"No, Leo, please." She changed her tune from outraged to pleading in record time, getting in front of me and clinging off my arm. "I can't. I can't go. Alcohol is all I have, it's the only thing that keeps me sane. Keeps my mind off Isabella." Her voice cracked and I brought her in for a hug.

I knew that she didn't drink for the pleasure of it. She had demons to hide, a closet full of them that constantly banged to be let out. Alcohol was her way of muffling those screams.

I hated doing this, taking away her one outlet. Tough love wasn't harsh just on the receiver, but I had to. "What would you do if you lost me too then Mom, huh? What if you woke up one day and I wasn't there anymore?"

"I would kill myself," she said without hesitation, her trembling arms holding on to my biceps. "I already outlived one child, I wouldn't survive it a second time."

My heart bled for her. I was doing the right thing. I wanted my mom back, the sweet and considerate one, the one that always showed up, at whatever cost.

"I'm sorry to break it to you, Ma, but unless you get some help, that's what's going to happen. I won't be there for you anymore. Even nuns have a limit, and mine is not greater than theirs. And the thing is, I don't think you're willing to change without some sort of initiative."

"And this is it? This is your initiative? Locking me away to some prison so I'll be brainwashed to fit in?"

"Please, it's a super expensive rehab center where you'll have more luxuries than you do your own house." I left the fact that her most important luxury wouldn't be there out.

"Think about Dad." I hit her where it really hurt. While she loved me, she worshiped the very her husband walked upon. She'd probably kiss his feet too if given the chance. It infuriated me because the bastard didn't deserve that kind of love and devotion. "Wouldn't you like for him to be around more?"

I saw the moment she changed her pace. Her eyes lightened, and her hands loosened on my forearms. "Is this really why he isn't around anymore? Am I the reason why?"

You deserve better, I wanted to scream at her, shake her out of her stupor, but I couldn't. I didn't want to lie again either, so instead, I settled for dodging the truth. "What do you think?"

Her gaze turned from torn, to unsure, to troubled. But finally, surety glimmered behind her grey depths as she spoke the words I always longed to hear through a deep heeded sigh. "Okay, I'll do it. I'll go to rehab."

Even though she was going for all the wrong reasons. Doing it for other people and not herself, I'd take whatever win I could get, hoping she'd understand why she needed to do this further down the road.

The atmosphere was somber in the car as I drove her to the rehab center later that day, but a wave of peace hit me when she was ushered inside. It wasn't like they would fix her up, and she'd come back brand spanking new.

Her wounds weren't ones you stitched up easily, but at least they could show her how to channel her pain differently.

Chapter 19

ELIANA

"**A**re we there yet?" My feet bounced impatiently on the floor of the car.

I'd slept for thirteen hours. A rejuvenating, dreamless sleep my exhausted self, needed like air. When I woke up, I found Leo trying to pack his R8 with our belongings. Safe to say, the sport's car wasn't made for that kind of heavy lifting. My car was a no-go since it was too recognizable according to Leo's newly gained abilities as a spy. So that was how we ended up in a more nondescript Volvo, cruising through the roads of Astropolis, headed to Rose Falls.

Rose Falls was a town approximately an hour away, famous for its beautiful array of cascading waterfalls and booming real estate market. Instead of an hour, though, Leo had stretched the journey to two after taking some back roads that were supposed to be "short cuts". The sun was getting low, and I, impatient.

"Has anyone ever told you what a horrible road trip partner you are?" he asked, as if it was my fault it was taking him ages to reach our destination.

"I haven't been on any road trips before," I'd found out the hard way that long car rides weren't for me, hence my unprecedented impatience right now.

"No wonder."

"Has anyone ever told you what a great driver you are?" I replied, aiming for the same level of pettiness.

"Not really." He grimaced after taking a sharp left.

"No wonder why," I mocked back.

"Hardy har har, Narcissus."

It took him thirty more minutes and a lot of back and forth later, over if we're going to be following the instructions of the GPS or not, to finally find his way around.

He pulled up a long uphill road, and I shivered, the hair on the back of my head standing up to full attention. Bishop pine trees closed in all around us, and the last house I saw was several miles back... when the road was still gravel. A full moon peeked behind the branches, and the scenery around us looked like a Halloween poster brought to life. The only thing missing was some fog.

"Did you lure me here to kill me and feed the evidence to the wolves or something?" My skin crawled.

I jumped when his hand landed on my thigh, slithers of warmth and a bite of danger seeping into my skin.

"Don't be ridiculous," Leo said, the crescent smile wrinkling his face was unnerving as he led us deeper into the secluded forest. "There aren't any wolves around here. I'd probably feed you to the coyotes."

"It's comforting to know you're this well informed."

"Don't worry, babe, no wild animals will get a bite in before I do." His perfect teeth gleamed in the dark.

"Are you sure you're not the wild animal?" I mumbled under my breath, but he caught it and chuckled.

Leo squeezed my thigh before slowing down, shifting the gear to park and killing the headlights. My eyes took a second to adjust to the bone-chilling darkness, but the view was worth it.

A soft-lit, rustic gem stuck out as I peered through the windshield. The roof was sharp, the edges high over the massive windows, looking like spears ready to gouge a giant's eyes out. Artificial yellow lighting illuminated the wooden structure, nestled between the trees. A traditional home, with a modern twist. It was big, three stories high, yet it still maintained a certain warmth, radiated through the logs that were used to build it.

Cold air rushed to the interior of the car once Leo pulled my door open. I'd been too distracted and didn't notice when he got out of the car.

"Are you coming?" he asked, his jean jacket in hand, revealing a tightly knit body that his black shirt did a poor job at disguising.

God, we'd be secluded in this cabin for who knew how long, and I couldn't keep my eyes off him from day one. I couldn't even count on the weekdays, so I could avoid him on campus, Christmas break was in a week.

I stepped out of the car, and a nippy breeze had me shivering in my knit dress. Although Astropolis was freezing in December, Rose Falls, because of the elevated altitude, was even worse.

"Here." Leo held up the jacket for me.

"Thank you." I stepped in, sliding my arms through the sleeves. It reached my mid-thighs and carried his pine scent. "Let me help you with those." I reached to take my suitcase, but he tugged them away from my grip, his eyes lingering on my bruises.

"I can handle the two suitcases, Eliana." Strapped with the load, he made his way to the residence. The protectiveness was... it was sweet, but I didn't want him to start treating me differently because of recent events.

Swallowing a sigh, I followed in his wake.

A flourishing garden unfolded around us as we walked up the hill. Mini artificial waterfalls and streams of water decorated the lush surroundings. "What? Were the actual Rose Falls not enough, you had to have some cataracts of your own?"

"I'll let you know this house was designed by Aaron Ford."

Astropolis's very own resident architect. He was so sought out he'd moved in the neighborhood permanently after checks started reigning in his bank account. It was absurd how much gullible rich folks were willing to pay for white and beige empty spaces, just because they bit into the idea that minimalism was trés chic.

"I think he's overrated anyway." I shrugged.

Reaching the cabin door, he turned to me before unlocking it, one dark eyebrow cocked. "You're just saying that because he dissed your painting at the Dane Peace Convention last year, and Serena got to win the competition again." Wisely, he ducked inside the cabin after spewing out the words.

"I mean, come on! Her idea was a white dove just as a

figurine this time, as if we've never seen it done before. It didn't deserve first place," I scoffed. "Whatever, all you have to do to win these days is suck up to people, and I'm not doing that. No, thank you." I crossed my arms under my chest, and Leo's gaze took a nosedive.

He sucked his lips through his teeth as he apprised me how the frigid air impacted my body. "I wouldn't be so sure about that if I were you."

I rolled my eyes at his double meaning.

Brushing past him, I moved inside, admiring the dome-like structure of the roof. The furniture was lived in and aided the charm of the place. As did the stunning windows that overlooked the back deck.

I couldn't see too far out, but I did notice a hot tub nestled under a covered part of the veranda. The idea of having a soak sounded very appealing after a long day. Although I had spent much of it sitting or lying down, it still had taken a toll on me.

I felt Leo's body press in behind me and ambush my senses. He stared at my reflection in the mirror, dropping a kiss on the crook of my neck. "Want me to get the jets on the tub running?"

It didn't take long for his jacket to meet the floor and for his arms to replace it. They circled around me, pressing against my womb until warmth swirled in my insides.

"What, no grand tour of the house?" I tried to form a cohesive question, although I was pretty sure it came out like a jumbled mess.

"You'll get intimately acquainted with every surface soon enough." He pushed me forward, and my hands gripped the glass as his palmed my ass.

"Vertical ones too, I hope," I croaked.

"Especially vertical surfaces." He thrust his hips forward, and my mouth fell open with a moan on auto-pilot. My head rested on his chest, and his hands slid upward, teasing my breasts with a ghost touch before closing in around my neck.

"I'll take the tub first." I strained to speak against his punishing grip.

"Strip, and I'll think about it."

His lips traced the curve of my shoulder, leaving a trail of goose bumps on my skin. Leo's touch was the sweetest form of hurt, nicotine you became addicted to. I was surprised my dress didn't melt away at his order. The reactions my body reserved for him were bizarre.

La petite mort—that was what the French called orgasms, little deaths. And that was exactly what Leo was to me. A rough diamond that split my skin and charred my soul, making me die a thousand little deaths. But what if we sealed the deal? What would become of me then?

An uncanny fear swirled deep in my gut, and I detached my body from his before he had a chance to react. I welcomed the coldness, scared of the heat of his battle.

"What are you doing?" he asked, and I took in the very obvious strain in his pants.

I think it was mad.

Mad at me.

"I-I uh... I'm hungry."

It was true, technically. I hadn't eaten since before we started the trip. And because I was a little shit that couldn't help stirring shit up, I slid a sleeve off.

"So am I." Leo licked his lips.

"For actual food." I slid the other sleeve off, and my dress slipped a little, revealing the lacy front of my scarlet bra. I was sure my skin took a similar hue when his eyes touched every exposed part of me.

"My mouth *is* watering." His chest vibrated with a growl, and the dress dripped from my sweaty grip. The snug material caught around the flare of my hips, and impatience flew behind Leo's greens as he advanced forward.

"Then you should cook us some dinner while I get the hot tub ready." I put a hand on his chest, cutting his approach short. Coincidentally, my dress slipped to the floor at the same time.

The gold flecks in his eyes flared and threatened to take us both up in flames. Within a second, my hand was caged behind my back, and he was grabbing my ass in a way that I was sure would bruise, branding his identity on my body.

"Are you trying to torture me, Narcissus?" he mouthed against my lips, stealing my slight intake of air.

His tongue triggered a shockwave of pleasure when it came out to play, licking the seam of my lips. I didn't open, but he didn't request. He thrust inside my mouth with one punishing stroke, swallowing every sense of logic with his utterly dominating nature.

My blood raced, and my heart felt close to flying out of my chest. Good god, desperation clung to my core as I tried to combat his greed. Needles pierced through my resolve with each lavish stroke of his tongue and grind of his hips. I glided my hand past the hard planes of his stomach, cupping his sharp jaw.

Leo was a man on a mission. His mouth ate me up, making it difficult to breathe. I flicked my tongue over his bottom lip as I tried to slow us down ever so slightly. And he took it upon himself to sink his teeth on mine, out for blood.

Losing my sense of self whenever he was around was a done deal, but with each passing day, I felt more and more like we were becoming an entity. Our movements were in tune, breathing in sync, and hearts fighting a war we both knew was a lost cause.

A hybrid mix between a groan and a growl escaped his mouth when I leaned back, after his appraisal turned leisurely. Gulping air greedily, I avoided the questions in his gaze by staring at his wet mouth and smearing the remnants of my pink lipstick on his lips with my thumb.

"Make me some dinner, and then I'll give you dessert." I looked up at him, my resolve trembling at the sheer male beauty. The urge to slip out of my soaked panties right then and there was immense.

"I want you naked and on your hands and knees when I return, Eliana. Ready to be fed in more ways than one," he hissed into my skin, and fire rained down on every cell of my body.

"Yes, sir." The authoritative term slipped from my mouth before I could stop it. Judging by his shit-eating grin though, he loved it.

"You should practice what you preach more." He kissed the side of my face, then let me go. "Get your sweet ass in the tub, I'll be back." Shaking his head, Leo took one last toe-curling look at me before his heat dissipated completely, disappearing down a hallway that led to the kitchen.

If I thought I'd be glad to have him playing by my rules, the throbbing pain in between my legs indicated I'd duped myself. But something held me back.

I wanted to be the card dealer for once.

Approaching the tub, I fixed the desired temperature and jumped inside, sighing when the hot water touched my freezing skin. I couldn't see much, save for the silhouettes of the trees, obstructing the view of the starry purple sky and the water as it fizzed. The jets picked up their tempo, alleviating some of the pressure between my legs.

It wasn't like I didn't want to have sex with Leo. In fact, I wanted it a little too much, all things considered. It was just... I was losing control. I always maintained the upper hand during sex. I liked the power, craved it, because the last time I didn't have any, everything went to shit.

My first time.

Naïve little old me wanted to play with the big boys when I was fifteen. It was during a summer in Nice. My mother was too busy downing bottles of Rosé. Dad had a stroke of inspiration back at the hotel room, and me? I was too busy getting fucked in a changing room by a French guy twice my age.

It wasn't involuntary or anything like that. But he sure as hell took advantage of my age and limited experience with the opposite sex, looking for a girl to rail and bail.

Shaking my head, I snapped the band of my bra free. This was different, it had to be. Water rushed around my breasts as I followed Leo's instructions, but I hesitated when it came to my panties. The thrill of wanting to know what he'd do, if I disobeyed him was too high for me to actually follow through.

Leonardo

I agreed to make her dinner, I never said it was going to be good.

The pan sizzled as I sauteed the onions, whipping up the food in record time. I'd called ahead and gotten the fridge stocked already. Finding the ingredients for the pasta wasn't that hard. My execution, on the other hand? Well... let's just say it could've been much better.

The pasta came out a little soggy, the tomato sauce a little runny... but it was still edible. Considering my cock was harder than the wooden spoon I used to stir up the sauce, I was surprised I'd even cooked and wasn't nailing Eliana four ways into heaven right now.

She deserved it, though. Deserved to be taken care of. I'd wanted to fuck her since for-fucking-ever, and still did, that would never change, but I wanted to cherish her too. Make the grass on her side of the field greener for once, instead of watching it wither away and dumping a healthy dose of poison on top.

I took it upon myself to shed my clothes before making my way to the deck. The whisk hanging from the wooden appliance rack gleamed, egging me on. Whatever, I was willing to accept the status of a whipped man if it meant I got the gorgeous and very naked blonde in my hot tub right now.

Eliana's wet strands stuck to her cheek and bare back as she twisted around at the sound of the sliding door. We took each other in like it was the first time. Her gaze traced every dip and curve of my body, and I couldn't take my eyes off her slick shoulders. I couldn't see much beyond the fizzing water, but even the sight of her face had my dick jumping with joy.

This was happening.

Eliana Roux would finally be utterly and unholy mine.

"That was quick." She cocked an eyebrow, transfixed on the body part that insisted on defying gravity every time she was around.

"What can I say? Someone was impatient to get reacquainted with you." She squared her shoulders as I jumped inside. Her breasts played peek-a-boo with me, almost popping out of the water and then disappearing again into the fizz. "You ready to eat, baby?"

She hummed a yes, reaching for the plate and frowning when I held it away, setting it on the edge of the jacuzzi. "On my lap. I'm an all hands on deck kind of chef, and that means your pretty little mouth is only getting fed by me tonight."

Lust and apprehension illuminated her face, but she hugged my shoulders, and her thighs came around me, straddling my lap. Fuck, feeling her bare breasts slide against my chest was like electricity coursing through my veins. I dropped a kiss on her collarbone as I circled my arms around her. It was distracting, so distracting I didn't immediately feel the barrier between her cunt and my dick.

"What's this?" I asked, my hands reaching for the offensive piece of fabric.

"My panties," the smart ass replied, tongue swiping over her bottom lip.

"You like pain, Eliana?" I tugged on the underwear, making sure it scraped against her clit, setting the bundle of nerves ablaze. "Like it when I rip your panties off?"

Eli didn't reply, just kept grinding on my hand as I moved the fabric. Her head was thrown back, and she was smiling. She knew what the fuck she was doing. "Oh, but you love it. I wonder how you'd feel after I burn the lot of them. You won't be needing them much anyway."

"You'll do no such thing," she said on a moan.

I stopped abruptly, and she whimpered, losing the much-needed friction.

"No," Eliana breathed out. "Why... why did you stop?"

I wasn't playing again into her hand tonight. She wanted her panties? She'd keep them... for the most part. This was as torturous for her as it was for me, and if there was anything I excelled at, it was making her suffer.

"You said you were hungry, no?"

Her face dropped, and my libido flared.

I twisted the fork in the marinated pasta and brought it between us, following the movement of her bee-stung lips as they wrapped around it. Then off to her throat as it worked with a swallow, hollowing out. I got the urge to bite it all over, leave purple marks on her porcelain skin.

I fed her, not touching any part of hers, except for my cock poking her lower belly. Eliana was stubborn, and I didn't fall far behind, but I wanted her to come to me this time around—and come for me, but that was a given.

She shook her head when I offered her another bite, nails raking my chest and disappearing under the water. I almost dropped the plate of pasta when her hand wrapped around my dick, squeezing tight.

"I'm full, or well... craving to be," she complained against my lips.

My mouth dove to lick up some of the tomato sauce decorating the corner of her lips, trying to keep my eagerness at bay. "How full are we talking about? One finger? Two?" I fisted the offending fabric disguising her pussy and the way the lacy scrap melted away with a tug was laughable. "Three?"

I smiled when outrage shone in her eyes.

"Full of your dick, Leo. Get on with it already." She twisted and turned over my lap, but I held her hips steady.

"Water is not a great lubricant." I pinched her ass, and she rewarded me with a moan and a pump of my erection. "Turn around and grip the edge of the tub, ass up," I bit through my teeth.

She stopped playing hard to get. As willing as a cat in heat, her glistening body turned around, revealing that ample ass that drove me crazy and equally wet pussy, spread enticingly wide.

I couldn't resist getting a taste, even though I was all but ready to combust. Angling her leg on the tub, so her clit was in direct contact with a little pressurized fountain, I dove in, fucking her sweet cunt with my tongue and spreading her ass cheeks wide for me.

"Oh fuck," she cried out. "That never gets old."

Nor did her taste. A mix of sweet and salty bloomed on my tongue as I continued working her. I licked and nibbled on her pretty pink lips, sucking in the full effect of her taste. Cum started dripping down my chin and her back arched when I prodded her tight hole. Eliana's whole body convulsed as she came screaming, slicing through the silence of the forest stretching beyond.

God, I loved the pipes on this woman. Especially when she used them to scream my name.

By the time Eliana got down from her post-orgasmic cloud, I was already sheathed with a condom I conveniently brought along. Everyone always raved about how fucking fantastic going bareback was, but the prospect of mini Leos running around was enough to hold me off the temptation.

Breathing hard, I got on my feet behind her, the head of my cock already poking at her entrance. I was more than fucking ready to root myself home after being denied entry for so long.

Eliana twisted around before I could sink in all the way, gripping my shaft with bright red nails, the color of sin. Sin, because I was a pump away from shooting my load all over her back like an overworked virgin.

She traced along the edges of the condom, a small smile tipping her lips. "Are you clean?"

"Yes," I croaked, and then cleared my throat. "Why?"

"So am I. And I'm on the pill." Eliana bit her lip, check-mating me in a box of peril. "I want to feel you bare, Leo. Please baby, I don't want any barriers between us anymore."

She could've asked me to paint the sky fucking red, and I would've pulled all the stops to make it happen. Fucking her bare? I didn't have to think about it once, not twice. Mini Leos be damned, I was going to savor my woman until we both needed IVs for all the fluids we'd lost. Make her mine, in every way that mattered.

"Take the condom off and spread your legs," I told her, giving her a chance to back out.

She didn't hesitate.

I was bare in a matter of seconds as Eliana worked the protection off carelessly. We were being sloppy, like fucking teenagers, but we didn't care. All I wanted, needed like the air I breathed, was to see pleasure in the vulnerable eyes that were staring back at me.

I didn't dare look away from the baby blues that had slaked my appetite until only one person fit in my menu. Her whole body was trembling, and I gripped her hips like my life depended on it, finally sinking into Eliana Roux.

Going from *persona non grata* to a first-class ticket to Eliana town felt surreal. Tingles saturated my body, and I had to thrust once to realize that this was, in fact, not an out-of-body experience.

Eliana Roux.

I was fucking Eliana Roux.

She was tight.

Tight and mine.

So fucking mine.

I thrust again, going balls deep, and a moan ripped from both our mouths at the same time. This wasn't just fucking. It was putting your life on hold until you'd relished in the girl of your dreams. I wanted to paint her every shade of filthy, but not at the cost of coming prematurely. So I went slow, torturously so.

"Leo," she groaned, throwing her head back, long blonde hair smacking against her tiny back. I pulsed harder inside of her. "Faster, please."

The water rushing over her clit also hit my balls. I tried to think of anything else under the sun, other than how she was cutting the circulation off my dick with her tight as sin pussy. "Just give me a second, babe."

But she didn't.

Eliana took control. Moaning as she slammed her bouncy ass on my cock, fucking herself until her walls quivered around me. What the fuck was wrong with me? I was no amateur and was not going to ruin this for either one of us.

Locking up every single muscle on my body, I grabbed her hair—mindful of her attack—guiding her up until her back arched, meeting my torso. Her tits were left exposed to the harsh air as I met her thrusts with brutal ones of my own.

"Ahh," Eliana cried out at the workout her pussy was getting impaled and stretching around me.

"*Ahh*, is right, sweetheart." Holding on to her throat as I fucked her from behind, my other hand traveled to her puckered nipple, pinching it until Eli was gasping for air. "You just couldn't wait to get fucked, could you? Couldn't wait to feel my cock rearrange your insides."

Her moans vibrated against my hand on her neck as she milked my dick for all it was worth, squeezing it to death. My thrusts became harder, and faster, again, and again, and again. Being inside her was addictive, stronger than any roll of Sativa or Indica could ever be. It was as if her pussy dripped gold, and I was a miner that was capitalizing on it.

I couldn't get enough.

The deeper I drove, the more I wanted.

Our reflections gleamed on the sliding doors, and I had a full frontal. Eliana's cheeks were flushed red, her eyes closed in euphoria, and her perky breasts smacked against the arm I kept branded over her ribs.

Her beauty was the kind that sucker-punched you every time you saw her. There was nothing subtle about Eliana. Neither her looks nor personality could ever fly under the radar. Her delightful screams on the other hand, now *they*... they broke the fucking radar.

"Leo," she panted, and I bent my head kissing and biting her earlobe. "You feel so good, baby. Don't stop. You feel so fucking good."

Her arousal coated everything, my dick, my balls, her ass. It stuck between us as I thrust into her. She didn't hold back either, though. Eliana took what she got and gave it back in earnest, meeting my thrusts until the sound of my balls smacking against her ass overshadowed everything else.

Her pussy spasmed around me, and she let out cry after cry, holding on to my hand as she came for a second time.

Holding back became damn near impossible. Heat kept building up in my veins the more her cunt contracted.

"Yess..." My voice trailed off as I didn't lessen my pace. "Is that what had you in such a mad rush?" I taunted like an asshole.

I was pretty sure she wasn't hearing me, though, even though she kept chanting, "Yes. Yes.". She was lost in the little bubble I created for her, riding the high until there was no road to veer off to anymore.

Her lungs emptied out and she nearly collapsed in my hands, but I wasn't done yet. I had six years of repressed needs to make up for, and she'd best believe she was getting out of this fifty shades of exhausted.

"Oh, no, baby." I pulled out, missing her heat immediately. She was limp as a rag doll as I turned her around, setting her spent body on the ground. Not wasting a single second, I pinned her thighs under her ears, keeping them open, and slipped inside of her again with a shudder. "You're not off the hook that easy."

"Leo, I-I don't think I can come again," she whined, exhaustion clear in her voice, but I knew she could. The more drained we felt, the sweeter was the release. Her eyes locked on mine, eyebrows slumped, and I saw a mixture of desire and tiredness behind them.

"That was just the appetizer, Narcissus. Do you really go to a five-star restaurant, not expecting a full course meal?"

Her back bowed off the ground at my words. "You're going to have to start cooking more and more than if this is what the full service of Leonardo Bianchi gets me." Eliana laughed with her whole body, delirious in her need.

I was thrusting inside of heaven. Sheathed to the hilt with her warmth and tightness, I never wanted to leave. I couldn't stop wanting her, and when she came for the third time, I knew I was chained to her for life.

Legs spread wide, tits bouncing by my thrusts, a thin layer of sweat illuminating her angelic face and body, I finally decided to let go. The image of Eli unraveling on my dick too much for me to bear.

My cock roared with blood, and I came, shooting inside of her tight channel. I spilled every drop of cum inside of my fucking obsession. And in that moment, the thought of mini Leos or Elis didn't sound as appalling as it fucking should.

My mind went blank when the thought crossed my brain.

"Jesus Christ," I mumbled, trying to catch my breath. Shaking my head, I closed my eyes as we both started to touch ground again slowly.

Blame it on the hormones.

Yup, the hormones.

Eliana's arms came around me, and she tugged me down for a kiss I got lost in. The sweat of our chests combined, sticking together. Kind of like my heart was trying to beat out of my chest and attach itself to hers.

It was like a weight had lifted, and we were free to explore each other lazily. I took my time getting to know her mouth, smoothing her hair, a mixture of sweat and water, away from her face. I reveled in her taste, drowning out pesky thoughts that had me blacking out.

Eliana broke the kiss, her lips parting slowly from mine, cerulean colored eyes searching for something in my greens. "Leo, I-I..." she stuttered, tugging the hair at the nape of my neck.

I raised a brow, waiting for her to finish her sentence and

trying to ignore the influence that doe-eyed look held over me.

But she never did. She closed her eyes, sealing her secrets behind a wall of dark lashes, kissing me again until we were both drowning in each other.

Chapter 20

ELIANA

I woke with a start.

A heavy hand strewn over my waist crushed my body under its weight, gluing me to a hard chest. It was suffocatingly hot, and I hurt. Everything hurt. My body felt like it had survived a car crash. My breasts were sore, and the space between my legs throbbed. It was a sweet pain, bringing back memories of last night... and early this morning.

Leo had the stamina of a bull. Either that or he was on some high-performance drugs. No square inch of my body was left unexplored. It was as if he was looking for hidden treasure under my skin.

I wasn't complaining. God, no. But my heart was acting weird. It was beating faster than normal and felt heavier than usual. It weighed me down. Every time Leo would kiss me, touch me, or simply look at me, I entered a rabbit hole with no way out.

I blinked several times, adjusting to the light pouring in from the windows. A sheet blanketed us. It wasn't nearly warm enough for the highland climate of Rose Falls, but being glued to a warm-blooded male did have its virtues.

Like a python, Leo's arms tightened unconsciously around me when I tried to stretch to ease the tension in my shoulders. Turning around was a struggle, but I grappled in his arms until I twisted around and had a front seat view at Leo's unruly curls.

His hair was one of the features I loved most about him, all mussed and sexy, brown with gold highlights. It looked worse for wear today, stray ringlets grazed his forehead, and I reached to touch the strands. I'd tugged it through hell and back when he took me on a tour of paradise yesterday.

Leo was a *break-your-heart-and-leave-it-shattered* type of gorgeous. I continued tracing his features with my index finger, committing them to memory. That stubborn curve of his jaw was now relaxed, his full mouth slack, and heavy lashes fanned his cheeks. I reached to caress his bottom lip with my thumb, eyes heavy by his beauty.

A brute type of beauty.

I got why everyone was so enamored by him. He was a lethal combination of smart, scary, and sexy, a holy trinity that had you pulling at your hair as you offered him your heart on a silver platter.

Sharp teeth connected with my finger, and I pulled back, gasping. His brilliant green eyes popped open, and another gasp escaped, but not out of fright this time. "You like feeling me up while I sleep, Narcissus?" he *tsked*, smirking. "That's not creepy at all."

My cheeks filled with heat at being caught. "What can I say? We all have our quirks."

"Hmm, I guess I forgive you." He rolled me to my back, his weight delightful on top of my naked body. Saliva pooled in my mouth when I felt his engorged shaft on my thigh. "There are weirder kinks to have."

I lost my train of thought once his mouth connected with my neck, licking and blazing a heated path lower toward my raised peaks. His tongue flattened on my nipple before he sucked it in his mouth and an embarrassing squeak came out of my mouth.

His early morning enthusiasm reflected deep in my core, and my folds got slicker. I guessed this was what the saying, *can't get enough of someone,* meant. Even on three hours of sleep, we were inclined to make up for lost time.

Leo molded his hands to my waist, tugging me closer so my legs fell open on either side, facilitating his body better. "I d-don't remember ever asking for forgiveness," I stuttered to the ceiling, aching for him.

He stopped, head snapping up, and I reckoned I should've kept my mouth shut. "Is that so?" His brows arched. "Would you be willing to receive the punishment for your indiscretions instead?" His smile was all teeth.

Call me crazy, but I longed to feel them scraping down my skin.

"I might." I brought my hands to his neck, bringing him down for a kiss.

Leo's teeth sunk in my bottom lip as his fingers played with my clit, spreading my wetness until I was panting and losing the battle between our tongues.

"Let's see how long it takes you to apologize then, baby."

He plunged inside me with one vicious thrust that had my insides squirming. My back arched off the mattress, and he swallowed my silent scream in his mouth as I tried to accommodate his entrance.

Leo followed his harsh intrusion with sharp thrusts, stretching me out, until the bed rocked with us and the headboard started a rhythmic slam against the wall.

Thump. Thump. Thump.

He drove into me like he was possessed, hunting me down and destroying my body from the inside out. I tilted my hips up every time he slammed home, eager to meet his thrusts. He was the one doing the fucking, but I was no submissive either.

"Leo," I moaned into his ear, my voice barely audible over the sound of skin hitting skin, as he attacked my jaw and decolletage with kisses, biting into my inflamed flesh.

"Ready to give in, baby?" he asked against my skin, hearing me anyway. His plunges never lessened in power, and I recognized that there was a punishing edge to his movements. The friction between us tore me apart as much as it pieced me back together. He wanted it to hurt, and I took it anyway because I loved his kind of pain.

"Not in this lifetime," I breathed out. Heat flared down south, and my clit swelled when he stretched tall above me. He held my neck in a tight grip and took in my naked body with hungry eyes.

My breasts bounced, and I was so close. Butterflies fluttered in my womb, and I kept my eyes shut tight as I prepared for the force of the impending orgasm... *that never came.*

"What? What are you doing?" I asked, frustrated when he stole my release. His thrusts slowed, and while I felt every glorious inch of him still sliding inside me, it wasn't enough.

Sweet and slow didn't do it for me. I needed brute and beastly today.

"What's the magic word?" he taunted, and his lips ghosted over the arch of my knee as he threw my leg over his shoulder, allowing for a more direct approach. Driving deeper yet still steadily.

He stopped his thrusts altogether once I started writhing underneath him again, and I felt like I could burst. "Please." My moan was loud. Ready.

"Close," he growled, rewarding me with one harsh thrust.

"I'm sorry," I tried again.

"That's better."

This time, he kept a brisk pace, and my head pressed harder against the pillow as momentum built up again. I squeezed my eyes shut tighter, fisting the sheets until my nails ripped the Egyptian cotton.

"Look at me, Eli," Leo's voice boomed with a command I obeyed.

My gaze strayed to the point where his body connected with mine, trailing past his thick corded muscles honed through years of physical activity and up to his face. His devastating, smirking face.

"I lied," he stated, as if we were discussing the weather, and he wasn't ruining the walls of the cabin with the force of his hips.

"About what?" The hazy fog clouding my thoughts cleared up a tiny bit.

"I love it when you look at me. In fact, I might enforce a rule where you're not allowed to look at anyone else but me." His smirk got wider, and so did the distance between my legs.

"You're delusional," I cried out.

"Is that what it is? Or are you unwilling to accept the truth? You do what I tell you to do and when to do it, baby. Whether directly or indirectly, we always cave into each other."

Fuck me, he was right. I was in so deep I feared there was no way out anymore.

But none of that mattered right now. I was lost in the vigorous slam of his groin against mine as he pushed inside of me relentlessly. Leo reached down with his other hand, and a roll of his thumb on my clit was all it took.

We both came apart, my pussy squeezing his dick in a vise grip, hungry for his cum. My leg on his shoulder trembled as the orgasm took and took from both of us until we were drained.

And because if anything, Leo was a man of his word. During round number *I lost count*, he decided to keep his promise of intimately introducing me to the vertical surfaces of the house, as he drilled me against the shower wall. Teasing my breasts like they were his favorite chew toys. Apparently, I wasn't averse to some gasoline fueling the fire. But I guess I should've known that.

I welcomed the fresh breeze in the veranda, resting on a cushioned outdoor chair. It tightened my pores as I took greedy sips of coffee. The wind picked up a bit, but I was prepared today. Armed with some jeans, Malone Souliers booties, and a lavender, fuzzy sweater.

The view I wasn't able to see last night was purely magnificent in broad daylight. Spreading before us, across several acres of unadulterated forest land was a beautiful river. Sunlight bounced off of it, reflecting into stunning rainbow hues in the atmosphere around us.

And if I strained to listen closely, I could hear the running stream of the waterfalls cascading down the side of the rocky range. Or maybe I was mistaking it for the sound of the wind, shifting through the tree branches. Either way, it was the calmest I'd felt in a while.

"The view is incredible," I proclaimed, feeling the scorching coffee spill down my throat. I didn't even care. I was so exhausted, I would inject the coffee in my veins if I could.

"It is, isn't it?" Leo said, averting his gaze once I turned to look at him. Weird. "My family used to spend Christmas and New Year's here when Isabella and I were younger."

"Was it like a tradition of sorts?"

"You could say so. We always looked forward to it. Mom would cook homemade food, and my father put on ESPN and bore us to death with football stats. We were almost normal for two whole weeks."

He gazed wistfully at the black railing on the edge of the deck as if replaying a memory in his mind. I didn't have any siblings, so I couldn't imagine how losing one felt—let alone a twin. My family never was any semblance of put-together either, so I also couldn't relate with how it was for the rug to be pulled from beneath his feet, and for everything to change so drastically.

"What happened? Why did you stop coming?" I asked the question that was implied. Leo looked uncomfortable, fiddling with the sleeves of his gray turtleneck, the scrambled eggs I made him sitting untouched.

I cooked breakfast (or well, lunch, seeing as it was way

past twelve p.m.) since he made dinner. It was only fair I returned the favor, sans the sex. I was spent.

"Some traditions hold others are forgotten." He shrugged like it was no big deal. "Isabella and I entered our teens, and the last thing we wanted to do was spend weeks secluded in a cabin when all our friends were out partying."

Friends—I knew those friends. We used to run in the same social groups until I was cast out. We were all spoiled rotten back then, kids that were handed everything. And the majority of those friends stayed the same, except for Ares. Despite Leo's casual attitude, I could tell that his past priorities bothered him.

I outstretched my hand, tangling our fingers together on the table. "Consider this year a continuation of that custom then. We'll cook together, watch football" —as much as I hated football— "and anything else you'd like to do."

It would be a first for me. I usually spent the holidays alone. Mom was off to tropical vacation number a zillion for the year. And my dad, while a more involved parent, lacked the whole Christmas spirit. His art always came first, and when you love what you do, it becomes your life.

He jerked his head, eyeing me with an indecipherable look, a smile tugging at the corner of his lips. "I'm down." Leo brought the back of my hand to his lips, pecking my skin. "Especially for the 'anything else you'd like to do' part." This time he left a little open-mouthed kiss on the inside of my wrist.

God, I was down for that too. I was starting to crave his presence. While I liked our previous gasoline throwing standoffs, this warm, steady fire that had taken over between us, played on my heart-strings like nothing else.

"So, what's the plan for today?" I cleared my throat, breaking the hold I'd gotten all too consumed in.

"We could go check out the falls if the weather holds up." He finally took a bite out of the eggs I'd prepared. "I haven't been there in forever."

"Do you even remember the road then?" We'd have to walk through a forest, with no visible paths as far as my eyes could see from atop the hill. "Because I don't think a stable GPS connection is possible in this kind of environment."

"Such a city girl. I pegged you for more of a risk-taker, Narcissus."

Of course he had. I'd defied him, cursed him, kissed him, and now had sex with him. Risk-taker should have been my fucking middle name. But seeing as I already had one Leonardo Bianchi and a whole bunch of murderers hunting our asses to deal with, it was best if I didn't add a black bear to the list.

"Forget it, Leo," I deadpanned, shoving the rest of my food in my mouth.

"Alright, what do you want to do?"

I chewed slowly as I thought. It was Sunday, and while we had no classes, we should really focus on our studies more. My stomach churned as it always did at the thought of college. I didn't like my major, but Leo excelled in his. He had already started applying for his master's degree, judging from the dozen college pamphlets I saw on his desk during my stay in his room.

All highly competitive and all far from Astropolis.

The realization that this was all fleeting solidified in the air around me. Playing house with Leo was nice, but I knew from the start it wasn't going to last. We'd eventually go our separate ways. He would inherit his father's billion-dollar company, marry the perfect girl with far fewer issues and baggage than me. And I... I just hoped I'd live to see another day.

I swallowed hard.

Get your head in the game. Focus on what you came here for. Isabella and Francis, this is all for them. You and Leo? Never happening, girl. Have your fun, but keep it clean.

"I want to drive to Long Beach. We still don't have a plan, but at least this time I'm confident you won't storm in, guns blazing."

"Are you implying I don't think before I act?"

"I'm not implying it, I'm stating it. You've got one hell of a temper, Leo." He probably was the most hotheaded person I'd ever come across.

"This wasn't the risk I had in mind." He leaned back, crossing his arms and plowing me with the force of his gaze. "I want to go, but I don't want you to come with me."

"Well, lucky for me, this is the twenty-first century, and women can make decisions for themselves. Besides, if anything goes down, I'll just throw you in front of me."

"Is that so? I know you can handle my load well, baby, but I hadn't pegged you for a professional weightlifter."

I cleared my throat, feeling my blush spread past the neckline of my shirt. Freaking bastard, he always knew what to say to get me wired.

"Right, let's go. It's a two-hour drive, and Lord knows, you might stretch it to four again." I let his words fly, gathering my plate and cup before heading inside. He followed suit, still laughing to himself at the innuendo.

I threw on a coat and reached for the handle, but before I could open the door, Leo closed in behind me, dropping a scorching peck on my cheek from behind. "Thank you," he whispered, his minty breath skating across my skin.

"What for?" My hand tightened on the knob.

"For not giving up when you had every reason to."

"You want some?" Leo asked.

Parked a few feet away from the waterfront property, Leo offered me gummy bears. We grabbed at a gas station stop an hour ago as we waited for something, anything to happen. You couldn't blame my arm for flicking his outstretched hand away after I'd repeated several times that I did not want any freaking gummy bears.

"Rude." He cradled his hand on his chest as if I did any real damage.

"We've been waiting here for forever now," I complained, shifting in my seat. My ass was starting to get numb.

The two-story house was cute. Upper middle-class. It had some pretty pots of flowers on the front. The blooms ranged from red, to yellow, to pink. Apparently, uniformity wasn't in the dictionary of whoever lived here.

While not bad, the home wasn't my father's style. His eye in real estate always went to intricate, albeit cold pieces. This wasn't that. This was homey, the kind of place you'd expect a large family, gather around a fire pit on the rooftop while the waves crashed ashore.

"What did you expect, Narcissus, that the universe would suddenly reveal all of its secrets if you just showed up?"

"No, but I at least—" I cut my sentence short when I caught movement in my peripheral vision.

Like a seagull hunting for fish, my eyes descend upon the object of my fixation. I squinted my eyes against the glare of the sun on the sidewalk. It was a man, probably not much older than me. I couldn't tell, though, seeing as he had his back to us and was walking to the house.

"Son of a bitch." I heard Leo curse next to me. "I'm going to fucking kill him."

"What's the matter?" I asked, but I was too late to the party. Leo exited the car, leaving the driver's door open, and jogged to the moving target.

Fuck.

So much for me being sure he wouldn't do anything rash.

I should get him a leash.

I climbed out of the truck swiftly and locked the doors. "Leo!" I whisper-yelled, power-walking in his direction. By the time I managed to catch up to him though, he was already swinging the stranger around holding on to his collar roughly.

"If it isn't the guy with the death wish." Leo got in his face.

I stepped around him, searching for the source of his contempt. My heart slammed against my chest when I took the person in. I locked my gaze to the curly mop of hair that belonged to none other than Cole.

My supposed friend Cole.

His eyes flicked to me when I gasped in horror. The reusable grocery bags he was holding met the pavement, and he looked like he'd seen a ghost. Like he couldn't believe we were standing here.

"Don't fucking look at her," Leo snarled, looking ready to tear him apart.

"Oh god, Leo! Stop!" I managed to get between them before he lost all sense of sanity. We didn't know why Cole was here, and I was hoping there was a very reasonable explanation behind this.

I pasted my body on Leo's and tried to tug him back, giving Cole some space to breathe.

"What's wrong with you, you fucking cunt?" he wheezed, now able to breathe again. He looked from Leo to me like we were a bunch of freaks. "What the fuck, Eliana? What are you doing with this loser?"

"I'm so sorry." I winced, elbowing Leo behind me when he tried to push forward. This was why you couldn't rely on men. They lacked finesse.

I had to think fast.

"We were walking on the beach, and someone attacked me out of nowhere and stole my purse. He was wearing a similar blue shirt as you. Leo here must have confused you for him." Lie after lie, the words flew out of my mouth before I could filter anything.

Leo's hands tightened on my waist, and I was rooted on the spot. The path leading to the white beach house was just a few inches away.

What are you doing here, Cole?

"We're very sorry," I apologized again, and Leo mirrored my statement gruffly after a shove from me. "Do you live nearby? We'll help you with the bags." I gestured to the spilled groceries.

"Okay, this is weird on so many levels." Cole shook his head, breathing normally once again. "When did you start going out with him?"

"Since none of your business," Leo interjected. "Answer her question, asshat."

I was going to kill him.

I whipped my head around, telling him to shut up through my narrowed eyes. For all we knew, this could be a coincidence. Cole was... he was good to me. He helped me with Serena, made me laugh with his ridiculous texts and tags. We'd gotten very close in school since we shared most classes. I refused to believe he wanted to hurt me.

"What is this, twenty fucking questions?" Cole asked, livid. "No, I don't live nearby. I was shopping at a specific grocery store catering to vegans, as you can see." We all turned to look at a very crushed lettuce.

I started to express my regret again, but the door from the house snapped open. My first instinct was to duck. Alas, the person's words made me freeze in my spot, leaning to Leo for support.

"Cole, what's taking you so long? Bring the groceries inside already." A woman's voice sounded, but I was too caught up in watching Cole's sour face to turn around.

"What was it you said? You don't live here?" Leo chimed in, his tone low and threatening.

Cole wasn't able to come up with another lie, though. The color drained from his face when the woman suddenly materialized next to him, looking at us through curious brown eyes. "Who do we have here; are these your friends, Cole?"

There was an air of familiarity when I looked at the woman. She had tight curls, and her skin tone was a tad too dark to be considered tan. It shone, speaking of an easy life, and didn't give much away in terms of wrinkles. I could see slight similarities between her and Cole in the flare of her nostrils and full lips.

Leo hugged me to his side as he took it upon himself to introduce us to the woman. Her name was Lylah, and she was Cole's mother, and they *did* live in the neighborhood.

In the very house my dad frequented.

My stomach churned when her eyes flashed upon hearing my name. The bad feeling in my gut intensified when Cole wouldn't meet my eyes when they invited us inside for a cup of coffee.

I opted for chamomile tea instead. My lips didn't touch the ceramic cup containing the piping hot liquid, though. I was too busy scanning the place as Leo grilled Lylah for answers.

This is such a nice property, and how long have you lived here? The questions fleeted past my ears as I stayed unceremoniously quiet for once.

I stripped the beige walls with my eyes. There was nothing left to look at, though. They were already bare. No signs of frozen moments between a happy family. The only person featured in Cole's baby pictures lingering in the hall when we walked past was Lylah. A mother and her son, no father in sight.

My throat felt dryer than haystack as I started reaching my own conclusions. I hung on the details of Cole's face, Leo's chatter with Lylah mere background noise. He squirmed under my blatant stare.

His gray eyes were so similar to the ones that raised me. The only difference being specks of brown, breaking through the sea of silver. His upturned nose, the boyish set of his jaw, his much lighter skin tone.

I wanted to throw up. I pressed my hand on my stomach,

trying to keep the bile threatening to spew down. God, how could I be so stupid? How did people always manage to stun me? Deceive me?

"Will your husband be joining us anytime soon?" My question sliced through their conversation. It was rude and nosey, intensifying the preexisting tension in the air.

"No, I'm not married," Lylah answered reluctantly.

"Divorced?" I persisted.

"N-no, I was never married."

I laced my fingers with Leo's under the table to assure myself that this was real. Albeit clueless, he squeezed my hand, rolling his thumb over my knuckles. Cole shifted uncomfortably in his wooden chair once my attention snapped back to him.

"What's the matter, Cole? Cat got your tongue?"

"Eliana, I..." He started but never followed through with the rest of his sentence. He heaved a deep sigh, reclining in his wooden chair.

"You what, you fucking liar? Or should I say, *bastard*?" I scoffed.

His silence perturbed me. Lylah's too. They knew what I was talking about, and they weren't denying it. Needles of discomfort pricked my eyelids as the world shifted beneath my feet. The one thing grounding me right now was Leo's steady presence beside me.

I didn't want to lose it.

Fuck, I *couldn't* lose it.

I needed answers.

I pulled a big breath in my lungs, and it came out scattered. "Were you ever going to tell me?"

"I was. I swear I was going to tell you." His response was frantic. "I wanted to ease you into it. I couldn't really say it outright. Think about it. You would've thought I was a crazy person." He laughed like one at the end of his sentence.

"You had no idea of knowing what I'd think," I yelled, and everyone jumped.

Calm down.

Breath in through your nose, and out through your mouth.

Oh, who was I kidding? Not even my old therapist's advice held ground right now.

"Okay, someone needs to tell me what the hell is going on right fucking now," Leo hissed, putting an end to our fight.

"You want to do the honors?" I asked Cole, my brows raising. "Get the opportunity to come clean for once? Might feel good to get things off your chest." I taunted.

He shook his head at me but proceeded to destroy whatever integrity remained between me and my parents. "Francis Roux is also my father. Eliana is my half-sister."

Lylah whimpered by Cole's side and a slew of curse words left Leo's tongue.

And here I was. Little old Eliana, the most naïve, dumb bitch in the world. *Claire this, and Claire that.* I criticized her for everything, judging her extramarital activities when daddy dearest wasn't far behind himself. But of course, who else would bear the brunt of a failed relationship if not the woman?

She had an affair.

He had a second fucking family.

I pushed down the wave of tears that came at me. I shifted my gaze to Lylah, any shred of respect fleeting out the window.

I wouldn't ask for details. I didn't want to know anything about their relationship. Another wave of nausea hit at the mere thought. I breathed slowly, focusing on the matter at hand—the reason why we showed up in the first place.

"Was Francis here the day and hour, a girl's body from the case was pronounced as deceased?"

Leo stiffened at the mention of Isabella.

"He was." She pushed out with a sigh, massaging her temples with her fingers. I didn't feel an ounce of sympathy. So she had to deal with the headache of *one* confrontation. I had had to put up with all kinds of shit from my parents ever since I was old enough to walk.

I was surrounded by evil and sinners, and the fear that I'd end up like them paralyzed me sometimes. I just wanted to be fucking normal. I didn't want to deal with secret families, or babies, or engagements, or half-sibling, and stepsiblings.

It was funny how we didn't appreciate what we had until it was gone. I went from complaining about being alone to craving that sense of solitude once again. The voices in my head were getting too much for me to deal with.

"Then why didn't you say something the day of the trial?" Leo sneered. "I don't assume it was because you didn't want to ruin any families?"

He did have the perfect alibi.

Why didn't he use it?

Lylah's face twisted at Leo's jab. "Francis didn't want me to. He knew something was going on behind the scenes and didn't want me and Cole involved. He'd rather take the fall than involve us."

But he was perfectly fine with abandoning me.

Bitterness swirled deep inside me, and a tangy taste bloomed in my mouth, taking over with vigor. I realized it was blood when Leo tugged my bottom lip from the confinements of my teeth. They were all looking at me, and I wanted to crawl inside a hole and die.

Forever an orphan. I was convinced now more than ever that my parents never gave a shit about me. So what? I had myself, and that was all that mattered. Right?

"I'm truly sorry, Eliana. I didn't mean for this to happen. I couldn't go against Francis's wishes, and I also didn't want to put my son in harm's way."

"I see." I nodded.

I was beyond over this conversation. All I wanted to do was go home and cuddle up in my favorite villain's arms until he eventually left me too.

Leo got my disposition without me having to spell out anything to him. His chair scraped against the wooden floors as he got up, taking me with him too.

"Wait. What are you going to do now?" Lylah asked me.

My father's wishes or not, she withheld valuable information, and in the eyes of the law that was considered as aiding and abetting.

No one was ever supposed to find out my family's best-kept secret. Both sides kept their mouths muzzled when it came to each other because if one went down, the other one couldn't help but follow.

"Nothing she'll share with you," Leo answered on my behalf, and I could've kissed him right then and there.

"Eliana, can we please talk, alone?" Cole insisted, hands clenched on top of the table.

I realized no part of this was his fault. However, I couldn't look at him without being reminded of my father's betrayal. It cut deep. Deeper than Claire's because I never saw this one coming.

"No." I shook my head, letting Leo lead me to the exit.

"All the talking is done, Cole. In fact, I'd be grateful if you stayed as far away from me as possible."

We left that godforsaken place as fast as our feet allowed us to. I wished I'd never stepped foot inside. When I did, it claimed a piece of my soul, and I was already running short. I didn't have anything more left to give.

I didn't miss how the person that was supposed to destroy me was the one that spooned me to sleep that night as my sobs wrecked his shirt. Leo held me close, wrapped his arms around me, and shared some of his strength.

Chapter 21

ELIANA

Vindication.

That was the running theme of the day.

The rumor mill had spread while I remained MIA on social media. The video where Serena went apeshit and got arrested had gotten over five hundred thousand views. And was being exploited for eye-catching articles by every news outlet in Astropolis.

People were tweeting, sharing, and talking about it everywhere. Carter called me every single day until I blocked his number. All the students in Dane were discussing it too. Whispers accompanied me everywhere I went, but this time hateful side-eyes and sarcastic snickers didn't follow.

Serena Laurent was a social piranha, and it was all my doing.

Red rimmed eyes stared back at me as I splashed my face with some cold water in the bathroom. Either the mirror was playing tricks on me, or my complexion had truly gone to shit.

I looked sick, no better than I did at the beginning of the school year. I was treading on thin ice. One more misstep, and water would swallow me whole. Every time I eradicated a problem, two more reared their ugly heads in its midst. It was like I was battling a Hydra, and the fact that I didn't possess Herculean power was becoming painfully obvious.

A bathroom stall creaked on the far left side of the bathroom. I didn't pay it any mind. I continued lathering my hands with soap, trying to drain my hectic thoughts.

"I never thought you had in you, you know." Serena's voice startled me. I snapped my gaze to the mirror, catching her reflection behind me. Poison swirled behind her honey-colored eyes, and my hackles raised. "You were the perfect doormat for so long. I guess I never took into consideration that when you're surrounded by monsters, you start to become one yourself."

She sauntered to the sink next to me, fixing her hair and straightening her red leather jacket and black skirt. Even fallen from grace, she looked more put together than I ever would. "You must be ecstatic, I presume. The snake finally got what she deserved, huh?"

"It's not my fault your head grew too big for your body, Serena." I turned the faucet off, tilting my chin up. "We both know you're not the victim here. I don't have any time for your games."

"It's never your fault, is it? But of course, Eliana can never do anything wrong. Her hair is always shiny, her smile always perfect, her body more toned than Teyana fucking Taylor's. I bet you shit gold too, don't you?" She chuckled. "I used to lose sleep wondering what it took to shine brighter than a Roux. Even at the bottom of the totem pole, you gleamed brighter than the peak."

I tilted my shoulders back. Her jealousy pooled around me as she sank her teeth in my character. Serena's description didn't represent me in the slightest, but she was so lost in her envy, her vision was clouded.

"Why are you telling me this? Am I to blame for your shortcomings too?"

"Oh no, not at all." She shook her head, lips twisting into a painful smile. "I am telling you this for me. Because no matter how untouchable you seemed, I finally realized that you're not all that much better than I am. My insecurities are mine, but you aren't without your own. Ain't that right little miss perfect? Wasn't I the one that drove you past your breaking point?"

I blinked, biting my tongue. "So what if you were? You want an award for being a shitty human being?"

"I want you to stare at the mirror and take a good look at who you've become, Eliana. We're both shitty, honey. The only difference is that I've been this way longer." She flipped her hair over her shoulder. "Welcome to the club."

My stomach lurched at her words. I thought I'd feel good, powerful. I'd finally showed her up, but all day I was having flashbacks to when I went through the same thing. No matter how much I tried, I didn't enjoy hurting others like they hurt me.

"You and I could never be part of the same club. I don't deny being a beast, but we're not the same kind of animal, Serena. What you're experiencing is a counteract of your viciousness."

"Is it? Carter is threatening to send me off to some god-awful boarding school for the rest of the year, so congratulations. You managed to get rid of me while your real enemies are still sitting pretty in their imaginary thrones."

I winced. The Pyrrhic victory hung heavy on my shoulders. "Their thrones are made of glass."

"They might be." Retrieving a lip gloss tube from her backpack, she proceeded to put some color on her ashy lips. "But then again, no one ever mastered breaking them."

"Was that why you never tried? Or did you fear losing as much as they did if you came out successful?"

It was her turn to wince, and I got my answer.

A humorless smirk took over my lips as I stepped away, fixing my backpack on my shoulder. "I never claimed to be a virginal queen, Serena. I get petty, jealous, and spiteful as much as the next girl, but at least I have a backbone, and I sincerely hope you find yours. If not for yourself, then do it for Amelia."

The lip gloss she was holding slipped from her fingers and rattled on the sink. Her eyes got misty, like they always did at the mention of her mother. *Good.* An influx of emotions built inside my chest, and as much as I hated the bitch, I hated what she had become more. She'd grown so accustomed in her mean girl persona, she'd lost herself. She'd lost the ability to feel and see anything beyond the narrow walls of her mind.

No matter how much I didn't want her to fail, it wasn't my job to help her find her way anymore, so I made a beeline for the door. I'd shown her the courtesy of pointing out her wounds, stitching them back together was on her.

"Eliana?" Her soft-spoken question stopped me mid-stride.

I tilted my head to watch her, but she wasn't looking at me. Her head was bent as she continued examining herself in the mirror, and I noticed, for the first time that same as me, she was sporting very similar red rims around her eyes.

"Yeah?"

Serena's shoulders shook as she took a deep breath. "You forgave Leo."

A statement, not a question, nonetheless I deigned it with a response. "I did."

"Why?"

Such a simple question. Then why did it make my mouth run dry and my toes curl as my heart picked up its speed into NASCAR mode?

"He apologized." The response flew out of my mouth like butter. I rubbed my hand along the back of my neck, over the cold sweat that had accumulated there.

"Is that really all it takes?" Serena raised a single brow at me through the mirror.

"Why? Do you want to try your luck?"

"No," she snorted as she turned to look at me. Her shoulders were slumped, posture passive, and I could tell she was enjoying this just as much as I was. "I was just amazed by how well you continue to lie to yourself after all these years." She got closer, her small statue inches below me. "We're not thirteen anymore, Eli."

"Could have fooled me," I replied, swallowing hard. She was leading to a dead end, I'd found my way to one too many times, and I didn't like it. Dead ends made everyone skittish, and I was no different.

We'd both changed a lot during the past two years, but our ability to read each other remained static. That was usually the case when you shared a childhood with someone. She could see past my bullshit with little effort.

"You didn't forgive Leo because he apologized. You did

so because you love him." She pointed her finger at me. "You didn't care that *I* saw him first. You just had to have him. And Leo being Leo, he took one look at the ice queen and couldn't help but want to melt her frigid heart."

She didn't touch me, but she might as well have pushed me. I stumbled back from the weight of her words, the sky-high walls I'd build crashed, and all it took was a few sentences.

Leo did not want to melt my ice-cold heart. He wanted to conquer it, leave its mark on it and move on to other viable territories. Once the novelty wore off, his attention would wean.

I didn't love him.

I couldn't be stupid enough to love him.

"Do you know what they say? We tend to attach ourselves to the people that remind us of our parents." Her hand came to my hair, tugging at a gold strand as she forced my flighty gaze to hers. "So who's really the coward here, Eliana? Me for not taking a stand? Or you for trading in one demon for another?"

My chest shuddered as I swatted her hand away. "Shut the fuck up Serena. You have no idea what you're talking about."

"I mean, I get it. Wind feels better than fire." A sugary sweet smile spread on her face before she snapped her mouth closed. "But get off your high horse, honey. Earth is where humans are supposed to be."

I got home late.

My feet were blistered from dancing my ass off for the

past five hours, and every muscle groaned like my body had gotten crushed under a Mack truck. A Christmas performance was underway at Bella's, but I chose to sit this one out and help out with the choreography instead.

I could never escape the limelight, but at least I could try and blend in. Foreign eyes on me were something I did not need at the moment.

I fumbled with a keyhole, knowing who waited for me inside. No matter how dog tired I was, practice after school had been a good thing. I managed to avoid Leo throughout the whole day. It wasn't hard to do since we didn't share any classes together.

Serena infiltrated my mind like poison. I knew my relationship with Leo had an expiration date since day one. That this was just a fun exploration until we reached our goal. Yet her words still swirled around in my brain like a broken record.

Leonardo Bianchi could've been temporary in my life, but he was permanent in my heart. He'd tattooed his name on it with big fat letters, and like the typography slut that I was, I couldn't help falling for it.

The door flew open, and I squeaked, stumbling back and losing my balance. I heard Leo curse under his breath and snapping to action, catching me before my ass met the cold ground underneath.

"I got you, I got you," he repeated and I clung to him.

"God, where were you going with such speed? You startled me." I said as he straightened us up. He looked good—I'd be shocked if he didn't—in his red, Neil Barrett hoodie and gray sweatpants.

Yup, real good, all eight inches of him.

I bit my lip.

Gotta love sweatpants season.

"You were about to drill a hole through the door, so I thought I'd help you out." Leo grinned, ushering me inside and taking my coat.

A delicious aroma permeated the air of the hallway. It smelled like Christmas had puked all over the wooden floors, like cinnamon with a touch of spice. My stomach growled in response.

"Well, what kind of multimillion-dollar cabin does not have light outside of the door?" I frowned, following him to the living room.

"The kind that houses monsters, sweetheart. We only come out in the dark." He winked back at me, and my heart dipped.

Leo wasn't someone you came across a lot. The arches of his body, the square of his jaw, they looked as if they were carved by a sculptor. And his eyes—*his eyes* were a brilliant green that left you dizzy. He was unnatural almost.

Rare as a blood diamond and deadly as one too.

He had everything he needed.

Charm, money, power, *adoration*.

What did he want from me? Was I really letting a monster slither his way into my heart?

"You coming?" Leo asked, and I realized I'd stopped short, lost in my thoughts.

Fuck, I could not let Serena influence me like this. What did she know? She was just a sad little girl that got called out on her shit and was looking to lash out. Besides, what if I had a thing for monsters? *Belle* certainly did, and she came out winning. And if *I* didn't, I was rich enough to afford therapy. After all, what was one more scar when I had an entire collection of them?

"Yeah." I mobilized my feet again.

"What's going on in that overactive brain of yours?"

"Just wondering who'll be the one you take a bite out of next." I tried to sound smart, but my stomach growled again and I blushed.

"Lucky for you, I'm on a diet and you're the only person on my menu." A small smirk developed on Leo's lips. "But let's feed you first, I like a woman with some meat on her bones."

I rolled my eyes. I didn't know if I should consider that an insult or not, but my retort caught in my throat when I caught sight of the dining table. It was brimming with food. A roasted turkey sat in the middle, surrounded by all kinds of seasonal dishes. Green beans, mashed potatoes, cranberry sauce, *hell,* there were pies as well.

"Are you expecting any friends?" I asked, inspecting the pretty gold silverware.

"No, this is all for us."

"It is?" I whispered. "You cooked all this for us?"

I walked closer to the table, and my eyes grew misty when I saw that he'd taken it upon himself to put up a Christmas tree too. It stood across the fireplace, making the room brighter with its fairy lights.

I didn't know what to think.

"Well, no, not really. If I had, it wouldn't look as pretty as it does now, and I imagine it would taste way crispier." Leo pulled out a seat for me, grinning. "But I did set everything up, I think that earns me an A for effort."

This was surreal. The wood in the fireplace crackled, and the lump in my throat grew. I hadn't celebrated Christmas in so long, I'd forgotten what it felt like to have people by your side this time of year. To not be lonely when romance hung heavy in the air.

"You can take the whole alphabet," I croaked, getting closer, but I didn't sit down.

"I'll settle for a kiss—*for now*." His head tilted to the ceiling. I followed his gaze up, and low and behold, he'd hung a mistletoe... *right above my chair*.

An unladylike snort came out of my mouth, and I chuckled. "You've really thought of everything."

"Always." He cupped my cheeks. "When it comes to you, I always think of everything."

Warmth spread in my chest as I looked in at his eyes and crooked smile. No one had ever put all this effort into *me*. Not any other guys. Nor my family. But *he* did, and I'd cherish this memory forever.

My eyes stung, and emotions that had built slid down my cheeks. A frown marred Leo's face as he wiped my tears, tugging me closer, concern lining the creases of his face. "What's wrong?"

"N-nothing," I stammered. "I-I've never done this before. I've always been alone during the holidays, while everyone gathered with their families. This is happy tears."

By the end of my speech, he'd closed his mouth on mine, and I tangled my hands in his hair. Little bursts of electricity zinged down my body as his mouth moved on top of mine. My heart pumped blood faster at the thought of getting used to this. I couldn't fathom finding this kind of chemistry again with someone else.

The kiss didn't go much further. It was sweet and all-consuming at the same time. I pulled back before I ruined it with my snot, smiling into his mouth. He pecked my nose, and I sniffled, pulling a laugh from him. "My next goal? Making you cry happy tears in bed."

I laughed. "Alright, Casanova, let's eat first."

Dinner was nice. Leo cut the turkey, and I fixed the food on our plates. He told me about the progress his mom had made in the rehab facility. She was having a rough time, but at least she was pulling through, and that was all that mattered. A stab of guilt pierced my heart as he talked about her, and I didn't go easy on the wine.

I didn't drink much anyway, but tonight I just wanted to feel lighter. Embrace the present and not worry about the past or future like I always did. Leo aided the process of taking my mind off things, and I enjoyed his chatter, especially when his eyes lightened as he talked about his future career and all the plans he had about transitioning his father's big oil company into a greener path.

"What about you?" he asked out of nowhere. "Do you know what you want to do after you graduate?"

I took another swig of the bitter white wine, and maybe it was the alcohol coursing through my veins, but I found the power to admit out loud what I'd never told anyone, out of fear that they'd think I was less than.

"I'm thinking of dropping out."

"What? Why?"

I proceeded when I didn't see any judgment in his eyes, just genuine curiosity. "I never really liked biotechnology. I didn't really hate it either. I went into it because college was supposed to be the answer to a stable future. Living off my inheritance didn't sit right. I thought Dad won his money at the expense of others, and I couldn't possibly sleep well at night with that knowledge tugging at my conscience."

"That's fair." He nodded. "Besides, you still have plenty of time to figure out what you want to do."

"I know what I want to do." I shrugged, wiping the precipitation off my wine glass. "I want to open my own dance studio, but it probably won't work. No one here would sign up. They wouldn't want to associate with someone like me. Even if we manage to clear my dad's name, my mom is still likely involved."

And as crazy as it sounded, I didn't want to move away from Astropolis. I was a creature of habit and stubborn as fuck. They wouldn't drive me out of here.

"Anything is possible, Eliana." Leo took my hand, trapping it under the heat of his fist, and I looked at him. His face told me he believed in me more than I ever would. "You can step away from your parents' shadows and build your own presence. Social media is everything, and with the right plan, you can sell anything you want. I know *you* can do it. Look at everything you've overcome to get here."

I shook my head and bit my lower lip. His words filled me with hope. His trust in me was touching. "You're really determined to make me cry today, huh?"

He smiled, kissing the back of my hand. "Let's keep this between us, Narcissus. Or all my street cred will go down the drain."

I laughed again for the thousandth time that night. My cheeks hurt from smiling so damn much. And when we went to bed, barely able to catch our breaths, our limbs a delicious tangled mess, I thought I could get used to this.

I also prayed that he wanted the same.

That he wasn't ashamed of sleeping with the enemy.

Chapter 22

LEONARDO

Six weeks passed like water. It was funny how time flew when you weren't a miserable fuck for once in your life.

I got her a red pair of *Casadei Blade* pumps—I'd found her searching for online—for Christmas. I got to fuck her wearing fuck all but those heels too. The blade-like stilettos dug in my back soon as the clock struck midnight, January first. You could say we started the new year off with a bang.

I hadn't received any calls from Ethan. I wasn't too broken up over it either. Trying to juggle *that shitshow* while preparing for graduation nearly crippled me. We both needed some time to just unplug and act our fucking age.

I knew the whole situation with Cole still bothered Eliana.

He called at least once a day until I picked up and threatened to cut his dick off. I guess he valued his reproductive organs more and hung up on my face. I got it though, I don't think I could go a day without fucking Eliana now. If there were any sex world records, we'd probably broken them all by now... *okay, most. I'd be realistic, there were some freaks out there.*

The police still hadn't gotten back to Eliana about the break-in. And now, *that*, I had a problem with. They weren't even trying to hide what a bordello of corruption they'd become. But unless they wanted to burn like whores in hell, they'd get off their asses.

"Are you ready to order yet, sir?" one of the waitresses at Café Nova asked me again.

I hadn't ordered anything for the past thirty minutes I was sitting here. Alessio Bianchi ran by the mantra, *you're not late, everyone else is simply early,* like the princess that he was. The only reason why I'd agreed to meet with him in the first place was because I needed his connections to keep Eliana safe.

But I think I'd suffered through watching people order overpriced lattes, just to take a thousand pictures by a pink and purple flower wall, for far too long. Whatever, if he wanted to be a cunt and ignore his family, I guess I could be that way too, when he grew old enough to need assisted living.

"You know what? I changed my mind. I won't be—" I started but was cut short when an all suited up Alessio Bianchi graced me with his long-awaited presence.

He rocked a tan that stood out against his silver watch and white dress shirt. His brown hair held highlights that weren't previously there. I could see what held him off so many months. *Definitely an important business transaction, most likely in Cabo, Mexico.*

"Could you give us a second?" he addressed the waitress

first, falling into his chair. "We'll call for you when we're ready."

I interjected before the petite brunette burst a blood vessel. She was looking at us like she wanted the ground to swallow us whole. I ordered a doppio espresso for him, and a café corretto for me—heavy on the brandy. Judging by the dark circles under his eyes when he removed his aviators, he looked like he'd seen better days. And I needed something stronger to deal with him this early in the morning.

I'd left Eli sleeping in bed when I could've woken her up with my head between her legs, but duty called. I already knew why he'd called me here. He'd caught wind that mom was in rehab.

"What happened? Were all your personal drivers unavailable?" I tore into him as soon as we were left alone.

"As a matter of fact, I drove myself today."

"That explains it then," I scoffed. "Did you lose your way? It's been a while since you last stepped foot in Astropolis."

He smoothed his hair back, stifling a sigh. "*Hello, son. How are you?*"

"Fine. Not thanks to you."

I took a sip of my coffee when it was placed in front of me. My blue cotton shirt I was clung to my back despite it being January. This was going to be tricky. I hadn't even thought about how to breach the topic of Eliana, let alone how to talk to him about it after I put Mom in rehab without his consent.

"So, what's this all about?" I asked, playing dumb.

"You really don't know?" He raised a brow.

I did, but rule number one of *interrogation for dummies*:

never confirm any speculation first. I leaned back on the bistro chair, legs wide as I waited for him to get on with it.

"You shouldn't have signed your mom in at Lake House," Dad spit out.

"The only thing I regret is not doing it sooner." I shrugged.

"I guess the thought of consulting with her husband and your father didn't cross your mind, huh, Leonardo?"

"It's not like you've been much of a husband or a father these past four years. Otherwise, you would've listened the last three-thousand times I tried to talk to you about Mom's drinking problem." I took another casual sip of coffee. "If you like to sit and watch while your wife wastes away, then that's on you. I attended Dane *because* that way I could take care of her, but I don't plan on living with my parents until I turn fifty."

"You have no idea what I've been doing for the past four years, so don't sit around passing on judgment like you're omnipresent." He almost sprayed his espresso all over me.

I fixed him with a narrowed gaze. His mouth was just begging to be split open so he'd put a sock on all the lies. "It's not that hard to guess, but here, let me try. Was it Destiny, Chastity, or *wait...* Jewel?"

He gave me a blank expression, yet his eyes seemed more alive than they had in years. Every time I spoke to him before, I wasn't sure if he was listening to me or not. His mask was starting to chip, though.

"What? Am I still wrong?" I questioned, shoving my balled fists in my pockets. "All three then? *Ah*, I see. One person is too vanilla for you now?"

"Enough!" Alessio's chair scraped back with a screeching

sound as he slapped the table. His roar echoed around the tiny café, and people all around took curious glances at us.

"Lower your voice," I hissed through my teeth. "I can make a scene too. You have a very excessive list of debauchery I could broadcast at any moment."

He retreated at my threat. People already hated the rich simply because they were *rich*. When their dirty deeds met the world of social media, they exploded. I could ruin his reputation with a simple touch of a screen.

"You have no right coming back and demanding answers as if it's your prerogative. You can't expect respect when you won't show any in return." I set him straight. "And as for Mom, she *will* stay in rehab until I'm confident she is better. If you try to mess with her recovery in any kind of way, I will end you."

I fucking would.

I didn't care about his money or the eight-figure inheritance that was undoubtedly waiting for me. I'd made enough connections these past four years in college and scored internships with top companies. I didn't need him. I could pave my own path.

"I see." Alessio took a deep breath, setting his identical gaze dead on me. "I'm sorry you felt abandoned. That was never my intention."

I'm sorry you felt abandoned.

You did fucking abandon us, asshole.

I bit my lip, refraining from wasting any more of my energy.

"Barbara can continue her treatment. I wasn't aware things were that bad—I just didn't want to draw any unnecessary attention to our family. Lord knows we get an abundance of scrutiny as it is." He closed his eyes, exhaling through his nose. "*I love her. I do.*"

"I'm not the one you should be saying that to," I spoke flatly. He nodded solemnly, and I was having a hard time believing he was being so agreeable. This was a turn of events.

"I also wanted to talk to you about something else." He smoothed some lint off his pants, back into his proverbial diplomat mode. "Carter Laurent invited us to attend his daughter's birthday party."

"*Serena's* birthday party?" Considering how we'd left things last time, I was sure my ears were playing tricks on me. She didn't have any reason to invite me there unless she knew I wanted to stab Carter as much as she did.

"I think that's her name."

He didn't even know her name, yet he was telling me about this, why?

"Anyway, I'm going to need you to cancel whatever plans you have for next week. Since your mother can't be here, you'll accompany me. Consider it a learning experience," he prompted. "Niels Van de Berg will be there, and we've been talking about how we can cut back Europe's reliance on Russia for gas."

Dad never enjoyed Carter's presence. Not that he had ever flat out said so, but his disregard for him had. People started to notice, and Carter has been trying to suck up to him for years now. I guess he studied him long enough to know that the Dutch energy minister would get his attention.

"Yeah... I'm going to take a hard pass." He could've invited the queen of England and I still wouldn't have attended. I kept my contempt to a minimum though, he didn't know what hid behind Carter's businesses.

He shook his head. "I wasn't asking Leonardo. You will come."

"I'm sensing there's an or else coming." I crossed my hands over my chest.

"Or else your little vacation with Eliana Roux is going to be cut short."

What. The. Fuck.

Fucking.

Bastard.

There was no way he knew. Maybe he'd heard we'd gotten closer together, it wasn't like we were trying to hide it anyway, but I'd been careful. So fucking careful when we relocated. I'd even stretched the journey to four hours making sure we weren't being followed.

This was a bluff. It had to be.

"What are you talking about?" I demanded.

"You know very well what I'm talking about." It was his time to act casual while I stewed in my fucking corner. "And you probably care a little too much about it, considering she's got you talking to men like Ethan White."

I went still, searching for some equilibrium in this messed-up plot fucking twist, but came up blank. For an absentee father, he sure has been keeping tabs on my life.

A blinding inferno raged inside my skull, and before I got the chance to burn him with it, he peeked at his watch. "*Fucking* with the enemy is not the way we roll in this family, Leonardo. You're exempt this time because I'm late for a meeting, but we'll be talking about this in length son of mine." He drawled, rising to his feet. For once, I was at a complete loss of words.

"I expect to see you at the party."

ELIANA

Sand was everywhere.

Inside the pockets of my jeans, in between my toes, tangled in my loosely hung hair. It was ironic really how such a small entity could be so chaotic, yet I'd never felt more peaceful.

It could be the fact that I had a front-row view at a seagull trying to steal a couple's picnic. The chuckle that escaped my mouth turned into a cough when the girl caught me staring and glared. I retracted my gaze quickly, to the foamy waves crashing by the shore.

"Eliana?" I twisted around at the sound of my name falling from Cole's lips.

I never believed in forgiving and forgetting. Putting your trust in someone that betrayed it in the first place was plain dumb to me. But if I managed to forgive Leo for *way* more than omitting the truth, then I could forgive Cole too. *My brother Cole.*

"I got your text. You wanted to talk?" he said stiffly, as if he wasn't sure if I was still mad or not.

I tried to push the bitterness that clung to my heart down, patting the sand beside me. In truth, a piece of my soul would always be jealous. Cole had gotten our father's protection, while I was left for dead. Blindfolded in the dark.

However, that wasn't *his* fault. I couldn't blame him for other people's choices.

He sat next to me, most likely staining the hell out of his white pants.

I didn't give him any time to settle before I started speaking, looking out at the ocean. "When I was twelve years old, a little asshole at a barbecue party almost drowned me in the pool."

Cole made a choking sound. "Why would he do that?"

"I kneed him in the balls for trying to kiss an unwilling Serena. No means no, and he needed a little kick to learn that lesson." I shrugged, a rueful smile taking over my lips at the memory. He'd screamed like a little bitch. "He was the son of the senator at the time and thought he was a big deal because his father pocketed hush money from the rich. My mom got to the scene first and she freaked."

"Did she get in trouble for pulling him off of you?"

"Huh." An unladylike snort escaped me. "More like she would've let him drown me and hid the evidence if Dad hadn't walked in right behind her a few seconds later."

Cole's head made a sharp turn in my direction at my confession. "She wouldn't have done that, she's your mother."

"In her mind, her role as a socialite with a big circle of influence comes first." That was a fact I begrudgingly accepted a long time ago. Not all mothers connected with their children the way we wanted them to.

Despite that, it was still hard to swallow every time I thought about it. I closed my eyes, sighing before I continued. "Anyway, Francis proceeded to berate the kid publicly, which got us kicked out of social functions for a while. Mom was ready to disown both of us. He didn't care though. He took me out for ice cream for a week straight after."

I rested my cheek on my knee, turning to look at him.

Questions swam in his eyes at my sudden departure down memory lane. Oh, how good it felt to hold all the cards for once. To drive and have everyone else follow.

"When I broke my leg at a dance recital when I was thirteen, he was there every step of the way. Even refused to leave when the doctor ordered him out."

"That's not the smartest way to go about it." Cole cringed.

"You're right, it's not." I smiled and his eyes lit up too.

The medical staff didn't appreciate his resistance, that was for sure. But me? Little Eliana loved having her daddy's attention. I didn't have any grandparents and my parents didn't have any siblings. Like me, they were only children. Dad was the light in my void.

"So you can see how I'd always been daddy's little girl. He always told me I was the brightest star in his sky." I sighed at the memories Cole's identical gray eyes induced. "When I found out his words were nothing but lies, though, that same sky came crashing down on me."

"I understand," Cole said, hands toying with the hem of his shirt. "Although, I don't think he lied. He talked about you like you hung the moon."

At least you knew I existed.

I bit my retort down. My guilt for not visiting my father's grave ever since the funeral toyed with me every step of the way, but there was a reason why I let it gnaw at my insides freely. I had to forge my own path to healing and ultimately forgiving him for all the things he did and didn't do.

I reached for Cole's fumbling hand and embraced it. "Moral of the story, I want to say I'm sorry. I found my peace in placing all of the blame on your shoulders when you were just a kid. I admire how you reached out to me and I-I love our friendship, and I don't want to lose you."

A stunning smile took over his face, and any lingering negativity went out the window. He tugged me forward, and I fell into his embrace, basking in his woodsy scent. This would take some getting used to, but I finally—*finally* had someone on my team. Wasn't that how siblings were supposed to be? Always there for each other.

"I am sorry too," he started, once we came apart. "I should've told you earlier, I was just nervous, and my mom thought it would be best if I kept my mouth shut. She pleaded with me to come back to New York with her before she left."

"She thought I'd blab." It wasn't a question, but he nodded anyway.

In all honesty, I would've. If I hadn't gotten to know Cole as well as I had, I wouldn't care about what happened to him. He'd become more than a brother in name only, and I didn't want him caught in the crossfire.

"How did they meet, do you know? I've been trying to place your mom, but my mind comes up blank every time."

"My mom's an artist too. She used to be an intern at Dad's Gallery, and that's how they met. She didn't run in the same social circles as him, it was simply a chance of fate. At least that's what she tells me." Cole shook his head when he caught the far-off look in my head, proceeding to change the uncomfortable subject.

"Soo..." He stretched out the word, placing his hands on the sand behind him. "You and Bianchi, huh? How did that come to be?" He wiggled his brows in question.

"How much time do you have? 'Cause that's a long story."

My ringing phone pulled me short from opening my car door. After declining Cole's invitation to head on over to his house for coffee—I told him not to push it—I was on my way to Dane.

I was going to do it.

I'd drop out.

There was no point in me wasting any more effort and money on something I didn't love doing.

Officer Allen's name flashed on my screen, and I slid it open quickly. It'd taken them about a month and a half to call me, but I'd answer anyway. "Hello?"

"Eliana Roux?" His gravelly voice sounded through the receiver.

"Yes, this is she," I replied, hopping in the car so I could hear better. The air ravaging the open space was making it hard for me to listen over the whistling noise in my ears.

"We're going to need you to come on over to the Astropolis Police Department, Ms. Roux. We have some news regarding the state of the ongoing investigation."

Chapter 23

ELIANA

They'd found them.

The rest of the missing girls.

They'd fucking found them.

My lungs burned as I tried to keep up with the choreography, but my head wasn't in the game. I was floating back to yesterday, the detective's words replaying in my thoughts.

"Do you recognize his voice, Ms. Roux?" the detective asked, pausing the video feed on the wall-mounted TV.

"I do."

I did. The low timbre of the intruder's voice with an underlying growl spoke to my nightmares, making the flames rage. I felt his ghost touch pressing around my neck as I tried to swallow.

"That's him. I know it is."

The police officer nodded, a grim look on his face. He was younger than most of the staff, probably in his early twenties judging by the lack of wrinkles on his tan skin.

New blood.

Yet, he held the most authority. I could tell from the way his colleagues shifted uncomfortably around him.

"I thought so. We're sorry for keeping you waiting this long, but the deeper we dug into the suspect, we found ties involving him to a human trafficking ring on the east coast. Brooklyn." He scrubbed a hand down the length of his face, and my blood pumped faster.

"Do the names Zena Steele, Kira Vang, and Emily Haviliard ring a bell, Ms. Roux?"

They were alive.

They were alive.

And my dad wasn't that prime suspect, judging by the onslaught of questions that followed about my relationship with Carter and Claire.

"Eliana, what's wrong with you today?" The head choreographer appeared in front of me, cutting off my non-existent rhythm. "You're missing all the steps, messing up the whole choreo."

I rested my hands on my knees as I started up at her tight face. I didn't even want to come to work today. I had yet to tell Leo what happened. He wasn't home when I got there yesterday, and I passed out on the sofa, waiting for him. The only indication that he'd spent the night in the cabin was that I'd woken up tucked in bed. I didn't know why he was being so distant, but it probably had something to do with his father being back in town, so I tried to push the worry that welled up in my heart down.

"I'm sorry, Kate. Can we take five? I'm expecting an important phone call and it's eating away at my focus." A little white lie never hurt anybody. I wasn't expecting a phone call. I had to make one. Even though this wasn't a conversation I wanted to have over the phone, I felt like I'd burst if I waited any longer to tell him.

"Alright." She sighed exasperatingly, her black hair sticking out of her ponytail. "But make it quick, the performance is on Friday and we still have a long way to go."

I nodded, and she clucked her tongue before heading on a smoothie run with the rest of the dancers. My stomach clenched as I watched them disappear out the door. I hadn't eaten any breakfast, and the fact that I'd made it through a full dance rehearsal with just a few sips of water was a remarkable feat on its own. Still, the thought of putting anything in my mouth made me queasy.

I didn't waste any time retrieving my phone from my backpack. I leaned against the floor-to-ceiling mirrors, sat on the laminated floors, and hit call. My stomach twisted like an origami when the shrill rings led to a voicemail.

Where the fuck was he?

A devastating thought fleeted through my mind, and I tightened my hold on the phone as it went to voicemail for a second time. What if he knew? What if he already knew and he didn't need me anymore? I knew he liked me, was in lust with me, but that wasn't enough for him not to discard me.

Dropping my head, I curled inward, my phone slipping on the ground.

I didn't think I could do it. Learn to live without him again after he filled my life with color. I didn't want to go back. I loved his dirty jokes, his devastating smirks, the way he encouraged me to go after my dreams, and his protective bursts. I loved his nocturnal nature and how he'd drain my sleep with a single kiss.

I loved him.

Fuck me, I did.

I loved him even when I hated him.

And that was a problem.

Serena was right, but I prayed that was the only truth in her words. I couldn't have fabricated all the chemistry between us. It was a product of years' worth of bad blood and repressed feelings. He wouldn't throw me away that easily, would he?

God, I wanted to turn my brain off.

When had I turned in this codependent, pathetic girl? Besides, I was sure it was nothing. People got busy.

I took a deep breath and a hungry sip from my water bottle, letting it wash all of my worries down. Only, I was all too eager, and the liquid went down the wrong pipe. A hand connected with my back, delivering "helpful" blows that made me choke harder from the shock.

"Hey, are you okay?" I heard a voice behind me, and whoever it was smacked harder.

I managed to get my breathing under control and turned around. Jet-black hair, longer on the top and faded on the sides, and jade green eyes, greeted me as he squinted at my curled up form on the floor.

"Yes, I am now." I winced at my sore throat, and he helped me get on my feet. "Thank you."

"Ah, no problem. I couldn't let you die now, could I?"

It was barely a cough until he made it worse, but okay. "No, I guess you couldn't."

My eyes traveled from his formal navy suit to the expensive watch on his wrist. It looked like it weighed him down every time he went in for a handshake. And he looked like he'd just gotten back from a trip to the dry cleaners, so immaculately put together.

This club got a lot of customers that were well-off, but

usually not this early in the morning, and he wasn't part of the staff. Even though his features struck me as familiar, I knew I hadn't seen him before. "If you don't mind me asking, what are you doing back here? This part of the club is closed to the public."

And it's nine freaking a.m.

"Saving pretty girls apparently." He leaned his shoulder on the floor-to-ceiling windows, and they bowed slightly inward at his weight. I tried not to cringe... much.

While one could argue that I suffered from daddy issues. Older men weren't my thing. And this guy looked like he was pushing forty if the touch of white along his temples was anything to go by.

My phone on the floor pinged with a text, capturing both of our attention. Leonardo's name flashed bold, and I felt this sudden need to get rid of the stranger so I could see what Leo said.

"Well, thank you again." I tilted my body to the exit subconsciously. "But you should leave. You'll probably get in trouble since you're not authorized to be here. You take a left after you pass the bar to get to the bathroom, if that was what you were searching for."

Did I expect some gratitude for the warning? Maybe.

Did I get it? No.

The man started chuckling as if he knew something I didn't. "Wow, you really don't remember me, do you?"

An eerie feeling washed over me as I shifted from foot to foot, taking him in again. I came up blank though and shook my head. "I'm sorry, I don't. Do we know each other?"

"Considering I pay your salary and you warm my son's bed, you really should." He delivered the information coldly, sucking any good-natured humor from the air.

Air punched out of my lungs as realization gripped me. Of course, he looked familiar. Leo was basically a mini-me figure of his dad. But the man he was when I'd last seen him wasn't there anymore. His once shallow gaze had regained its glow, and mine was starting to pack some heat as I grasped his words.

My mouth opened and closed like a fish.

I didn't know what to say.

I didn't know how he knew.

"You've grown into quite the young lady, Ms. Roux." Alessio's gaze glowered down my lackluster sports outfit. Not in a lustful way, more so like examining a bug under a microscope type of way. "First you take my daughter away, then my money, and now you want my son too? You're running on quite a greedy streak, aren't you?"

Selfish. Selfish. Selfish.

A lump settled in my throat.

I stuck with this job even after learning that the Bianchis owned it. It might've been just another investment for them, but that didn't mean I had the right to capitalize on it. Especially when it donned Isabella's name.

I was defaming her memory, yet I couldn't let go of her brother. He'd gotten his hooks on me deep and was off the negotiating table. The only way I'd let him go was if he took my heart with him.

"I-I will resign from the job tonight," I offered, not mentioning Leo.

Alessio gave me a sardonic smile in return. "Yes, you will. You'll also let my son be if you know what's good for you, Eliana."

"Excuse me?" I took a step back, but he didn't have to follow me to make me want to flee from the room. He stayed in place, calm and collected, while my chest flamed with pressure. "Are you threatening me?"

"You can take it as you want." His ever-present smile stayed glued on his lips. Ridiculing me. "Although I'd say I'm simply sparing you the heartache. Whatever you two have got going on will never work. And you know why?"

Most people just stared at a car crash about to happen. I participated actively because my whole life was a damn accident I was aiding along. And old habits die hard.

"Why?" I graced his rhetorical question with an answer, my heart beating out of my chest as the loose threads in my story started unraveling.

Alessio detached from the mirror, recognizing he had me in his snare. "Because I know my son. I know what he is capable of and where his loyalties lie. He might've had his fun with you, but that's all it ever was. Fun," he sneered. "Leonardo doesn't betray his family. And you? You'll never be part of our pedigree."

He breathed fire in my soul, sending my deepest insecurities raging, as if he knew exactly where to hit. It was as if I was an open book when it came to Leo, and everyone could read my weakness for him with minimal effort. Too bad for me, they always insisted on ripping out pages along the way as well.

My skin chilled as I used the remainder of my fire to spew my own poison. Defend myself even though it was time to back down. "I never asked to be, but that didn't stop your son from wanting me."

"Greedy and conceited too?" He brushed past me. "I think it's time to reevaluate your life, little girl."

From that day on, I was exempt from ever stepping foot at Bella's again. Boss's orders.

I gnawed on my thumb as I stared at the satin, black box I found outside the door when I got back to the cabin. A silver ribbon was wrapped around it, beckoning me to unravel the knot at the middle. I wasn't expecting any deliveries, so I'd been debating opening it for the entire afternoon.

It could be Leo's, and I didn't want to be that kind of girl. The one that snooped through his things. Even though the last text I got from him said that he was working with Ares on a project and was going to be late, I wanted to trust him. He'd earned it.

I realized I was letting people influence my perception of him way too much. Yes, we had a murky past, but he hadn't been anything sort of perfect ever since we started investigating this shitshow. Leo deserved a fair chance. We both did.

But I guessed taking a peek at the cream envelope attached on top wouldn't hurt. It could very well be a package for me.

I swiped my sweaty hands on my thighs as I leaned forward on the couch, reaching for the box on the coffee table. I didn't let myself rethink my actions and swiped the card from the top. The handwriting rivaled every doctor's note on the planet, and I had to squint to make out what was written.

Stars stop shining long before their light fades before our mortal eyes.

Do you really believe yours can withstand the darkness of the universe?

Do what has never been accomplished?

The night sky is nothing but an illusion, Ms. Roux.

Don't be remembered as the fool that bought it.

My hand tightened around the paper until crinkling sounds filled the space of the living room. It wasn't signed, but I had a pretty good idea who'd sent it. There was an address scribbled on the bottom, one I knew all too well.

The invitation was clear. The challenge stuck out like a sore thumb.

A fool. Conceded. Greedy. Liar. Air-head.

The thinly veiled insults aimed for my heart. No one wanted to see us together. We didn't belong with one another in the world's eyes. There was gravity in levity's space and everyone wanted to know why, pick apart our relationship until something gave.

I shouldn't do them the favor and bend to their wills, but I wanted to show them that they were wrong. My night sky was real, and they could shove their reservations where the sun didn't shine.

With a newfound gusto, I tugged the box open and just... stared. Wind fled from my lungs faster than one could say Mississippi five times.

The gown was gorgeous.

I pulled it out and held it up, staring at the asymmetrical

chiffon number. The draped details of the dress made it look like water. It featured a color so blue, waves immediately came to mind, darkening at the bottom of the flared skirt, reminding of the abyssal bottom of the ocean. I caressed the fitted waist, biting my lip.

It was certainly eye-catching, but its history held as much weight as its beauty.

The first and last Falco X Fleur collaboration. It was the engagement dress Saint's mom had worn the day she and the Fleur heir were supposed to announce their future marriage to the world. The two biggest and oldest fashion houses in the world, coming together. The event was very well documented, so was poor Celia's face when her betrothed never bothered to show up.

The walls of the cabin grew narrower, and the air turned stuffy. Alessio wasn't playing around. His cunning messages closed in around me, but I was determined not to let them crush me.

Game fucking on.

"Eliana, what are you doing here?" My mom spotted me the second I stepped foot inside. I was the only one dressed in blue in a sea of black. Her hands curled around her slightly rounded belly, and I sliced my gaze up again.

A crowd had gathered to celebrate Serena's birthday. Middle-aged men in stuffy suits were in the majority. Her father's friends, seeing as her own, had discarded her like a ratted shirt that didn't withhold the test of time. Exactly what she did to me.

"Attending my sister's birthday party. What does it look

like I'm doing?" I smiled. I was entering enemy territory armed with nothing but some bold red lipstick. I had to flaunt it.

Claire's brows furrowed at my statement. "Oh, I wasn't aware she had invited you considering..." Her voice ceased flowing.

Yeah, considering I'd fucked her over. Not even mommy dearest could force them to invite me to events after that. Alessio Bianchi had though, and you couldn't say no to a Bianchi. Lord knows I tried.

He was here too. Alessio was surrounded by Cole and a pale, lanky guy, but his attention was on me. Nice dress, he mouthed, and I resisted the urge to flip him off. His eyes were identical to Leo's, and when he stared at me like he'd love to see me burn at the stake, it brought back unwanted memories.

I brought my gaze back to Claire, who looked very close to throwing me out, to avoid another scene. "I guess your stepdaughter doesn't share everything with you then. Besides, I've come bearing gifts." I shook the black Chanel bag I was holding. I wasn't keen on getting her anything, but I couldn't show up empty-handed.

"Okay," she sighed. "You can stay. Serena is finishing up in her room. I think it would be best if you dropped off your gift personally and apologized."

Why, thank you for allowing me to be part of your life, Mother. Don't go looking too excited now.

"Sure thing." I was pretty sure my smile looked more like a grimace by now. Why shouldn't I apologize for getting assaulted by a psycho?

Alessio gave me an ominous smile as I made my way upstairs. It was one thing dealing with young adults, scorned forty-something-year-olds hit way harder. Or paid other people to do the hitting for them depending on who you asked.

Shivers broke along my back the closer I got to Serena's room. She didn't deserve any apologies from me, and she wasn't going to get one. Time and time again she'd shown she didn't care about our friendship, but I wasn't blameless, I'd give her this last gift. I suspected she didn't have much on her name, and Carter wouldn't be left with a lot either once the state made their case against him.

I didn't bother knocking. I wanted to surprise her, maybe even shock her a little because I knew she wasn't expecting me.

I pushed the door open and just froze.

Everything suspended.

My chest grew tight, and my heartbeat faltered. Air caught in my throat as tears pricked my widened eyes. My limbs became numb, and the gift slipped from my fingers.

I couldn't feel a thing.

No outside force could measure up to the mindfuck that stood before me.

Leo was pressed against the wall, hands creasing Serena's silky dress as he held her waist in a tight grip. Serena was plastered against him, holding his head hostage, her red fingernails peeking through his dark tresses. Mouths fused together, they looked like extensions of each other. Like they lived and breathed for one another.

Venom thawed the ice around my heart, and a steady fire blazed beneath my skin. It felt like I was on the receiving end of a bullet as it pierced through my soft tissue and unleashed its poison slowly.

"What the fuck?" My high pitch sliced through the air.

If I wasn't about to spew the contents of my stomach all over Serena's pristine white carpet, I would have laughed at how quickly he pushed her off. Serena stumbled and fell to the floor, her tailbone cracking at the impact, the sound echoing in my ears.

Leo's gaze locked on mine, eyes flashing with shock. All I could see was the pink lipstick imprinted on the contours of his mouth. A beacon that another had touched what I'd naively thought was mine.

Stupid. Stupid. Stupid.

I am so fucking stupid.

"I see Ares grew boobs and put on a wig since the last time I saw him." My throat burned as I tried to sound out the words. He'd taken everything from me. My trust, loyalty, time, all the while painting me in clown colors.

"You're a piece of shit, Leo," I spat, my feet unfreezing.

"Eliana." He took a tentative step toward me. "Fuck, baby, I can explain!"

I didn't want to hear it. I took a step back just as he took another step forward, then turned around and fucking ran. I ran from my monster before he got another chance to destroy what was left of my tattered heart.

I tore through the hallway with the speed of a hurricane, Leo hot on my heels. He couldn't explain shit. I'd seen everything with my own two eyes. He'd betrayed me, and worst of all, it was Serena he'd done it with. I ran faster —harder.

"Eliana." He breathed harshly, right behind me. "Wait, please!"

We reached the staircase, and his shouts attracted the attention of all the guests. About a hundred pairs of eyes rubbed off on my body, taking in the train wreck before them

335

with hungry gazes. Me, tripping over my skirts, and Leo, shouting like a manic—like a cheater.

I almost slipped in my attempt to get as far away from him as possible. My legs burned with the effort to keep going. "Stay the fuck away from me!"

My vision blurred, and I followed the bright lights of the illuminated patio to find my way outside. I couldn't see clearly in front of me as hot tears stained my cheeks. He'd fucking kissed her when he knew how much she'd hurt me. Why did I always forget that he'd hurt me just as much, though?

Love blinds. Love fucking blows every imperfection, every tiny red flag to the wind, leaving one lightheaded. Drunk on the feeling of being wanted.

"Eliana! Stop!"

A few feet away from my car, my lungs collapsed, and I struggled to breathe as exhaustion took hold of my body. Sadness, tiredness, and loss, all swirled together in the pit of my heart, like an angry swamp.

Leo caught up and spun me around with a sigh of relief that grated on my nerves. He held my squirming body tight as I struggled to break free from his touch. "Fucking let me go!"

"Baby, please, listen to me." He sounded out of breath. Desperate. "I didn't kiss her, Narcissus."

"Unless you fucking stumbled, your mouth landed on hers and your tongue happened to roll out of your mouth, then yes. You did fucking kiss her, you asshat," I roared, hitting his hard chest with my balled fists.

"She kissed—"

I did what I should've done a long time ago. I hooked my leg up and kneed him straight in the balls.

"Umpf." A haphazard sound escaped his mouth as he slowly slid to the ground, face red. His arms stayed wrapped around my midriff like steel bands, no matter how much I clawed at his skin.

"It was my mistake, trusting you. You still call me Narcissus, for god's sake, when the only vain motherfucker here is you." Leo struggled to speak as I battled to detach him from me. He was gripping my waist tight. Exactly like he'd done with Serena some mere minutes ago. I bet she was loving this. She'd probably dance on my grave too, if I died first.

"Whatever this was, it's done now, Leo. We're completely fucking done. Let me go."

I thought I heard him mumble *never*. But it was too late.

The damage was done.

My dream shattered, and he was the one that held the hammer.

Leo loved breaking things more than he loved life itself.

I slapped his clinging hands off and took a step back as he struggled to stay upright. My eyes flicked to the guests that had spilled out of the house, looking at us and capturing our grade F Greek tragedy on film.

I bolted before Leo could come after me again. He stood up as soon as my ass met the leather of my car's seat.

Too late again.

I floored it. My eyes stayed glued on the rearview mirror when he started running after the vehicle, pathetically trying to catch up with the motor's power. I stared at him until he became nothing but a dot.

Until darkness encompassed my white dwarf, swallowing him whole.

Chapter 24

LEONARDO

She'd left everything behind.

I checked her place. *Not there.*

Cole's? *Not there.*

Bella's? *Not there.*

The cabin? *Not fucking here.*

Oh, but she could run. She could run all she wanted. The thrill of the chase made the bite of the capture juicer. And I planned on sinking my teeth in so deep, she'd have no choice but to sit and listen. Listen to the truth, she was all too eager to write off. *My truth.*

I burned a hole through the bedroom's carpet as I checked through her stuff. Her orange-scented body wash sat in the bathroom, her pointes were by the closet doors, and the shelves were still filled with her clothes.

I didn't know why I went through every drawer as if I was going to see anything I hadn't before. I've been checking every day for the past seven days, calling, driving to the Roux

Manor. And kept finding nothing save for empty calls, barren spaces, and memories.

She just up and left and wasn't showing any signs of coming back.

I never kissed Serena. Not at her birthday party or ever before. It did cross my mind. Eliana wore her heart on her sleeve. Even when she played tough, I could see her weak spots from miles away. But I never wanted to play up *that* weakness all the way, not when I craved her pain, and certainly not when I couldn't fucking breathe without her.

I didn't tell her about Serena's birthday party because I didn't want her to get upset, and once there, I figured I'd fucking wish Serena a happy birthday. I wouldn't have if I knew it'd end up with her shoving her tongue down my throat. The road to hell is paved with good intentions.

I had a feeling I knew who was behind all this.

The person that insisted I show up in the first place. The one that was pronouncing around with a pep in his step, acting like a twenty-year-old rather than his actual age for the past few days. My father had been all smiles and just short of farting rainbows when Eliana floored it all the way to God knows where.

On cue, I heard the door downstairs slam shut and abandoned my work in the closet, taking the stairs to the living room. Alessio was setting two cups of coffee on the kitchen counter when I appeared in the doorway.

"Oh, good, you're up already," he said, shaking his hair out of his hat and fixing up his slightly damp suit. Rain pelted over the roof of the cabin creating a rhythmic strum that rolled with the tension in the room.

"I don't know why you insist on staying here, but the hour drive from Astropolis is eating away at precious time.

You're accompanying me to some of my meetings today at BB Oil's headquarters. You're a few months shy of graduating, and you're going to have to start showing up more at the company that's going to be yours one day."

"Maybe I don't want it to be," I said and he stopped dead in his tracks, holding his coat and looking at me as if I'd lost my mind. "I mean, why should I, right? That company is your pride and joy. You've been more attentive to it than your own family."

"You have no idea what you're talking about." He set his coat down, stepping closer.

"Then why don't you enlighten me?" I matched his gait, stepping in his personal space. "Where have you been for the past four years, *Dad*? Why are you all of a sudden making a return now? Apparently, you didn't have any mistresses, and it hasn't been work keeping you away."

"Tell me." I pushed him a step back when he took too long to answer. His nostrils flared, but I didn't stop. "Where." *Shove.* "Have." *Shove.* "You." *Shove.* "Been."

"Stop it," he roared, shoving me back.

"Or what? Are you going to orchestrate another scheme with *Serena Laurent?* Up for round number two of bullying people that are thirty years your junior?"

"If it means keeping the little whore out of our family then yes, I'd do it a thousand times over."

I didn't know what came over me. One moment, my hands were firmly planted at my sides, and the next, I'd cocked my right arm back, packing a punch with the force of an avalanche straight to my father's face. His head reared back, his body flailing to the floor as he groaned out in pain and surprise.

"Don't you ever call her that again. Her name is Eliana

Roux, *use it*. She's a million times better than you will ever be," I spit out, fire pumping through my veins.

"What is the matter with you?" he yelled at me, blood dripping from his nose to his moving lips. "You'd hit me over her? Your own blood for a girl belonging to a family that killed Isabella? Your sister?"

"It wasn't Francis that killed Isabella," I snapped.

"Yeah, but it *was* her mother, wasn't it?" He threw the words at me like they weighed nothing. I stood rigid when he got back on his feet, face decorated with the color of rage, just like the rest of him. "You really want to know what I've been doing for the past four years, you ungrateful brat?"

I didn't let my shock show as Alessio's chest grazed mine with every furious breath he took. He continued talking, decorating my white dress shirt with spittle of saliva and blood.

"While you were busy fucking your little toy, I was all over the country, trying to put a cap to the mess her family started. The police couldn't be trusted, so I took matters into my own hands while trying to keep BB Oil afloat. I wanted them all to pay, every single person that was involved in my daughter's death," he raged, and I felt this sudden itch on my knuckles. My fist was begging to meet his face again.

"So you fucking knew? All this time you fucking knew that it wasn't Francis behind Isabella's death, and yet you told us nothing? Let us stew in misery and lies?"

I couldn't look at him, because if I did, I was afraid he'd end up in a grave and I, behind bars for patricide. I stepped away, raking my hands through my hair. All this time Eliana and I spent searching for answers he knew all along. My mother became a shell of a person because my father was too busy hiding the world from us.

"*I suspected.* What motive could Francis Roux possibly have to abduct four young girls and kill one of them? Money wasn't a problem for him, and the story of Francis being mentally ill sounded like folklore. How could one person pull this off, and where did the other three girls wind up?"

A sour taste filled my mouth at his words, and I wanted to bring down every wall in this cabin. "And why didn't you make us privy to your suspicions? Were mom and I too stupid to grasp what you had to say?"

"I wanted to protect you." He followed as I stepped out to the balcony. Harsh raindrops soaked me to the bone, yet I didn't care. I needed some air. "I came across people viler than you could ever dream of when I started digging deeper into this case. Dirty cops, sex traffickers, *murderers.* I never want you to come across people like that, and for as long as I am alive, you and your mother never will."

"It was up to us to decide if we want your protection or not," I screamed over the sound of the rainfall, turning to look at his slouched form. "Keeping someone in the dark is more hurtful than sharing the fucking truth. We *deserved* the truth."

"You want to fucking know what the truth is? Want to see what I've seen?" my father scoffed, darkness permeating his eyes. "Victims, beaten bloody and raped right in front of me while I couldn't do anything? Force-fed drugs, so they weren't lucid enough to fight back? I couldn't get them out of the hellholes they were imprisoned in until I had sufficient evidence. Until I'd found the other three girls that went missing right along with Isabella."

Bile rose up my throat at his words and the visuals that overtook my brain. And maybe I was naïve and wouldn't have lasted a day, but I wanted justice for my sister. I would've done it for her.

"And did you? Did you find them?" I swallowed my fury and disgust down, moving to the most pressing matter at hand.

"I did. Kira, Zena, and Emily. I will never forget their names. The first thing that popped in my head when we finally found them in a ratty Brooklyn whore house was 'I'm glad Isabella died before they'd killed her soul too'." His voice cracked, and my eyes stung as the rain washed away some of my anger.

I didn't want my sister dead. I wished no one had touched her in the first place, wished I'd been more fucking attentive. But unfortunately, I had to live with my bastard ways for the rest of my life. If what he was saying was true then I was thankful she escaped a fate worse than death too.

Dad's head snapped up when I placed my hand on his shoulder, squeezing. I couldn't forgive him just yet, the need for revenge thrummed through my veins and seeped through my pores, and he'd taken that option away from me.

"I want everyone that was involved to suffer." My voice was low, threatening.

"They paid the price. I made sure that everyone involved in Isabella's case was put away for good. There's still a long way to go, but I can't do it anymore, Leo. I did my part for my daughter and pointed the police in the right direction for future cases, but after that, I had to get out. I was suffocating, and now I have to see a therapist regularly to lessen the burn of the memories," he admitted, his voice barely audible.

Even my jackassery knew an end, and I couldn't help bringing him in for a hug. Dad sighed over my shoulder as I slapped his back. "I see you have no shortage of white knight syndrome." I tried to lighten the mood and he released a huff.

Tough crowd.

"There're only two people left that have yet to receive any form of punishment, save from their miserable existence," he said once we came apart. "I'm pretty sure you know who they are."

"Carter Laurent and Claire Roux."

He nodded, confirming my statement. His jaw locked tight at my mention of Eliana's mother. That didn't deter me though. My mind was set. Her egg donor's actions didn't define her. I didn't give a shit about how forbidden or scandalous us being together was.

Eliana Roux was it for me.

I wanted to see my ring on her finger one day.

Her walking down the aisle to me.

And eventually, my baby rounding her tummy.

She might not see it yet, but there would be no version of our story where she didn't end up with me. I might be a bastard, but I'm her bastard. And she might be a bitch, but she's my bitch.

"You love her, don't you?" Alessio asked, sorrow lacing his voice.

"I do," I answered without hesitation. "I've loved her ever since the first time I saw her. Eliana is nothing like her mother, and she has been with me every step of the way since I started looking for answers."

I could tell he wasn't satisfied with my answer. His shoulders remained drooped, like they carried the weight of the world on them. He'd adjust though, all in due time.

"Alright." He heaved a sigh. "If that's who you truly want, I can't do anything about it. Well, not without getting punched again." Dad cringed, pressing his hand on his nose. "I guess I taught you well, you've got a fucking mean right hook."

I shrugged. "You deserved it, old man. Now let's go inside before you catch pneumonia and we have to rush you to the hospital."

He came at me with a mock punch and I side-stepped him, laughing. "Do you think we could pay the little lovebirds a visit before the police get involved?" I raised a brow.

"Damn it, Eliana, answer your phone. Where the hell are you? I don't like this cat and mouse game we're playing, baby, and you know patience is not a fucking virtue I possess. When I find you, *and I will find you*, you better keep your ears open and listen to what I have to say. I'm mad, sweetheart, you've got my blood pressure through the roof, and all that energy will have to go *somewhere*. *Two days, Eliana*. I'm giving you two more days to come out by yourself. If I don't see you by Friday, just remember... you asked for it."

I hit end call with more force than necessary and barely resisted smashing the phone against my car's windshield. First came shock, and now I was basking in anger. The irony of our situation didn't escape me. I was supposed to be the cheater, yet I felt like I'd been cheated. Robbed of the opportunity to defend myself and hurt by her jump to conclusions, by her *lack of faith* in me.

I was no saint, but fucking hell, I'd all but been a nun with a streak for the darker things in life for her. I didn't give her any reason to doubt my loyalty. Why would I look at other girls when I had my personal wet dream rolling around in my sheets every night? Her legs open, her cunt warm and inviting?

I took a deep breath, trying to calm Leo junior, before abandoning my phone on the center console and joining my dad outside. Sexually deprived *and* angry. Carter was in for a treat today.

"Did Ares take care of Serena?" he asked as I stood beside him, a few steps and a door away from the cause of my bloody dreams. Neither of us retracted our gaze from the entrance.

"Do you have to say it so ominously?" I scoffed. "Yes, he took her out on a date like I asked. Carter and Claire are home alone." It wasn't like Serena could stop my boot from breaking every bone on Carter's body, but we figured the fewer witnesses, the better.

Everyone wasn't equal in the eyes of the law. The disparity of power was painfully obvious. First serve was the one percent, but even among us, we had those that were overly ambitious. This was an eat or be eaten world, and Carter and Claire had sowed more than they could reap. It was past time their bubble burst.

"Let's go then." Alessio nodded, and my nails bit the skin of my palm.

I took the stairs first, and we waltzed inside the Laurent mansion like we owned it. And we did. The guards were paid off, the cameras shut, and the grounds swept off staff.

It was just us, and them.

Lion and sheep.

Who was who, only time would tell.

The inside looked like an insane asylum. White dominated every other color in the mansion, and it made sense considering the people it housed. Some hid their sins behind religion, while others hid behind a shield of mock innocence.

The perfect family, perfect house, perfect *life*.

The perfect lie.

But lies always had a way of coming out.

Our steps echoed across the empty halls as we made our way to the dining room. It was twelve p.m., even snakes had to eat occasionally.

Dad grabbed my shoulder a second before they filled our sight. His eyes burned with the need to let him go first, let him protect me like he had done countless times before, let him take revenge for his sole daughter. But I couldn't. My need for revenge extended to Eliana too. They wouldn't only pay for their sins against my sister. They'd answer for the bruises and cuts on Eliana's skin too, their abandonment and disregard of her.

No one harmed the people I loved and got away with it.

Dad shook his head at me, a careful resignation, and I took a step past the foyer. Plush dark green chairs broke the dominion of the white, a gold table sat amidst them fostering food and vases filled with fragrant gardenias. The air smelled rotten to me, though when I caught sight of Carter sitting at the head of the table, his fiancée flanking him on his right, her back to us.

"Bon appétit," I said, good naturedly. They both choked on their drinks, wine and orange juice, at my intrusive voice. Red liquid sloshed out of Carter's glass and soiled his pants at his abrupt turn. Two sets of horrified gazes settled on us.

I basked in their fear as I sauntered toward them. Claire remained sitting, rooted in place, while Carter slowly rose to his feet, unsure whether to greet us or run for his life. "Alessio, Leonardo, what are you doing here?"

"Why, we came to pay you a little visit." I patted his back until his hip met the corner of the table and he fell back down on his seat with a hiss. I wrapped my hand around the nape of his neck when he glared up at me.

"What's going on?" I heard Claire ask as my father positioned himself behind her, ready to hold her back if she interfered. "Where's security?"

I'd never in my life raised my hand on a woman, but I'd been very tempted to do so with her. Her lack of dignity made for my lack of respect. It was often said that behind every successful man was a woman, and I had no doubt Claire didn't come without her shortage of ruthlessness. I wouldn't touch her, but I'd bury her so far down with legal charges she'd lose the light to find her way up again.

"Are you enjoying your meal, Carter?" I smiled down at him. From the ascension of his chest, I realized it didn't look very friendly.

"What the hell is this?"

"Answer the question." I forced his stare back to the prawns on his plate. "Are you enjoying your fucking meal?"

"I am." He gulped, unsure.

"Good, *good*." I patted his back again roughly. "Enjoy the last meal you'll ever be able to chew properly."

"Are you out of your min—" He never got to finish his sentence. One second his mouth was full of empty words, and the next blood was seeping from his lips as I slammed his head on the plate. A dull thump echoed around the room, mirroring Claire's scream.

"Do you know who will never get to enjoy a meal again, Carter?" I hissed, fisting his hair in a tight grip and pressing his head down harder until his groans of pain reached my ears. "*Answer me.*" I slammed his head back down again, craving to see his skin split open, like Eliana's. I needed his suffering like I needed air.

He released muffled words and I grinned grimly as I pulled his head up. "What was that?"

"You're g-gonna... you're gonna p-pay for this," he said in between stolen breaths. His fiancée matched his statements, but my dad didn't even have to hold her back that much. Claire twisted and turned, unable to do anything because of her condition.

"Isabella is the correct answer, you piece of shit." I let go of his hair only to deliver a blow to his ratty face. Carter's nose became a fountain of blood as his head snapped back from the impact. His chair followed the movement of his body, and it toppled on the ground with his limp weight on top. The white-collar man writhed at my feet, trying to regain his strength and failing miserably. Embarrassingly.

"It's easy to hide behind others, isn't it, Carter? Sending people to beat up your stepdaughter, trafficking young girls, framing your closest friends, *murdering my sister.*" His face twisted with my every word, and he opened his mouth to no doubt deny everything. I didn't give him a chance to do so.

I swung my right foot back, hitting his ribs as one would a soccer ball. Carter wasn't bouncy though, he was breakable. The cracking sound his smashed bones produced danced in my eardrums, making me want to hear it again until he was nothing but a lump of blood and pain at my feet. And so I did. I hit the pathetic excuse of a man again and again until a fraction of my bloodlust subsided.

"Leonardo!" My father's stern voice leashed me to reality again, seeping through the staccato rhythm of my foot connecting with Carter's stomach.

I let up long enough for Carter to mutter his threats

through heaving breaths and cut up lips. "I'm g-going to k-kill you, you fucking delusional b-bastard."

A laugh evaded me "With what? Your words? Or the brilliant mind that got you in this position? Bloodied up and knocking on death's door beneath my feet. It's done, Carter. The police know, and we know. You aren't getting away with what you did."

Shock fleeted through his eyes, but he didn't bother denying anything. Antagonizing me was his top priority.

"Your sister was ever the optimist too." He spat out a mouthful of blood, staining the soles of my shoes as he smiled up at me with contempt. "I was told she begged and begged for you to find her. Held out hope till the very last minute."

A red hue overtook my vision, and I felt weightless as I bent down, striking out and wrapping my hand around his neck. "And you? Would you like to outmatch her, Carter?" His face looked ready to burst from the pressure I applied, and a sick satisfaction roiled deep in my stomach. "I'll make you cry like the little bitch that you are, don't worry about that, but I won't stop there. No." I shook my head.

"Your life? It's mine now. I'll make sure you sink so low, you'll drown in your sins. I'll drag out your end until you're fucking begging for it. Your fiancée, kids? You'll never get to see them again. In fact, make sure you get a good look at the last female you'll ever get to see because the only action you'll ever be able to get from now on is when you drop the soap in the shower."

Spittle flew from Carter's mouth as I tugged his body up. His feet hovered a few inches above the floor, and he managed to hit my shin and scratch up my arm in his fight to breathe. I didn't feel it though, I felt nothing but resentment burning a path from the top of my head to the tips of my fingers.

"You hurt Eliana? Your bruises will be permanent. You rob my sister of her life? I'll deprive you of yours. You should've kept the money you spend on ruining people's lives and tried to better yours, Carter. A stupid fuck like you never gets his hands bloody, yet the trail of sins still managed to lead us to you."

I let go of his neck, and he slumped against the wall, taking in hungry breaths. If he were a smart man, he'd be pleading for his death right now. I was a sliver away from giving in without much encouragement. The only thing that held me back was my dad's tension from the back. I didn't want to rob him of some fun time of his own.

The future was still long, and I had a *lot* of money to waste on crooked guards. We'd see each other again.

With that promise in mind, I brought my knee to Carter's stomach, and he wheezed as he bent over. I took the opportunity to hit his nose too, and a sick crack graced my ears. Carter recoiled on the floor, curling into himself.

Breathing hard through my nose, I turned to my father that had taken in the scene with hungry eyes. Claire looked about ready to pass out, tied in her chair. Her pregnant belly stood out, but I couldn't find it in me to care. She should be grateful. That unborn child was the only thing that saved her today.

"Even if Eliana forgives you," I addressed her. "I promise you, I won't."

I patted my dad's shoulder as I passed him by. "All yours."

Chapter 25

ELIANA

You'd think I'd be used to this by now.

Learned to roll with life's punches, but instead, I let ambition get the best of me and threw intuition and experience into a flaming pile of trash. In the span of eight days, I lost everything I never really had a claim to in the first place.

Alessio Bianchi made sure both Carter and Claire were locked behind bars for life. Obstruction of justice, sex trafficking, and even drug dealing, were some of the many felonies listed.

I couldn't escape it. The news was blasted on every news channel out there, and I think even the president had something to say about it. The case didn't stop with them. There were multiple other parties involved. Word on the street was that Carter and Claire wouldn't make it much longer in prison.

They had major dirt on other players that were rumored to be of high status as well. Alessio Bianchi was a mastermind. As much as I didn't like him, I had to give it to him. He made sure they lived for this very reason. Constantly wondering if you'll survive to see another day, I imagine, must be a very torturous way of living.

"Good afternoon, Ms. Roux," Ben, the receptionist at the hotel I'd been staying at, greeted me.

I nodded at him as I made my way to my room, where I'd hole up under the covers, order room service, and stare at the TV until my eyes felt raw. I couldn't find it in me to care for Claire, but hell, if I wasn't obsessed with seeing how this would go down. She might have been the woman that gave birth to me, yet for what it's worth, I knew her as much as the next stranger did. The trophy wife image she always projected crumbled overnight, and now everyone around her was put under a microscope.

I pushed the button for the fortieth floor and stepped back as the elevator started to fill in. At least one good thing came from the instability of this whole week: I finally found my imaginary balls and dropped out of college, despite the staff's insistence that I was ruining my life.

I was Eliana freaking Roux. My father was a disgraced artist and Mom a famed con. I survived through lows and highs before I could do it again. Leonardo Bianchi was nothing but another bump in the road. He wasn't worth my tears or the empty Ben & Jerry's tubs in my trash can.

He is nothing, I whispered to my heart that insisted on tightening painfully every time I thought of him. His chocolate hair, brilliant green eyes, and empty words would be nothing but a memory soon.

I hoped and prayed.

LEONARDO

Her days were up.

Cunning little thing, she'd hid right under my nose.

Eliana had taken up residence at the Ritz Carlton, a mere thirty-minute drive from my home. The gray marble slabs felt slippery beneath my shoes as I made my way to her door and swiped the card key. My creep levels were through the roof, but I wasn't losing any more sleep over something that could be resolved in seconds.

So, yes, I did bribe the receptionist. Yes, I had her tailed when she showed up on campus today. And yes, I didn't care about the lines I was overstepping. Just like she didn't give a shit to hear my side of the story.

I plowed inside with determination, scanning the plush interior of the suite. It opened up to a living room with gray amenities and dark wood flooring.

And no Eliana in sight.

I moved farther in. Half-eaten plates of food lay forgotten on the dining table, overlooking the Astropolis public garden, and the steady buzz of the shower in the bathroom on the far left pierced my eardrums.

She wasn't here, but her clothes were. The eye-catching white fabric of her sundress lay on a heap on the floor, followed by her slippers, and some very interesting red undies that made for a trail to the bathroom. One I so wanted to follow, but I settled for getting a drink from the wet bar instead.

I'd freak her out plenty when she came outside, there was no need to accelerate the process.

The sound of the shower ceased flowing, four sips of my whiskey in. My heart galloped in my chest, but I rested my left ankle on my right knee and settled back in my chair as I waited for her to exit.

A picture of arrogance that showed its first cracks when the steam that spilled out the bathroom door lessened, and a *very* wet and *very naked* Eliana took its place. My eyes widened as my eyes took in what I'd been deprived of this past week.

No robe.

No towel.

Just pure flesh.

The tables had turned.

Her pink nipples were puckered and screamed, *hi* and *suck me,* in about a hundred different languages in my brain. Fat droplets of water donned her skin, and glided slowly down her toned stomach and cinched waist, leading to a mouth-watering triangle that held a fine dusting of blonde hair. The arch of her ass proved to be kinkier than her tits, however, by screaming, *bite me,* and *smack me.*

I licked my lips as I gawked. Busy making all kinds of promises to her body parts. It flew past my brain that she'd noticed me. Albeit, her shrill scream alerted me that she was very much aware of my presence.

"What the hell are you doing here and how did you get inside?" She squealed like a deflating balloon, crossing her hands over her breasts in an attempt to hide her body from me.

Too late, baby, I've already seen it all. And I'll keep seeing it every day for as long as we both shall live.

"I told you, you had two more days to come out. You didn't, so I came to find you instead." I shrugged, barely sticking to the charade of keeping my cool. I had a raging boner and a lot to say.

"I don't take orders from *you*." Her eyes spit as much fire as her mouth, as she crossed the slight distance to her king-sized bed, tugging on the blush silk robe that lay on top and hiding all that creamy wet skin from me. "And what part of getting fucking lost didn't you understand?"

"Get lost in what? You? Because I can definitely do that." I took a sip of my whiskey, eyeing how the damp robe conformed to the contours of her body.

I was egging her on, and we both knew it.

I wanted her to come to me. Rile her up enough, so she craved for me to taste her kiss of war.

She didn't respond to reason, but she'd respond to my body.

Eliana fell right into my trap and stormed over, bringing with her the scent of a woman scorned—orange with a hint of cinnamon. My lungs froze at the hate displayed clearly on her face, but I didn't lose hope. Hate meant she still cared. I'd take anything over the resignation that'd stood over her drooped shoulders when she ran away from me.

"No. Get lost as in go to hell and let the devil have you for lunch." She knocked the glass of whiskey from my hand, and it crashed, breaking on the floor next to us. The grin that took over my face was automatic.

I was in the premise of a kitten in severe need of a declawing, and I'd give just that.

I locked her wrist in my palm before she could retract her hand and brought her down on my lap. Her body shivered with barely contained rage and she sucked in a breath when she felt my erection rubbing against her ass.

"You're disgusting!" She writhed on top of me, struggling to leave, but I latched my hands on her waist and plastered her chest on mine until she had no more space to move. *That's right, baby. You're going to stay there until I've said my piece.*

"Think about what you saw, Na—" I started, but she looked a second away from scratching my eyes out, so I relented. "Think about what you saw. Serena threw herself at me, I was trying to hold her off."

"A: I'd rather not think about that scene ever again. As a matter of fact, I wish I could unthink both Serena and you. And B: You were trying to hold her off by going Colombo all up in her mouth, real clever evading techniques there, buddy."

"I froze. We both heard footsteps outside of the door, and then, next thing I knew she was inches away from my face and attacked my mouth."

Her eyes squinted at my statement, contemplating. Yet, the defiance of her raised chin showed me she was miles away from accepting my explanation.

This scared her.

I scared her.

Eliana wanted to believe I was cheating on her because painting me as the bad guy came naturally to her. After all, why would Leonardo Bianchi tell the truth? The ever-present mistakes of my past never came back to bite me in the ass.

"You don't believe me, do you?" I blew out a breath.

"Why should I, Leo?" Her mouth twisted in a painful

smile. "You never gave me any reason to believe you, and we never put a label on anything. You even lied and said you were working on a project with Ares. Honestly, I think I would've reacted way better if I'd caught you kissing him over Serena."

She balled my shirt in her fists, and she was right. I wished I hadn't lied, but I couldn't change the past. All I could do right now was tell her the truth and prayed she believed it.

"My father was adamant that I attend. He used you against me. Somehow, some-fucking-way, he knew we were living together, and he threatened to show you out. Or do worse if I didn't show up."

"Your father?" Realization sparked behind her blues and her hands smoothed out, her palm resting flat over my heart. "He was the one that invited me too. Said you were only having fun with me, and I was a fool for believing your lies."

I clenched my teeth so tight I feared they'd break as Eliana relayed the information. "I know. He was the one that pulled the strings and arranged everything. But trust me, baby, I made sure he paid for it, and he won't be making the same mistake twice."

"What did you do?" She eyed me warily, and I fished her hand from my chest, pressing a kiss on the inside of her wrist. A rush of calmness washed over me when she allowed it.

"Let's just say his nose didn't thank him for what he did."

"You hit your dad?" Her mouth dropped open in shock.

"I did. I could never betray you, Eli. You're special to me. Always have been, ever since you threw me in the pool when I tried to kiss you for the first time. A little spitfire I couldn't wait to tame."

The corners of her mouth pulled up at the memory. I realized I'd never told her what she meant to me before, never admitted I had feelings that went beyond being sexual. If even just the tip of the iceberg got her this happy, then they needed to give me an "I'm a douchebag" sign, so I could wave it on the side of the road.

"Is that the only reason why I'm so special to you? You just want to tame me?" she questioned, her head tilting to the right. Her voice barely traveled, feather-light and unsure.

I opened my mouth to voice how much she meant to me. That the past few months, she was the one thing that kept me going. How her light shone past the dark clouds of my misery, breaking them apart one glowing smile at a time. How I admired her even when she drove me crazy. I loved how she stayed true to herself. I admired her strength. And if I could just bottle up her scent, I'd take it everywhere with me. I couldn't go back to being without her. Couldn't fit that thought in my brain.

Alas, the words took too long to travel past my lips, seeing as I had the emotional availability of a freaking cucumber. Her eyes hardened immediately, and all the advance I made in getting her to soften up went down the drain. She slipped past my hands and stood up swiftly before I could stop her.

"You know what? It doesn't even matter." Eliana fixed up her robe, cinching the belt tighter, and opened up the distance between us. "What you did or didn't do doesn't matter. We would've never worked, Leo."

"What are you talking about? We were working just fine, Narcissus." I followed close behind but stopped dead in my tracks when she whipped around, fuming.

"Don't fucking call me that." She pointed her finger at me, a flush took over her face, and worked its way down the valley of her neck, disappearing under her robe. "Like you said. *Were*. Past tense. We *were* working just fine because no one actually knew that we were together o-or fucking. I don't even know what we were, but one thing I know for sure is your dad won't be the only one opposing this. Didn't you see what happened when the tabloids caught wind of our little showdown outside of the Laurent's mansion?"

"And? What happened next, Eliana?" My blood pumped in my veins when she didn't answer. She retracted her gaze, staring at a blank spot in the wall. She was past logic. She simply didn't *want* us to work.

"I'll tell you, since you seem to be at a loss of words all of a sudden." I rolled my shoulders to keep from storming over and making her look at me. "Five days later, those very same tabloids had a juicer, more lucrative story in their hands. Carter and Claire's arrest. And poof, just like that, our *forbidden* and *unorthodox* love story was forgotten." I used air quotes for the very same words used in the articles of those trashy news outlets. "Besides, you seem to be forgetting about Astor's party, sweetheart. I made it pretty fucking clear who you belong to there, and no one had shit to say."

"Well, maybe they suspected. It's not the same as knowing. You know what though? Fuck them. Let's say we don't give a shit about what strangers have to say. What about your mom? She's in rehab now, but she'll get out eventually. What about then Leo? Won't she have something to say?" Eliana hit me where it really hurt and she knew it. Her confident stance lessened the farther she hit the nail right in the head. "I don't want to be the reason you're alienated from your family."

My mom was a weak spot for me. Eliana was right again. I didn't know how she'd take it. Her son, dating the girl whose family was responsible for her daughter's death. Living with her and eventually putting a ring on her finger. All signs pointed to a downward spiral and I didn't want to do that to her.

I loved my mom, but Eliana had my heart. I'd do my best to make it work, but if push came to shove, I'd choose the person I couldn't live without. I'd choose the person I couldn't fucking breathe without.

"You get it too now, don't you?" she continued. "We aren't meant to b—" Her voice cracked before she could finish her sentence. Eliana cupped her mouth and turned her back on me when tears welled up in her eyes.

I broke out of my stupor and went after her. I'd already made her cry multiple times in the past. I never, *ever*, wanted to be the reason tears graced her eyes again.

Her shoulders shook under my touch, and it felt like someone was bouncing a hair tie off my heart. I hauled her in my arms and she buried her head in my chest, soft sobs racking her delicate form.

"Look at me, baby." I tugged her chin up and cupped her face when she opened her bloodshot eyes and slayed me with that beautiful blue gaze. Bending down, I placed a kiss on each tear-stained cheek and then each eyelid, tasting her sadness and absorbing some of it so she wouldn't carry this burden alone. "We are not over and as for if we're meant to be or not, that's for us to decide. No one else gets to make that decision for us."

I stole whatever resistance she had left with a kiss on her pink lips and tasted tears there too. And maybe I was deluding myself because of my wants, but I swore hope and desire laced her mouth-watering taste too. I tangled one hand in her wet hair letting the other wrap around her waist. Eliana's mouth opened for me and her minty pants matched mine.

I backed her up against one of the columns that separated the bedroom from the living area, groaning when she wrapped her arms around my shoulders and her breasts rubbed against my chest.

I could do it. I could slip her flimsy robe off and take her right now, I knew she wouldn't resist. The bed was a few feet away. Although the wall, the floor, the couch, fuck, even a bed of nails would work for me as long as Eliana was naked and willing. But I didn't. I detached my mouth from hers as soon as her moans hit the back of my throat, exploding with sweetness.

Eliana wasn't a simple fuck for me, and this wouldn't be how we solved our problems. My dick wept as I got a good look at her thoroughly kissed red puffy face and hooded gaze.

"We're two consenting adults. We get to be the only ones holding the reins in our lives. I don't care what anyone else has to say and you shouldn't either." I nudged her nose with mine and she let out a small sigh, slipping her hands down my pecs.

"You're right. I shouldn't care. I've lived my whole life being judged for every minuscule detail. First, it was my mom fretting over what I should wear, and how I should talk. Then my dad went to jail and the whole world got involved."

Me and my bitch pack were part of that world too. The unsaid words dangled between us, like rotten fruit. I'd done a stellar job of putting her on a pedestal just so people could take their swipes at her.

She stopped fumbling with a button from my shirt and

met my gaze head-on. "For as long as I can remember, you've always been in my life. Friend, lover, foe. I've gotten to sample every side of you, and I guess I just need some time to think everything over, Leo. I need to learn who I am without you."

My body went rigid and my breath sliced in half.

"You want to see other people?"

Over my dead fucking body.

"No, I-I don't know." Her nose scrunched up as she thought about it. "I'm not really interested in dating right now. I just want to take some time to discover myself. Anyway, now that Carter and Claire are dealt with, we don't have to stay together. Our job—or I should say your father's job is done."

Again, she could see other people only when I was six feet under. I kept that thought to myself, recognizing that the ice I was treading on was fragile.

"Time?" I repeated.

"Yes." A smile slipped on her lips, and I didn't understand the reason why. "Time and space." She finished off her sentence by pushing me away and freeing her caged body.

Time and space.

Time and freaking space.

I could give her that. It would kill me, but I could give her that. I waited eight years for her. What were a few more weeks? Or months? Or maybe yea—

I stopped that thought before it had a chance of developing into a rabbit hole. I was willing to give her time, but I also wouldn't go crazy. Anything over a few months was non-negotiable, dating other people was off the table too. She didn't need to know that, but I'd make sure any poor sods that came close to her knew that they were running the risk of having their dicks amputated.

"Okay." I breathed hard through my nose. "You want time? I'll give you time. But this, us? We're happening, baby. You're not off the hook yet."

Chapter 26

ELIANA

I sold the mansion.

It'd been unlivable for a while now. Bad memories and spilled blood shrouded every corner. It wasn't a decision I took lightly. Writing off my entire childhood didn't come easy. The good would stay with me no matter what, though. It was the bad I wanted to get rid of, and the mansion had become an emblem for all the shit in my life.

Not to mention, after my mom's arrest people had taken it upon themselves to transform my front gates into a flower garden, and two months later, it was still blooming. Strangers showed up at all hours of the night, filming and whispering theories about what really went down between husband and wife. They took sides and fought over who the real victim was. The insane artist or the self-absorbed trophy wife?

My dad was the resounding winner of that debate, receiving the majority of the support.

One person that was always forgotten?

Me.

I faded into the shadows of my parents' limelight and learned to appreciate it. I didn't expect this kind of response, but I guess our vanity made us the star in everyone's story. When the realtor came to check the house, clutching her pearls in awe at the high ceilings and salivating all over the marble floors, I didn't feel any sense of loss. My chapter in their life was done. Now all that was left to do was say my goodbyes.

"You must be feeling quite loved, huh?" I murmured, caressing the letters engraved on the tomb.

Francis Ambrose Roux.

That was it.

No, *in loving memory of,* no, *a wonderful husband, father, and son.*

Nothing.

That was the single thing we'd been in charge of, and we chose to leave the engraving on his tomb blank. My father, ever the planner, had made funeral arrangements in advance. A macabre thing to do in retrospect. In a city like Astropolis, where real estate was held on a higher pedestal than active cemeteries, you had to be prepared for your death.

Opulence surrounded him even in death. He didn't spare a dime when it came to building this place. He thought his family was going following him here. There were two extra burial niches, and I didn't pay them much mind at first. I assumed maybe he'd thought of future generations.

The dots connected now, though.

Lylah and Cole.

"God, you were arrogant. Did you really think your wife and mistress would agree to be buried in the same place?"

If anyone walked past right now, took a peek through the stained glass windows, and found me talking out loud in an empty room with a tomb in the middle, they'd probably phone the local insane asylum to come leash me. I needed to speak, though. I didn't want to be stifled with emotions anymore, so dragged down by my thoughts, I felt exhausted by the end of the day. I found talking cathartic, like I could finally sort through so many open tabs in my brain.

"I guess in the grand scheme of things, you weren't so bad." I sighed, leaning back against a marble pillar. "You weren't bad at all, actually. You were an incredible father, with a shitty habit... lying. But hey, at least you didn't try to kill me, so that's something."

I cringed when I realized how passive-aggressive I sounded. I had a right to be mad, to not want to forgive and forget. I had to do this for me, though. Stewing over past events wouldn't do me any good in the long run—at least that was what my shrink said. It was unavoidable, really. You didn't have the parents I had and came out without needing some sort of professional help.

"Okay, let's try this again." I rubbed my sweaty hands on my thighs.

"What you did was bad. I know Claire didn't hold back either. You were married, but that was about it. You two led separate lives. I can't help thinking though that you were the instigator of everything."

My stomach knotted up as it always did when my mind wondered about this topic. I slid down the pillar slowly, resting my elbows on my knees as my ass touched the frigid ground.

It was six a.m. I'd woken up at the butt crack of dawn with the sudden desire to be rid of all the things that weighed me down. And I didn't know what it was, but I felt more at peace around the dead than I did with the living. Their sorrow rubbed off on my skin, blending in with my inherent melancholy until an oil canvas full of dark, angry strokes stood in the place of my heart.

"Cole is only nineteen, Dad, about to be twenty in two months. The same age as me. He will be the same age as me for three whole months," I stressed, raking my nails through my scalp. I might have dropped out of college, but the math wasn't hard to calculate. "You betrayed her first, and I hadn't even been alive for a whole year yet."

My words echoed inside the mausoleum, making it harder to work the sentences past the knot in my throat. I'd never forgive my mom for what she'd done, but in a way, I sympathized with her. I knew firsthand how being Dad's second choice felt like. The bitterness that laced my soul after I first found out who Cole was still lingered.

"In a way, I can't help blaming you for not having a relationship with her."

The downhill road to blame town was a slippery slope, and I'd had—I'd had Leo to help soothe the burn. He didn't let my walls build back up, he'd nipped the blooms of my resentment right in the bud, one soft word, touch, and dirty joke at a time.

But who did my mom have?

Carter.

The overachieving lawyer, one with an agenda longer than The Lord of The Rings. A failing man, looking for a vulnerable victim to take advantage of. Claire fell right into the hands of the wolf, betrayed and alone.

"Was that why you were always so attentive?" I whispered, the thought hitting me like a ton of bricks. "Did you feel guilty and were trying to make up for it? Or were you trying to show her up by proving to everyone that you were the better parent?"

I banged my head on the pillar, trying to stop my brain from forming any more connections. I didn't want to know. What had knowing ever gotten me besides heartbreak and pain?

One was dead, and the other would soon follow.

I was fighting a losing battle.

There was no point in lingering in what was or could have been. I'd never get an apology from either of them, and they could never right what they did wrong.

Not to me and not to each other.

I had to move past them. Break the chains that anchored my chest to the ground and soar. I deserved the good in my life, and I had enough self-respect to give myself the chance to become something more than the Roux's broken daughter.

I straightened up, dusting off my bottom, and reached for the bouquet I'd brought along. Daffodils, the flower of pardon and rebirth, because new beginnings required symbolic starts.

"I forgive you, Dad." I slid the posy in a clear vase by his name. "I hope you managed to forgive yourself too before you left."

I caressed the green marble surrounding the crypt one last time as I backed away, eyes lingering on the flowers. The botanic name for daffodils was Narcissus, according to the florist that prepared the bouquet for me.

Leo had been giving me my much-needed time. It wasn't like I could escape him entirely. We lived in the same town after all. But he was distant, and the interactions felt unnatural. Like I was expecting for him to either sneer at me or kiss me until my lips started bleeding, yet he did neither.

He just gave me what I asked.

I wasn't so sure I wanted it anymore, though.

I missed him.

I missed him so fucking much, and the fact that I knew his door was always open made it so much harder to stay away.

Wrapping my jacket tighter around me, I opened the gate, and a savage gust of wind hit me right in the face. My hair went flying all around, meeting all four directions. It was like south, east, north, and west all came out to play at the same time. Something landed on me as I tried to get my mane under control.

A little bloom with white petals and a yellow center.

I loved my new home.

It was way smaller than my previous one, a single-story, with great panoramic views of the Atlantic and an open floor plan. Multiple doors exited to an outdoor deck that allowed for breeze and sunshine to become one with the earthy-toned furniture.

It reminded me so much of our trips to Istanbul when I was younger. The colors of the sunsets, the smell and sounds of the ocean, transported me to my summers spent by the Mediterranean Sea.

"How about now? Is it up to your standards, milady?" Cole asked, twisting his upper body up on the ladder and addressing me.

Hanging up string lights by the edge of the roof, over the

sliding doors leading to the deck, he looked quite vexed as I surveyed his work. I took a sip of lemonade, letting the cool liquid freshen up my mouth a little bit before swallowing. "A Hard Day's Night," by the Beatles pumped out of the speakers, and I drummed my fingers on the wooden table, going along with the beat.

"Hm, you might need to bring the right side a bit upwards. Glue the spot right by the nail, yeah, right there," I confirmed, pointing at the same place as him. "It will still look a bit droopy, but it's okay."

It wasn't, but when his *face* went droopy, it sure made mine light up.

"Man, who knew having a little sibling would be this much fun?" I laughed at his glare, arching a playful eyebrow.

"Yeah, well, I think I'd like a refund," he grumbled, climbing off the ladder and planting his ass on the chair across from me.

I poured Cole some lemonade while we soaked up the sunshine. I kind of envied his ability to hang out in the sun without sunscreen or a hat and still tan while I took on the shade of a boiled lobster.

"I'm afraid that's not happening." I shrugged, handing him the glass. "We have years of the older sibling bullying the younger one to catch up on."

"Isn't it supposed to be the other way around? Also, you're like a year older. Stop flaunting it in my face."

"Is it? I must have missed the memo. Even seconds count, so you better believe that's a year I'm taking full advantage of."

He rolled his eyes, and I smiled as I took a sip. Cole and I had always acted as siblings in a way. Save from that one time, I thought he was hitting on me. Now I shuddered every time I thought about it.

He, on the other hand, didn't mind using it as an excuse to make fun of me. I moaned and groaned about it, acting annoyed, while at the same time putting him in charge of transporting my luggage on moving day. And Cole did it. He took care of everything with a smile on his face the whole time because he thought he'd out-snarked me that day.

"Leo, came up to me today," he spoke out of the blue, ruining my mojo. "He was waiting for me outside my econ class."

I had a gaping hole the size of Mars in my chest, and every time Leo's name was mentioned it made itself known, contracting and forcing me to shut my eyes and take a deep breath.

I wasn't a masochist. I didn't like hurting. But I never wanted to bring him into the difficult position of having to choose between me and his family. His mother was in rehab, for Christ's sake. I reminded myself that every time I felt weak and my phone looked mighty inviting.

I wouldn't rob him of his family.

Wouldn't take the role my mom left vacant.

"Really?" I asked, toying with the ice chips in my glass, sucking one in my mouth. "What did he want?"

"He wanted to know how you were holding up with the move and all that." Cole paused, cringing when I dumped the ice back in the glass. Whatever, it was freezing my brain. "Said if you needed any help, you should give him a call. I think he also mentioned something about a dance studio space being available on Mason's street... or Clement Avenue? I'm sorry, remembering is not my strong suit."

I pursed my lips, staring at him. "How does he know I started looking for dance studio space?"

"Probably the same way he knew, Rhys, the barista across the street from Bella's, asked you out."

"Wait—what? What happened to Rhys?" I frowned, leaning forward.

"When I stopped by the next day, he wouldn't look near my vicinity until he realized you weren't with me. I'm no detective, but it seemed like *someone* had a talk with him. It's good that you didn't actually go out with Rhys. Poor guy would've likely ended up in a ditch somewhere."

A shriek of anger bubbled up to the surface, but I swallowed it down. I didn't want to send Cole off, screaming.

So this was Leo's space and time. Lying to my face and scaring every guy off behind my back. He was acting like a fucking caveman, and I didn't appreciate it. Rhys was one of the sweetest guy's I'd ever met, regardless if that didn't do it for me.

No, my obsession was with mean assholes who made me lose my breath. The ones that turned me cruel with their actions. The ones that gassed up the steady fire in my soul until we both lived in a constant stream of heat.

"Fucking asshole." I cursed out a stream of expletives as I reached for my phone.

"What are you doing?" Cole asked, alarmed.

I didn't answer, just continued hitting the letters on the keyboard hard enough to crack my phone's screen. I felt Cole sliding behind me, taking curious peeks at my phone, soon as I hit send.

Eliana: Stop trying to fish information from Cole, and stop scaring my dates away!

Eliana: Time and space! Open a dictionary.

"Oh, now you really told him!" Cole breathed in my ear, and I shot him a look over my shoulder, recognizing the sarcasm in his voice.

We both focused back on my phone, like two kids waiting for their shot of candy. A lick of anticipation spread warmth inside my chest after finally stepping out of the mold of cordial politeness that stifled us.

I breathed faster when a ping soon followed.

Leo: I would've asked you, but I wasn't sure if you were ready for a question containing so many syllables yet.

Cole ate up the text faster than I did and guffawed. "He's right. You look like you're ready to run away screaming every time you see him in public."

My scowl deepened, and I elbowed his stomach. He doubled over further, giving me enough time to shield the next texts that came through from his intrusive gaze.

Leo: Your dates can fuck off.

Leo: I am giving you time. If you're looking for a ride, though, you remember the way home, baby.

I set my phone, screen down, back on the table, not missing a beat, even when I heard the screen crack. A buzz hummed beneath my skin, in response to the razor blades Leo threw my way.

I didn't fit in his home.

Chapter 27

LEONARDO

"**B**reathe, would you? You look like you're about to faint," I instructed as Dad and I walked through Lakehouse Recovery Center's halls. It looked like a palace, if I'd ever seen one, featuring private beachfront villas, landscaped grounds, and sparkling chandeliers.

"How much does the treatment here cost?"

"Let's just say the price of anonymity doesn't come cheap." Quite the opposite, it came at about twenty-thousand dollars a night. Sometimes I wondered if the excessive price point was just so the patients were simply too broke to buy drugs afterward. "There is no need for group sessions here, and the patients' personal information is closely guarded."

"You did your homework, huh?"

"Yeah, I didn't want to put you in an early grave, but it seems just the prospect of seeing your wife after months might," I teased, taking a peek at his pale face as we stopped in front of her room. Although I shouldn't be taking any jabs at him, I had skeletons of my own in my closet. "And I think this is a good time to tell you, I might've... sort of... insinuated that you had a hand in her attending rehab."

"You did what?" His green eyes widened and he leaned his suited frame against the wall by her door. Anxiety made his frame weak, and I had just added to that.

It had been a couple of months since I'd last seen Mom. I'd kept up with her over the phone though, I knew she was getting better day by day, learning to detach herself from her constant companion. Alcohol was like that one toxic friend that provided you with momentary comfort, but when your back was turned, did its damned best to break you.

At first, she refused to answer my calls. In the eyes of the law, her decision to come here was hers, but we both knew I'd coerced her into it. I still didn't regret it. I never would. It didn't make me feel like any less of a jackass though. Thankfully, time heals all wounds, and by the second month, she'd reluctantly started picking up my calls. Our conversations ranged from curt five-minute phone calls at first to full-blown hourly sessions a few weeks after.

I knew what to expect, but Dad didn't.

"Um, I told her that you wanted her to go to rehab too, and if she didn't go willingly, then you'd intervene." Even I cringed as I spoke the truth. Dad stared at me like he wanted to strangle me, his left eye twitching and I rushed to patch things up. "I'm sorry, but I had to do it. Mom values your word above everything else, she wouldn't have come otherwise, and she *needed* the treatment."

He sighed, and if it were possible, I bet fire would be blowing through his nostrils instead of air. I did take responsibility for my mistakes. I could've handled the past better, yet what happened, happened. Eliana, Barbara, Isabella all were weighing heavy at my consciousness at the time, and Alessio was the easy target. The one that had to be sacrificed to save everyone else.

It sounded harsh, but his name had been permanently stamped on my shit list.

"Fuck," he huffed harshly, scrubbing a hand down his stubble, ridding some of the tension on his body. "And of course, you waited until the last minute to tell me. We're going to talk about this later."

We both turned our gaze toward the door. A plaque with the number 201 was plastered on top of it. I didn't do it on purpose. My head had been rather preoccupied with a stubborn blonde whose last name rhymed with blew.

Because she was blowing me off big time.

I bit down on my bottom lip hard enough to sting and swiped my fingers through my hair. This was not the time to think about her. "Consider your debt to me paid. You didn't tell me about years of pursuing an active investigation. The way I see it, you come out on top."

Alessio shook his head, but I could tell he agreed. We both had bigger battles to fight than each other. Namely, Barbara Bianchi and Eliana Roux. And I planned on using up all my reserves.

The unspoken agreement between us led me forward, and I gripped the handle, throwing the door open slowly to not startle anyone inside.

Mom looked... she looked better.

Perfect even.

Her cheeks were flushed with a healthy glow, and her skin tone had transitioned from a pale white to a normal beige one. Her brown hair, gray eyes, high cheekbones, *everything* looked so... healthy. She seemed capable of standing on her own two feet, no crazy falls, no dragging feet. Nothing.

Mom was stone-cold sober, her eyes clear as two fresh-water lakes as she jumped in my arms in greeting. "Leo!" she exclaimed, hands wrapping around my broad shoulders.

With ease, I tucked her tiny, sweat covered frame under my embrace, reveling in the fact that I couldn't feel any ribs poking out from her sides. I still thumbed them, making sure she was eating well, and she squirmed in my arms, giggling.

"Stop it!" She managed to wiggle her way out of my embrace, cupping my face in her hands. "What are you doing here? No one informed me you'd visit today."

"Aren't you happy to see me?" I teased, and a spark of mirth passed through her expression. While the unanimous decision was that I looked more like my dad, personally I had a different opinion. It was true, appearance-wise, I was closer to my dad, but my actions and personality were more like a shadow version of my mom's. My heart overflowed with joy, now that I was finally getting that piece of her back. She was very much alive, smiling, and happy.

"Of course I am," she scoffed, rolling her eyes. "I just wasn't expecting anyone today."

"Well, we wanted it to be a surprise, hope you don't mind." I leaned in, kissing her forehead.

"What are you talking about, why would I mind? And— wait... who's *we?*" Mom took a step back and peeked over my shoulder. The gray in her eyes deepened, and the tempera-ture in the room dropped by a thousand degrees when she looked at her husband.

"Barbara." I heard Dad's voice. He sounded calm and collected, but I couldn't turn back around to see him. My mom had latched on to my forearms with a bruising grip, and I stayed put because she needed someone to hold on to.

"Alessio." She mirrored his greeting, her previous enthusiasm lacking. Her gaze zig-zagged between me and Dad, not knowing what to make of the two of us together and likely feeling much like I did when Dad first came back in town.

"Come on." I threw an arm around her shoulders, leading us to the couch by the windows. "We have a lot of catching up to do."

Mom's room was spacious. It managed to fit a king-sized bed, an en-suite bathroom, and a mini living room and kitchenette fully equipped with a mini-fridge. She had opted out of a private villa when we first came, and I supported that decision. I didn't want her to be lonely, and it looked like she had been keeping busy. A pink yoga mat lay abandoned on the parquet floor, the soft murmur of an on-screen instructor mere background noise as we relayed what she'd missed the past few days.

By the end of our recount, she was shaking like a leaf. I could tell my dad wanted to reach out, but my mom's grip on the suede couch became knuckle white when he leaned closer. Rejection sloshed through his bones, and he slumped back on his armchair, never taking his eyes off her.

"And you kept this from me? From us?" Mom's tone was low but uneven. Betrayal was evident in her stance, and she etched farther away from him. "For four years you let me believe in a different version of the story. You *left* me and stripped me of the choice to hear the truth. The truth about what happened to my daughter!"

"Mom." I stepped in, tugging her to me, and she melted in my chest as sobs racked her body. "I know it's a lot to take in, *trust me*," I stressed, side-eyeing Dad, who looked like he was sitting on a crown of thorns. I had time to chew on his lack of finesse when it came to dealing with this situation, so I was speaking from experience.

"I already made sure Dad understood the gravity of his mistakes." I refrained from mentioning what really happened, didn't want to overburden her. "Please, let's try to take this one day at a time. I'm worried about you."

She didn't reassure me in any way, just kept sobbing against my chest. I felt every painful sniffle down to my heart. Mom was vulnerable and sheltered. She was a wonderful person with a heart of gold that for the longest time looked at the world through a green-tinged plexiglass. Money made the world go round, but they didn't bring the world to you. She was breakable, ever so fucking breakable. I wouldn't let it go past the breaking point this time. Would do my damned best not to.

"I want a divorce," she muttered against my shirt, and my gaze flew to Dad's. Thankfully he was too lost in his own misery to hear her weak admission. He stood frozen, wanting to help, but unable to.

"Shh..." I smoothed my hand down her hair, tugging her head back so she would look at me. "We're going to take this one day at a time, okay? There is no need to make rash decisions. We have all the time in the world... well, I'd like to believe you guys have at least fifty more years."

Her eyes crinkled slightly at my joke, and I swiped the tears that gathered on the sides. "Take the time to digest everything. We're all together now. You want to have daily crying sessions together? We'll do that. You want to attend therapy? We'll do that too. Whatever you want, I'm always here."

"Me too," Dad threw in, and she sucked in a breath.

I bit my tongue because if *I* had about a thousand retorts to his little comment, Mom must've had a million. He needed to show her he'd be there for her, or else I'd back any decision she took all the way.

I kept her chin tucked between my fingers until I had her rapt attention. "Together. We're gonna work everything out together."

She nodded, and a loud exhale fought its way out of my mouth, but I didn't let it out yet. It would probably stay lodged there for a few more months. I wanted my family happy, and that included Eliana.

Happy and by my side.

Then I'd be able to breathe and sleep well.

"Okay." She nodded again, pressing her eyes closed. "But I'm only doing this for you, Leonardo. Lord knows you've suffered enough, forced to grow up before your age and take care of me. I'm sorry, I want you to know that. I'm so damn sorry for stealing your childhood away."

Yeah, by the time Mom had started drinking, I'd lost my virginity a couple hundred times over and been a dick to more people than I'd actually dicked. There was no ounce of childhood left in me. Big towns will do that to you. Rich towns will take every bit of innocence, twist up and shred it to pieces. Both combined left you with a slot of little assholes running around amok. No wonder we were all fucked up.

"You didn't steal any—" I started, but she cut me off, her hand floating between us.

"I did. I'm no better than they are. They stole my daughter's life. They probably ruined their daughters' lives as well. I remember both of them. Eliana and Serena. Isabella always used to gush about their time together when she was younger." She shook her head wistfully, staring at her knotted hands. "What separates us from them, really? We were so lost in our own anger we couldn't see past it and you paid the price."

"You're confusing grief with anger, Barbara." My father spoke out, not able to hold back anymore. "Could we have handled things better? Yes. But that doesn't make us equal to the antichrist."

"You have no room to talk. You weren't here," she snapped at him. "The sins of the parents should never fall on the children's shoulders, but that's all Leonardo has been doing. Paying for our incompetence."

"I am not a child." Unless children were six feet and some inches tall and could grow a beard, then I could safely say that that argument could be put to rest. "Whatever it is between you, either work it out or don't use me as the driving point behind your arguments. And Mom, we're all allowed to grieve. You didn't steal anything from me, quite the opposite. I've lived a very privileged life and am extremely grateful for all that you both have given me."

They both shut up after that, losing their bite as soon as they'd gained it. I continued talking, since the air was drenched in sin, I took the liberty to add my own mark. Let Mommy know how innocent her child had been through the years.

Noble and good.

I wish.

"Don't paint me as a saint when I've been anything but one. You found comfort in alcohol, Dad buried himself in the past, but me?" I scoffed, rubbing my hands over my jeans. "I found solace in reaping misery out of people. I made sure Eliana Roux's every day turned char black. Was a dick to everyone in my life and am still convinced they suffer from some degree of Stockholm syndrome for sticking it out with me."

"What?"

"Yeah, although I'm not sure my *dickness* is a fleeting thing. Ares still swears by it." I cracked a smile at her wide eyes.

"*Dickness* is not a word. And what do you mean you turned Eliana's days black? What did you do to the poor girl?"

Poor girl.

The words stuck out to me, like two quick knife wrist flicks.

The first thing I realized from those two short words was that there was still hope. Mom didn't hate Eliana. I'd get to keep both of them.

For the first time in never, I'd get to have my cake and eat it too.

The second thing was Eliana was no poor girl. She'd dropped out, gained a family member, and started building her career. She was shooting for the sky, and I had no doubt she'd land among the stars.

I was the poor boy. I needed her more than she needed me. I was stuck, and she was flourishing. I was the pain she'd never asked for. She didn't want me, but I didn't know how to fucking live without her.

No more time.

No more space.

It was time to get my ass in gear.

"It's a long story."

"And it's still not done," Dad added wistfully.

Eliana

I looked like I'd French-kissed a ladybug.

My lips were scrubbed raw because I couldn't decide on a lipstick. I went with a clear gloss instead, sealing the debate with a thick layer of extra shine.

I felt nervous. My skin was buzzing with anticipation, which spoke volumes for the current state of my social life, or lack thereof. Maddy invited me to the grand opening of her friend's new restaurant downtown, and it would be the first time I showed my face in public after my family's hundredth scandal.

Shaking my head, I sealed the tube and dropped it in my clutch. It was now or never. I couldn't live my entire young adult life behind the four walls of my home. Besides, my dress deserved its moment to shine. The pleated baby blue number, outfitted with a sheer, beige-hued overlay, hung off my body like a dream.

Slipping on some nude pumps and a coat, I grabbed my keys off the console and opened the front door only to come up short. A man stood crouched before me, and his jet-black head snapped up at my terrified gasp. The green eyes that greeted me weren't the ones that dominated my dreams. No, they were the ones that'd shattered them.

"Do you want to kill me prematurely, is that your plan?" I clutched my chest, hoping to slow down the rapid beat of my heart.

It was the second time Alessio Bianchi had snuck up on me unexpectedly.

He let out a chuckle as he stood up, his suit wrinkling with his movement. It didn't sound ironic or mean. A hint of nervousness peaked below as he ran a hand through his hair, looking over my shoulder and inside my house.

"Oh, I didn't know you were home."

"So you thought to look under my door to confirm that theory?"

I wouldn't even ask how he got my new address. It wasn't like I'd moved miles away from Astropolis. I was still within city limits, but far enough to separate myself from the toxicity surrounding the town like an overcast cloud.

"I was just tying my shoelaces, that's all."

My gaze swept down his disheveled outfit. The lapels of his gray suit flapped slightly as a light breeze ravaged my front porch. His white dress shirt was loose, a few buttons up top, revealing a dusting of sparse hair on his chest, and paired off with some Gucci loafers.

My eyebrows rose sharply as I replied. "Tying the nonexistent shoelaces on your loafers?"

His eyes fell to his feet, and we both examined them, an awkward silence stifling the air. "Would you look at that? There really aren't any. You'll have to excuse me. It seems old age is catching up with me."

Riiight... forty-something was considered equal to eighty and suffering from cataracts now.

"Okay... um, is there a reason why you're here? I'm in a bit of a rush."

Count on me to lose my backbone when I most needed it. I didn't want to know what he was here for. I was afraid it would go kind of like last time. In any case, I shut the door behind me, leaning against it to get some of the weight off my heels.

"It was pointed out to me that I might have been a bit unfair the last time we met."

A wave of surprise rushed down my body, even though what he was saying was very *"the sky is blue"* news. I searched his face for any signs that this was a joke, but the lines on his forehead remained harsh and determined. He meant it.

"A bit unfair?" I questioned, a cunning smile pulling on my lips.

"I was *very* unfair. And mean," he corrected, sighing through his teeth. "I would like to apologize, Ms. Roux. I had no business meddling in something that didn't involve me. Your relationship with my son took me by surprise, and I acted before I could think it through."

I could tell this was taking a lot out of him. He kept fiddling with his clothing as he spoke, going against his polished nature. He was apologizing to his enemy, and I didn't feel the need to rub it in his face. Regardless of his agenda, he'd done me a favor.

Alessio's past words captured the essence of how unrealistic mine and Leo's expectations were.

We were way in over our heads.

No one could heal while our relationship kept the painful past stitched together.

"You don't have to apologize." I swallowed the lump in my throat as I released the words. "I had some time to think about what you said as well, and it wasn't all untrue. You were right, we are both too young and nothing can ever flourish when it lacks support."

A relationship was a multifaceted aspect of life. Like humans needed oxygen, food, and sleep, like plants needed sunlight and water, relationships couldn't survive solely on love. If the habitat was hostile, you'd seldom see spurts of growth.

"No, I wasn't." He shook his head at my words. "I was nasty for no reason, and I thought Leo was doing this just to get back at me."

"And was he?" The breath I was trying to pull got stuck in my lungs.

"No, of course not." Alessio was quick to confirm, running his hand through his hair again. "I'm making this worse, aren't I? What I wanted to say was that I miscalculated my steps and added one more person to my shit list than I should have. Contrary to my past actions, I care about my son and want to see him happy. If that's with you, then so be it."

"Well, don't spare me any compliments now." I rolled my eyes, ungluing my back from the door. "And call me Eliana, I'm not my mother."

"I am well aware of that, *Eliana*. You're truly not. You seem quite capable of taking care of yourself, and I know you helped my son look for answers even at the risk of going against your own blood. Your father would be proud of you for doing the right thing."

"Thank you, but I'm afraid I can't take all the praise. My French descent and fat inheritance do make it easier for me to roll through life unperturbed, unlike less privileged people in my position."

"Yes, but you could have also turned out to be nothing but a brat, blowing your money away, one party at a time. There are two sides to every story."

My chest swelled with pride at his approval, like a peacock raising its feathers. My need for validation trumped my pride. It had been too long since I heard a *job well done*. "I'm still young. You never know what might happen."

Alessio smiled, quite condescendingly, in fact. He most

likely thought I was all talk and no bite, and I could actually vouch for it. I was a bit of a prude and an introvert, all things considered.

"I'm willing to bet otherwise if what Leonardo has been saying about you is to be believed."

There was that painful thump again.

The ever-present shallowness in my heart.

The ice sheet I kept trying to build around my emotions didn't stand a chance whenever I heard his full name. It hit the frost around my heart with the same viciousness lava flow had ravaged the whole of Pompeii.

"What has he been saying?" I shifted my clutch from one hand to the other, airing out my sweaty grip.

Thump, thump, thump.

Stupid heart.

Stupid me.

"I believe that's not for me to share." He took a step back, and despite being severely late for the opening by now, I didn't want him to leave yet. Not when he threw me a bone and I was hunting for the full steak.

I stepped forward, but I was no match for his gait. He retreated, the space between us opening up. "I'm sorry again, Eliana. Children shouldn't have to pay for their parents' sins. I hope you can find it in you to forgive me. "

With that, he lowered himself in his bright red Ferrari, stepping on the gas and after a blink, nothing but a cloud of exhaust emissions stood in its place.

Dammit.

Goddammit.

Under any other circumstances, I would've forgiven him on the spot. He had no reason to apologize in the first place.

Sure his words stung, his rejection even more so, but he had every right not to want me around.

I tried to brush off the fact that he'd left me hanging, but my shoulders were unnaturally stiff as I headed on over to my car. I was ready to get trashed on cheap beer and feel my head pound as obnoxious pop music blasted through the speakers. With some wishful thinking, a night out would help me wipe the long-lasting effects the Bianchi clan had left behind.

A white spot on the gray driveway caught my attention, and I squinted as I tried to make it out. A folded piece of paper lay discarded, where the Ferrari was not too long ago.

I picked it up, trying to flatten the wrinkled page as best as I could.

My heart pulled short at the hand-drawn image inside the folded letter. The page was yellowed, but I could make out the girl on the sketch as clear as day... because it was me.

My wide-set eyes looked alluring, slanted in an almond shape that gifted me the whole 'just woke up' look. My hair was fanned out all around me, like a blonde halo of loopy ringlets. I was lying on a bed, I could make out the outline of a pillow below me, pushing out my chest that was donned in a bralette. The fullness of my upper lip almost met with the bottom of my nose as I smiled. My face was illuminated at its highest points, my cheekbones looked sharp enough to cut through skin as the artist had experimented with shadow play.

This wasn't me.

This was past me.

The happy one.

The one that lived despite the severity of her world and didn't just survive.

The one that had that one person that made everything worth it. Every struggle, every breath, every day.

A tear rolled down my cheek, smearing the initials at the bottom of the page.

"L.B."

I rolled my thumb over the salty substance, wiping it away and making it worse at the same time. I didn't want a drawing. I wanted to live out the sketch.

I wanted him.

Consequences be damned, I wanted Leo.

Chapter 28

ELIANA

GRADUATION

The crowd spread before me like a colony of ants. The soon-to-be graduates, in their shiny golden capes, mingled with each other on Dane's ginormous football field. Expensive notes of perfume lingered in the air. I stuck out like a sore thumb between parents donning pearly smiles and misty eyes as they waited for the ceremony to begin.

I was a spectator, not a participant.

A college drop-out. A national gossip hot-topic. A recipe for disaster.

Everyone was looking at me. The look in Leo's eyes as he gazed at me from across the field made it all worth it, though. I'd taken the first step. A tentative slide in the right direction and accepted his invitation to attend his graduation ceremony. And so far? I wasn't regretting it one bit.

I smiled at him from my place on the sun-bleached red

bleachers, and even from miles away, his signature smirk and wink had my heart racing. I didn't know how he managed to pull that ghastly yellow color off when everyone else looked like baby chickens.

"Gosh, barf much? I preferred it when you could barely look at him." Cole accompanied his complaint with retching sounds, shifting on his seat.

I snapped my gaze to his, relishing in the sarcasm painted on his face. "Jealous, squirt?" I tried to mess up his hair, but he swatted my hand away before I could touch his precious locks. "Don't worry, I promise you'll still get my undivided attention."

"Eliana?" The airy voice traveling from behind my back cut my torment of Cole short.

The smile on my face froze when I turned around. Barbara Bianchi stood on the steps of the aisle, an elegant black dress wrapped around her slim figure. Alessio wasn't far behind. He loomed over her head, a permanent frown etched on his face.

"Mrs. Bianchi?" I asked, dumbfounded.

"Hi!" She grinned tightly, gesturing to the empty space next to me. "Do you mind if we sit with you?"

My throat tightened as I shook my head. "No, of course not."

Yes, yes, I mind.

I was a vehement believer that women should stick together, that we had more power in numbers. I'd even been described as overtly feministic by my mother once, when I defended a woman that had "broken up" her friend's marriage, by saying her cheating husband should get just as much, if not more scrutiny.

The irony wasn't lost on me now.

We were as cunning as we were smart. We caught sly glances, wicked jabs, and undercutting remarks in the air and were proficient in bouncing them back. Most of us were cursed with an overload of emotional intelligence, and that was why I held my cards closer to my chest when dealing with women on opposing fields.

Alessio was ruthless, but Barbara had the power to gut me.

The sweat from my thighs stuck to the plastic bleachers as I scooted over and adjusted my blue sundress before sitting back down. I took a sharp breath when Barbara leaned over me to shake Cole's hand.

"I don't think we've met. I'm Barbara, Leo's mother and this is my hu—" She cleared her throat. "This is Alessio, Leo's dad."

Alessio mumbled a quick hi, leaning closer to Barbara, but didn't bother with a handshake. Cole took her hand in his, a polite smile plastered on his face. "Cole, nice to meet you. I'm Eli's brother."

From another mother. If it were anyone else, Cole would've probably slid that tidbit in, but even he wasn't oblivious to the tension gripping the air.

"Ah, so I heard." Barbara straightened up, and I didn't miss how she avoided touching her husband. "It's amazing how you two get along so well already. We could hear you laughing from atop the stairs," she said. I didn't know how to infer her words. Was she being malicious or was she genuinely surprised?

"We had our fair share of difficulties, but I decided to take him in after he wouldn't shake off of me." I grinned tentatively, taking the high road.

Cole scoffed next to me, but he didn't have a rebuttal. It

took Leo threatening to chop his baby maker off for him to stop calling every day. He'd have a stellar career in groveling in the future. I'd already told him so.

"Well, I'm glad you kids have each other. Siblings are eternal, even if friends change and lovers leave. I too, had a sister, but unfortunately, she lost her battle against leukemia when we were still young."

"I'm so sorry to hear that," I muttered, watching as Alessio inched his hand slowly to hers until he'd engulfed her tiny fist in his.

Unlike both men in her family, Barbara was on the smaller side of the human spectrum. She looked like a pixie, with brown hair, cut in a stylish bob beneath her ears and an upturned nose, that got even tinier when she wrinkled it.

"Oh don't worry dear, I've learned to live with it. It's not true what they say, *time heals all*... but it does mute the pain. I visit her grave quite frequently and promptly talk to her and Isabella's headstones for hours on end like a proper lunatic."

"You do?" My gaze snapped to hers as soon as the words left her mouth. I was taken aback by the kindness in her eyes. I was taken aback by this evening as a whole. My baby step had turned into a leap as it turned out that Barbara didn't harbor any hatred in her heart for me.

"Yes. It helped me get through some tough times and shed some of my anger. It is almost as if they're there, looking over me and rolling their eyes at my insistent chatter." A sense of understanding passed between us. A connection charged the air, and she shook slightly, regaining her smile again and shaking her hand from her husband's grip. "Anyway... no need to talk about all that, today is a happy day."

"I understand." My whisper got lost in the excited

chatter of the throng. We settled forward as the professors started rolling out. I sought out Leo, finding him sitting in the front row, flanked by Saint and Ares on either side. "You must be quite proud of your son; he's top of his class."

"The proudest. Not only because of his academic achievements. Leo has always been smart, although his baby pictures might give a different impression. I'll have to show them to you sometime," she said casually, and my heartbeat faltered. "He has a heart of gold too, and that's what I'm most proud of."

"Yes, he's quite something," I said and blushed when she threw me a sly smile.

"I wanted to thank you."

"Whatever for?"

"For taking him along when you pulled yourself out of the mud. Both of you are survivors, but I have a feeling you were the pioneer. Thank you for not leaving my son behind. I'll never forget it." Barbara squeezed my hand and focused on the ceremony as a voice rang from the speakers, welcoming everyone.

There was power in admitting your mistakes. I'd been wrong. So dead wrong. My heart sputtered in my chest, flapping in its attempt to be revived again. Barbara's statement breathed life in my forbidden dreams, ridding every corner of my soul off the slithering smoke that lingered. It was as if I could see pieces of shattered glass gluing back together behind my prolonged blink as I turned to look at Cole.

"I told you so," he mouthed at me.

He had. My little brother saw the best in people. Cole was convinced not everyone was a lunatic in this town. He saw things through a fresh set of eyes, as opposed to me, constantly shrouded by the weight of people's opinions. My enemies had succeeded in one thing, and that was piercing through my soft tissue until they'd drained me of my confidence.

With Barbara's blessing branded on the back of my brain, I powered through the need to run to Leo. I stewed in my seat, going through the motions. Clapping when it was required and laughing when one of the professors cracked a corny joke.

Too many sweaty handshakes and diploma exchanges later, Leo's turn finally arrived. The dean called his name, and I joined the rest of the people on my bench in shouts of pride and joy, clapping until my palms felt raw. I was proud of him. So damned proud, and fuck... just a little bit turned on?

An educated man was attractive.

Leo retrieved his diploma, but as he set out to make his way off the stage, he veered in the last moment, sauntering toward the podium. My brows met my hairline as a team of football players swarmed the stage from each side, with Saint and Ares leading the packs. They formed a human wall around Leo as he tapped the mic, testing it.

"What the hell is going on?" I asked no one in particular.

"I have no idea," Barbara replied anyway, leaning forward.

Hijacking.

They were hijacking the ceremony, but Leo didn't care as he flashed his pearly whites at a horde of groaning students.

"Good afternoon, ladies and gentlemen." His voice rang across the student body and their relatives.

"Hey! What do you think you're doing?" I could hear the staff's confusion all the way from the stands. The air shifted, and small-talk ceased as Leo captured the undivided attention of a few thousand people.

His natural-born confidence shone through, though. He wore his smirk like a suit of armor, ignoring the world behind him and showering the crowd upfront with his undivided attention. "For those of you living under a rock. Hi, I'm Leonardo Bianchi... some of you may know me as Bruised Balls."

He did not just say that.

I choked on my next breath, laughter mixing with disbelief, and Cole had to slap my back to get me to function again.

Oh, but he did.

Laughter rose like smoke all around me, and I wanted to crawl in a hole. It seemed the headlines the day of Serena's party weren't missed. Especially the one poking fun at his family's company.

BB Oil—Is The Bianchi Oil Empire Really Named After Their Only Heir's Bruised Balls?

Spoiler alert: Enemy's daughter, Eliana Roux, was spotted kneeing the young playboy, outside her new stepfather's property. Take a look at the ball-busting video below.

That particular video was blasted on every gossip site long enough for me to swear off phones forever. I might've not lasted long, but it was the thought that mattered.

"Fuck... well, I guess the nickname was not all false. Thank you for that." He nodded toward the gaping press members in the audience that was here to document some politician's speech later on. He was giving them a juicer story and every camera honed in on Leo's face. "But it wasn't just my balls that were bruised. It was my heart too. That's what happens when you disappoint the person you love."

His gaze found me in the crowd, and I froze under the full force of his brilliant green eyes. Had he just said the L-word? His heart might have been bruised, but mine was close to shattering. It beat so fast, I rubbed my hand over it, aware of the ache that spread down my body like stretching vines.

"So to confirm everyone's speculation. Yes, I am in love with Eliana Roux. I have been ever since I was old enough to know what love was. My feelings weren't sudden or out of the blue. Eliana has owned me wholly for the past ten years. Whether it was love or hate or both mixed together, I couldn't get enough of her, and I still can't. I never will. She's my endgame, and I'd rather die than live without her so the scrutiny of every rando means absolutely nothing to me."

He had just said the L-word.

Accompanied by my freaking name.

In front of at least five-thousand people.

He was blasting my insecurities in the air by making me face the music. And the best part? The shocked gasps, snide remarks, and side glances barely registered in my mind. Barbara fisted my other hand, but I couldn't turn to look at her.

"I wanted to come up here today, to drive home the point of how many shits I give on everyone else's opinion about the matter. Around minus a thousand for those looking for specifics. Have at it. Make your outrageous headlines, sell your lies, because I know the truth..." He had lost his smile now, his forehead troubled, hands fisting each side of the podium. "... And Eli will too after today, because as much as I love her, I've really only shown the opposite."

Test me, his pursed lips screamed as his aura nailed

down even the harshest of critics. He was declaring war on everyone that liked to run their mouths.

A layer of heat blanketed the back of my neck from the weight of the glares, but Leo was there to blast them away.

"Eliana, you ruined me the moment you threw me in the pool when I tried to kiss you for the very first time. For all of you pervs out there, we were unfortunately very much clothed."

Nervous laughter bubbled up my throat. I was so lost. His words were dancing around my head, letters swimming and mixing together. My vision turned blurry, and even more giggles escaped me when laughter rang around me again.

"My god, even when he's trying to win her back, he's crass as ever." Barbara sighed in resignation, directing her voice to Alessio. "He got that from you."

"I think he's doing fantastic, learning from the best. After all, I won you over, didn't I?" Alessio replied.

I tuned them out as Leo tore out the mic from the podium, much to the professors' protests. He walked down the small steps of the stage, the green lawn crunching beneath his weight as he made his way to me.

"You were my very own Narcissus," Leo continued and if I thought I was frozen before, I'd turned into a fucking icicle when the nickname escaped his mouth. "So fucking unattainable and perfect, but you wanted nothing to do with me, and I wanted everything from you. Do you know the story of Echo and Narcissus, my love?"

I shook my head no.

Oh, I knew it alright, but I wanted him to say it. I craved his rampage on my heart for just a little longer. His stomping all over it stopped feeling invasive. He wasn't here to conquer and leave. He was here to stay, make his mark and revel in us.

Because he loved me.

He loved me enough to shout it in front of a football field filled with people.

I bit my lip to hide my smile, despite the tears streaming down my face when I saw the glint in his eyes as he approached. He knew I knew, yet still humored me.

"Well, let me shift the genders a bit, so the rest of our audience doesn't get confused. I've known most of these fuckers for four years now, and I'm still amazed at how they managed to graduate."

"Some of them probably never will if you don't wrap this up, Bianchi," the dean countered from a second microphone, fighting a smile. The human wall of football players was still intact, but they didn't struggle to hold anyone back. "And stop swearing, for God's sake."

"Sorry, Mr. D, just making another boring graduation memorable here." Leo, ever my little anarchist, smiled conspiratorially at me, stopping a foot away from the railing that separated us. The vines closing in around me struggled to take him in too, but I held them back, my hands trembling to touch him.

"Once upon a time, in a land far away, where togas were all the rage and Greek gods got to fu—" He cut himself off as some poor mothers readied their palms over their children's ears and Barbara gasped for the zillionth time next to me. "Love whoever they pleased, there lived a huntress called Narcissa. Said huntress was drop-dead gorgeous. Ocean blue eyes that crystallized when she was mad, wavy golden hair that looked like they'd absorbed the sun. No one could take their eyes off the stunning beauty."

"I think he's talking about you," Cole said next to me, and a mixture of snot and tears threatened to overtake my laugh.

"Thanks for the clarification, dude," Leo countered.

"Anytime."

His focus was back on me. The look in his eyes was final and his face grave. He was nervous. Uncertainty permeated the air and my position of power tasted bittersweet.

"So Echo, the poor sod, never stood a chance against her either. He fell. Fell down the rabbit hole until he couldn't make sense of his feelings. The more he learned, the more he looked beyond the beauty's shield, the more he loved what he found. He was screwed, utterly and unequivocally screwed. But Narcissa didn't want him, so he strived to gain her hatred instead when he figured out he couldn't get her love."

Done with the barriers, Leo ate up the distance between us, jumping over the fence with ease. His proximity did wonders between my legs, and his words melted my faux resistance with ease.

I took the hand he stuck out between us without a second thought. Leo jerked me up, cradling my head in his palms. The microphone, the laughs, his family, mine... everything melted away as his skin hummed against mine. I was hyper-aware of his soul laying beneath my feet in pure surrender.

"Your arrows pierced my heart until it bled black, Eliana," he whispered against my mouth. "I never thought we'd get to have this, but what do you say? Do you want to rewrite the ending in our story, baby?"

"How can you be so sure I won't fall in love with my own

reflection?" I taunted, enjoying the curve of his lips on my cheek.

His eyes danced with mirth. "I'll give you something prettier to look at."

"Bastard." I flicked his nose, and he captured my fingers in a free hand, bringing my wrist to his lips. My pulse stalled, and acceptance all but flew from my mouth. "Okay, if you must insist, I guess I'll have you. But that's it, Bianchi. You're stuck with me forever."

"Even when I'll sometimes annoy the hell out of you?" he baited, knowing full well the scars we'd inflicted on each other would never fade. Both the good and the bad. His name was carved into my soul. Nothing ever came without a cost between us.

For Leo, I was willing to risk my heart, though.

"That's the thing, baby." I threw my hands around his neck, pressing closer. "I am bound to you. You can't leave without taking my heart with you."

Leo's eyes turned molten, and neither of us could wait anymore. We attacked each other's mouths just as cheers and catcalls assaulted our ears. My body came alive, like haywire. Our kisses of war progressed, rapturing into a kaleidoscope of love. A rainbow burst behind my eyelids, colors swirled and came alive with a vibrancy that had me gasping for air.

I murmured a weak protest when he stopped all too soon, forgetting where we were, getting lost in our beautiful, chaotic world that razed everything to the ground. My heart was overflowing, bleeding all over Leo's fists as he held it tight.

"I love you, Narcissa." He smiled into our kiss.

"I love you more, Echo."

Epilogue

ELIANA

Six Years Later

R ough hands encircled the contours of my waist. The touch was branding, consuming, and achingly familiar. A plop sounded as the lemon I was squeezing slipped from my hand and down to the juice bowl below. Spittle stained my dress and the quartz countertop.

"Hm... I'm really digging this dress," Leo said, hands trailing down the skirt, and bunching up the white floral fabric. "The South Carolina housewife look is definitely becoming. Makes me want to lick sweet tea off your pretty skin, sweetheart."

My boyfriend made good on his statement. His teeth dug into the tender skin of my neck before he followed up the sting with a long lick that spread goose bumps down my spine. He was insatiable. Ever since we'd gotten to Santorini, I couldn't breathe without sharing his air. I wasn't complaining though, life back home was hectic, and we needed some time away to recharge... and fuck.

Horny Leo made for a cranky Leo.

"You've got a very overactive imagination there, babe," I gasped out, nails digging into his arm that dipped past my panty line.

Going straight for the kill, he inserted two digits inside of me, his thumb rolling over my clit. I didn't know where he found this much energy after spending hours in the hotel's gym, but I wasn't about to complain, not when the anticipation of the high rolled over my senses.

"I'm afraid you're right." He tugged on my earlobe with his teeth, his minty breath teasing my decollete. I rested my head back on his chest, pressing my ass harder against his hard-on when he curled his fingers just right. "There probably isn't any sweet tea on this side of the world, but I can more than settle for ouzo."

His other hand fisted my hair, tugging my head back until his lips found mine. I moaned into the warm heat of his mouth, tasting a bit of the Greek liquor on his tongue. The delightful licorice taste hit the back of my throat, spreading a stinging sweetness over my body as he continued to work me with his fingers. One more, two more fingers pushing inside of me, and euphoria blasted in my womb.

"Oh, god!" I came embarrassingly quickly, my cheeks flashing with heat. He didn't mind though, Leo said he loved my responsiveness, how I seemed to always be wet around him. I told him that wasn't scientifically possible, but I was kind of starting to believe it too now. He was the whole package, brains, looks, an absolutely filthy mouth that I loved. I had a hard time keeping my hands off him.

Leo chuckled against my mouth, pecking the skin around

my lips. "I take it you're not opposed to that idea, huh, Narcissus?"

I turned around, weightlessness gripping my movements, just in time to catch the moonlight seeping from the open balcony doors and illuminating his face. I sucked in a breath, running my palms flat over his naked chest. Sweaty, rugged, and all mine.

Time had been good to him, and life had been kinder to both of us. Leo's mom was in her third year of being clean. She had a relapse shortly after exiting rehab, but Alessio was there every step of the way much to her disbelief. He had a lot of free time now that Leo had taken over the majority of the workload at BB Oil. He'd be ready to become head of the company as soon as next year.

"Only if I get to be fed oysters on the beach, while you hold an umbrella over my head to shield me from the sun," I joked, negotiating. "If I'm gonna be a sticky mess, I should at least get something out of it."

"Well, now you're just hurting my feelings, babe." Leo engulfed my hand in his, kissing the back of it and tugging me closer. "I always give more than I get. Besides, my aphrodisiac will hold your interest much more than oysters will."

"Why?" I asked haughtily, smiling up at him. "Are you packing bigger pearls behind your shell?"

"You best believe my pearls are bigger. There's no shortage of them either, you just look at me and they keep on coming."

I threw my head back on a laugh and squealed when he gripped my waist tight, circling my legs around his midriff. I held on, locking my ankles behind his back and curling my fingers in his black strands. "Their value would decrease then, though. An abundance of something makes for lack of need."

"And yet you're just as needy as when I first saw you, if not more." He leaned forward, proving his point with a dizzying kiss. Humid summer air shifted around us as Leo moved, leading our tangled form to the balcony.

"That's because you're my happy drug." I toyed with his five o'clock shadow, my breathing hoarse. "I can live without pearls. I can't live without you."

His answering smile was stunning. "My gorgeous prima ballerina."

Prima ballerina.

He had an extensive list of nicknames for me, and this was by far my favorite. I'd even named my dance studio in downtown Astropolis after it. I started calling him my lucky charm after my business took off. People were more open to supporting me than I expected, but Alessio, Leo, and Cole helped a lot. The three men had a stellar background in business and marketing and were able to paint me as a fucking angel. Charities, fundraising galas, community work, you name it, I did it. I had to get rid of the negative stigma that surrounded me somehow.

I was happier than ever, teaching kids that were bursting with talent and collaborating with artists I never thought I'd have the chance to meet. Leo was especially overjoyed when I introduced my dancing skills in the bedroom.

I installed a pole in our bedroom for his birthday last year. The nickname of the untouchable prima ballerina all but flew out the window after all the nasty things he did to me pressed against it. Prima ballerina in the streets, pole dancer in the sheets. That was how he switched between my aforementioned double personalities.

"Woah, what's going on?" I asked as he set me down on my feet.

The starry sky filled up with bursts of color. Dark blue turned into an array of red, green, and golden tones that lit up the Mediterranean with their reflection. Like a moth drawn to light, I pressed forward, hands fisting the iron railings as I stared.

"Pre-celebratory preparations in case you say yes."

"Yes to what?" I twisted at the waist and almost fell forward when I saw him down on one knee.

A swell of emotions gathered in my throat as his hands fiddled around with the pockets of his dark gym shorts. He pulled out a blue velvet box, but my eyes never strayed from his, my heart accelerating and almost beating out of my chest with its ferocity.

I didn't know why I was so overwhelmed. We were basically married already. Leo was my confidant. We lived together, cooked together, christened every part of our new house in Astropolis... Hell, we even had a joint bank account. Marriage was nothing but a piece of paper confirming what we already had, but I thought we'd never get to this point. From open war to openly in love. Proud of each other and so damn happy.

"Eliana Roux, I can't remember how life was like before you. Before I got to hear your sweet laugh every day, your smart-ass replies, smell your addictive perfume all over my clothes. I can't remember what it was like not sleeping next to you every night and waking up sweating my balls off because you love to press up against me as if our furnace is broken."

"Are you complaining?" I asked, my voice thick, struggling between laughing and crying happy tears.

"Never. Because I don't want to remember. That life was gray and dull." Leo snapped the lid of the box open and the oval-shaped diamond sparkled as bright as the fireworks. "I want you, baby. I've always wanted you, and my obsession is only getting stronger by the day. Will you marry me? Will you be mine today and forever?"

I didn't think.

I didn't have to.

I just acted.

With a squeal that I didn't know the origin of, I attacked Leo's squatted form. He grunted, falling back on the tiled balcony floor, and smiled like a lunatic when I started littering every inch of his face with wild kisses.

"Silly boy, I've always been yours," I spoke, explosions still going off behind our tangled bodies. "Yes, baby. Today, tomorrow, and forever."

LEONARDO
One Year Later

"Who spiked the eggnog again?" Eliana stormed into the room with the air of a thousand armies. Dressed in an ugly oversized sweater and knee-high socks with little reindeers on them, she looked like my definition of a Christmas miracle as she glared at a suspicious-looking Saint.

"What's the matter, princess?" He threw his arm over the cushioned back of the brown leather couch. "This is an all adults household. If you expected virgin pina coladas, then you shouldn't have joined," Saint bit out.

He'd been on edge ever since we arrived on his

Christmas retreat in Aspen for Christmas. Eliana, Ares, me, Saint, and their girls, or you could call them their flavors of the month. Neither of them had much luck in getting anyone to stick around. Not because they couldn't, because the motherfuckers had it all, looks, power, and money, girls practically tripped over each other in their attempt to reach them. They chose to not get attached, choosing quantity over quality.

I'd kept my mouth shut, giving him a wide berth, knowing full well the hoops his father had him jumping through, but shit was getting annoying. No one talked to Eliana like that.

"Watch your mouth, asshole, before I make you eat the snow outside." I smacked his head, and he hissed at me as I got off the couch to check on Eli. She hadn't been feeling well recently. At first, I thought it was something she ate, a stomach bug, but she kept puking her guts out every morning for the past week, and I was starting to get worried.

"Are you okay, babe?" I palmed her red cheeks to check if she felt hot, but I graduated from business school and worked for an oil company. My doctor skills were utter shit... unless we were talking about the bedroom. My disobeying nurse was one sexy piece of ass, and I had the utmost fun getting her to fall in line.

"Do you want to go see a doctor?"

"No, no." She shook her head hard, her blonde strands flying around her shoulders, but I didn't miss the way she paled at my question. "I-I'm fine."

"Eliana, what's the matter?"

Her gaze sliced to the guys cuddled up with the girls (whose names I kept forgetting) by the couch next to the fireplace, pretending like they weren't listening in on us but doing a poor job at it. All conversation had ceased in the decorated living room, and all you could hear was us and the crackle of the fire.

"Kitchen. Now," I growled at them, more than I did her.

Leading the way, I held on to Eli's hand, bursting into the kitchen and settling her squealing ass on the wooden countertop.

"Tell me what the hell is going on, now. You've been puking nearly every morning, you won't touch your food, and as much as I'll rip Saint's tongue out if he ever talks to you like that again, he has a point." Parting her knees, I took my place between them, thumbing the fuzzy fabric of her socks. "On top of all of that, you refuse to go to a doctor. The way I see it, you have two options here. You either tell me what's up, or I'm strapping your ass in the car and taking you to a physician ASAP."

Her eyes took on a glossy sheen, her little nose wrinkling in a grimace, and I felt like I'd kicked a puppy. I took a deep breath through my nose, trying to lighten up, but fuck, I was going crazy with worry. An apology was on the tip of my tongue, but I stopped when Eliana shot off a reply so fast I failed to comprehend whatever the hell she said.

"Slowly, Eliana. I have some difficulties reading between the lines when there aren't any lines to begin with." I bit my bottom lip, staring at her.

My girl looked too pale for my liking.

She released a deep sigh, shoulders sagging and hands toying with the loose threads of my shirt as she released the words sluggishly. "I missed my period this month. I didn't think it was a big deal at first, you know? My cycles aren't always regular. But then—" Eliana cut herself off, hand freezing on my chest.

I clutched her hand in mine, gripping her chin and pulling her head up so I could look at her expression. It was crestfallen, as if she held all of the world's problems on her shoulders and as her fucking husband I felt incompetent. Whatever it was, she shouldn't have to go through it alone.

"Then what?"

"Then, I started feeling queasy. Certain foods made me want to barf." She cocked her head to the side. "Either that or it could have been Ares, swapping spit with Sofia during dinner. Seriously, they might have as well done it in front of us."

I cringed at the unwanted memory. "Focus on the matter at hand, baby, the last thing I need is to be reminded of that."

"Right." She swallowed, her feet swinging on either side of me. "So, one thought led to another, and yesterday, when I didn't join you guys skiing, it was because I... I took a pregnancy test."

"What?" I thought I heard wrong. I slanted my head, trying to regulate my breathing. "What did you say?"

"I took a pregnancy test and-and it came out positive." Eliana's voice was thick and low, heavy with emotion.

Positive.

My heart rioted in my chest, my blood pumping faster. Eliana was pregnant. My wife was pregnant with my baby. A dad. Oh god, I'd be a fucking dad. A thousand different fears came at me with viciousness, but the slither of happiness in my gut was unmistakable. I didn't know anything about kids, yet I couldn't wait to hold mine. A tiny little soul that was all Eliana and me.

I dropped my gaze to Eli's belly when I should've started with her face instead.

"I'm sorry."

I stopped cold when she apologized.

"I'm so fucking sorry. We talked about kids before, and we both agreed to wait a bit longer because of our careers. And I swear I-I tried to be consistent with taking my birth control pills, but Leo, I'm not sure I'm not entirely to blame. There could have been days where it slipped my mind."

"You have nothing to fucking apologize for," I said harshly, and realized I should soften up when her head snapped up, eyes wide. I cupped her cheeks, bringing her closer to me until there wasn't any wiggle room between us. "It takes two to tango. We're not machines. We all forget. And, baby, with the amount of sex that we have, even if you had been consistent with your birth control, it was bound to happen eventually."

"You're not mad?"

"Are you kidding me? I can't fucking wait to see what the little squirt looks like." I dropped my hand on her stomach, pressing against her still flat belly. "I adore you, and that means I adore everything that comes with you."

I kissed the top of Eli's head, willing to absorb some of her fears. Her hands came around me, squeezing tight as she pressed her forehead on my shoulder.

"But what if we fail Leo? What if bad parenting is hereditary? Lord knows there are countless studies out there proving that we get a lot of behavioral traits from our parents."

"Behavior is not hereditary, Eli, it's learned. I'm sure we'll make mistakes, countless of them, but baby, we'll also learn from them. Our pasts don't define us. They make us stronger. Just you worrying about not wanting to make the same mistakes your parents did, shows you're already proactive and dedicated to giving our baby the best life it deserves."

A sigh. One of relief this time, as she tilted her head up to look at me. Protectiveness gripped my chest the more I looked at the gorgeous woman that would give birth to my baby. "So you're really happy? You want this?"

"As much as I want to live, breathe, and fuck you every day." I kissed her mouth, once, twice, until she pulled away, her frown turned upside down.

Eliana threw her hands over my shoulders, tangling her hands in my hair like she loved doing. "You realize this means I'll look like a bloated whale for the next nine months, right?" She smirked. "That means no more adventurous positions for you, there, buddy."

"I don't need any crazy positions, Narcissus. You're all I need."

"My happiness." I dropped a kiss to one eyelid.

"My love." And then to the other.

"My lives," I said, kneeling down and kissing the flat tummy that held my baby.

The End.

Acknowledgments

It took me three rewrites to finally be happy with Leo and Eli's story, and honestly, if it weren't for the people on this list, I don't think I would have made it.

To my parents—Even though I'll probably die of mortification if they ever read my books—your faith, support, and encouragement means the world to me.

To Marzy Opal—I wouldn't have done it without you, girl. I am so grateful for your friendship, advice, and feedback, you are a freaking gem, and I love you times a thousand. I can't wait to meet you one day and hug the shit out of you.

To the best friend a girl could ever ask for, Jessy—thank you so much for being my free therapist. The amount of times I was ready to give up were infinite, and you were the only thing that kept me going, I mean it. Kiss of War wouldn't be published without you and all our late-night talks. I love you to the moon and back, and I thank God every day, I have someone like you in my corner.

To my sister—thank you for letting me borrow your laptop whenever I wanted, to write this book and not hating me for it. I appreciate it.

To my wonderful betas, Marzy, Sonia, Ketlli, and Jessy—y'all are freaking angels. Thank you for making my words shine and working with me on such a tight deadline!

To the Rona Writers aka Sharon Woods, Katie Lowrie, J. C. Hawke, Billie Lustig, Sonia Esperanza, L.J. Findlay, Jessica Grace, A.R. Thomas, D. Lilac, and Khrista Teresa—

thank you for always hyping me up, and for being there whenever I have a question (I seem to never run out of them, I know). Your advice has been invaluable, and going through this self-publishing journey with all of you has been amazing.

To my lovely editor Amy Briggs—thank you so much for working with me on such short notice! Your attention to detail is incredible!

To the Weeknd—he doesn't even know I exist, but I felt like I had to mention him since I only listened to his songs while writing Kiss of War.

Huge thanks to Savannah Richey from Peachy Keen for her wonderful PR services.

To the girls from Books and Moods—I am seriously obsessed with this cover! Thank you so much!

I would also like to thank all the wonderful bloggers and reviewers who took the time to read this book. Thank you for reading, reviewing, sharing, hyping my books up. I appreciate you so so much!

And of course, to you, the reader who picked this book up, thus allowing me to continue doing what I love. If you have the time, please consider leaving a brief, honest review.

Always grateful,
Clara Elroy

About The Author

Clara Elroy is an author of Contemporary Romance and New Adult novels that make your heart clench. Her love for reading began when she was a young girl, and would lose sleep because she wanted to read "just one more page."

Clara lives for reading and writing about flawed and relatable characters. She loves making sparks fly between stubborn men and the badass women that make them kneel.

When Clara's not typing away at her computer, you can find her with her nose buried in a book or writing biographies in the third person.

Yeah, she's cool like that.

Clara loves connecting with her readers, so please join her FB readers group, Clara's Firehearts, for exclusive excerpts, giveaways, funny memes, book talk, and more.

https://www.facebook.com/groups/clarasfirehearts

You can also find Clara at these places:

Website:
www.claraelroy.com

Newsletter:
https://bit.ly/3voOhiz

Follow on Amazon to be alerted of her next release:
https://amzn.to/3oEXmFw

instagram.com/claraelroyauthor

facebook.com/claraelroyauthor

goodreads.com/claraelroy

bookbub.com/authors/clara-elroy